D1027404

Delia and the Drifter

Westward
to Home · 1

Delia
and the Drifter

MELODY CARLSON

WhiteFire
PUBLISHING

This is a work of fiction. All characters and events portrayed in this novel are either fictitious or used fictitiously.

DELIA AND THE DRIFTER

Copyright © 2021, Carlson Management Co., Inc.
All rights reserved. Reproduction in part or in whole is strictly forbidden without the express written consent of the publisher, with the exception of a brief quotation for review purposes.

WhiteFire Publishing
13607 Bedford Rd NE
Cumberland, MD 21502

ISBN: 978-1-941720-45-5 (print)
       978-1-941720-46-2 (digital)

1

Pittsburgh, Pennsylvania
June 1884

DELIA BLACKSTONE NEVER LIKED FEELING SUSPICIOUS ABOUT ANYone. Particularly her own mother. But everything changed today. It all started right after breakfast, shortly after Father left the house.

Delia experienced mild interest when the unexpected stranger showed up at their front door. She didn't hear the actual words exchanged, but did note the sharp edge in Mother's voice as she directed the stranger to the front parlor. The old gentleman was obviously not there to see Father, but instead of playing host to the guest, like Mother would normally do, she took Delia aside.

"I need you go next door at once," she said abruptly. "Ask Mrs. Taylor if we can borrow her silver punchbowl…for this upcoming weekend."

"Why can't I just use the telephone to—"

"Would I ask you to do an errand that didn't need doing?" Mother gave her an indignant scowl.

"I just don't understand the urgency." Delia peered toward the front parlor, curious about Mother's strange behavior. "Do you really need me to go right this—"

"Good grief, Delia, you never questioned me about every little thing before—I suppose this is just one more delightful reward from your fancy education."

"I apologize, Mother." Delia tried not to react to the sting of harsh words as she agreed to perform what seemed a senseless errand. With her two years of university just finished, Delia was now grappling with her parents' general disapproval of her. They had grown critical of almost everything. From her schooling, her opinions, her aspirations…even her fashion sense—or lack of it.

As she hurried next door, Delia intended to keep this visit short. She knew a simple errand to borrow anything from the loquacious Mrs. Taylor could easily turn into a social visit with tea and cakes and questions. To her relief, after waiting several minutes for someone to answer the door, she was informed the Taylors were not at home. She relayed the punchbowl message to the servant, requesting that Mrs. Taylor call her mother later.

As Delia turned up the walk to her own house, she spied the elderly man already partway down the street. His gait was slow, with a slight limp, as he laboriously made his way toward the streetcar stop. Apparently Mother had little to say to the old man, since it appeared she'd given him his leave quite abruptly. But if that were the case, why was he invited into the front parlor in the first place?

Delia hurried inside and discovered her mother descending the stairs with a deeply furrowed brow. "Who was your visitor?" she asked

"No one of concern," Mother answered briskly.

Naturally, this only added to Delia's growing interest. "What did he want?"

"Nothing."

"Then why did he come here?" Delia studied her mother. Why she was being so secretive about this?

"I really couldn't say, Delia." Mother's voice was laced with irritation as she smoothed her periwinkle satin skirt. "Why are you so fascinated by that old man in the first place?" She narrowed her eyes with suspicion. "Perhaps he is a friend of yours?"

"Of course not. I was simply curious. You are acting so mysteriously, Mother. Almost as if you have something to hide."

"You can be most impertinent." She waved a hand. "Why are you not cloistered in the library with your nose in a book like usual?"

"Because I have read most of the books in that library. At least the ones that interest me." Delia followed her mother down the hallway that led to the kitchen. "But I *am* interested in your stranger—"

"Delia Adelaide Blackstone! Stop being so nosey! Do you honestly imagine that old man's visit had anything to do with you?" Mother pursed her lips tightly, her signal she was vexed.

"If he had nothing to do with me, I'd think you'd be more forthcoming." By now Delia's curiosity had blossomed into full blown suspicion.

"Honestly, Delia. I'm worried your fancy schooling has ruined you for all practical purposes. Why did we ever agree to such madness in the first place?"

"Because Great Aunt Adelaide paid my full tuition before she passed away," Delia reminded her. "There was no hope of getting that money back. Furthermore, I was most eager to learn."

"Well, I'm grateful it's over now. Why a young woman needs so much education is beyond me." Mother turned into the dining room, making a pretense of rearranging the bowl of pink peonies in the center of the large mahogany table.

"So you refuse to tell me about your mysterious visitor?" Delia picked up some dropped petals, holding the delicate pieces in her palm.

"Gracious me, Delia, do you think *everything* concerns you?"

"Possibly." Delia suddenly realized this might be the opportunity she'd been looking for since coming home from university last week. She needed to raise an unsettling subject, one that had grown even more disturbing last night—around this very table. She glanced over her shoulder. It seemed she and Mother were alone. "It concerns me…that you and Father are very intent on marrying me off," she said quietly.

Mother's brows arched slightly, but her mouth remained a firm line, her eyes averted from Delia's.

"I suspect that this morning's visitor is somehow related to your plans, Mother. That might explain why you wish to keep me in the dark about him. Tell me, was your unexpected visitor Henry Horton's father?"

"No, no, of course, not." Mother waved a hand. "That is perfectly ridiculous. You always imagine things."

"The man seemed of the right age," Delia continued. "Henry Horton must be sixty, and that old man looked well beyond eighty."

"Henry Horton is only fifty-two."

"That's ten years your senior, Mother. I cannot believe you wish to marry me off to a widower who is even older than my own parents." She glumly shook her head. "Am I such a burden that you must foist me off on the first man who comes around?"

"Henry Horton is quite a catch." Mother scowled. "As you know, he owns a prosperous steel mill. And as you know, you have no dowry. Furthermore you are not getting any younger, dear. Good grief, you'll be *twenty-one* in November. I was married by seventeen."

"So you have told me. Dozens of times."

"Then you tell me, Delia, how many men will be interested in an overly educated wife who is getting a bit long in the tooth?"

"What makes you think Henry Horton is *interested*?"

"He told your father as much, just last night. And it wasn't the first time he's mentioned you're a fine-looking woman." Mother smiled in a catty way. "Father believes Henry plans to make his intentions known *very* soon." She clasped her hands together. "Do you know how much this pleases us, dear daughter?"

"I'm sure your pleasure has nothing to do with Henry Horton's wealth." Delia didn't like being sarcastic, but sometimes it was impossible to hold back.

"What, pray tell, is wrong with being rich? Are you complaining that Henry's family owns one of the finest new steel mills in Pittsburgh? And if you are worried about playing mother to his three sons, don't concern yourself. The firstborn is older than you and the other two are nearly grown and away at school most of the time."

"So my wishes don't matter to you?" Delia peered into her mother's pale blue eyes. "You would see me married off to a man I don't even care for?"

"You would want for nothing, Delia. You could sit and read books all day if you liked. I hear that Henry has an impressive library with bookshelves that go from the floor to the ceiling. Does that not appeal to you?"

"Haven't you also heard that books can be borrowed from a lending institution without signing a wedding certificate?"

"Your education has made you most obstinate, Delia. Not an admirable trait in a wife, I should say."

"If wishing to have a say in the choice of my husband is considered obstinate, I suppose you're right." Delia suppressed the urge to raise her voice and throw a childish fit. But did her mother truly think that she couldn't see through this marriage arrangement? Delia knew her parents' finances were unstable—at best. She'd noticed that some of the servants had been let go this past year, and that some old paintings and costly carpets and furnishings were missing—assumedly sold to cover debt.

Delia suspected her family's money concerns were the main reason they were so determined to marry her off to Henry Horton. Never mind that the wealthy widower was short and round with stringy, thinning hair and smelled like stale tobacco and machine oil. Not that Delia was one to judge anyone based solely on appearances. But when she'd spoken with him last night, while he was their guest for dinner, all he'd talked about was the modernizations in his beloved steel factory. And when she remarked about the poor quality of the air near the steel mills, or the fact that many factories were unsafe workplaces, or that she was appalled to hear that they actually employed children, he had gotten rather annoyed with her. Not a good sign for a happy marriage.

"I should think you would be grateful," Mother said with a look of dismay.

"Grateful for what?"

"That your father and I are looking to your welfare, Delia. You should thank us for caring enough to secure your future."

"*My* future?" Delia frowned at her mother. "Do you honestly believe that I am unable to—"

"Where are the twins?" Mother used an urgent tone, as if the eleven-year-olds might be in some kind of imminent danger if left to their own devices—which might be true, but nothing new. Delia recognized the distraction tactic.

"I saw Julius in his room earlier," Delia said flatly. "I couldn't say where Julianne is keeping herself."

"Well, if you will excuse me, I must speak to Cook at once." Mother gave the peonies one last tweak then, with her bustled skirt rustling noisily, hurried toward the kitchen. Delia knew there was no real reason to converse with Cook right now. Mother was simply avoiding her.

Delia slowly went up the ornately carved staircase, ready to lock herself in her room until she figured a way out of this prearranged engagement plan that seemed to have taken on a life of its own—and without her consent. At the landing she observed Julianne dart down the hallway, away from Delia's room, with a guilty expression on her pixie face.

"What were you doing in my room, little sister?" Delia asked pointedly.

"Nothing," Julianne said curtly, and oddly similarly to their mother.

"Then why were you in there?" Delia persisted.

"I was, uh, looking for something." Julianne feigned innocence.

Delia smiled as she patted her sister's blonde head. "Come clean, little sister. Tell me what you were looking for. Perhaps I can help. Although I can't imagine I'd have anything of interest to you anyway. Mostly books and—"

"Oh, but you do." Julianne brightened. "Your earrings!"

Delia laughed. "You mean Great Aunt Adelaide's earrings?"

"Yes." Julianne nodded eagerly. "They're so beautiful." She frowned. "But I don't see why she left them to only you. What about me?" Her lower lip jutted out.

"You were a very little girl when Auntie passed away," Delia reminded her. "And, as I've told you before, I will pass some on to you—but not until you're old enough to actually wear them."

Julianne scowled. "A girl at my school isn't much older than me, and she wears earrings…sometimes."

Delia shook her head. "Mother would not approve." She reached for Julianne's hand, leading her into her room. "But show me which ones are your favorite. Perhaps they'll be the ones I give to you on your sixteenth birthday."

Julianne's eyes grew wide. "Truly?"

"Well, as long as you don't pick *my* favorite ones." Delia led her over to the dressing table where the carved box that Great Aunt Adelaide had left her was still open. For the most part, Delia wasn't overly fond of jewelry. And it only seemed fair she should share some of the pieces with her little sister…someday.

"*These* are my favorites." Julianne picked up the emerald earrings. Teardrops set in delicate gold filigree.

"Too bad, little one." Delia playfully tugged one of Julianne's ringlets, watching it bounce back into shape. "Aunt Adelaide would not approve of your choice. She always said that these emeralds perfectly matched my eyes, and she made me promise to wear them on my wedding day."

Julianne scowled.

"But these beauties." Delia selected a similar pair with blue topaz stones. "These match *your* eyes, Julianne." She held them up to her little sister's earlobes. "Oh, my!" Turning Julianne to face the dresser mirror, she continued. "These are perfect with your eyes. Look how pretty!"

Julianne smiled. "Would you truly give them to me?"

"When you are sixteen." Delia put the earrings back in the carved box.

Julianne looked longingly at them. "That's so long to wait. Couldn't I just keep them in my room? Just to look at sometimes?"

Delia firmly shook her head. She knew Julianne well enough to know she would probably sneak them out to wear to school. Chances are they would be lost long before she turned sixteen.

"What if I told you a secret?" Julianne said suddenly. "In exchange for the earrings."

"A secret?" Delia shrugged with disinterest.

"Yes! A secret that concerns *you,*" Julianne declared.

"What sort of secret?" She suspected it would be related to Henry Horton. Hopefully Mother wasn't planning an impromptu wedding, although that might explain her sudden need for a silver punchbowl. Come to think of it, Mother had even spoken of weddings last night.

"I was in the parlor when that old man came to the door a little while ago," Julianne said mysteriously.

"What do you mean—you were eavesdropping?"

"It wasn't intentional, Delia. I sneaked some sugar cookies from the kitchen, and I was eating them in the parlor when I heard Mother send that old man in there. So I had to hide quickly. I got beneath the round table, under the purple tablecloth, and just waited."

"You hid in the parlor while Mother talked with her guest?" Delia was both appalled and intrigued.

"Yes." Julianne nodded eagerly. "And I got caught too. Now I'm supposed to stay in my room all day as punishment." She wrinkled her nose.

"But instead, you go sneaking about in my room?"

Julianne shrugged. "I got bored."

"So what did you hear?" Delia fiddled with a garnet necklace, feigning disinterest.

"I can't tell you."

"If you can't tell me, why bring it up, silly goose?"

"Because I *may* tell you—if I didn't have to wait until I'm sixteen for those earrings."

"What makes you think I want to know your secret that badly?"

"Because, I *told* you, Delia. They were talking about *you*. And if I were you, I would want to know."

Was it possible Julianne really had heard whatever transpired between Mother and the elderly stranger? Even if Delia didn't approve of her little sister's eavesdropping habits or hints to bribery, wouldn't she be a fool not to find out about the mysterious visitor? Especially since it concerned her. In all likelihood it was related to this arranged marriage that her parents were so determined to force upon her. She had to know!

Philadelphia, Pennsylvania
June 1884

As he packed his bags, Wyatt Davis realized that some folks might consider him a *drifter*—and it didn't trouble him at all. Not many men could say they'd traveled close to 15,000 miles by the age of twenty-seven. But before his next birthday, Wyatt planned to have bragging rights to such a feat. His first 3,000 miles had been traveled partly by foot and partly by covered wagon when, at the age of five, he'd traveled with his parents along the Oregon Trail. They'd left Pennsylvania in 1863 after his father, crippled by the war, decided to move his family to Oregon.

Today Wyatt was returning to the West—and not a day too soon. As he put several pairs of new woolen socks on top of his satchel, he tried to remember why he'd been so doggoned determined to come to Philadelphia two years ago. Why was he willing to leave his ranch behind and head out on horseback for such a long trip? Certainly, it was a great adventure—crossing the Great Divide and the Great Plains and some mighty rivers—but had it been worth it?

When Wyatt set out in the spring of 1882, his plan had been to make enough money to set his property up as the best cattle ranch in his region. His primary goal was to get rich. At the time, it had seemed a good idea, but now it just seemed plain foolish. Money, he realized after twenty-one months of hard work and penny-pinching, wasn't everything. Spending twenty-one months working for his uncle in the city had been interesting and educational at first, but downright tedious in the end. He longed for the wide-open spaces of the West.

As he closed his satchel, he remembered his true motivation for coming out here. To get away from Maryanne. He'd wanted to escape the memory of the vivacious girl with her flame red hair and flashing blue eyes. Riding a horse across the entire country seemed just the way to do it.

When the Boswell family arrived out West in an ox-pulled wagon, Wyatt thought their sixteen-year-old daughter was the prettiest thing he'd ever seen. Although to be fair, there weren't a lot of attractive young women to choose from, so that alone gave Maryanne a distinct advantage. Perhaps if he saw her now, after being around all these fancy city women, he'd find her homely. Funny how one's perspective could change given time and distance.

Wyatt had made fast friends with Mr. and Mrs. Boswell. His new neighbors had been worn out from the trail and ill-prepared for settling in before winter. In need of a roof over their heads and with six mouths to feed, there was much to be done. Being neighborly—and wanting to be near Maryanne—Wyatt had made himself useful to the Boswells. So useful that he neglected his own homestead.

Prior to that distraction, Wyatt had been working the land his parents had acquired through the Oregon Homestead Act. As their only child, he'd inherited their acreage after both parents died within a year of each other. Just seventeen at the time, Wyatt felt the loss deeply. To assuage his grief, he threw his energy into improvements, but after a few years he realized it would take more than muscle and sweat to transform the 320 acres into the productive cattle ranch his father had dreamed of.

So when his buddy Jake Hardy invited him to partner in a

gold-mining venture in southern Oregon, Wyatt happily agreed. His drifter nature, first discovered on the Oregon Trail as a child, beckoned him. They traveled south, and after two long, hard years working a fairly worthless claim, he and Jake went home with a few hundred dollars in their pockets. Wyatt put his earnings right into the property. He enlarged the barn and purchased some livestock and had just started work on the leaky old packrat-infested cabin when the Boswells arrived.

Smitten by Maryanne, Wyatt set his own projects aside to help her folks build a small cabin and barn. Throughout winter and spring, Wyatt continued offering his assistance by clearing timber and putting up split-rail fences. As the year progressed, Wyatt felt certain he had a future with Maryanne. She seemed to confirm this with her flirty blue eyes and fiery hair. Then right after Maryanne turned seventeen, she went off and married Duke Martin, a man nearly old enough to be her father.

Although he was hurt, Wyatt had nothing against Duke. A decent and respectable man, making an honest living with his well-stocked mercantile, Duke Martin was a widower with two children. Still, it seemed unfair that he should win Maryanne. Especially after all that Wyatt had done to help her family and the sacrifices he'd made. Shortly before the wedding, Wyatt learned the truth—the Boswells had relied heavily on credit from Martin's Mercantile. Their account had grown impossibly large during their first year. When Mrs. Boswell discovered that Duke Martin fancied Maryanne, a deal was struck.

Wyatt could almost understand this, but when he questioned Maryanne about her upcoming nuptials, thinking she might have some resistance to being treated like chattel, he was surprised to discover that she seemed generally unconcerned. And that's when he realized that she had never loved him. In all honesty, looking back, he suspected that his pride was hurt more than his heart.

Wyatt decided it was time to drift again. Leaving his leaky cabin behind, he sold off what little livestock he owned then informed friends and neighbors that he planned to take the Oregon Trail *backwards*. Wearing Pa's old buckskins, Wyatt set out on horseback with a pack-mule loaded with provisions. He was a drifter.

"Wyatt?" His aunt's voice echoed through the small guesthouse he'd been staying in since arriving in Philadelphia. "You still here?"

"In the bedroom, Aunt Lilly," he called back. "Just finishing my packing." Lilly was his father's older sister and, next to his mother, one of the sweetest women he'd ever known.

"Oh, my." She let out a sad sigh as she gazed at the bags by the door. "You are truly leaving us…going back West after all."

"Afraid so." He put a comforting hand on her shoulder. "But once again, I thank you for your kind and generous hospitality. The only thing I'll miss about Philadelphia is you and Uncle George." He smiled apologetically. "But I'm just not a city person, Aunt Lilly. I crave the wide-open spaces, the mountains, the rivers and trees. I suppose I'm like my father in that respect."

"You are very much like your father." She nodded sadly as she handed him a paper wrapped parcel. "Something for your trip."

"Thank you." He took the package from her and, feeling its firmness, suspected it was a book. He and Aunt Lilly shared a mutual love of reading. In fact, that was one other thing he would miss about Philadelphia—his aunt and uncle's library.

"Although I understand your feelings, Wyatt, I do wish we'd been able to convince you to stay. Your uncle will be too old to keep running the boot factory in a few years. You would've been the perfect replacement for him."

"I'll admit that Uncle George's offer was tempting." He set the package on top of the socks. "If all I wanted was to become rich— and I'll admit that's how I felt when I set out on this trip—I would take him up on it. But I've learned a lot since coming east. I believe there's more to life than gaining wealth now."

She smiled, but her eyes were sad. "For a young man, you have good sense. Wise beyond your years."

He chuckled. "Well, most of my lessons were learned the hard way, dear aunt, but thank you for saying that."

"George is very sorry to lose you at the factory. Last night he told me how impressed he was by you—he said you have gumption. And, as you must surely know, your uncle is not one to dish out praise."

Wyatt nodded grimly at that understatement. As much as he liked and respected Uncle George, he was well aware of his uncle's austere disposition. With hardworking business ethics, he desired nothing less than the very best from all his employees. And Wyatt, working his way up into a managerial position, felt as if he'd never quite measured up to his uncle's high expectations.

"Before he left this morning, George said you were the finest employee to ever work at the Bauman Boot Factory."

Wyatt blinked in surprise. "He said that?"

She brightened. "Yes. Does that make you want to change your mind about leaving, Wyatt?"

As badly as he wanted to please his aunt, he knew it was impossible. "Sorry, I still need to go. But I do appreciate knowing that. Thanks for telling me."

"George asked me to inform you that your crates from the factory were delivered to the railroad station yesterday afternoon. I still can't fathom how you're going to manage to sell so many pairs of boots. I hope you won't regret it."

"Boots are valuable out West," he explained, not for the first time. "Especially in mining towns like Juneau." Buying the boots at cost, he expected to make a nice profit.

"You still intend to journey all the way up to the Alaska Territory? You're not the least bit concerned about wild animals or Indians?"

His smile laced with tolerance, Wyatt was well aware of how foreign his plans sounded to his citified relatives. "My friend Jake has been in Juneau for several months. He's already staked a claim for both of us. And his last letter was very reassuring. You really shouldn't worry, Aunt Lilly."

"It's hard not to worry when I read stories of miners being buried alive or freezing to death up there." She shook a finger at him. "And what about what you said, that you're not seeking wealth? Yet you run off to the wilderness to sell boots and search for gold. I don't understand." She shook her head in dismay.

He laughed. "Dear Aunt Lilly—I am headed to Alaska for the adventure and to spend time with my friend, but I'm not opposed to making a little money. I've had enough mining experience to know the odds are stacked against me hitting the mother lode. That's not why I'm going. But I also know that miners pay good money for supplies. Good boots can be almost worth their weight in gold."

"Despite your claim to be a drifter, you're a shrewd businessman. And you still plan to purchase tools in Pittsburgh?"

"Yes. Uncle George recommended a factory and even gave me a letter for the owner."

"And two weeks from now you will load all your goods onto a ship in San Francisco and sail to Alaska." She laid her hand on her chest. "You're a very brave man, Wyatt."

"It's an adventure," he happily reassured her. "And at the end of my adventure I hope to have enough funds to turn my ranch into all that Pa dreamed it could be."

"Your father would be so proud of you. I know how much he loved that land."

"It really is a beautiful piece of property." Wyatt felt surprised by how much he suddenly missed Oregon.

"When I've listened to you, describing the mountains and rivers and meadows out there, I can almost see it. In my mind's eye Oregon is very beautiful."

"Everything out West is beautiful." He fastened the buckle around his leather bag, cinching it tightly.

"The women too?" Aunt Lilly's brows arched. "Do you suppose

you will find a bride out there, Wyatt? Someone to share your beautiful ranch with you?"

Wyatt shrugged as the image of a redheaded flibbertigibbet flitted through his head—with absolutely no appeal. "The truth is I wouldn't care to be saddled with a wife right now." He reached for his satchel, closing it as well. "I'd rather remain a drifter for the time being."

"You are a good man, and a handsome one at that," she declared. "Any single young woman should be glad to land a husband as fine as you."

"Well, I'm in no hurry. Maybe someday the right one will come along. But I won't settle for just anyone." He winked at her. "I want a woman as wise and kind as you, Aunt Lilly. And just as pretty too."

She waved her hand at him. "I'm just a faded old woman. But back in my day…well, I did manage to turn your uncle's head."

"I've seen your portrait in the drawing room. You were a true beauty in your youth. And you're still a fine-looking woman."

Clearly touched by his words, she sniffed as she reached for a lace-trimmed handkerchief. "I hate to see you leave, dear. It's been like a breath of fresh air having you here." She dabbed her eyes. "I know you must be going soon. What time is your train?"

He checked his pocket watch. "Ten forty-five. I suppose I should be on my way."

"I told Peter to have the carriage ready and, if you don't mind, I'd like to ride to Broad Street Station with you. George would've come with us, but he had things to attend to."

"Uncle George already said his goodbyes." Wyatt reached for his jacket.

"The truth is I think he was afraid he would become emotional." She made a tsk-tsk sound. "That would be too unmanly for him."

Wyatt laughed as he pulled on his jacket and picked up his bags. "Is that all you have?" she asked. "Just three bags?"

"A rolling stone gathers no moss." He laughed. "To be honest, this is more than I arrived here with. I suppose I *have* gathered some moss."

Together they walked across the well-tended yard that ran between the guesthouse and the mansion where his aunt and uncle lived. "I'm aware that trains have rather nice dining cars nowadays," she told him, "but I asked the cook to pack you a hearty lunch. I'm sure it will be preferable to train food."

Before long, they were on their way, and to Wyatt's surprise, he felt a bit emotional himself. It was no small thing saying goodbye to his only living relatives. But not wanting to be unmanly, he contained it. "It's been a blessing getting to know you, Aunt Lilly," he said solemnly. "And Uncle George too. After Ma and Pa died, I felt alone in the world. With no family around."

"I always felt bad that your parents weren't able to have more children." She sadly shook her head. "It seemed that both your father and I were not blessed in that way."

Wyatt reached for her hand. He knew that Aunt Lilly had lost two children in a cholera epidemic. Just one more reason she had been so eager to keep Wyatt with them. "I will miss you," he said quietly.

"You will be in my daily prayers."

"Thank you. And we will remain in touch through letters," he assured her.

"Yes." She nodded eagerly. "And I will send you new books as promised, and you can write me your opinions of them."

"I look forward to it."

"So tell me your plans again, Wyatt. I want to know where you'll be and when. So that I can pray for you during your journey."

"I'll be grateful for your prayers." He paused to think. "Pittsburgh first. I'll spend the night at the Franklin Hotel and tomorrow I'll purchase tools and have them sent to the train station. Then I'll spend another night at the hotel and depart Pittsburgh on Friday afternoon. For the next week, I will be headed West. Destination San

Francisco. I should be quite comfortable in the berth I booked and, as you mentioned, there is a dining car. Not such a bad way to travel across the continent." He smiled. "When I think of how long it took to ride east on horseback, compared to how quickly one travels by train, I have to laugh at myself."

"But it was an adventure," she reminded him.

He squeezed her hand. "You *do* understand me."

"In San Francisco you board the ship bound for Juneau," she said. "Make sure you send me a letter after your arrival."

"I will write to you from several stops along the way," he promised as the carriage pulled up to the train station. "And just as you pray for me, I plan to pray for you and Uncle George too." He flashed her a mischievous grin. "Do you know what I'll be praying for?"

"I have no idea." She tilted her head to one side.

"I'm going to pray that you two will make the train trip out there to visit me one day. To see my ranch and all the beauty of the West."

"I believe we would be inclined to make the long trip—if it was to attend our nephew's wedding," she said with a twinkle in her eyes.

He chuckled. "Well, I suppose you never know."

"Because that is what I will be praying for, Wyatt. I plan to ask God to send you just the right woman."

He leaned over to kiss her cheek. "Thank you, Aunt Lilly—for everything." He saw tears glistening in her eyes as he reached for his bags. "We will remain in touch."

She waved her handkerchief with a trembling chin. "God bless your journey," she called as he climbed down from the carriage.

He waved one more time then turned, hurrying into the bustling train station. It was well and good that his sweet aunt planned to pray for his future wife, but like Wyatt had told her, he was in no hurry. He still had places to go and people to see…and a wife, if that was meant to be, would have to come later.

3

DELIA STUDIED JULIANNE FOR A LONG MOMENT. IF THIS WAS HOW her little sister intended to play the game, perhaps Delia should simply play along. Picking up the blue topaz earrings, she held them in her palm before her little sister. "Fine, Julianne. You tell me what you overheard between Mother and the visitor, and if you're telling the truth—and if it does concern me as you have insinuated—I will give you these earrings *before* you turn sixteen."

Julianne eagerly reached for the earrings.

Delia closed her fingers over the earrings. "First you must tell me what was said in the parlor."

"The old man wanted to see *you,*" Julianne began in a furtive tone. "He said he's an uncle or some sort of relative. I really don't remember that part. But he had something important he wanted to give to you. I think it might've been a letter. But he said he had to deliver it personally."

"Did he give it to Mother?" Delia asked eagerly.

"I don't think so. She asked him to give it to her. But the man kept saying no, that he had to give it to you himself. *In person.*"

"But Mother didn't offer to fetch me? I was home when the man arrived and then she sent me next door."

"She told him you were out of town, something to do with school." Julianne's fair brows arched. "But that was a falsehood, wasn't it?"

Delia grimaced to think Julianne had witnessed their mother in a lie. "Well, did you hear the man's name or where he came from?"

"Mother called him Richard, I think. And he said he could be reached at his hotel. I think he said the Franklin." She nodded. "That's right. He asked her to send you to the Franklin to speak to him."

"What did Mother say to that?"

"*Goodbye!*" Julianne giggled. "That's when she showed him the door. Bad manners, if you ask me."

"The Franklin…I read about that hotel." Delia was already reaching for her hat. She'd never been inside the Franklin but knew the location. It was one of the newest and nicest hotels in the city.

"My earrings, please." Julianne smugly held out her hand.

Delia dropped the pair back into the jewelry box, closing it with a snap before she turned to smile at her sister. "Because you told me what you did, Julianne, I have decided to give you the earrings when you turn *fifteen.*"

"Delia Adelaide Blackstone!" Julianne's eyes flashed angrily. "You tricked me! You lied!"

"I told you the absolute truth. I promised you'd get the earrings *before* sixteen. Fifteen is a whole year earlier." Delia pulled on her summer weight gloves and picked up her leather purse, checking to be sure she had correct change for the streetcar.

Julianne narrowed her eyes. "I'll tell Mother."

Delia smiled coyly. "Then we'd have to confess to Mother that you told me about her secret visitor. I don't think she'll like that, Julianne. Especially since she wasn't too pleased about you spying on her in the first place." Delia pointed at her door. "Now aren't you supposed to be in *your* room?"

As Julianne stormed off down the hallway, Delia locked the jewelry case, hiding it safely away in a hatbox on top of her wardrobe. Hopefully Julianne wouldn't go poking around up there. And now, curious as to this puzzling Richard visitor, Delia hurried out of the house without saying a word to her mother. She felt a little guilty as she waited for the streetcar, but not guilty enough to go back home. Not until she had a conversation with this mysterious relative anyway. Who was he and what did he want with her?

Delia felt a bit uneasy as she waited for the streetcar. Not because she was uncomfortable about being out in the world by herself—two years at the university had seasoned her. She wouldn't go so far as to call herself worldly, but she did possess an educated confidence for such undertakings now. Her nervousness was over the possibility that her father might happen along and spot her standing on the side of the street. Besides finding it embarrassing, which he would, he would probably question her whereabouts. And, since Delia was not inclined to tell an outright lie, she would be forced to confess her mission. Then, of course, Mother would find out.

Despite her willingness to question Mother regarding these unwanted marriage plans and her own future, Delia had always tried to respect her parents. She knew that children were supposed to obey their parents and, as a child, she had striven to do so. More, she felt, than young Julianne and Julius. But in Delia's opinion, the twins had always been a bit spoiled.

But as a grown woman, she felt confused. Did she still need to *obey* her parents? She felt she should always respect them—even if it proved a challenge. But just because they were her parents, was she expected to submit to all their wishes? To allow them to pick her future husband? A man she could barely stand to look at, let alone converse with? She did not think so—from the depths of her soul, she did not!

Delia peered down the street, watching for the streetcar and hoping her father's sleek black carriage wasn't coming this way. It was a bit early for him to show up for the midday meal just yet, but one never knew exactly when he'd decide to come home because he kept no real schedule. As a child, she had assumed that when he came home for lunch, it was because he'd been at work all morning. As she got older, she discovered that her father didn't actually have a job and, in fact, he seemed to have an aversion to work.

Born into a family with fading wealth, her father felt that holding a job of any sort was beneath him. He preferred spending time at his gentleman's club, in the company of friends. Or at the racetrack, where Delia suspected he'd lost a fair amount of his family's money. Although she questioned him on this once—and only once—he claimed that horse races were a small diversion and that his winnings greatly outweighed his losses. She found that difficult to believe—not to mention disturbing. Even more disturbing, she suspected her parents were living well beyond their means.

That was just one reason Delia had been grateful for Great Aunt Adelaide's gift of an education. In the event she had to make her own way in this world, she might at least be somewhat prepared. Although she knew her parents would be mortified if she were to seek employment, a career seemed highly preferable to marrying the likes of Henry Horton.

As Delia boarded the crowded streetcar, dropping her change into the wooden box, she was glad that she'd worn one of her sensible "university ensembles" today. The high-collared, long-waisted pale gray dress, with a conservative bustle, drew no attention to itself. Although the fine wool fabric was a bit warm for this June day, the understated style suited her and, in her mind, made her almost invisible.

Delia's mother had never been fond of Delia's "school girl dresses," as she called them. The mousy tans, grays, and browns were not among Mother's favorite color palette, and she made no secret of it. "Such a beautiful girl should be dressed in beautiful gowns," Mother often said. And sometimes, for special occasions, Delia would give in to Mother's whims.

Feeling like a porcelain doll, she would allow her mother to indulge her love for fashion by dressing Delia as she pleased. She knew that her mother missed the days when her own figure was shown off by full skirts with narrow waists. But after the twins' birth, Mother became more rounded and matronly. Not long after that, the silhouette of gowns changed dramatically. The waists grew longer and, instead of hoops beneath the skirts, they wore bustles behind, with a smooth profile in front.

According to Mother, these were just the styles that a tall slender girl, like Delia, could carry off with ease. "If she wasn't so obstinate," Mother would whisper to friends after apologizing for one of Delia's less than stylish dresses. Delia had heard, in one of her college classes, that mothers sometimes lived vicariously through their grown daughters—particularly when it came to fashion. And so Delia had tried to be patient and understanding with her mother, knowing it wouldn't be too long before this kind of attention was lavished on Julianne.

To Delia's surprise, her mother had gotten rather fashion-obsessed this past spring. Aware that Delia's school was coming to an end, she seemed determined that her daughter should look the part of a real lady. And despite the tightening of the family's budget, Mother had somehow managed to acquire an excellent selection of well-made gowns for Delia. Some that Delia actually admired.

"Your homecoming gift," Mother had explained as she made an exhibition of showing Delia the lovely garments and accessories. But after a day or two of hearing bits and pieces about Mister Henry Horton—and following last night's dinner party—Delia understood. The gowns were not a homecoming gift as much as they were *lures.* Mother wanted Delia to hook and reel in a wealthy husband—specifically Mister Henry Horton. And the sooner the better.

As the streetcar got closer to the city, factory smokestacks grew visible, and the blue summer sky gradually turned to a dull beige tone. Even the river was a rusty shade of brown today. Thanks to the steel industry, Pittsburgh had changed greatly since she was a child and, in her opinion, not for the better.

Delia got off the streetcar a couple of blocks from the Franklin Hotel. She wanted to walk the last bit, allowing herself time to think—and to compose herself. Who was this stranger? An elderly relative by the name of Richard? Why hadn't she heard of him before? And why had Mother tried to keep her from meeting him? Was it possible he was an undesirable person? Someone who wished ill on her? Although it hardly seemed possible that such an old man could be dangerous. Besides, she would be meeting with him in a public place. It seemed unlikely he could pose a hazard or take advantage of her.

As Delia walked into the hotel lobby, she held her head high. She was a strong, independent young woman. If this elderly stranger had ill intentions, she could easily manage him.

As she approached the reception desk, she realized that she didn't have a real name for the man she wished to see. "Can you help me?" she sweetly asked the young man behind the desk. "I'm trying to locate a guest. He came to visit my home this morning, but I was unable to see him and no one seemed to get his full name." She smiled hopefully. "Although the name Richard was mentioned. And he is an older man. Possibly in his eighties, I would venture."

"*Mr.* Richards?" the desk clerk offered. "He's an elderly guest here, and he did go out to meet with someone this morning."

"Yes, I believe that's it. My sister said it might've been Mr. Richards."

The desk clerk pointed to a sitting area across the lobby. "That's him over there. The man in the black suit with the newspaper."

"Thank you." She rewarded him with another smile then strolled across the lobby. Seeing other guests milling about, she noticed that most of them were dressed quite elegantly. Women in ornate and ruffled gowns, beaded purses, stylish hats…making her simple gray dress appear quite drab. As she approached the stranger, she felt a bit out of place. Perhaps her mother's sense of fashion was more finely tuned than Delia's.

"Excuse me," she said to the white-haired man. "Are you Mr. Richards?"

He laid down his paper and looked up. "Delia?"

She blinked. "How did you know that?"

He dropped the newspaper to the floor, slowly pushing himself to his feet, his eyes locked on her. "Why, you look just like your father."

Delia frowned. "I don't look anything like my father."

The elderly man leaned forward, peering into her eyes. "Yes, you do. You have the same green eyes." He pointed to her hair. "The same chestnut brown locks—and I'll bet they're wavy too. You are definitely your father's daughter."

"My father is fair-haired with blue eyes," she stated crisply.

"I'm sorry, Delia. I'm referring to your *real* father," he said. "Not your stepfather."

Delia felt slightly dazed now. "I—I'm confused," she admitted.

"Come, let's go sit someplace quiet. It's a bit early, but maybe you'd like some lunch."

"No, thank you." She stepped back. Was this man mad?

"How about a cup of tea?" he said gently. "I could use some myself. We have so much to talk about. I s'pect there's much you don't know. Things your mother never told you."

"Wh—what are you saying?" She studied him closely. Was he trying to trick her? "And just who are you, anyway?"

"I'm your father's uncle. Your great uncle. Your grandmother, Adelaide Williams, she was my younger sister."

"You mean my Great Aunt Adelaide?"

"Come, come." He hooked his arm into hers, slowly walking her through the lobby. "I'll try to explain everything over tea, dear."

As he led her toward the hotel's restaurant, Delia felt her head was spinning. What on earth was he talking about? *Her father was not her father?* Great Aunt Adelaide was her grandmother? Was Mr. Richards suffering from senility? With his wrinkly parchment skin and wisps of white hair, this stooped-back man might be a hundred years old. Was she a fool to take him seriously?

4

AFTER THEY WERE SEATED AT A TABLE BY THE WINDOW, DELIA TOOK
a long moment to steady herself. Attempting to carefully arrange her
words and, she hoped, get to the bottom of this mystery, she began.
"You say you're my great uncle, Mr. Richards." She slowly unfolded
a linen napkin, laying it neatly in her lap. "What is your full name?"

"I am Enoch Edward Richards."

"Enoch? I do recall Great Aunt Adelaide mentioning a younger
brother by that name."

"Yep, that's right." His light green eyes lit up. "Except that my
sister wasn't your great aunt. She was your grandmother."

"How is that possible?"

Before he could answer, a waiter came to take their order. Mr.
Richards ordered tea and biscuits and jam for both of them and then
turned back to Delia. "Adelaide was your father's mother. I mean
your real father. Not Jefferson Blackstone."

"You are saying that Jefferson Blackstone is *not* my father?"
Again she felt lightheaded. Was this man crazy?

"Jefferson Blackstone is your *stepfather,* Delia," he said gently. "I think your mother allowed you to believe he's your real father. But that ain't the truth. Your real pa is Winston Williams."

"Winston Williams," she said slowly. "I do recognize the name. He was my great aunt's son. He went out West, I believe."

"That's right. Winston did go West. But before that, he was a captain in the US Army. We heard he'd been killed in the war. But turned out that he was in a prison hospital down south. Took a shot in the leg along with a nasty head wound. Nearly died, and lost all his memory for a good long while."

"So you're telling me Great Aunt Adelaide was my grand-mother?" She was still trying to absorb this startling revelation. "And that Winston Williams, her son, is my father?"

"Yep, that's right." He nodded eagerly. "The Williams lived in Philadelphia. And your ma's family lived nearby. Winston married your mother, oh, about a year into the War Between the States, I reckon. You were born about a year later, in November."

She nodded without speaking. He did have her birthday month correct, but she still felt bewildered.

"Winston was injured in spring of '65, shortly before the war ended. Course, you were too young to recall any of that. Don't know that you ever laid eyes on your real pa." He sadly shook his head.

"But I still don't understand."

"Well, your ma, and everyone else, believed your pa was dead. She met Jefferson Blackstone in Philadelphia. For some reason he didn't serve in the war. The Blackstones were a wealthy, influential family, and your ma, thinking she was a widow…and with a baby… went and married Blackstone. I s'pect she never saw no need to tell you he weren't your real pa."

"Because she thought my father was dead."

"Well, yes…at first anyway. Although she found out—later on—that Winston wasn't dead. Your pa's memory eventually came back, and he made his way home to Philadelphia." He sighed.

"To find my mother married to someone else?"

The old man slowly nodded. "Your pa let your ma pick. She took Jefferson Blackstone."

Delia's heart twisted in sympathy for the soldier who'd survived the war only to discover his wife had married another. Truly heartbreaking. "I don't understand," she asked quietly. "It seems if my parents were already married and had a child together—that it would be law-abiding to stay married. Didn't she love him?"

"I can't answer that, Delia, whether she loved him or not. But it seemed that Jefferson Blackstone could provide for her. Your father, Winston Williams, didn't have much in the way of worldly goods."

"But you say he is Great Aunt Adelaide's son," she said eagerly. "I thought my great aunt was rather wealthy. What about that?"

"Adelaide was a poor widow back then. Her wealth came later—from Winston."

"But you just insinuated he was poor. Or something to that effect."

"After your ma made her choice, Winston went West to join me and my good friend Caleb. We'd been working a claim for pert near ten years with no luck. Winston had new ideas, and after a spell our gold mine started to show some color, but by then me and Caleb were weary of Pike's Peak, and we'd heard about a new rush in the Dakota Territory. So we sold our share of the claim to Winston and took off. We hadn't been gone a year when Winston struck the mother lode."

"That must've been hard."

He smiled. "Winston was generous to us. And he regularly sent money home to his mother too—and to you, Delia."

"To me?" She shook her head. "No, that's not true. My father—as you call him—never sent a penny to me."

"You got that wrong. He sent funds through Adelaide. She passed it along to your parents. And when Adelaide died, I heard she left everything to you and your family. Including the house she'd purchased with money sent from Winston."

"Great Aunt Adelaide did leave us an inheritance. I do remember hearing that. And her house too. That's true."

"And she paid for schooling for you. Ain't that right? Winston asked her to."

"Yes." She nodded. "She prepaid my college tuition when I was a child. I just finished two years. That was all the tuition that was paid."

"Two years of college schooling for a woman. Mighty impressive."

"My mother thinks it a waste of money." She paused as the waiter brought their tray, neatly arranging the tea things. It was difficult to grasp all this. And a small part of her still questioned the validity of this man's claims...and yet.

"Where is Winston Williams now?" she asked as she stirred milk and sugar into her tea.

"Still out West. Not mining no more. Runs a small ranch in Colorado."

"But I don't understand something, Mr. Richards—"

"Just call me Uncle Enoch. That's what your pa calls me."

"All right...Uncle Enoch...if all you're saying is true, why didn't my mother just tell me? She could've explained about my real father—if he is my real father. Furthermore, why didn't Great Aunt Adelaide tell me the truth? Why would she pretend to be my great aunt when she truly wasn't?"

"Your ma made 'em swear to an agreement," he said sadly. "She threatened to keep you away from him and Adelaide unless your pa stayed away until you became an adult. I reckon the Blackstones were embarrassed about the situation. Anyway, your pa kept his part of the bargain. And now that you finished up your schooling, your pa felt it was time." He smiled. "That's why I'm here."

"You came here to tell me that everything I've believed for the last twenty years is a falsehood?" Delia tried to keep her voice calm and even, but everything inside of her wanted to rage. "Your mission is to inform me that I've lived in a family that isn't what I thought? That I grew up thinking that I am Delia Adelaide Blackstone, but I'm really not?" She took a deep breath, hoping to steady herself in a world that seemed to be whirling out of control.

He frowned. "No, dear, that weren't my intent. You're still who you are, Delia. I only came to say you got a pa that loves you very much. A pa who'd like to meet you." He reached into an inner pocket, extracting a long thick envelope. "Winston asked me to give you this. It's his invite for you to go out to Colorado to visit him. There's train fare and a money order for your expenses. He's hoping you'll come see him."

She sighed as she fingered the long envelope. "I am so confused."

"I s'pect you are. I warned Winston it might be hard on you."

"Why didn't he come himself?"

"He's got his hands full with the ranch right now. Having some nasty disputes over water rights. A downright ornery neighbor, determined to stir up trouble."

"What kind of ranch does he have?" She took a sip of tea, trying to appear as if all was normal—as if her foundation wasn't being shaken at its core.

"He started out with cattle, but he's a clever man. Experimenting with all sorts of things. Got a nice little spot for it too. Tucked in a meadow between the mountains, it's protected some from the elements. Oh, it gets a little harsh some winters, but this time of year, well, it's heaven on earth."

"Heaven on earth?" She nibbled a biscuit.

"Lush green meadows, lots of wildflowers blooming right now. Sparkling clear streams and them snowcapped mountains against the bluest sky you've ever seen." He shook his head in a sorrowful way. "Not like this pitiful excuse of a sky in this filthy city. Can't believe what they'd done to Pittsburgh since last time I passed through these parts. Darn shame."

"I've had similar thoughts." She picked up the envelope. "You say that everything I need is in here? If I wanted to take my, uh, father up on his offer to travel to Colorado?"

"Yep. It's all there."

"Will you be going back there too? Will you accompany me on this trip?"

"Wish that I could." His face grew sad. "Unfortunately, my days living in the West are behind me now, Delia. It's beautiful country, for sure, but it can be rugged and harsh too. Getting too old for it." He grinned, revealing yellowed teeth. "Can you believe I'll be eighty-eight years old in August?"

"You don't seem a day over eighty." She smiled.

He chuckled. "Well, I'm on my way to Philly. Plan to leave tomorrow. Wanna look up some loved ones—before it's too late."

"So you recommend I go to Colorado?" she asked. "You feel this is a wise decision for a young woman?" She watched his expression closely.

He nodded firmly. "I most certainly do. I know your Grandma Adelaide would approve too. Nothing would please her more than knowing you met your pa. Her only son."

Once more she tried to absorb this. Great Aunt Adelaide was her grandmother and her son was Delia's real father…truly?

"Whether you knew it or not, Winston—*your real father*—sent your ma and step-dad money, through Adelaide, for the whole time you were growing up. He kept his share of the bargain." He peered curiously at her, as if questioning whether she would accept his invitation.

"I'm trying to understand this," she said calmly. "The idea of a father…way out West."

"Even though your pa made a new life for himself, he never got over losing you…and your ma too. He was generous out of love for you, Delia. He wanted you to have a happy childhood and good education. Now he just wants some time with you. Even if it's just a short visit. Just a few weeks even. And this time of year is beautiful in the mountains. Do you like nature?"

"I love nature."

"Then you go." He slapped his hand on the table, making his teacup jump. "You owe it to yourself, Delia. And, if you ask me, you owe it to your pa too."

Suddenly Delia remembered her own situation. Her mother had deceived her for all these years—and then there was the new plan to marry off Delia for the sake of money. "I've made up my mind, Uncle Enoch. I believe I will accept the invitation. I want to do this," she said with certainty. As soon as the words were out, she felt a sense of peace and assurance—as if this was the right choice.

"Good for you!" He let out a whoop that turned the heads of everyone in the restaurant.

"It feels like God's way of opening a new door for me," she confessed eagerly. "And I plan to walk right through it."

"You won't regret it."

"There's no time to waste either." She laid down her linen napkin and stood. The sooner she escaped Pittsburgh, the better it would be for everyone. "It's been a pleasure to meet you, Uncle Enoch. Thank you for delivering this." She folded the envelope smaller, sliding it into her purse. "Is there a way to be in touch with you once I get there? To tell you how it goes?"

"Your pa knows how to reach me. When you get to Colorado, he'll be over the moon—and no doubt he'll let me know."

"Thank you so much." She beamed at him. "I plan to set out as soon as I can book my train passage."

"You send a telegram to your pa. I reckon you'll attend to that when you get your train ticket."

"I'll do that." She patted her bag. "And everything I need to know is in that envelope? Where to go and all that?"

"It's all there." He stood up, extending his hand. "I'm right proud to have met you, Delia." Then instead of shaking hands, he hugged her. "Give this hug to your father from me. Never had a boy of my own, but if I did, I would've wanted one just like Winston. He's been like a son to me. I know you'll be pleased and proud to make his acquaintance."

"I'm sure you're right."

"Have a good journey, Delia."

She thanked him again and, feeling both disturbed and excited, she exited the hotel. Eager to get home—so that she could confront her mother with this startling revelation—Delia hurried to the streetcar stop. Oh, she knew there was still the remote chance that Uncle Enoch was a madman who'd invented this story, but the warmth in his eyes had convinced her otherwise. All it would take was one look at her mother's face when presented with this evidence, and Delia would have her answer.

5

DELIA TOOK A SEAT IN THE BACK THE STREETCAR, WHERE SHE COULD safely and furtively examine the contents of the long yellow envelope. Just like Uncle Enoch had said, it contained a generous money order as well as specific directions for her journey. After sliding those pieces back into her bag, she unfolded her father's letter. The first thing to strike her was that his penmanship was excellent. Judging by the way he formed his bold letters, his choices of words, and the structure of his sentences, he was a man of both confidence and education.

> *My Dearest Daughter Delia Adelaide,*
>
> *I must beg your forgiveness as I simultaneously attempt to make your acquaintance. A complex way to establish good rapport between father and daughter, but I hope you will be charitable. I have instructed my uncle, Enoch Richards, to enlighten you as to your paternal ancestral heritage before giving you this letter. As promised to your mother, I have kept my whereabouts and relationship clandestine until you became*

*of age. I hope that in time you'll come to understand
my rationale.*

*As my uncle will inform you, I wish to invite you
to venture into the wilds of Colorado. Do you know
we got our statehood in 1876, just one hundred years
after the birth of our country? Although our young
state is not even ten years old, I must confess that, after
seventeen years, this land does not seem overly unruly.
However I am aware that newcomers are sometimes
distressed by our "lack of civilization." I understand
that our local Indians, rough speaking miners, carous-
ing cowboys and such, do not put everyone at ease, but
I assure you that I will do everything possible to keep
you safe during your visit.*

*Enclosed you will find all you need to make your
journey. Upon your arrival, I will gladly provide
whatever you need to make your return trip, and you'll
be free to go whenever you wish. Although I do hope
you will grant us at least a few days of your excellent
companionship. I am so eager to become acquainted,
dear daughter. Words can barely express it. I have an-
ticipated this day for years. However, I want you to
know that, should you choose to decline my offer, my
love for you is unchanging – just as it has always been.
Use the money order as you like.*

*Please, send a telegram to inform me of your deci-
sion, Delia. Although I will understand if you are unable to come, I sincerely hope that you will prayerfully
consider making this trip.*

> *God's Faithful Servant and Yours as Well,*
> *Winston Edward Williams*
> *Double W Ranch, Cougar Creek Road*
> *Rainbow City, Colorado*

After she wiped her tears, she read the letter two more times then, seeing her stop was next, slipped it back into her bag. Winston Williams sounded like a genuinely good man. If all that Uncle Enoch had said was true—and she had little doubt now—she would have no compunction about making this trip. All that was left was to speak to Mother.

As she walked toward their house, she began to rehearse the words she would say. She suspected that most young women were not so cautious when speaking to their mothers, but Delia knew from years of experience that her mother was adept at manipulating a conversation to suit her own needs. Whether it was by distraction, emotion, accusation, or guilt, she knew how to get her way.

It wasn't until she was on the wide front porch that a fresh realization hit her. This house—the one they'd called home for the past six years—had belonged to Great Aunt Adelaide. She'd left it to their family when she'd passed on and, since it was much grander than their previous home, they had decided to live here. But, according to Uncle Enoch, it was probably her father—Winston Williams—who had paid for this home. How much he'd contributed to her life and livelihood—and yet, until today, she'd never even known of his existence. So very strange.

The house was quiet when she went inside. Because of the hour, she suspected that they'd already finished their midday meal, and she had no doubt that her absence was noticed. That alone would put Mother in a bad mood. She went upstairs to put away her hat and gloves, as well as to hide the envelope sent by her father. By now she was thinking of him as that—*her father*, her real father. After reading his letter, she believed it with her whole heart, and although it was a comfort to know she had one parent who seemed to genuinely care about her, Delia's feelings toward her mother had grown decidedly chilly.

"There you are." Julianne stuck her head out of her room.

"Here I am," Delia said in a flat tone.

"Did you find the old man?"

Delia considered her answer. "Did you tell Mother where I went?"

Julianne shook her head. "I didn't honestly know where you went, Delia. Did I?"

Delia smiled. "No, I suppose you didn't."

"Did you see him?" Julianne's blue eyes were big with curiosity. Delia nodded.

"What did he—"

"Delia?" Mother's voice trailed down the hallway from the direction of Delia's room. "Is that you?"

"Mother's in your room," Julianne whispered.

"Delia?" she called again.

"I'm coming, Mother," Delia said stiffly, pausing to give her little sister's golden ringlet another playful pull. "More with you later." Then, bracing herself for what was coming, Delia went to her room.

"Where have you been?" Mother demanded then waved her hand in a dismissive way. "Oh, never mind, dear. I have wonderful news for you." She held up what looked like a new riding habit. "Isn't this just perfectly stylish?"

Delia frowned at the sable brown velveteen habit. "Why are you in my room?"

"This came from the dressmakers while you were out." She held the jacket up to Delia. "You must try it on, dear, to make sure it's right. Although Miss Simpson had all your measurements and the other garments have fit properly, you just never know."

Delia removed the jacket from her mother's hands, laying it on the bed. "I need to talk to you, Mother."

"We *are* talking, dear. And have you noticed I'm not even vexed at you for going to town without informing me? Julianne said you had an errand to attend to. But I forgive you for your absentmindedness." Mother smiled brightly. "And now for my news, dear. It's very exciting. And I'm so pleased your new habit arrived. Just in the nick of time too. Do you remember how Henry Horton told you about his country home?"

"Yes, but we need—"

"Well, he has sent a wonderful invitation for us to join him there during the upcoming weekend. He wants to have a fox hunt on his property. Just imagine what fun that will be. And you are such a good horsewoman, Delia. I told him about how your great aunt insisted on your equestrian lessons and how much you enjoy—"

"Speaking of Great Aunt—"

"Do not interrupt." Mother waved a warning finger. "As I was saying, it seems that Henry has been a guest at a fashionable new hunt club in Newton Township. I believe it's called the Radnor Hunt Club. And now he wants to establish his own hunt club. Having this social gathering at his country home might be the beginning of—"

"Mother," Delia interrupted again. "We need to talk. Somewhere in *private*."

"Isn't this private?" Mother looked around the room.

"These walls are not sound-proof, and you might not want Julianne or Julius to hear what I'm about to say."

Mother's fair eyebrows arched high. "What on earth are you talking about?"

"I'm suggesting we go to the library for this discussion." Delia led the way, whisking past her mother and down the hallway, ignoring her protests that Delia should try on the riding costume. It wasn't until she was going down the stairs that she realized she still wore her hat, with her purse still dangling from her wrist.

"Today is Wednesday, Delia, so we don't have much time," Mother said as Delia went into the library. "If the riding habit needs alteration, Miss Simpson has promised that she will finish it on time, but only if we send it—"

"*Mother.*" Delia closed the library door, looking at her mother with a very stern expression, trying to remember the opening speech she'd been rehearsing in her head. "I have been to the Franklin Hotel, where I had tea with Enoch Richards. I know that he is my great uncle and that Adelaide Williams was his sister. I know that she was not my great aunt, but my grandmother. I know that she had a son named Winston Williams and that he is my father. I know that he was injured during the war and that you were married to my step-father when he returned. I know that my father, Winston Williams, with Great Aunt Adelaide's assistance, has been helping to support our family."

Mother's face was visibly pale as she sank into a chair, waving her hand like a fan in front of her face but saying nothing.

"I am sorry to shock you like this, Mother, but perhaps you can imagine *my* shock at learning these truths." Delia studied her mother.

"I was going to tell you, Delia." Mother paused to take in a deep breath. "Your, uh, your father felt it best to wait until you were grown."

"I am grown."

"Yes, well, you were at the university and—"

"Which father are you referring to?" Delia pressed. "Who felt it was best to wait until I was grown? Williams or Blackstone?"

"Williams, of course. We agreed to—"

"That's not how I understood it, Mother. I was told that you insisted on keeping this from me until I was grown. Are you saying that's not true?"

Mother waved her hand again. "It was a long time ago, Delia. How am I supposed to remember such details?"

Delia sensed deceit in her mother's downcast eyes, but at least she wasn't denying what Uncle Enoch had told her. "My father has invited me to join him in Colorado, which I intend to do."

"What?" Mother sat up straight. "You want to go to that God-forsaken country? Have you lost your senses?"

"I wish to meet my father."

Mother slowly exhaled, pursing her lips as if deep in thought.

"As your mother, I understand your interest in meeting your, uh, your father. It is understandable."

Delia blinked. "So you don't mind?"

"Not at all. But, as your mother, I must insist that Winston travel here to meet you. Not the other way around. In fact, I said as much to Mr. Richards when he was here."

Delia considered this, trying to remember the conversation at the hotel. "But my father needs to remain in Colorado. Uncle Enoch told me he has urgent matters to attend to there. Some trouble with neighbors."

"Trouble with neighbors?" Mother scowled. "He probably means the Indians. Perhaps he is worried about being scalped or burned out of his home. To think that he would invite his only daughter out there—to such a hostile and dangerous place. Haven't you read accounts of the Wild West in the newspapers, Delia? With all your education, I would think you would know more about the world than you appear to."

"Uncle Enoch has assured me that it's perfectly safe. As did my father in his letter. I am not the least bit concerned for my safety."

"Well, as your mother, I am."

"I appreciate that." Delia smiled stiffly. "I hope you will keep me in your prayers as I travel out there. I plan to leave as soon as possible."

"You cannot do this!" Mother stood with fire in her eyes. "Henry Horton is a very wealthy man, Delia. I expect a proposal from him soon. Possibly during the weekend at his country home, and you—"

"If you expect a proposal from him, I advise you to go carefully, Mother. You have already committed bigamy once. Do you really think it wise to—"

"Delia Adelaide, you horrible, wicked girl!"

"I'm sorry, Mother. But you need to understand that I do not intend to marry Henry Horton—*ever*. The sooner you accept this, the better it will be for everyone."

"But you haven't even seen his Pittsburgh mansion—it's a modern marvel with wonderful conveniences. And there's his steel mill too. And what about his country home that he's so graciously invited—"

"And I hope you will still go there, Mother. I'm sure that Fath—I mean your husband and the twins will enjoy it immensely."

Her mother's features softened. "He has fine horses, Delia. Valuable thoroughbreds with fine bloodlines," she said enticingly. "Some for racing and some for pleasure. I told him how much you love horses and riding and—"

"Perhaps my father has a horse or two," Delia said quietly as she went to the door. "Once I get there, I will write and tell you all about it."

"I forbid it!" Mother shouted. "As your mother, I forbid it."

"I am not a child, Mother. You cannot forbid it. Not legally and certainly not morally or ethically." Delia opened the door, but before she could get out, she heard her mother breaking down in tears.

"How can you do this to me, Delia? After all I've done for you?" She let out a loud sob. "This is the thanks I get from my firstborn daughter?"

Delia went over to place a hand on her mother's shoulder. "I'm sorry to hurt you, Mother. Truly I am. But it doesn't change my resolve. I *am* going." She looked down at her mother, noticing that no tears trickled down her powdered cheeks. Delia knew this was her final tactic in hopes of getting her way. As pathetic as this display was, Delia almost felt sorry for her. But her pity was more for her mother's weakness of character and for the way she had deceived Delia.

Instead of going up to her room, Delia walked out the door, heading back to the streetcar stop. Her plan was to go to the railway station to purchase a ticket and send a telegram. A small, angry, impractical part of her wanted to simply get her ticket and get on the train—and go. The more sensible side of her knew that Colorado was too far to go without packing properly.

As she rode the streetcar back into the city, she hoped that her mother would assume that she wasn't coming back, that she was gone for good. Perhaps it would give Mother some time to reconsider the role she'd played in this mother-daughter drama. Perhaps she might even be sorry by the time Delia returned.

As Delia waited in line at the train station, she pulled out her father's traveling suggestions, quickly perusing his instructions regarding trains. When her turn came, she smiled politely and greeted the ticket clerk. Buying a train ticket was nothing new to her since it was her way of getting to and from university. But she'd never purchased a ticket for such a great distance before. "I need a ticket to Denver," she told him. "With a sleeping compartment."

"When do you want to go?" he asked.

"As soon as possible," she told him.

He glanced at a chart. "The next available sleeping compartment, all the way to Denver, will be on Friday afternoon. I can get you on the 4:40." He looked up. "That soon enough for you?"

"That's fine." She removed the money order. "Can you cash this for me? And I need to send a telegram too."

She wrote out her telegram, asking her father to respond to her at the Franklin Hotel. As the ticket clerk attended to her business, he explained that her trunks could be delivered at any time before noon on Friday. "Up to three days in advance." He handed her a card. "Call this number if you need someone to pick them up, and then we'll store them and load them into the luggage car. Naturally, you'll want your smaller bags with you. Now, the Union Pacific has a first-rate dining car, but some folks prefer to bring their own food. And, of course, there are restaurants at the stops along the way." As he rambled on, she paid close attention, and soon her transactions were completed.

With her train ticket tucked safely in her purse, she boarded the streetcar again. For the fourth time, she read her father's letter. By now the words were familiar to her, and although it was a comfort, it was still very strange to think she had a father she'd never known about. A father she would come face to face with in less than a week. Her resolve to reach Colorado was stronger than ever now. Despite knowing that the next two days would be trying—mostly because of her mother's ire—she hoped that, with much to do, the time would pass quickly.

6

When Delia entered the house, she immediately knew her father was home. She frowned as she closed the front door, realizing that her mother's husband wasn't truly her father. All these years she had called him Father, but Jefferson Blackstone was no relation to her. None whatsoever. Furthermore, and in all honesty, she'd never felt terribly close to this man. In fact, she had often imagined he favored the twins over her. Perhaps it wasn't her imagination after all.

But the most difficult part of being Jefferson Blackstone's "eldest daughter" was her inability to respect him as the head of the house. Oh, she'd kept her thoughts to herself, but the older she got, the more she knew that he was not a good provider. And, besides betting on the horses and drinking to excess, he sometimes had a cruel streak that had chilled her to the bone.

Oddly enough, this new realization—that Jefferson Blackstone was not her actual father—was an unexpected relief. She stared in wonder at the familiar brass-tipped walking stick with the lion's head carved into the ivory handle. He usually carried the cane on the street with him. For as long as she could remember, she'd heard that he'd suffered some kind of knee injury—the reason he was unable to serve in the U.S. Army—but most of the time he seemed to walk just fine and the stairs didn't bother him in the least. Observing his soft kid gloves and black bowler hat carelessly tossed onto the hall-tree, she detected that although Mr. Blackstone was in the house, he was not in a happy state of mind. And the sound of angry voices coming from the library seemed to confirm this.

"She's *your* daughter," Mr. Blackstone yelled as Delia passed through the foyer. "Do something with her!"

"What would you suggest I do?" Mother retorted. "Shall I hogtie her and drag her to the altar for Henry Horton to forcibly wed?"

Delia paused at the foot of the stairs, knowing that she shouldn't be listening to this—and yet her feet refused to move. Frozen in place, she listened.

"She must marry Henry," Mr. Blackstone declared woodenly. "Remind her of what the Good Book teaches. Tell her that as a submissive daughter who wants to honor her parents, she *must* marry the man we have chosen for her. That's all there is to it."

Mother's bell-like laughter tinkled through the foyer, but there was no warmth in it. "Education has ruined her," she said. "Delia is stubborn and independent and strong-willed. If you ask me, that was her father's doing. I'll bet Winston planned this all along. He wanted her to become a willful, wayward daughter so that she could easily disobey her parents—that is why he paid for her education. It makes perfect sense now!"

Delia took in a quick breath. Was that really what Mother believed?

"Well, as I've said, she is *your* daughter, Jane. It's up to you. If you want to remain here, to maintain the life you're accustomed to, you must make Delia understand that she has no choice in this matter."

"How, pray tell?"

"I don't know. Think of something. When I consider all the years I have given that girl my name… I have treated her as my own flesh and blood. For her to repay me like this is not only ungrateful, it is a knife in my back."

"I'm sorry, Jefferson."

"Fix this, Jane. We need Delia to marry Henry. You must see that she does."

"I've tried, but she—"

"Tell her that if she chooses to go to Colorado, she is making the choice to leave this family for good. She cannot return—ever. I will not allow it."

"But Jefferson—"

"I mean it, Jane. She will not be welcome in my home."

"But she is—"

"*Tell* her, Jane!" he shouted. "Or I will."

"You don't have to tell me anything," Delia said as she pushed the library door fully open. "I heard you already."

"Delia!" Mother turned with a shocked expression.

"I didn't mean to eavesdrop, but I couldn't help but—"

"It's just as well." Mr. Blackstone came over to her, peering at her with a look of pure disdain as he shook his head in a disgusted way. "I meant what I said, child. If you are so ungrateful that you can turn your back on this family, the ones who have cared for you, supported you, loved you for your entire lifetime—if it is so easy for you to treat us in this manner, then you are not the fine young woman that I believed we had raised. Perhaps I never really knew you at all."

Delia was speechless as his words sliced through her.

Mother came closer now, taking Delia's hands in hers. "Tell me you don't plan to carry through with this plan of yours, Delia. You're not really going off to the wilds of Colorado, are you?"

Delia saw what appeared to be real tears in her mother's eyes and suddenly felt torn in two. "I only want to go visit him," she said meekly. "Perhaps for only a week. Or two at most. I got my train ticket today, and I was pleasantly surprised to discover it takes less than three days to get there—that with just a week and the return trip, why I could be back here by the end of June."

"How can you betray me like this?" Mother demanded.

"Betray *you?*" Delia frowned as she bit her tongue, refraining from demanding to know why her mother had betrayed her for all these years—why had she forced Delia to live out a lie?

"That's right. You're betraying all of us." Mr. Blackstone's intensity surprised her as he continued. "Not only your parents, but your brother and sister too. What are they to think when they discover you have left your family to travel out West to claim a complete stranger as your family? Shall we tell them you've lost your senses?"

"Of course, not. I'll explain where I'm—"

"I always thought you were such a fine young woman, Delia, so honorable and dependable." He softened his tone now. "I always speak highly of you with my friends. That is precisely why someone like Henry Horton took notice of you in the first place. Henry trusted my reports of your honesty and integrity." Placing a cool hand on her cheek, he smiled apologetically. "And Henry appreciates your beauty as well, Delia. Surely Henry's affections must mean something to you. Do you know how much the Horton Steel Mill is worth? I recently heard it could be in excess of ten million dollars." He sadly shook his head. "To think you would throw that all away for a foolish train trip—out to the frontier where God only knows what might happen to you." He made a tsk-tsk sound between his teeth. "Such a shame. A shame and a waste."

"Please, listen to him," Mother implored her.

"You claim to be a faithful woman, Delia," he continued. "You obediently attend church, even when you go by yourself. I've seen you reading your Bible in the parlor. How do you answer God's command—do you turn a deaf ear when the Bible instructs children to obey and honor their parents?"

"My father in Colorado…he is my parent too," she said meekly. "I believe it's his turn to be honored."

In response to that, Mr. Blackstone called Delia a foul name and stormed from the library, slamming the door behind him. Although the word stung like a slap, Delia recognized his honesty. Mr. Blackstone was simply showing her his true colors. Painful, yes, but it made it that much easier to go.

"Don't mind him," Mother said dismissively. "He is simply hurt and upset. He didn't mean what he said, Delia."

Delia searched her mother's eyes. "I think perhaps he did. And it doesn't really matter anymore, because my mind is made up. I am going."

"You ungrateful child!" Mother glared at her. "You are selfish and spoiled, and I cannot believe you are my daughter. You heard what your father said, Delia, if you leave like this, you will not be welcome in our home again—*ever!*" Now she too stormed from the library.

Delia stood there for a long moment, trying to grasp all that had just been said and finally realizing that perhaps it was pointless. Some things were just unknowable. And no matter what she did or said, there was no way to assuage their ill feelings toward her. She could only hope that in time they would forgive her—in the same way she knew that she needed to forgive them—and she suspected this was easier said than done. But perhaps with God's help it was possible.

Her steps felt leaden as she went up to her room. What had seemed like an adventurous trip was starting to feel more like a big heavy burden. Was she really up for it? Yet she knew she had no choice at this point. Her heart was made up—she was going.

In her room, she began to sort through her things, trying to determine what she would need for the trip and what should stay behind. Although her university dresses seemed sensible for travel and durable for life in the frontier, whatever that might entail, they were mostly winter-weight woolens. A bit warm for June. The finer gowns, the ones her mother had recently gotten made for her, were of lighter fabrics, but they seemed too refined for the western frontier. Besides, if her mother was still angry at her, Delia felt uneasy about taking them. What if they got torn or stained?

Finally, with everything heaped about her room and very few packing decisions made, Delia realized that she was hungry. Not only had she missed lunch, but the dinner hour was past too. Doubting that her presence had been missed very much at the table tonight, she poked her head out the door to listen for the members of her family. Not hearing anyone nearby, she slipped down the back staircase and into the kitchen where she quickly made herself a plate of leftovers which she carried back to her room unseen.

As she picked at the cold food, she felt like a true outcast. Did her parents really mean what they'd said in the library? Did they really plan to disown her if she carried out her plans to visit her father? And if they did, well, did it really matter?

Without packing more than a few personal items in her valise, Delia gave in to tiredness and went to bed. She would devote the entirety of tomorrow to packing.

After a night of tossing and turning, Delia felt even more out of sorts in the morning. It seemed unfair that, about to embark on a trip of this magnitude, she could not have at least a minimum of support from her family. As she smoothed out her university gowns, planning to put one in her valise and the rest in her trunk, she heard her bedroom door opening.

"I would have knocked," her mother said sharply, "but since this is my house and you are choosing to no longer live in it, I didn't feel you deserved such respect."

"Come in, Mother." Delia laid the brown wool dress on her bed and then, tossing some items from the chair, she motioned to it. "Care to sit?"

Mother sat on the edge of the chair with a terse expression. "I see you are packing," she said curtly.

"Yes." Delia picked up a nightgown, laying it atop the other clothes in the valise. "I need a few things for the train." She pointed to the trunk. "And a few things for my visit."

Mother frowned. "You are taking those ugly school dresses?"

Delia just shrugged.

"You know your father meant what he said last night, Delia."

"Which part are you referring to?" Delia made room to sit down on her bed, watching her mother's expression closely.

"You will no longer be welcome in this household if you leave." Mother looked evenly at Delia, her eyes narrowed ever so slightly.

"Then that is what it must be." Delia held her hands up in a helpless gesture.

"Have you lost your senses?" Mother's voice grew shriller. "Do you honestly think you can make it—a woman alone in this world? In the Wild West, no less?"

"I can't really say. But I know this. I have an earthly father in Colorado who loves me and wants to see me. Besides that, I have a heavenly Father who promises to take care of me." She smiled. "What more do I need?"

"You are a fool." Mother stood. "I have raised an utter fool for a daughter."

"I'm sorry you feel that way." Delia was on the verge of tears, but she wanted to appear strong.

Mother opened the wardrobe, slowly removing a sea green dress of voile and satin and lace—one of the gowns that Delia had actually liked. "Such a waste…an unfortunate waste." She turned to Delia, shaking the gown at her. "I want nothing left in this room!" she shouted. "Anything you leave behind will be given away. I will remove every trace of you from this house—every trace of you from my heart."

Delia felt the lump in her throat growing bigger. "Mother," she said in a husky voice. "I know you're angry at me and you might always be angry at me. And there's a part of me that's angry at you right now."

"*You* are angry at *me?*"

"For deceiving me, Mother. All these years when you led me to believe that Jefferson was my father. And if you'd had your way, I still wouldn't know the truth."

"It was for your own good."

Delia felt that was untrue, but with tears streaking down her cheeks, she didn't want to argue. "Even though a part of me is angry at you, I want you to know that I still love you. And if you ever get past this, I hope that we can reunite again."

Her mother's angry blue eyes filled with tears and for a moment, Delia imagined that perhaps the rift between them might be shrinking, and so she went over, attempting to embrace her. But her mother shoved her away.

"Get your things out of my house, Delia. If you go to Colorado, you are dead to me. Do you understand? *Dead!*" She rushed from the room.

Delia let her tears flow freely after she closed her bedroom door. The hatred still hanging in the small room made the air feel hot and close—so much so she could barely breathe. She had to get out of this place—the sooner the better. And if Mother meant what she said, Delia might as well take everything with her. But how?

Delia opened the window to let in some air and began to pace, trying to make a plan. Suddenly, as a whiff of lilacs drifted in, she knew exactly what to do. As a child, when she came to visit Great Aunt Adelaide's house, she had sometimes explored the attic where many old trunks resided beneath layers of dust. By all rights, those trunks should belong to her since the previous owner was really Delia's grandmother.

Delia hurried on up to the hot stuffy attic and started to examine the trunks, deciding which ones were sturdy enough to make a train trip to Colorado. And then, using an old rug, she slid them down the stairs and into her room.

It took until the mid-afternoon to pack and label everything, but when she was done, besides being sticky and dirty, she felt a sense of satisfaction. Her room was completely emptied of anything and everything that would remind anyone of her.

When it sounded as if her mother and the twins had gone out, probably to the park for their afternoon stroll, Delia slipped downstairs and put in a quick telephone call to have her trunks picked up and taken to the train station and they promised to get someone there by three. Next she called the Franklin Hotel, making a room reservation for the night. It was a bit of an extravagance, but thanks to her father, it was something she could easily afford.

She hurried back upstairs and, after a quick cleanup, sat down at her desk to write notes to her family members. She started with her mother, writing many of the things she'd already said and attempting to remind her that she still loved her. Next she wrote a brief note of gratitude for Jefferson. It wasn't easy, but she felt it was important. After that she wrote a brief note to Julius, saying she was embarking on an adventure in the Wild West. He should like that. And finally she wrote a note to Julianne, telling her to study hard—even if she was a girl—and to keep saying her prayers at night. And she put the blue topaz earrings in the envelope.

She was just setting the envelopes on the parlor mantle when she heard someone at the door. Relieved that it was just the stevedore, she watched as her trunks were loaded in the cart. Then, loaded down with her valise, leather case, and hatbox, she headed for the streetcar stop. She knew she could've called for a cabbie, but something about riding the streetcar, burdened down with her baggage and heavy heart, felt like a fitting way to depart her family home. And when a few tears trickled down her cheeks, she didn't even attempt to hide them.

7

IF DELIA HAD FELT OUT OF PLACE IN THE FRANKLIN HOTEL LOBBY while meeting Uncle Enoch yesterday, it was ten times worse this afternoon. Not only was she wearing one of her plainest school dresses, which looked even more drab—as a trio of young women in summery pastel gowns gracefully floated past—it was dusty and wrinkled too. To add to her overall unbecoming image, she had hurriedly pinned up her hair this morning and now strands were sneaking down, trailing around her face, which she suspected was still flushed from the heat of her rushed packing in her stuffy room. All the she had left to ease through checking in right now was good manners.

As she waited in line at the reception desk, with her luggage in hand, she felt certain she could pass for a cleaning lady—or, as her mother would say, 'something the cat dragged in.' She felt no surprise that the bellboy hadn't offered to carry her bags at the entrance. He probably thought she was too poor to tip him. No matter, she was strong enough to carry her own bags. Now if only she could get checked into her room, where she planned to clean up and transform herself into a normal human being again and, hopefully, get some food. If only there wasn't a line for the desk clerk!

Tapping her toes impatiently, she took in a deep breath and, trying to feign serenity and patience, she held her head high as she slowly surveyed the bustling lobby. So many well-dressed women in lovely gowns—as if they were attending a summer wedding, although she suspected they were simply guests of the hotel. It almost made her understand why Mother had been so put off by her university dresses.

Delia felt a surprised relief to realize that she'd had the foresight to pack a couple of the new gowns in her larger case. She hadn't really planned to wear them, but perhaps she would change her mind. She hoped the delicate gowns hadn't had time to become overly wrinkled. She set her bags on the thick carpet, willing the short line in front of her to move faster.

As she tugged at a glove that was concealing a less than pristine hand, she got the distinct feeling she was being watched. Although she couldn't imagine who would find interest in a ragamuffin girl like her, Delia looked around the lobby again. Off to her right, she noticed a tall, dark-haired man with nice broad shoulders. His eyes were fixed on her, but when she returned his stare, he looked away—affording her the opportunity to study him a bit more closely.

This fellow was positioned next to a pair of ornate iron doors for, as far as she could detect, no apparent reason. Or maybe he was simply waiting for someone. A wife perhaps. Because, she surmised, someone as attractive as this man would certainly be taken. Probably with a couple of small children too. He looked neat and respectable in his dark pants and stylish long coat. Although he had the appearance of a businessman, he did not appear to be the sort of man who sat behind a desk all day. In fact, he seemed more like a man who would look good upon a horse. Feeling embarrassed by that thought, Delia looked away. Had she actually been staring? Never mind that he was the one who'd started it.

To be fair, there could be any number of reasons why. Perhaps he was wondering why a fashionable hotel like this would allow someone like her to take a room. She was, in fact, wondering the same thing herself. Good grief, why hadn't she taken more time to clean up before she'd left the house? Of course, she knew why. She'd been in a hurry.

Feeling even more uncomfortable about her disheveled appearance, she turned her attention downward, taking in her black button-top shoes. Of course, they were so dusty they looked more gray than black. And they were a bit worn too. They had been serviceable shoes for school, with plenty of wear left in them, although they could use a good polish. Maybe she could get someone at the hotel to polish them.

The line moved forward one space, and now she had only one man in front of her. As she stepped up, she glanced to her right again, surprised to see that the handsome young man was still there. And, unless she was delusional, he was still watching her. At least it seemed that way. Feeling unexplainably bold, she decided to return his gaze, looking directly into his eyes for a few seconds. From this distance, she couldn't determine the color, but they were dark like his hair and brows. And as he returned her stare, there was an intensity that sent a strange shiver down the back of her neck, forcing her to look away.

As she took in a quick breath, Delia felt her face flushing again—and the lobby was quite cool and comfortable, especially compared to the stuffy room where she'd packed her trunks. Feeling unsettled and self-conscious, she glanced over her other shoulder, making a pretense of looking for someone. As if she were meeting someone. But mostly she was curious as to whether she was wrong about the stranger. Perhaps he was simply looking at something or someone beyond her and she had assumed he was watching her.

That's when she noticed the trio of fashionable young women again. The same ones she'd seen earlier. The girls seemed to be her age, perhaps younger, but definitely fresh-faced and pretty. Clustered like colorful birds, they were gathered around a display of magazines and newspapers for sale. As they chirped and laughed, Delia realized they were well worth a young man's attention. Of course, the stranger had been watching them.

Both relieved and disappointed that his intense attention hadn't been focused on her, she watched as the guest ahead of her took his key and moved away from the reception desk. Stepping up, she quickly and concisely gave her name, explaining she'd made a room reservation. "If it can be arranged, I will need a room with a bath," she said politely, "I was in a rush and unable to tidy up and change my clothes before I left."

The man nodded with a sympathetic expression. "We hope you're most comfortable during your stay here." He peered curiously at her. "Did you say your name is Miss Delia Williams?"

She nodded, feeling a bit guilty for using her father's name instead of Blackstone.

"That's interesting because we got a telegram this morning for someone named Miss Delia Blackstone, but it was sent from a Mr. Winston Williams."

"Oh, yes," she said eagerly. "That's my father. I'm sorry for the confusion. My name used to be Blackstone. It is Williams now."

He nodded, turning away to get something.

She felt a wave of nervous guilt. She didn't think there was anything illegal about going by a different name, but she wasn't absolutely sure either.

"Here you go." He set down the telegram along with a brass key. "Your suite will be on the tenth floor." He pointed to her right. "The elevator is over there, behind that set of wrought iron doors."

"Elevator?" She frowned.

"That's a device that carries you—"

"I *know* what an elevator is," she said crisply. "I'm just surprised that we have one in Pittsburgh."

He nodded with pride. "The first one. But from what I hear, there may be an elevator business in town before long. With all our steel factories, it seems a good idea."

"How very interesting." She took the key, gathered her bags, and thanked him. As she headed directly to the right side of the lobby, she could see that the handsome stranger was still there, posted right next to the iron doors as if he was a sentry. To her discomfort, his eyes still seemed fixed on her. Hadn't he been told that it was rude to stare?

Attempting to ignore the handsome, ill-mannered young man, she proceeded. Although she'd seen photographs of elevators before, she'd never actually seen one up close, and she'd never been inside one. As she considered the idea of riding up in a little box—for ten floors, which might be nearly a hundred feet—she wasn't even sure she cared to experience it. Even though the idea of climbing ten flights of stairs with two heavy bags sounded tiring after her long day of packing, perhaps she would opt for the exercise.

"Are you wishing to take the elevator?" he asked.

She looked into the young man's eyes, noting that they were an attractive mixture of pine green and dark brown. "Uh, yes…well, I was considering it."

"Nothing to be afraid of," he said in a casual way.

"Oh, I am not afraid," she told him—and it was true, she wasn't actually afraid, just a bit uneasy. "I simply thought I might enjoy the stairs."

"But you're carrying your own bags." He pointed to her load. "What floor is your room on?"

She frowned at him. While attending the university, young women were often warned about certain things—like not disclosing personal information or whereabouts to a perfect stranger.

"I'm sorry," he said quickly. "I'm sure that's none of my business."

"I believe I will take the elevator," she declared.

"Allow me." He opened the gated doors, waiting as she went inside, but when the floor jiggled ever so slightly beneath her feet, she stepped back out to solid ground. The handsome stranger smiled with amusement.

"It's quite safe," he assured her, still holding the gated door opened. "I've ridden on it a dozen times. Usually there's an operator running it, but he told me he had to see to something. He promised to be right back, but he seems to have vanished."

"I think I'll take the stairs." She glanced across the lobby, noticing that the stairs were all the way on the other side.

"You look a bit worn out," the man said with what seemed genuine compassion. "I'm happy to help you with operating the elevator. I've been up so many times that I know how it works."

"Well, I…"

"Come on," he urged. "I'll bet you're an adventurous girl. Everyone should have a ride on an elevator—at least once." His smile vanished. "Unless you're afraid."

"I am *not* afraid," she said for the second time. Then, taking in a deep breath, she stepped into the small box and, once again feeling the floor swaying slightly beneath her, she clutched tighter to the handles of her bags, as if that would help.

"It's perfectly normal for an elevator to move like that," he explained as he closed the doors on the outside. "You see, this tiny room is suspended with ropes and cables and weights. It has a steam engine down in the basement to move it up and down. It's not terribly complicated." He closed the doors on the inside. "And I think you'll be pleasantly surprised at how quick and easy this is—much better than lugging your bags up several flights of stairs. But you'll have to tell me your floor's number."

"Ten," she said stiffly. "Thank you."

He pulled a lever, and after a little jolt she could feel herself going up, and up, and up. And then, almost as quickly as it began, the elevator stopped. And the stranger stepped forward to open both sets of doors. "There you go. The tenth floor."

"Thank you," she said as she hurried out to solid ground. "That really was nicer than climbing ten flights of stairs."

He politely tipped his head then closed the doors. Still trying to grasp everything, she stood there for a moment, listening to the sound of the elevator going back down again. As she walked to her room, she could imagine just how silly she must've looked and sounded to that sophisticated man. Certainly not like a woman with a college education! But she was tired and under great duress—most assuredly not her usual self.

Her room felt decidedly luxurious with a thick carpet, a comfortable looking bed, a pair of soft plush chairs, and a handsome marble-topped table. Best of all was the bathroom. What a treat to have a bathroom all to herself—with hot water right out of the tap! But before she did anything, she opened the telegram. What would she do if her father had changed his mind? Perhaps the Indians were restless, or he simply felt it inconvenient to have a daughter out there getting in his way. To her relief, the telegram was warm and welcoming, and he promised to be waiting for her at the station in Colorado City, which was about an hour's drive from his ranch.

As she ran water into the tub, pouring in some of the hotel's bath salts which smelled of lavender, she realized that for one night, she would feel like a princess. After that she had no idea what sort of accommodations she would have. After all, she was journeying to the wilderness of Colorado. What could she expect? Certainly not indoor plumbing! So for now, she planned to enjoy this.

While the tub was filling, she opened her large case, removing the pale green dress and laying it out on the bed. Fortunately, it hadn't had time to get too wrinkled, and the shirred layers of voile fabric with its lace trim seemed to hide any rumpled imperfections. She removed the bone-colored shoes her mother had raved about a few days ago. Although they were button-tops, they seemed much more delicate than her black ones. And there was no denying they complimented the light-colored dress.

This was just the sort of ensemble that would fit in with the trio of giggling girls down in the lobby. Not that she wanted to imitate their frivolity, but at least she wouldn't stick out like a sore thumb either. Besides, she told herself, this might be one of her only opportunities to dress like this. At least for a few weeks, or however long she remained at her father's ranch. Because she doubted this lovely gown would be appropriate for the wilds of Colorado.

After her relaxing aromatic bath, she took her time in dressing carefully. Layering on the proper undergarments, including the corset, which she probably didn't need, and the bustle which the gown required. All in all, she dressed herself in a way her mother would approve, finally brushing and arranging her hair in a style that her college roommate Beatrice had recently taught her to do, swept out from the sides and piled high on top, secured with combs and pins.

As she looked at her image in the dresser mirror, she couldn't help but giggle—not unlike those silly girls downstairs. Her transformation was so complete that she wondered if anyone, including the handsome stranger, would even recognize her now. She hoped not.

She secured her golden watch brooch onto her bodice and then, for a final touch, opened Great Aunt Adelaide's jewelry case, removing the emerald earrings. It wouldn't be the first time she'd worn them, but she could count on one hand the other occasions. For some reason, it felt fitting to wear them tonight. It was as if she were making her own personal declaration of independence, and she felt certain Great Aunt Adelaide was cheering her on.

Checking the time on her watch, Delia was surprised to discover it was not even six o'clock. And yet her stomach was rumbling. With all her packing, and not having had a thing to eat since mid-morning when she'd snuck fruit and cheese from the kitchen, she decided that an early dinner was just what she needed. She started to take her old leather purse with her, then remembered the pretty little beaded bag her mother had gotten to go with her new wardrobe and decided to give it a try. The big question was whether it was large enough to contain the small book of essays she'd been carrying in her other purse. When she discovered the book fit, she dropped in her room key then slipped on the white lacy gloves and headed out of her room.

She felt a bit self-conscious as she walked down the long hall toward the elevator. It wasn't that she'd never donned formal attire before, but this ensemble felt much more sophisticated than anything she'd ever owned. Clearly, her mother had been trying to make her appear womanly and grown up—and well off. Not just the gangly schoolgirl, like Mother had accused Delia of playing for too long. But being here in this fancy hotel and dressed in these fashionable clothes, she was completely outside of her normal life. So much so that she felt she could be part of a theatrical production.

As she pushed the call button next to the elevator doors, she wondered if that might be the best way to carry this out. As if she were in a play, she would simply pretend to be someone else. As she heard the sound of the elevator making its way upward, it occurred to her that she truly *was* someone else. All her life she had imagined herself to be the daughter of Mr. and Mrs. Jefferson Blackstone or Pittsburgh, when she was actually the daughter of Winston Williams of Colorado.

When the elevator doors were pushed open by a short man wearing a burgundy velvet jacket, the idea came to her. If she truly were a different person, perhaps it was time to adopt a different name. As she exchanged greetings with the operator, her mind was made up. From here on out, she would be known as Delia Adelaide *Williams.*

By the time she exited the elevator, strolling into the lobby, she knew that it was true. She really was Delia Williams. And it felt right. Holding her head high, Delia Williams walked gracefully through the elegant lobby. Even though she had never been comfortable with dining alone in a public restaurant before, she was ready for it now. After she made it clear that she was meeting no one, she was shown to a small table against the wall.

Despite her hunger, Delia was determined to exercise her best manners. She laid her napkin on her lap, taking her time to survey the menu. When the waiter returned, she politely gave him her order and after he left, feeling a bit conspicuous for sitting alone, she removed her book of essays by Ralph Waldo Emerson and started to read. She was about three-fourths through the book and, although she'd read it in college, she was enjoying it from a slightly older perspective this time. Certainly she did not agree with all of Mr. Emerson's philosophies, but she found many of his thoughts to be sensible and practical.

"Good evening."

She looked up, expecting to see the waiter bringing her food, although it was a bit quick. Instead it was the handsome stranger who'd helped her with the elevator, smiling down on her as if he believed that they were actual acquaintances. She did not know what to say.

8

WYATT HADN'T BEEN SURE, AT FIRST, THAT IT WAS REALLY THE SAME girl. Or should he say woman, because she seemed much more grown up now. He had observed her walking across the lobby, looking very much like royalty, and despite his resolution to avoid females in general for the next few years, he found himself feeling pulled in. Not only by her beauty, which was undeniable, but there was something else too. Something he'd noticed when he'd watched her waiting for the desk clerk.

She had caught his attention from the start. Not only because she'd been wearing such a dull serviceable dress—although that had aroused his curiosity—but more to do with the way she carried herself, the way she held her head, the way she didn't seem too intimidated to look him in the eye. And those eyes! He didn't know that real people had eyes the colors of emeralds.

And now, like the pauper transformed into a princess, she had emerald earrings that matched her eyes. Her gleaming chestnut hair was piled on her head, and her gown—although he was no expert—was lovely.

"Hello?" She looked up with a perplexed brow.

"I apologize for interrupting." He suddenly realized he'd overstepped the bounds of etiquette. This was something Aunt Lilly had warned him about numerous times. The way people behaved on the East Coast was not the same as in the West. Why had he forgotten?

"You are not interrupting," she said with what seemed a tinge of amusement.

He looked down at the book in her hand, feeling a surge of hope—perhaps he could rescue his misstep. "I noticed you're reading *The Conduct of Life*," he said eagerly. "I enjoy reading Emerson too."

Her eyes lit up. "You do?"

"Yes. If you don't mind me asking, which chapter are you reading?"

"I have just finished the one on beauty."

He nodded. "Ah, yes. What did you think of it?"

She looked ill at ease as she smiled politely. "I enjoyed it. I've been thinking on one line in particular." She opened the book, searching the page. "Here it is: 'We see God face to face every hour, and know the savor of nature.'"

She could have knocked him over with a feather just then. That was his favorite line of the whole book, but to make this claim felt so unbelievable that he knew he would appear false. And so he simply nodded. "That is a good line." He made a slight bow now, something he'd never done before in his life. "Forgive me for not introducing myself earlier—I completely forgot my manners. I am Wyatt Davis, and I would be pleased to make your acquaintance."

She looked a bit taken aback, but her smile remained in place—a most engaging and beautiful smile. "I am Miss...." She paused, perhaps to determine if he were truly trustworthy, then continued. "Miss *Williams.*"

"I'm pleased to meet you, Miss Williams. I've been living in Philadelphia."

"I've been to school in Philadelphia," she confided. "But my family home is in Pittsburgh." Her eyes seemed to darken with sadness for a moment.

"I'm only in Pittsburgh for a short while and don't know anyone here." He spoke quickly and mostly to stretch out this moment. "But it's been an interesting visit so far." Even more interesting after meeting her.

"How have you enjoyed our *fair* city?" The way her green eyes twinkled made him believe she was speaking facetiously, which indicated a sharp wit—a good trait when paired with kindness.

"Your steel mills are quite impressive," he told her. "I spent most of my day at the Horton Steel Factory. Henry Horton has created a modern wonder."

It suddenly seemed that the light in her eyes went out. "So I have heard," she said woodenly.

"You're not fond of the Horton Steel Factory?" He studied her face, trying to discern what he had said to offend her.

"I have no opinion on it one way or another." She reached for her book now, opening it as if to signal this conversation was over.

"Excuse my intrusion," he said awkwardly. "Please, enjoy your dinner, Miss Williams." And feeling like an ill-mannered fool, he tipped his head and stepped away.

Because he'd made his dinner reservation for seven, he had no reason to remain in the restaurant and, eager to make his exit since he'd clearly said or done something ignorant, he slipped back out into the lobby. He considered returning to his room, but since he had only twenty minutes until dinner, he decided to bide his time with the *Post-Gazette*.

Instead of reading the newspaper, which he positioned in his lap, he replayed his conversation with Miss Williams. Oh, he knew it was impertinent to walk up to an unfamiliar woman and attempt an introduction, but it wasn't as if they were complete strangers. After all, he'd helped her with the elevator. And, to be fair, hadn't they engaged in pleasant conversation at first? When she'd read that Emerson quote, he'd been nearly floored. So, he asked himself, what went wrong?

Rather than attempting to answer this impossible question, he decided to consider the incident in its entirety. Wyatt Davis, a country bumpkin from what easterners referred to as the Wild West, had allowed himself to be taken in by a sophisticated citified woman, who was obviously was well off. He could tell just from looking at her. Although she hadn't seemed like that when they'd first met. This afternoon, she appeared somewhat vulnerable and out of place, clearly uncomfortable in the elegant hotel lobby. Then she shows up at the restaurant looking like a queen. It made no sense. But it also added to the overall mystery that had initially attracted him to her.

Still he could hardly believe that he'd been pulled in by a woman's wiles. Perhaps that was the wrong word since it wasn't as if Miss Williams had tried to trap him through deceit. Or had she? He'd spent these past two years (after the way Maryanne had toyed with his heart) managing to keep females—even the pretty ones his aunt had introduced him to—at arm's length. What was wrong with him now?

Sternly reminding himself he was about to embark on what he expected to be a year-long adventure, he asked the question: Why would he go out of his way to make the acquaintance of *any* woman? Particularly a wealthy city woman. Was he mad?

And with his train leaving tomorrow, did he honestly believe that striking up a conversation with a beautiful Pittsburgh woman was sensible? While he waited for his dinner reservation, he went over all the many reasons he needed to put Miss Williams, and women in general, out of his mind.

Until he attained the funds required to transform his ranch into a place where a decent woman would care to live, he needed to keep himself to himself! If and when that time should come, he would need to find someone suited for the rugged lifestyle of ranch life—not an overly indulged gentlewoman.

Delia didn't know what to think as she pretended to continue reading her book. On one hand, Wyatt Davis was attractive, well spoken, and quite pleasant. On the other hand, those charming characteristics could be her undoing. After two years of university life, she knew better than to engage with strange men. Especially ones with so much natural charisma. But for Mr. Davis to make that comment about Horton Steel... She'd felt her blood run cold.

For several minutes, furtively glancing about the restaurant for anyone connected to her parents, she wasn't even sure she would be able to eat. But eventually her food arrived, and her appetite revived. Satisfied that no one was going to swoop in and attempt to carry her away, she began to eat. It was the first real meal she'd had in two days.

Dabbing her lips with the napkin, she glanced around the restaurant again, still trying to make sense of the strange encounter. Had this young man been sent here by her parents? Although, other than leaving her father's address in Colorado, she hadn't disclosed any other details regarding her trip in her note to Mother. She certainly hadn't shared her plans to spend the night in a hotel in the city. She had actually insinuated that she would already be on the train by now. Even so, Mother might have guessed the truth.

Delia knew that her mother could be doggedly determined at times. And losing the hoped-for alignment with Henry Horton had seriously aggravated both her parents. So much so that it was possible they'd gone to extreme measures. But if they truly had sent Mr. Davis here, what was their intention? Did they think a smooth-talking stranger could entice her to give up her plans? Or was Mr. Davis a private detective who was right now telephoning her parents, advising them of her whereabouts? Perhaps she should eat quickly and skip dessert. Just in case they planned to show up and create an embarrassing scene.

But, short of kidnapping her—and she knew they wouldn't do that—how could they possibly force their will upon her? No, she finally decided as she finished up her meal, she was simply overreacting. Her sensibilities must be strained from disagreeing with her mother over the past couple of days. Still, despite the temptation of cherries jubilee, she declined dessert.

As much as she would enjoy lingering in the fancy lobby—now that she no longer felt like a vagabond—she was unwilling to risk an unfortunate encounter with her angry parents. Before going to her room, she stopped by the front desk. The same desk clerk from this afternoon warmly greeted her and, she felt certain, didn't recognize her.

"I do not wish to be disturbed." She gave him her name. "If anyone should call for me, please, do not give out my room number or even disclose that I am here."

"Be assured that guest information is private, Miss Williams. It is our policy."

"Thank you."

"You're welcome. Enjoy your visit."

Looping the beaded handle of her delicate purse around her wrist, Delia held her head high as she strolled across the lobby toward the elevator. The place was bustling with guests, and she could feel eyes on her, but she didn't care to acknowledge it. Whether she was being watched by Mr. Davis or just another curious guest, she told herself she did not care. It did not matter. All that mattered was getting up to her room without being stopped by her parents.

To her dismay the elevator was already in use which meant she needed to wait or take the stairs. But to reach the stairs meant another stroll through the lobby. Not to mention a trek up ten flights. So she decided to wait, and instead of glancing around the lobby like she was tempted to do, she removed her book of essays and made a pretense of casually reading it while she waited for the elevator.

It was only seven thirty when she was back in her room and, although it seemed a bit early to turn in, she was exhausted from the past two days. And so, after checking to see that her door was securely locked, she prepared for bed. It was such a luxury not sharing a bathroom with her younger brother and sister or the women in her college dormitory that she was determined to take her time and thoroughly enjoy it. And so, feeling quite decadent, she indulged in another bath. She had never had two baths in one day before. She doubted she ever would again.

As she poured bath salts in the warm water, she wondered about Mr. Davis. Wyatt Davis—if that was his real name. Just who was he anyway? If he was a detective, someone her parents had hired to find her, how would he have recognized her? Perhaps her parents had given him her high school graduation photograph? But how would they have contacted him so quickly?

Waiting for the tub to fill, she ran the timeline through her head. If Mother got home shortly after she left, she could've read the letter and called someone even before Delia got off of the streetcar. And it was possible that Mr. Davis worked for the hotel. She'd read somewhere that some of the larger hotels employed detectives. As she turned off the tap, she remembered their introductions—perhaps she'd thrown him off by using the name *Williams*. Anyway, she would try to keep to her room as much as possible tomorrow.

As she soaked in the lavender-scented bath, she wondered why such a delightful young man should want to be a detective. Not that she really knew him well enough to call him delightful—although he had made a good first impression upon her. But what would motivate a person to wish to snoop around in other peoples' affairs? Perhaps for the adventure? Or the money? She sighed. She didn't like to be judgmental, but it didn't seem a very honorable profession.

It wasn't until the water began to cool that she questioned why Mr. Davis would bring up the Horton Steel Factory the way he did. Especially if he was trying to be discreet and win her trust. Unless he had hoped to provoke a reaction from her, possibly to confirm his suspicion that she was really Delia Blackstone—not Miss Williams.

Oh, it was too much to figure out, and it was starting to make her head hurt. Better to take a book to her bed and attempt to relax. And so, feeling clean and comfortable in her soft batiste nightgown, she opened up the book of essays again. And, as if to taunt her, her eyes fell upon the quote she had shared. She read the words aloud again. "'We see God face to face every hour, and know the savor of nature.'" His expression upon hearing that sentence had surprised her—his eyes, which had reminded her of mossy woodlands, had lit up, almost as if Emerson's words had struck a chord. But then he'd simply called it a "good line." Not good communication in her opinion. But then, if he was a hotel detective like she was imagining, he probably did not wish to engage too intimately. And it was just as well since she had no use for a busybody snoop who earned his living spying on others.

9

WYATT ROSE EARLY, AS WAS HIS HABIT, AND AFTER QUICKLY DRESSING, hurried down to the hotel lobby in the hopes that he would see her again. He had loitered about the lobby for most of the evening, watching for her—to no avail. The girl was making herself scarce, and he figured it might be his own fault.

Not spotting her anywhere, he strode toward the restaurant, glancing around to see that only two tables were filled and those were with businessmen. But then it was rather early for breakfast. Hopefully she hadn't left her room yet. Finding a morning paper, he positioned himself in a spot where he could see both the elevator and stairs. His plan was to pretend to read the paper while he watched for her.

Oh, he knew he was being ridiculous. Especially since he had absolutely no intention of engaging with her. He had promised himself that he would say nothing more than a polite "good morning" and then move on. It was just that he wanted to see her again. For just one more time he wished to simply gaze upon her and, in a sense, print her beautiful image into his memory bank...something he might draw on from time to time. Perhaps while up in Alaska, chilling his bones while searching for nuggets, he would garner some warmth from the memory of those emerald green eyes and that gleaming chestnut hair.

His plan, if she ever came down, was to use the newspaper as a screen until she reached a certain spot in the lobby. Then he would casually lay it down, slowly stand, and leisurely stroll toward her— on his way to the restaurant. It all seemed quite feasible and, he hoped, innocent.

But by nine o'clock, he was ravenous. He usually had breakfast two hours earlier than this. He was just starting to question his good sense when the elevator doors opened and out she stepped. Not dressed nearly as elegantly as last night, she wore a sensible tan gown with a high neck and very little frill. Similar to the gray one she'd had on yesterday, only cleaner and less rumpled. But the severity of the gown, especially compared to what the other women, now milling about, were wearing, made her resemble a teacher or even a minister's wife.

Looking away from her, as if he hadn't seen her, he laid down his paper and stood, heading for the restaurant where, to his relief, she appeared to be going too. As far as he could tell, she hadn't observed him. Not wanting to appear overly interested, he kept his distance as he followed her. It wasn't that he disapproved of her relatively plain dress, it was simply that it intrigued him. Why did this woman go around like a schoolmarm by day and a princess at night? Baffling.

The maître d' was speaking to Miss Williams and then gestured to Wyatt who was now waiting behind her. "Are you together?" he said more to Wyatt than to her.

She turned and, seeing Wyatt, frowned slightly. "No, we are not," she crisply told the maître d' and he excused himself then took her to a table.

Chuckling upon his return, he smiled at Wyatt. "Such a lovely woman, it is too bad she did not wish your company."

Wyatt chuckled too. "Yes, too bad. If it's not too much trouble, can you seat me where I can see her face—but not too close?"

The maître d' grinned. "Certainly."

Wyatt did his best to appear nonchalant as he was seated nearby. Focusing his attention on the menu, he furtively glanced her way when she wasn't looking toward him. To both his pleasure and dismay she was even prettier than he remembered. Despite her plain dress, Miss Williams was beautiful.

The waiter took her order first and, as a result, she was both served first and finished eating first. She seemed eager to get away from him and without even returning his smile, she turned and hurried away. He let out a disappointed sigh as he spread a liberal amount of raspberry jam on his toast. What did he expect? Besides, he had promised himself that he was only going to look at her. Wasn't that just what he'd done? He should be relieved.

Delia hadn't been surprised to see Mr. Davis waiting for her in the lobby. And she certainly hadn't fallen for his guise behind the newspaper. He'd clearly been watching for her. And he'd intentionally followed her into the restaurant too, and, unless she was mistaken, he'd bribed the maître d' to seat him nearby as well. But at least he was still eating. That gave her the chance to hurry over to the front desk to inquire about remaining for a few hours past check out time. She explained about her train departure time, and the desk clerk kindly agreed to let her stay.

Feeling a bit relieved, but still concerned about Mr. Davis, she went over to peruse the newsstand, picking out a new novel to take on her trip. After purchasing it, she hurried back to her room where she planned to remain until three. That was her reason for eating such a late breakfast, so that she could skip lunch and avoid any more encounters with Mr. Davis. More than ever, she was certain he was a detective—and all she wanted now was to get securely on the train without any intervention from her family. Once the train pulled out of Union Station, she would be able to breathe more easily.

She used her time to repack her bags, read, and have a nap. Despite her concerns over Mr. Davis and her parents, she felt surprisingly relaxed by the time she went down to the lobby to ask for a cabbie to transport her to Union Station. And seeing no sign of Mr. Davis in the lobby, she thought perhaps she had managed to evade him after all.

At the station, she went to the ladies waiting area, where she sat and read until she heard the announcement that her train had pulled in. Taking her time to gather her bags, she made her way through the crowds. She was nearly to the platform when she heard the announcement that her train was now boarding. Feeling like she was home free, she pulled out her ticket, waiting in line to board.

Just as the conductor checked her ticket, she looked up and saw him—Mr. Davis was already aboard the train, staring down at her with a furrowed brow. "Move along, miss," the conductor said as he handed her bags to a porter. "We need to keep our schedule."

With a fluttering heart, she hurried aboard. How had Mr. Davis been allowed to board without a ticket? Perhaps he'd said he was telling someone goodbye. But how had he known that she would be on this train? Furthermore, what did he intend to do about it?

"Porter," she said to the man carrying her bags. "Can you please show me to my berth?"

"That's what I'm doing, ma'am." He maneuvered through the crowded aisle of a coach car. "Right this way."

Before long, she had tipped the porter, and she and her luggage were safely stowed in her berth. Although the space was a bit tight and not as luxurious as her hotel suite, it was surprisingly nice, and she was relieved to be behind a locked door, which she had no intention of opening for anyone—and she would not venture out until the train was well on its way. Even then she would be cautious. Why on earth had he followed her here?

By the time the train pulled out of Union Station, she realized she was very hungry. It was a bit past five, and she hadn't eaten since breakfast, but her plan to enjoy an early dinner seemed hampered by the chance that Mr. Davis might still be on board. Although why he would be was a mystery. What did he think he could do—forcibly remove her from the train at the next stop? If he so much as laid a finger on her, she would make so much noise that everyone aboard would hear.

With hunger getting the best of her, she decided to venture out. She cautiously opened the door, looking both ways before she emerged and started for the dining car, which the porter had explained was toward the front of the train.

She began to feel some relief when she reached the dining car without a sign of Mr. Davis, but when she pushed open the door, she felt her heart lurch to see him sitting at a table midway through the car. By himself, he was staring out the window with a cup of coffee in front of him—but his eyes looked troubled.

"Are you meeting someone, ma'am?" the steward asked her.

"No. I'm dining alone."

Mr. Davis looked up at the sound of her voice, locking eyes with a perplexed expression. "Hello, Miss Williams," he said in a stiff voice.

"Hello, Mr. Davis," she replied crisply.

The steward smiled. "Oh, would you like to be seated to—"

"No!" they both declared simultaneously.

"Yes, yes, right this way," the steward said apologetically. "Nice table right up front, ma'am." As she sat down, taking a seat with her back to Mr. Davis, the steward began to tell her about the special of the night.

"That sounds lovely," she told him. "And I'd like tea as well. Right away, if it's not too much trouble."

After the steward left, she simply sat there, wishing she'd had the foresight to slip the Emerson book in her purse for a distraction.

She stared out the window as the city was giving way to neighborhoods similar to where her family lived, only perhaps not as nice. She wondered what they were thinking about her. Would Julianne and Julius be hurt by her abrupt departure or would her letters help them to understand? And what about Mother and…Jefferson, as she was starting to think of the man who she'd assumed was her father—had they really sent Mr. Davis to spy on her? And if so, why? What would it accomplish?

Finally, she felt as if she were about to boil over like the tea kettle that was probably heating her water for tea right now. And, before she could stop herself, she was on her feet and approaching his table, where once again he was gazing out the window.

"Mr. Davis," she said abruptly.

He turned with wide eyes. "Yes?"

"Why are you following me?

"Wh—what?"

"Did my parents send you?"

"No, of course not."

"Are you telling me the truth?" She peered into his eyes, trying to determine if he was on the level or simply employing some sort of detective trick. "Are you a detective who's—"

"I have no idea what you're talking about." He looked very puzzled, but she knew it could be an act.

"Then why are you on this train?" she demanded. "The same train as I—"

"I booked this train from Philadelphia—"

"This train just departed Pittsburgh," she pointed out hotly. "You were in Pittsburgh, Mr. Davis. I demand that you tell me the truth, sir."

"I started my trip from Philadelphia to Pittsburgh on Wednesday. I stayed in the Franklin Hotel for two nights. I was attending to business there. Now I am on my way to San Francisco."

"So you weren't sent by my parents?" Delia felt the warmth of embarrassment climbing up her neck. Was it possible she had imagined the whole thing?

"On my honor, Miss Williams, I do not even know your parents." He locked eyes with her with such a sincere expression that she knew he was telling the truth.

"I'm so sorry," she said. "Please, forgive me."

His somber expression melted into a slow smile. "I do forgive you, Miss Williams. But I must admit you've aroused my curiosity and, if it's not too much to ask, I wish you would join me and, please, explain yourself."

Flustered and seeing more people were coming into the dining car now, she took the seat across from him. "I suppose it is selfish for two lone travelers to tie up two tables," she said.

"Yes, it's only polite that we share a table." He waved to the waiter who was coming with a tea tray. "Over here, please. Miss Williams and I have decided to dine together after all."

"Very good." The steward set down her tea.

"And I will have the special as well," Mr. Davis told him.

After the steward left, Delia didn't know what to say.

"Would you mind telling me why you assumed I was a detective?" he asked with amusement. "Was I doing something suspicious?"

She sighed as she tried to decide how much to say. "I left my family rather abruptly. Although I am an adult and have every right to go my own way, I was worried they would attempt to force their will upon me." She added a spoonful of sugar to her tea.

"What would their will be?"

"To marry the man of their choice," she said plainly.

"But not of your choice?" His dark brows arched with interest.

"Not by any means. The man is very wealthy, but not someone I'd care to be wed to." She suddenly remembered something. "In fact, you may be acquainted with him, which is one reason I suspected you were in cahoots with my parents."

He frowned. "I can't imagine I know this person."

"Mister Henry Horton of Horton Steel," she said flatly.

He looked somewhat shocked. "Are you serious?"

She nodded grimly.

"He is more than twice your age and…" He let out a slight chuckle. "I can see why you're on the lam, Miss Williams."

She sat up straighter. "I am *not* on the lam, Mr. Davis."

"I'm sorry. You gave me the impression you were fleeing your parents."

She took a slow sip of tea. "That may be partly true," she confessed. "But I am also on my way to visit my father." Without going into all the details, she gave him a quick explanation about having a father in the West.

"How far out west?" he asked with interest.

"Colorado," she said and, not wanting to continue disclosing her information, she decided it was time to question him. "Is this your first time to visit the West?"

"Hardly." He took a sip of coffee.

"You've been west before?" She estimated that he was a bit older than she was. But probably not much. And judging by his well-tailored suit, he must come from money.

"I live out west."

"But you said you came from Philadelphia, Mr. Davis."

"That's true." He smiled warmly. "Please, call me Wyatt. When people call me Mr. Davis, I feel they're addressing my father."

She nodded, unsure as to whether she could actually call him by his first name.

"So I'd been working in Philadelphia for the past couple of years, but I'm on my way home now. Well, not home exactly. I'm on my way to Juneau in the Alaska Territory."

"Alaska? I thought you said you were going to San Francisco."

Now he explained how he planned to take a boat from California to Alaska and how, once he got there, he would work a gold claim with a friend and sell supplies to miners. "I plan to spend a couple of years there. After that I'll go home to Oregon."

"Your home is in Oregon?"

"That's right. Been there ever since I was five years old. My folks brought me out on the Oregon Trail in 1863. My pa got shot up in the war. He decided to take us to the West for a fresh start, but the trip was hard on him, and I think working the farm took its toll too. He passed on about ten years ago. My ma followed him a few months later."

"I'm sorry."

He nodded. "I'd been working the ranch myself but decided to take a break from it by visiting my relatives in Philadelphia. But I'm done with city life now. Can't wait to get back to the wide-open spaces."

They paused as the steward delivered their soup and then, to Delia's surprise, Mr. Davis asked if he might say the blessing. "Thank you," she told him. "I appreciate that."

He bowed his head and said a sweet simple blessing that, she felt, gave her a quick glimpse into his soul. And she liked it.

"So how long do you plan to be in Colorado?" he asked as she dipped her spoon in the broth.

"I'm not sure. My father said I should at least stay a week or two."

"A week or two?" He frowned. "That's not long enough to see much of anything. Colorado is beautiful country. Which part did you say you were headed for?"

"His ranch is near Colorado City."

"That's mining country there. In the mountains."

"Have you been there?"

"No, but I've read about it. When my buddy Jake and I decided to be miners a few years ago, we considered heading that way, but decided on Southern Oregon instead."

"My dad went to Colorado to mine too," she explained. "He

was injured in the war. My mother thought he'd died." She paused, unwilling to admit to him—or anyone—that her mother had committed bigamy, even if it was unwittingly. "Anyway, my father went out to Colorado, and from what I've heard, he was successful in the gold mine."

"From what you've heard?" He puzzled. "Have you never spoken with your father?"

"I've never really met him. I mean, perhaps as a very small child…but I can't remember him at all."

"So this will be like meeting him for the first time?"

She nodded solemnly.

"Are you looking forward to it?"

She considered this, wanting to answer honestly. "I am looking forward to it, but now that I'm on my way, I suppose I'm feeling a little nervous."

"That's understandable." He looked more serious now. "And a woman traveling alone in the frontier… Not to be an alarmist, but that's reason enough to be a bit uneasy. Do you mind if I give you a small piece of advice?"

"What's that?"

"As we get further west, be wary at train stops. Don't wander around these rough towns by yourself. And be cautious with strangers. I don't like to paint a bad picture of the West, but some places are worse than others when it comes to lawlessness. And you can't trust everyone."

"You mean the way I trusted you at the hotel?" she asked in a teasing tone.

He laughed. "No, you handled that just right. You're good at giving the cold shoulder, Miss Williams. I suggest you keep it up until you are safely with your father."

She nodded and, although she didn't plan on admitting as much, she felt much safer knowing that Wyatt Davis was onboard this train. She just wished the train wasn't traveling so fast—and that she had more than just two days to become acquainted with this interesting young man. And yet, she questioned this sentiment. What difference would it make when he was headed off to some remote mining area in Alaska for the next couple of years? Perhaps it would be better for her, more specifically her heart, to continue to maintain a safe distance from Wyatt Davis.

10

DINNER WAS STRETCHED OUT WITH DESSERT AND COFFEE, BUT BE-cause the dining car was filling up, Wyatt invited a pair of business-men from Pittsburgh to share their table. When the men began to discuss the modernizations at the steel mills, Delia politely excused herself. As she walked back to her compartment, she felt saddened to depart Wyatt's company—and then she felt irritated. At herself.

"Don't be a violet," she told herself as she closed her door. It was a saying she and her best friend from college had coined. A woman in their dormitory, Violet Van Horn, was a hopeless romantic. Notori-ous for "falling in love" in an instant and getting her heart broken at leisure, no sensible young woman wanted to be like Violet.

Delia considered preparing for bed, although it wasn't even eight and she didn't feel the least bit tired. In fact, she felt restless. So she decided to pay a visit to the observation car. She'd passed through it on her way to and from the dining car and was impressed with how elegant and comfortable it looked. As she went inside, she could see that most of the plush seats were taken, but since this car had big windows and skylights, she decided to simply stand in the corner for a bit to enjoy the view.

For a few minutes, she stood peering out the window in the rear of the car, enjoying the pastoral scenery of the countryside in the dusky evening light. When it grew too dark to see outside clearly, she changed her attention to the interior scenery. Gazing at fellow passengers, she noticed two things. First of all, the women on the train were outnumbered by men by at least two to one. The second thing she noticed was that the women, even those in traveling garb, were quite fashionable in their summer gowns and Delia, in her somber beige dress, looked plain and drab compared to them. Or perhaps she simply looked studious, she told herself as she started to make her exit.

On her way back to her berth, she heard a man call out, "Miss Williams." Of course, it was Wyatt. She turned to smile politely at him.

"I was just coming into the observation car," he said, "when I noticed you leaving."

"It was crowded in there."

"I noticed." He pointed toward the end of the train. "Want to see something?"

"See something?"

"A way to get some fresh air." He reached for her hand. "Come with me."

She felt pleasant tingles rushing through her at the touch of his hand, and it was impossible to decline. "Where are we going?"

"I found an observation deck on the back of the smoking car."

"Oh…are women permitted in there?"

"We'll just pass through." He led her through a coach car and then through the smoking car, where several gentlemen were enjoying cigars and pipes. She gave them an embarrassed nod as they hurried through.

"Here we go," he said as he opened a door that led outside to a small platform with a small bench. "Welcome to the great outdoors." He waved his hand to the bench. "Care to sit?"

"Thank you." She sat down, nervously smoothing the front of her skirt. Although she knew she was doing nothing wrong, she felt as if being here with Wyatt like this, in the dark of night toward the rear of the train, was somewhat wayward.

"See the stars?" He pointed upward.

"Oh, yes."

"There's the Big Dipper," he said.

"Yes," she exclaimed as she saw it. "And the little one too."

"And the North Star."

For a short while they both just sat quietly, side by side in the darkness, with only the stars overhead and the rumbling sound of the engine up front and the wheels vibrating over the tracks. *Don't be a violet*, she warned herself.

"My apologies for not including you in the conversation at dinner."

"No apology necessary. It wasn't a conversation I cared to join in."

"I figured as much, but I was disappointed when you left."

She glanced at him, barely making out his features in the darkness, then quickly turned her attention back to the night sky.

"I hear that we will be stopped in Chicago for nearly two hours tomorrow evening. Some passengers plan to have a quick dinner in the train station."

She simply nodded, unsure of how to respond.

"I wondered if perhaps you would join me for dinner, Miss Williams."

"Oh…?" She swallowed nervously.

"I don't mean to be too forward. But I'd like to get a glimpse of Union Station. It was built a few years ago, and I hear it's quite an architectural masterpiece, with some good places to eat too."

"Well, that does sound interesting." And now, despite her sensibilities telling her to say no, she accepted. "I'd love to have dinner with you. But on one condition."

"Yes?"

"You must stop calling me Miss Williams. My first name is Delia."

"Delia," he said slowly. "That's a pretty name."

"Thank you." Knowing she was at serious risk of becoming a violet, Delia suddenly stood. "Now, if you will excuse me, I think I will turn in. It's been a long day."

He stood too. "Yes, I'm sure you must be somewhat exhausted from fleeing from detectives."

She laughed. "I'm embarrassed to admit that is probably true."

"Well, I'm relieved that we straightened that all out," he said as they passed through the smoking car. Before long they were standing in front of the door to her berth, and feeling nervous and awkward, she quickly thanked him for showing her the observation deck then told him goodnight.

As she closed and locked the door, she felt her heart fluttering—and she knew that she was crossing some invisible line. She was turning into a violet! As she prepared for bed, she sternly told herself that she could cancel her reckless dinner date with Wyatt tomorrow. She would explain that it wasn't prudent, or perhaps even feign a headache if necessary. But somehow she would nip this violet in the bud before it was too late.

Delia was relieved that the dining car was so full in the morning that she was seated at a table with another couple and an elderly gentleman. It wasn't that she didn't wish to see Wyatt—she most assuredly did! But at the same time she wanted to put some space between them, she wanted to protect her heart.

After breakfast, she saw him sitting in the observation car with an opened book in his lap, but gazing out the window. However, when he noticed her coming down the aisle, he smiled brightly. "Care to join me?" He waved to the seat across from him.

Not overly eager to return to her stuffy berth and inexplicably drawn to this handsome young man, she sat down. "What are you reading?"

"*Life on the Mississippi* by Mark Twain." He held up the book.

"I've heard of it but never read it. Is it good?"

"Very good. It's biographical. About when he was a steamboat pilot on the Mississippi. Before the war. My aunt gave it to me before I left Philadelphia. She's an avid reader." His smile diminished. "I will miss my aunt and uncle—and their well-stocked library."

"Are they the relatives in Philadelphia?" For some reason she was trying to understand Wyatt's history, but it felt like sewing together different patterned quilt pieces and not being quite sure of the order.

"Yes. My uncle owns a boot factory. I worked for him for a couple of years. He wanted me to stay on there, take over management for him. But I had to turn him down."

"Philadelphia is a pleasant city," she said absently. "I enjoyed going to the university there."

"You attended the University of Pennsylvania?" His brows arched in disbelief.

"Only two years." She wished she hadn't mentioned this fact. She knew how disconcerted some men were about educated women. And so, to change the subject, she began to ask him about various points of interest in Philadelphia, discovering that they had enjoyed many of the very same spots.

"You sound as if you're somewhat fond of Philadelphia," she said. "And yet you spoke disparagingly of the city last night."

"I must admit to being charmed with the big city…at first. It was such a change from all that I'd grown up with. And it was interesting to work with my uncle. Especially since my education had been, well, less than traditional." He frowned. "And rather paltry compared to yours."

"You do not strike me as uneducated, Mr. Davis."

"Wyatt." His eyes twinkled. "Well, my father was fairly well-educated, and he taught me at home. A rather stern taskmaster too.

Especially in regards to mathematics and natural science. My uncle was impressed with my ability to work figures in my head." He held up the book again. "And I've always been a reader. I suppose I got that from my mother. But books are not easily come by in the frontier. Although my aunt has promised to send me recent publications once I get a mailing address." He chuckled. "Receiving mail can be a challenge…when you're a drifter."

"Is that how you would describe yourself? As a drifter?"

"I've done more than my fair share of drifting. By the time I get back to Oregon, I'll have trekked around ten thousand miles."

"My word!"

"And I've pursued various occupations."

"Such as?"

"Well, aside from ranching on my own property, I've worked as cowboy for another rancher—a man with close to a thousand head of cattle. I helped him round them up and drive them to market. That was what made me think I wanted to develop my ranch into something similar, on a much smaller scale. And I think I mentioned my stint as a gold miner. That took me away from home too. Then two years ago, I rode on horseback, taking the Oregon Trail backwards all the way to Pennsylvania."

"You are an adventurer."

"Or a fool." He smiled sheepishly. "Traveling by train is much more convenient."

"Then you worked in your uncle's boot factory," she said, filling in the blank. "And now you are off to search for gold in Alaska?"

"Yes, drifting west and then north." He shrugged. "See, I am a drifter."

"But you have roots," she pointed out. "Your home—your ranch in Oregon."

"That's true. But sometimes I think those are my parents' roots. Not mine."

"But you spoke of how much you love the land."

"I do love the land—I love the wide-open spaces and the freedom of riding a good horse over the next rise. I'm not even sure I want to be tied down to my ranch in Oregon anymore. Perhaps when I'm finished in Alaska, I'll decide to sell it."

She blinked in surprise at what seemed an impulsive statement. "I suppose you truly are a drifter. Where do you think you'll wish to drift to after Alaska? The Orient perhaps?" Although she was partly teasing, she could tell by his thoughtful expression this was not outside of his realm of possibilities. Even more reason for her to proceed with caution. Perhaps she should break tonight's dinner engagement now.

"What sort of plans do you have?" he asked abruptly. "After your visit to your father's ranch in Colorado."

"To be honest, I haven't thought that far ahead." She frowned. "Although I'm worried that I may have burned my bridge at home."

"Burned your bridge?"

Delia knew she'd said too much. She had never intended to divulge her full story—not to anyone. And yet, Wyatt had been quite forthcoming to her. What difference would it make if she shared parts of her story with a drifter? What were the chances their paths would cross again?

"My parents told me that if I left, I was not welcome to come back." As she said this, she felt a tightness in her throat. "And it isn't that I wish to live in my family home forever. In fact, I feel confident that I can make my own living. But it does hurt to be, well, cast out."

His eyes were sympathetic. "Well, your father sounds like a good man. Didn't you mention that he'd been a miner before becoming a rancher?" He grinned. "That's my kind of fellow."

She peered curiously at his well-tailored clothing. "If you don't mind me saying, I have difficulty picturing you as either a miner or a rancher. You look more like a businessman."

He laughed. "Then I better warn you that as soon as we're beyond St. Louis—the jumping off spot—I'll be shedding these city duds for good. And I suspect I'll return to my western dialect too. As we head into western territory, you will start to see my true identity."

"The drifter?"

He shrugged. "Among other things." Now he nodded toward her. "Speaking of appearances, I have been curious as to yours. When I first saw you the other day, you had on a similar gown..." He paused, looking a bit uneasy, as if he was concerned he might have stepped over some invisible line.

"Please, continue," she urged. "I'm curious as to your observations."

He nodded. "Your appearance was, shall I say, different from other female guests at the hotel. So much so that you captured my attention—and my curiosity."

She couldn't help but smile over this. To think that her drab university garments had garnered the attention of such a handsome man was rather amusing.

"When you showed up at dinnertime dressed like a queen, I couldn't figure you out," he finished. "I felt certain you were playing some sort of game. But what?"

So she explained about her serious university dresses and how much her mother despised the dull drab colors and styles. "She tried to transform me into a fashionable young lady in the hopes of luring in a very wealthy husband." Delia smirked. "Poor Mother. She must be thinking I was a very poor investment. But she told me to take everything with me. And none of it would've fit her, and my little sister is only eleven."

"You have a little sister?"

She explained about the twins. "Of course, I now understand that we're only half siblings. And I understand why my stepfather clearly favors them. A lot of things are slowly beginning to make sense."

"So when did you find out about your real father?"

She considered this. "Three days ago."

He looked shocked. "That's a lot to take in."

She sadly nodded. "It hasn't been easy."

"Well, you seem like a strong person, Delia. And your father sounds like a good man. I have no doubt that good things lie ahead for you."

She wished she could have that same certainty. His question about what she would do after her visit in Colorado was disturbing. What *would* she do? She had no solid plan, no real ideas...perhaps she should start figuring it out.

11

AT LUNCHTIME, WYATT SAVED A PLACE AT HIS TABLE IN THE HOPES that Delia would happen along, but not seeing her anywhere, he finally surrendered the spot to a talkative Virginian with a large handlebar mustache. It wasn't until Wyatt was just finishing up his meal that he noticed Delia entering the dining car.

With a book in her hand, she seemed preoccupied. Or perhaps she was simply trying to avoid him. Just the same, he greeted her and was rewarded by her beautiful smile. "I recommend the chicken salad sandwich," he told her.

"That sounds good." She looked around the crowded car.

"You may have my seat if you like." He stood. "I'm finished here."

"Thank you," she said primly.

"And I suggest we meet on the platform at Union Station in Chicago," he said as he moved past her. "I'm looking forward to a good steak dinner."

Her brow creased slightly, as if she was having second thoughts, but before she could speak the steward stepped between them and quickly cleared a place for her at the table. And, not wanting to give her a chance to renege on her previous agreement, Wyatt hurried out.

As he went to his berth, Wyatt questioned his actions. If Delia had wanted to back out on dinner, why didn't he let her? Did he really want to dine with a reluctant dinner guest? Furthermore, was it a mistake to continue fostering a relationship that had no future? Because if he was thinking rationally—which was difficult to do in her presence—he would have to admit that the chances of winning a girl like Delia were slim. He'd been over it in his mind several times already.

For starters, he was headed for Alaska. He had promised Jake that they'd work their claim together for at least two years. Besides that, he had invested in supplies to sell in Juneau. Items that would have the strongest value in a remote mining area like that. If he wanted a good return on his investment, he would have to follow through with his plan.

In the meantime, a fine woman like Delia would not be available for long. He knew it. Even dressed in her plain gowns, she turned heads. Someone would snap her up. And since she'd clearly been raised with affluence, he suspected she'd be attracted to a man who could provide for her in a similar fashion. Besides all that, she was college educated! That alone should scare him away. And yet, whenever he was near her, he felt anything but scared.

Feeling restless and agitated, he decided to spend some time on the observation deck behind the smoking car. As fast and convenient as train travel was, it was also confining. But at least the countryside, between the towns that were farther apart and growing scarcer, was wide open. The flat prairie wasn't as beautiful as the landscape out west, but compared to the populated city, it was a welcome relief.

The more Wyatt thought about the potential with a woman like Delia, the more he realized it was a fool's dream. And he wouldn't be surprised if she remained on the train in Chicago. He wouldn't even blame her. What was the point? Tomorrow they would arrive in Denver and she would step off the train and out of his world… forever. Why had he been so insistent that they should share another meal together? Perhaps he just enjoyed pain.

Around five o'clock, Wyatt returned to his berth with an idea. He had warned her that he would return to his western garb soon, so why not now? If she saw him dressed like a cowboy, she might decide to pass on dinner with him. And, if she did, it would be for the best. So, removing the expensive suit that his aunt had insisted he needed to work in management at the boot factory, he put on a pair of dark trousers, a white shirt with a narrow tie, a brown buckskin vest, and his hat and riding boots. *Goodbye, city slicker.*

The train pulled into Union Station at five forty-five and Wyatt was one of the first ones to get out. Waiting out on the platform, he watched as passengers emerged from the various cars. Looking for the girl in the drab beige school dress, he was surprised—and more than a little uneasy. When Delia gracefully came down the steps, a porter offering her a hand, she had on a gown that was similar from the night at the hotel. Only this gown was a soft shade of purple. Lavender perhaps. Anyway, she looked like a queen. And he looked like a cowboy.

"Delia," he said apologetically as he went to meet her. "I didn't know you were dressing for dinner."

She looked at him and then down at her gown with an uncomfortable expression. "I didn't know you—I thought—"

"I know I said I planned to remain a citified gentleman until St. Louis, but something about being in Chicago made me feel we were already in the West. Do you mind?"

She shook her head no.

"You look *beautiful.*" He linked his arm into hers, lest she decide to run away.

"You look…" She studied him closely. "Like a cowboy."

He laughed. "Are you embarrassed to be seen with me?"

She smiled. "Not in the least."

Knowing they looked incongruous together, he led her through the terminal. As they walked, he explained that a fellow traveler had told him the best place to dine. "He said to let them know that our time is limited." As they strolled, he pointed out some of the architectural details of the terminal.

She gazed around with wide eyes. "Very nice."

As they entered the restaurant, Wyatt grew concerned. What if they refused service to cowboys? To his relief he noticed a similarly dressed man already seated, and before long, they were led to a table.

Wyatt apologized again for his rustic apparel. "I didn't really think it through," he admitted.

"I think you look quite nice as a cowboy," she said as she laid her napkin in her lap. "No more apologies."

As beautiful as Delia looked in her lavender gown, Wyatt wasn't sure that he didn't like her plain dress better—mostly because it was so doggone distracting to be seated with such a beautiful woman. It didn't help when others looked her way too. They were probably curious as to why the princess was dining with the cowboy.

"This train terminal was finished ten years after the Chicago fire," he informed her after they'd placed their orders. "In 1881. So, it's still fairly new."

"It's a beautiful building." She glanced around the restaurant. "And this is a lovely departure from the train." She smiled. "I was starting to feel a bit confined."

"I know just what you mean. At least you get to end your trip tomorrow. I won't be in San Francisco for two more days."

"Have you been in San Francisco before?"

"Never. I plan to spend some time there, getting more supplies and seeing the sights."

"These supplies you plan to sell in Alaska… Will you open a store?"

"A store of sorts. But probably not like you're imagining. I plan to set up a wall tent at first. Partly to live in and partly to sell my wares." He grinned. "I never considered myself a businessman before, but it might be interesting."

"Perhaps you'll get so good at it that you'll want to partner with your uncle by opening up boot shops in other frontier towns."

He chuckled. "I doubt that."

They made casual conversation as they dined. He was pleased to discover that Delia was well informed on a wide variety of topics, and he enjoyed hearing her opinions on everything from politics to fashion. Not surprisingly, she was in favor of suffrage and opposed to certain ridiculous fashions that restricted a woman's freedom. And, although he hadn't given it much thought, after a bit of discussion, he was inclined to agree.

As much as he didn't want to rush dinner—or this time together—he was unwilling to miss their train. Mostly for her sake, although it would be greatly inconvenient to him.

"I wonder if we might find a shop that's open," she said as they were exiting the restaurant. "I'd like to purchase a travel journal."

"I noticed a newsstand on our way," he said. "We can check to see."

To her delight, the newsstand was still open and actually had some rather basic journals for sale. "Perfect," she told the man as she paid him. "Just what I need."

He checked his watch to see that they still had ten minutes and, wanting to enjoy the feeling of her delicate hand resting on his arm, he strolled slowly, pointing out various points of interest in Union Station and relaying to her some of the facts he'd read about regarding its construction. "Someday I'd like to spend more time in Chicago. It sounds like an interesting city."

"But I thought you disliked cities?" She gave him a sideways glance.

"I prefer wide open spaces," he clarified, "but a city can be an interesting place to visit."

"I see." She nodded. "I suppose that goes with being a drifter. You probably appreciate all sorts of different experiences."

"Exactly."

She held up her journal. "Do you write about your experiences?"

"As a matter of fact, I do. I'm currently on my fourth travel journal, and I plan to pick up a fifth one in San Francisco."

"Impressive." She looked at him with sparkling eyes as they stepped onto the platform where other passengers were milling about, preparing to board the train. "You are not an average sort of drifter."

He was thinking that she was not average either. Not in any way, shape, or form. Delia was the kind of woman a man could dream about…and never meet. And yet, here she was standing right next to him, smiling up into his face as if she truly enjoyed his company. Was he really willing to part ways with her tomorrow? Forever?

"I plan to sit outside on the observation platform behind the smoking car again tonight," he said quietly as they boarded the train. "Would you like to join me? I might even be able to talk the steward into bringing us some coffee or tea."

"Coffee sounds lovely," she agreed. "Give me a few minutes to drop off my journal and pick up a shawl and I'll meet you out there."

"Perfect." As she headed for her berth, he located his favorite steward and, giving him a tip, arranged for their coffee to be delivered in about twenty minutes. Then, heading back to the observation deck, he sat down to wait for her. And to think. As completely mad as it sounded—they'd only known each other for a couple of days—he knew he was smitten. The feelings he had for Delia were completely different from the way he'd felt about Maryanne.

But they were bound for two different worlds. He had made a commitment to work the gold claim with Jake in Juneau. Was if fair to expect that she would wait for him? For two long years? What sort of woman would agree to something like that? Perhaps a desperate one. But Delia was not desperate.

Besides, he decided as the train began to move, what did he really have to offer her? An undeveloped ranch in Oregon? A bunch of boots, wool socks, and mining tools? Not very tempting for a woman like Delia Williams. And, if he was being honest with himself, a bit presumptuous on his part. As much as he believed he truly loved this woman, he was in no position to take a wife—and he knew it.

"There you are," she said as she came out onto the platform. Still dressed in her pale purple gown, although she'd removed her hat and now wore a soft white shawl, she sat down beside him. "What a beautiful night."

"And coffee is coming," he said brightly, masking how he truly felt.

"Thank you again for such a wonderful dinner," she said. "I'm so glad I got to see the Chicago station. It was really quite grand."

"Are you excited about meeting your father tomorrow?"

"Excited and nervous," she said quietly. "What if he doesn't like me?"

Wyatt laughed. "I can't imagine how he wouldn't love you, Delia."

"Really?" She sounded sincerely surprised.

"Do you honestly think he wouldn't?"

"I don't know." Even though the light from the sky was dim, he could see her frown. "Besides my Great Aunt Adelaide, who was actually my grandmother because she was my father's mother, I never felt as if my family loved me. Not truly."

"Surely they loved you." Wyatt couldn't imagine anyone not loving Delia—especially her own parents.

"I suppose my mother loved me in her own way. But not in the same way she loves the twins. Knowing what I know now, about her first marriage with my father, I can almost understand. I was probably a constant reminder to her of something that had gone wrong." She sighed. "And my stepfather, well, I wasn't even his own flesh and blood and yet he was forced to pretend that I was."

After a long pause, Wyatt responded. "I'm sorry you didn't have the love you deserved in your childhood, Delia. But I have a feeling your father is going to make up for that now." This was his one consolation—that Delia's father sounded like a man Wyatt could relate to. A miner turned rancher—now, that was familiar territory. And if Delia and her father formed a close bond, it was possible she would want to remain with him in Colorado for more than just a week or two. And if she did remain with him, perhaps Wyatt could remain in contact with her through letters—while making his fortune up north. He could only hope.

"I feel like that too," she said dreamily. "As if finally connecting with my own father is going to change everything. As if my life will finally make some sense."

"I'd really love to hear how it turns out for you," he said. "Would you consider remaining in touch through letters?"

"I would love to correspond with you," she said eagerly. "Will you be able to get mail all the way up in Alaska?"

"It's slow and unreliable and expensive, but yes, the mail makes it up there. My friend Jake and I have already exchanged several letters. Jake's last letter made it to me in about three weeks' time. But that was to Philadelphia."

"Then give me your address before we reach Denver and I promise to write. I'll send you a letter right after I meet my father and if it takes three weeks, it will get there just a week after you arrive."

"I will write down my address and give it to you in the morning," he said as the steward arrived with a tray. After adding cream and sugar to their coffees, Wyatt thanked the steward, adding a second tip on the tray.

"My pleasure." He bowed then went back inside.

"I suggest we make a toast," Wyatt said as he held his coffee cup up.

"What shall we toast?"

"To our friendship," Wyatt said.

"Yes, I like that," she agreed. "To our friendship."

They clinked the coffee cups together and, looking into each others' eyes, they both took a sip. And, although it wasn't quite like what he'd imagined earlier—him on one knee asking for her hand in marriage—it did give him hope. And for the time being that would have to be enough.

12

AFTER A SOMEWHAT SLEEPLESS NIGHT, DELIA ROSE EARLY. SHE KNEW her restlessness had been partially due to her unexpected feelings toward Wyatt—she had fallen by way of the violets. But she'd also felt anxious about meeting her father in Colorado City later today. As a result, she'd finished reading the novel she'd purchased in Pittsburgh and suddenly realized that she might not have too many more chances to buy more books for the next couple of weeks—or however long she remained on her father's ranch.

After packing her bags, she went to the dining car for an early breakfast in the hopes that Wyatt would be there. To her dismay, he wasn't. Since the diner wasn't very busy, she took a table by herself. As the steward served her tea, she inquired about the next stop. "Is there a place where the train will be in town for more than just a few minutes? It seems that since Chicago, the stops have been fewer and quicker."

"Not as many towns out here."

She looked out the window—nothing but flat grasslands for as far as the eye could see. This must be what Wyatt referred to as the "wide open spaces," but it felt unsettling to her—so much vast nothingness, for miles and miles. She didn't like being dramatic, but it was the sort of landscape in which one might spot a band of Indians. Not that she felt fearful of Indians, but she had read of brutal attacks not so very long ago. And probably not so very far from here.

"The train makes a stop in Kearney," the steward said. "To take on water and fuel and make deliveries and such. Usually takes about thirty minutes."

"Do you suppose this place, Kearney, would have a place to buy a book?"

"Kearney—used to be Fort Kearney—has grown into a big place." He grinned. "Well, for these parts anyway."

"How far to Kearney?" she asked as she stirred her tea.

"Oh, about ten minutes, I'd say."

She told him she'd have breakfast later and, after hurrying to drink her tea, she got her purse and prepared to get off. She looked up and down the train, hoping to see Wyatt so that he might accompany her, but when the train slowed down without spotting him, she looked out the window to see that, indeed, this place appeared to be a good sized town. Surely it would be a safe place.

As soon as she was on the platform, she asked the stationmaster to direct her to where she might purchase a book. Distracted with loading some barrels and crates, he pointed her toward Main Street, saying, "The mercantile carries some books."

As she hurried along, she noticed several saloons, and then some shops, but everything seemed to be closed up, and the street was fairly deserted. And then of course, it hit her. It wasn't quite eight o'clock—she'd gotten up so early that it seemed later to her. This was too early for shops to be open. Feeling silly, she turned around and was just heading back to the train station when someone roughly grabbed her by the arm, spinning her around.

"Wha's a pretty little thang like you doing all by herself?" A grubby, unshaven man grinned down at her with rheumy eyes, his greasy hair hanging down in his flushed and sweaty face.

"Let me go!" she yelled, trying to pull free.

"Come on now, shweetie, don't you be—"

"Release me, you brute!" With her free hand, she swung her purse at his head, just missing him.

"You're feisty little thing, ain't you?" He leaned toward her, smelling of cheap whiskey, dirtm and sweat. "Come on, honey, jus' give ol' Buster a kiss an—"

Turning her face from him, she tried to wrench away, but in the same moment felt the man being lifted from the ground—and just like that her arm was released. Nearly falling over, she turned to see what had happened, and to her surprised relief, there stood Wyatt, holding the man up in the air. With an angry expression, Wyatt gave the horrid beast a good shake then tossed him down onto the dusty street.

"You keep your hands off the ladies!" Wyatt shouted at the startled man. "And you might want to start running before the law gets here." He kicked the dirt next to the man, making a cloud of dust sail up into his face. Sputtering and swearing, the man stumbled to his feet then took off in a staggered run that was almost comical—except that Delia was too upset to laugh. "And lay off the whiskey!" Wyatt yelled after him.

Still shaking and barely able to stand, Delia fell into Wyatt's arms. "Thank you," she cried in relief. "Thank you!"

"Are you all right?" he asked urgently.

"I'm fine. He just scared me out of my wits, that's all." She took in a quick breath, trying to steady herself, although her knees were shaking so badly, she wasn't sure she could stand, let alone walk. She couldn't remember ever feeling so frightened.

"Why did you go to town on your own?" he demanded as he peered into her face.

"I know, I know—it was foolish. I just wanted to get a book. And then I realized the shops aren't even open yet—and that awful man, he just came out of nowhere and—" She broke into embarrassing sobs.

"Come on." With one arm still snugly wrapped around her waist, he began walking her back to the train station. "Let's get you out of here."

"You warned me." She tugged her handkerchief from her purse and, using it to blot her tears, felt like a silly child. "I'm so glad you came along, Wyatt. I don't know what I would've done."

"I'm thankful I found you when I did." His tone suggested that he was a little shaken up too. "I had a bad feeling when the porter told me you'd left the train, but I never expected you to find trouble so quickly. Why didn't you heed my warning about going out alone?"

"I don't know why," she said meekly. "I assumed the town would be safe. I can see now that I was headstrong and foolish."

"It's not your fault, Delia," he said soothingly. "You'd think a lady would be safe on the streets in the daylight. But the trouble is you never know."

As they walked back to the train, she explained about her sleepless night of reading. "It was my last unread book. I just hoped to find a book or two in Kearney—to take to Colorado City with me. But perhaps they'll have a bookstore there."

"I'm not sure about that, but I'll give you some books," he told her as they went into the station.

"I can't take your books."

As they prepared to board the train, his arm slipped back down to his side. She knew it was the proper thing to do, but she had liked the secure feel of having it around her. She'd never experienced a feeling like that before—so right…so perfect. But at least he took her hand, helping her up the steps.

"Have you had your breakfast yet?"

"No, but I'd like to go to my berth first," she murmured. "To wash up and—" Her voice broke. "I just feel so foolish."

"Take your time, Delia. I'll get us a table."

She tried not to take too long, splashing cool water on her face, smoothing her hair back into place. She just wanted to feel like she was under control again, trying to convince herself that it wasn't such a horrid ordeal. After all, she was alive and well. And it had been rather exciting being rescued by Wyatt. Besides, this was the Wild West. What did she expect? However, beneath her bravado, she wondered—what if Wyatt hadn't come along just then? She didn't want to think about that. And, in the future, she would be more careful.

She found Wyatt sipping coffee at a table in the front of the dining car. "Thank you again," she said as she sat across from him. "I've been wondering how you happened along just then. How did you know where to find me?"

He nodded to the steward who was setting a coffee in front of her. "This good man told me you'd gone into town by yourself." He reached out to shake the steward's hand. "I'm most grateful too."

"Glad to be of help."

"I took the liberty of ordering you a coffee," Wyatt said as the steward left. "Thought you might need it."

"Thank you." She attempted a smile. "Seems that is all I've been saying to you this morning. *Thank you.*"

He waved his hand. "Anyway, like I was saying, I'll give you some books, ones that I've already read. It'll lighten my load."

"I can't take your books."

"Then I will *loan* them to you."

"But how will I return them?" she asked.

"I suppose I'll have to come back to pick them up." The corners of his mouth turned up ever so slightly. "And if I don't, you'll just have to keep them."

She smiled with amusement. "What sort of books do you have? I must warn you, I'm fairly well read."

He scratched his chin. "Let's see…I have *Ben Hur* by Lew Wallace. I've read that book twice over the past couple of years and highly recommend it. Another one of my favorites, one that I've read

more than enough times, is *A Tramp Abroad* by Mark Twain. Have
you read either of those?"

"I actually haven't. You really don't mind loaning your books to
me?"

He grinned. "Not at all."

They met back in the observation car mid-morning. Wyatt
handed her the two books he'd mentioned earlier and, when she tried
to refuse what she knew were some of his best loved books, he insisted. "I've written my address in Juneau in the Mark Twain book,"
he explained. "As well as my aunt and uncle's names and address in
Philadelphia." He smiled apologetically. "Just in case."

"Thank you." She handed him a card on which she'd written
the address her father had sent to her. "And this is where I'll be for
a while." She frowned. "Although I can't really say for how long.
Perhaps my father will take one look at me and decide that I'm a
greenhorn and put me back on the train."

Wyatt laughed. "Well, you might be a greenhorn, but I doubt
your father will send you packing."

She sighed as she gazed out the window where the prairie seemed
to stretch for eternity. "I'm not sure what I think about your wide-
open spaces," she confessed. "I'm afraid I find it slightly disturbing—
there's so much of it…it just seems to go on forever. I feel rather lost
in it."

"I'll grant that this is some wide-open space," he said. "But it's
not exactly the sort of land that I'm drawn to. I prefer a landscape
with mountains, rivers, trees…the kind of country I left behind in
Oregon."

"My uncle described the place where my father lives in a similar way…mountains and meadows and a lake or stream. Perhaps
it won't be as desolate as this." And now she asked him to describe,
in more detail, the land he left behind in Oregon. After that she
inquired about the time he'd spent mining gold and then about his

expectations for San Francisco, the boat trip, and Alaska. And the minutes and hours passed quickly. Like the train, there was no stopping the time as it raced along.

"I made a lunch reservation for us," Wyatt told her. "I hope you don't mind."

"Not at all. I had hoped to have one last meal before Denver. The steward told me that the train from Denver to Colorado City has no dining car."

"Then we should go in." Wyatt stood, offering her his arm.

As Wyatt led her to the dining car, she realized how much had changed between them since their first meeting at the Franklin Hotel in Pittsburgh. And, with a small lump in her throat, she realized that they would be parting ways in less than three hours.

"You seem sad," Wyatt said after they were seated at a table by themselves. "Are you still upset over the incident in Kearney?"

"Oh, no." She waved her hand. "I've nearly forgotten that."

"Well, don't forget it completely," he warned. "I do think there was a lesson to be learned there."

She nodded. "I couldn't agree more."

"Then why do your eyes look sad to me?" he asked.

She took in a deep breath. "I think I am sad to lose your companionship," she confessed. "You have been a good friend to me, Wyatt. It won't be easy to say goodbye."

He just nodded, waiting as the steward sat down their soups and then, as usual, he said a short but sincere blessing. But as they started to eat, she felt uncomfortable, as if she'd revealed too much. And so she decided to change the subject.

"I suppose I'm filled with a lot of conflicting emotions. I do feel sad for the way I left my mother, the way we quarreled. I will be writing her a letter as soon as I get settled."

"And you will be writing me a letter too," he reminded her.

She smiled. "Yes, of course. That will be my *first* letter. But after that, I will write my mother an apology. Although I have no idea how I will word it, I'll do what I can to repair my burnt bridge with her. Although I suspect it may take some time."

"Perhaps it will encourage you to remain with your father longer," he said with what seemed like hope. "To give yourself more time. If you stayed there long enough, maybe your mother would miss you and regret trying to force you into a marriage for money."

"You could be right. I just wish I knew more about where I'm going and what I'll find there," she said wistfully. "I wonder if my father might live in a small one-room-cabin, like I've read about in books."

"I'm sure that's a possibility. When my parents settled, more than twenty years ago, they built a one-room-cabin. My father had always planned to enlarge and improve it, but there was so much to be done on the property and given that he had a hard time getting around with his bad leg…well, it just didn't happen." He frowned. "To be honest, I'm not sure I'll be doing many improvements to the cabin myself—not straight away. I think I'd be better off putting my time and strength and investment into building up a cattle herd— that's where I'll have my livelihood. It's possible your father has done the same."

"Yes. I'm preparing myself for a rugged sort of lifestyle." She smiled nervously. "I'd like to be helpful while I'm there, but the truth is I've not had much experience in the womanly areas of cooking or housekeeping."

His brows arched slightly—was it from surprise or amusement?

"I know what you're thinking," she said quickly. "What use is a woman who can't cook or keep house?"

"I never said that."

"The truth is my mother didn't think it was proper for her girls to work in the home. That was why we had servants. Certainly, not as many now as when I was growing up." She frowned. "But sometimes I would sneak into the kitchen. Cook taught me how to do a few things…and I suppose it cannot be terribly difficult to learn."

"Take it from me, cooking is not that hard." He grinned.

"Do you know how to cook?"

"Sure. I'm a bachelor. If I didn't know how to cook, I would've starved by now. I know how to cook most kinds of meats and vegetables. And I even make a pretty good biscuit. Although I wouldn't go so far as to brag about my cooking skills, I sometimes made money at the goldmines by selling hot meals—and I got no complaints."

It was embarrassing to think that this young man, who called himself a drifter, was also a good cook—when she barely knew how to boil water for tea. "Well, I just hope that I'm not too much of a disappointment or a liability or even an inconvenience to my father." Once again, she changed the subject, asking Wyatt more and more questions about himself, wanting to know as much about him as possible before their time together ended.

When they finally finished up—a very long lunch—she knew that it was only a matter of minutes before they reached Denver. Hopefully she wouldn't make a complete fool of herself by breaking into tears.

13

WYATT FELT HIS HEART BEING TORN FROM HIS CHEST AS HE AND DE-
lia parted ways. In fact, it was hard to simply breathe. Some might
blame the high elevation for this, but he knew it was because of
Delia. Watching her slender form from the observation deck where
he had gone specifically to see her for as long as possible, she looked
so fragile and vulnerable that he felt a strange stab of guilt—as if he
had abandoned her. Of course, that was ridiculous, but it was how
he felt. As if he somehow was responsible for her welfare and he was
letting her down.

And yet he had gone out of his way to help her with her bags,
to ensure her trunks were unloaded and ready to be put on the next
train, the one that would take her south to Colorado City. And because her train wouldn't depart until three fifteen, she was the one
left standing on the platform, bravely waving goodbye to him as his
train continued its journey west. Everything in him wanted to grab
his bags and leap from the train, run to her side and proclaim his
undying love.

He could blame his watery eyes on the train cinders as he
watched her waving her white handkerchief and getting smaller, but

he knew it would be a lie. He pulled off his hat, waving it back and forth energetically, until she was no longer visible. Feeling like he'd just lost his best friend, he slumped down onto the bench. Why hadn't he followed his heart and gotten off in Denver? After all, he was a free man…a vagabond…a drifter. Who could tell him what to do or where to go?

Yet he knew that wouldn't be just highly impractical, but downright foolish as well. He and Delia both had important business to attend to—business that didn't require being bound to another. She needed to meet her father, on her own terms. And if she felt a real connection with him, perhaps she'd decide to spend a significant amount of time on his ranch. His prayer was that she would be so taken in by the natural beauty of the West that she would want to stay put—just long enough for him to sell his goods in Alaska and make good on his promise to Jake. His goal, no longer to get rich, was simply to accumulate as much money as quickly as possible, and then get out.

After that, he wasn't entirely sure. He could reinvest in the Oregon ranch, like he'd originally planned, or he could take up something entirely different. Travel and exploration had been hugely appealing during his last year at the boot factory. Perhaps it was during that spell that he first began to see himself as a drifter. That was how he'd felt when he'd started out on this trip—like an unfettered explorer out to see and experience the world at large.

But meeting Delia had changed everything. Something in him had been pulled in so that now, as much as he longed to see new places and experience new things, he also wanted Delia by his side. But that would not be easily done. Women didn't usually take to the road and the vagabond life. They wanted homes and roots and children. Things he'd imagined he'd wanted at one time. Perhaps he still did, he wasn't even sure. Or maybe this would just turn into another learning experience like the one he'd had with Maryanne. Because, if he were being totally honest, how could he expect that someone like Delia would want to cast her lot with him...a drifter? It was irrational.

Not only that but he knew, by the time he was finished with his Alaskan expedition, Delia would quite likely be married. After all, what man in his right mind wouldn't want to take dear Delia for a wife? She was intelligent and beautiful...and genuinely good and kind. After hearing her story these past two days, he knew the only reason she wasn't already married was because she'd been tucked away in college—ironically not so very far away from where he'd been tucked away in his uncle's boot factory. For some reason Wyatt saw God's hand in this. But he also knew that if Delia's mother and stepfather had gotten their way, Delia would probably be at an engagement party today—her own.

As he made his way through the cloudy smoking car, Wyatt questioned whether Delia would actually write to him like she said she would. Not that he thought she was the type to break a promise, but more because he thought she'd get busy and simply forget. He could imagine a bunch of suitors lining up on her father's doorstep. Good women, in general, were scarce in the West. Women like Delia—well, they were just plain scarce.

Delia was relieved that the Colorado City train arrived in Denver right on time. Partly because she needed the distraction of boarding and getting seated to numb the ache inside of her. And partly because it looked like a thunderstorm was brewing over the mountains and she hoped that she and her luggage, waiting for the train, wouldn't be soaked.

With help from the porter, her trunks and bags were soon on board and she was seated in a coach car. This train wasn't nearly as new and elegant as the last one, and her car was about half filled. Mostly male passengers—and many of them seemed overly interested in her. She did a quick perusal of the rough looking characters. Most looked to be miners or cowboys, although a couple were dressed like businessmen. She felt curious eyes returning her gaze and so she turned to peer out the smudgy window. Once again, she realized that a lone woman traveling in the frontier wasn't terribly common.

For that reason she held her head a bit higher and, remembering Wyatt's advice, decided to avoid conversation with anyone on this relatively short trip. Instead she kept a watch on the weather outside. She was still amazed at the size of the sky out here and then, as flashes of lightning and the sounds of thunder rumbled through the train car, she felt a wondrous sense of awe. Almost as if God was playing in his heavens.

Finally the sky grew dark and heavy and the rain came pouring down in sheets, drenching the grassy plains and, unless she was imagining it, turning the previously faded grass a few shades greener. And then, just like that, the sun came out and the world looked sparkling clean. She opened the window and breathed in the freshly washed air, inhaling deeply. She wondered if Wyatt had experienced the rainstorm too.

The train was scheduled to arrive in Colorado City a little before six, and she knew her father's ranch was more than an hour's ride from the town, which meant they should get home before dark. It was strange to think of her father's place as "home," but that is what she was starting to tell herself. Hopefully it would be more of home than the house she'd inhabited with her mother and stepfather and half siblings for all those years. Because the honest truth was that she'd never felt completely at home. And it wasn't the house's fault because she had felt very much at home in that same house when it had been owned by Great Aunt Adelaide—rather *Grandmother* Adelaide. She still had difficulty grasping that.

But now she was on her way "home." And even if her father's house was just a one-room cabin, she was determined to make the best of it. She remembered reading what turned out to be one of her favorite books several years ago. Although it had been written for children, she had enjoyed it immensely before handing it down to the twins. *Heidi* was the story of a young Swiss girl who went to live in a tiny cabin with a grandfather she had never met. At first there was difficulty, but in the end the two unlikely characters won over each others' hearts. In some ways, Delia thought she might be in for a similar experience—and she was ready for it. Even if it meant she had to sleep in a hayloft and milk cows. Truly, it could be fun!

And so much about this trip had already proven fun and exciting. Even nearly being abducted by the drunkard in Kearney seemed almost amusing now. Not so much that she would be that careless again, but in hindsight, it was not truly a life endangering event. At least that was what she was telling herself. Be cautious not fearful.

The only fly in the ointment, as her mother would say, was parting ways with Wyatt Davis this afternoon. Just thinking of it now was painful. As if someone had laid a small boulder upon her chest. She took in a quick breath, trying to shake it off, but found she couldn't. It was too late. She had finally succumbed to the very thing she and her friend had disdained throughout college—she had given into becoming a *violet*. She'd allowed that attractive young man to steal her heart—and now she was paying for it.

Oh, she didn't blame Wyatt for this offense. How could he help it if he was helpful and charming and witty and generous and oh-so-very handsome? And it wasn't as if she had been forced to spend time in his company. There had even been times when she had brazenly sought him out. No, she was getting what she deserved, and as much as it hurt, there was a sweetness to the pain.

She intended to keep her promise too—in fact, she was controlling herself from pulling out pen and paper right now—and she would write to him as soon as she got settled into her father's home. Perhaps tonight. Even if it were by candlelight in the hayloft like little Heidi. She would write and tell Wyatt all about it. Every little detail. And somehow she knew that he would be amused by it.

As the train rumbled south, heading directly toward the mountains, which Wyatt had told her were indeed the "Rockies," chugging up and down with great determination, she allowed herself to daydream about Wyatt and the short time they'd shared together. She was telling herself that, if that was all they would ever have, a few brief days, she would try to remain grateful for it. And if, by some miracle, their paths crossed again—and she prayed that they would—she would be overflowing with gratitude! As she admired the scenery all around her, she could understand why Wyatt was so fond of this part of the country. In her opinion, this landscape was much more attractive than the flat plains and prairies. Although it was rugged, it was beautiful.

The train made good time, and at a quarter before six, she heard its whistle blow as it steamed into the station. Looking up from the book that she'd started midway through the trip, she was surprised to see that Colorado City was really quite large. For some reason, perhaps because it felt like the end of the line, she had expected it to be a little mining town. But this was a booming big city. From what she could see, it was bigger than Denver. She found this both reassuring and slightly unsettling. Based on what had happened to her in Kearney and what Wyatt had told her about mining towns, she imagined that there could be a lot of unsavory characters in these parts.

Fortunately, she need not be concerned. Her father would be waiting at the train station—they would be home before dark. She realized it might be difficult to spot him—since they'd never met and he'd made no plan to identify himself—but she did remember Uncle Enoch saying that she looked very much like her father. She had his coloring.

As she stepped down from the train, she took in a deep breath, bracing herself for whatever came next. She looked through the faces in the small crowd, expecting to see a pair of green eyes searching for her, a rugged hand waving to her, calling her name…but she didn't.

Seeing her trunks and luggage piled on the platform, she decided to wait there. It was possible that her father got waylaid somehow, but she felt certain he must be on his way. She waited for several minutes and finally sat down on the largest trunk, wondering what she should do.

"Miss Blackstone?" a man's voice called out.

She stood, shielding her eyes with her hand from the sun which was low in the sky. She saw what looked like a stationmaster approaching her. "Yes?" she said eagerly.

"Miss Delia Blackstone?" He asked urgently.

"Yes. That's who I am."

"I have a message for you."

She held out her hand.

"No, it was a phone message. It seems no one can pick you up tonight. The man asked that you might stay in a hotel."

"Oh?" She nodded with uncertainty. "Well, of course, I can do that."

"He recommended a new hotel called the Elk Horn."

"The Elk Horn?" She imagined a decrepit hunting lodge.

"We can arrange to have your luggage sent." He directed her inside, where before long, she was all set and riding in a hansom cab through what seemed to be a very attractive and good-sized town. This did not feel one bit like the Wild West. Not only that, but the air was clean and fresh. She felt like she couldn't get enough of it, but then remembered Wyatt explaining that because of the high elevation, people had to adjust in regard to breathing.

"Here you go, miss." The cabbie stopped in front of a large and elegant building. "The Elk Horn."

Surprised by the grandeur of the castle-like four story building, she paid the cabbie and, while he got her luggage unloaded, went inside to inquire as to a room. The lobby was grand and beautiful, and she realized that the reason they called it the Elk Horn was probably because of the enormous elk antlers adorning the tall walls. Although she knew nothing about hunting, she could not help but be impressed.

Although everything about the Elk Horn was impressive and well planned and lovely, she felt distinctly let down over the fact that her father had not shown up. She hoped he wasn't having regrets over her visit. Perhaps he felt apologetic for his own humble abode, and that was why he wanted her to stay at such a grand hotel—so that she might enjoy one last night of luxurious civilization before joining him at his ranch.

Despite her disappointment over her father, she decided to make the best of it, enjoying a fine meal and all the comforts of a well-appointed room. She wished her mother could see this place. All her fearful warnings about the hazards of the West seemed sadly informed. The West—at least at the Elk Horn Hotel—was surprisingly sophisticated. So much so that even her rather finicky mother would be impressed.

The bed, Delia soon discovered, was the most comfortable one she'd ever slept in. God bless her dear father for wanting her to enjoy this one last night of blissful elegance—what a delightful welcome to Colorado City!

When she woke up, she felt rested and eager to begin the day. Hopefully there would be a message for her in the lobby. When there wasn't, she told the desk clerk of her whereabouts and was just on her way to the restaurant for breakfast when one of the bellboys came over to her. "A gentleman just arrived for you." He nodded over to the fireplace, where a man stood with his back to them. "The man in the dark brown coat."

As she approached him, Delia could see that, like her, he was tall and thin. But his hair, which she'd expected to be chestnut, was rather tawny, but perhaps it had grayed with the years.

"Hello?" she said tentatively, just a few feet away. "Father?"

The man turned around and she was surprised to see a much younger face than what she expected. This man couldn't be more than thirty. His eyes were blue—startling blue—and his expression was serious.

"I beg your pardon." She started to step away.

"Miss Delia Blackstone?" he asked expectantly.

"Yes, although I go by Miss Delia Williams now."

"I'm pleased to make your acquaintance, Miss Williams." He extended his hand. "I'm Marcus Vincent." He gently took her hand. "Welcome to Colorado City."

"Thank you. I was expecting my father to come—"

"I have some bad news for you, miss, and I'd just as soon get it out."

"Bad news?"

"Your father...well, he has passed on."

"Passed on?" Delia felt a dull buzzing inside her head. "What do you mean? What are you saying?"

"Your father, Winston Williams, is dead."

"*Dead?* When did he die? I got a telegram from him just a few days ago and—"

"He was shot. Just yesterday afternoon, miss."

"Shot?" Delia felt dizzy, and the buzzing in her head was getting louder.

"I'm sorry to be the bearer of bad news..."

His words blurred together as Delia's world turned to black.

14

WHEN DELIA CAME TO, THE MAN WITH THE BRIGHT BLUE EYES WAS staring down at her with a perplexed expression. "Are you all right?" he asked with concern.

"Yes…yes." She sat up from where someone must've eased her down on a couch. "I'm sorry. It's just such a shock. Did I understand you correctly? Did you actually say that my father is *dead?*"

"Yes. I'm sorry." He took a glass of water from one of the hotel employees. "Here, drink this."

She took a small sip, still trying to absorb what she'd just heard. "My father was *murdered? Is* that what you said?"

"We don't know that it was murder. It's possible it was an accident," the man clarified. "He died from a gunshot wound."

"Are you suggesting that someone *accidentally* shot my father?"

"It happens. Someone could've been hunting or target shooting. It's not that unusual."

"And my father is truly *dead."* She said the word again—trying to force her brain to accept it.

"I'm very sorry for your loss, Miss Williams. That's why no one picked you up last night."

"And who are you? I forgot your name?"

"Marcus Vincent."

"Mr. Vincent," she said slowly. "How do you know my father?"

"I'm his foreman. Been with him for about ten years." He glanced over at the small crowd that had gathered around them.

"I see." She pressed the back of her hand into her forehead. "What am I to do now?" She felt tears welling up in her eyes but hoped she could hold them back, especially since the onlookers were already too curious.

He studied her for a long moment. "The best plan is to put you back on the train and send you back East. Back to your folks, where you'll be safe."

"Oh…" The tears began to trickle down now. "I can't believe I'll never meet him…that he's dead. That I'm too late." And now she let out a choked sob.

"I know this is difficult," he said, "but you must understand that—well, since your father is dead—there is no reason for your visit."

"But he wanted me to come—to see him and his ranch." Despite the strangers looking on, she crumbled into tears. "I don't know what to do."

"You poor little thing." An older woman rushed over and sat next to Delia on the couch. "Do I understand it right? Your father just died? And you arrived too late to see him?" She wrapped a comforting arm around Delia's shoulder, offering her a handkerchief.

Delia nodded, using the handkerchief to blot her tears. "Only one day too late," she sobbed. "But I—I came as soon as I could."

"You poor darlin'." The gray-haired woman shook her head. "And you say you've never met him? Never even seen him?"

"Not that I remember. He left when I was very small."

The woman turned to Mr. Vincent. "This man died yesterday? Is he still laid out? Or have you buried him yet?"

"He's still laid out," Mr. Vincent answered with a frown. "We planned a funeral for tomorrow."

"Then you can't put this young lady back on the train going east. You best take her home to see her dearly departed father. It's the least you can do. Allow her to say her final farewell."

"Yes," Delia said eagerly. "That's what I want to do." She looked up at Mr. Vincent. "Please, take me to my father's ranch. I need to see it...and I need to see him." And now she broke into fresh tears.

"You heard the young lady," the older woman declared. "Take her to her father's place—straight away."

"All right," Mr. Vincent reluctantly agreed with a furrowed brow.

"Thank you for your help," Delia told the kind woman. "I don't even know your name."

"I'm Maggie O'Neil," she said. "My husband Rocky O'Neil owns the Shamrock Mine just south of here."

"Thank you for your kindness, Mrs. O'Neil. I do—"

"Please, call me Maggie."

"And I'm Delia. Delia Williams," she said. "My father—the man who died—is Winston—"

"Heavens to Betsy—I *know* who your father is!" she exclaimed. "My word, I can't believe it. Someone shot Winston Williams?" She turned to Mr. Vincent. "Is that true?"

He just nodded, turning his felt hat in his hands.

"Oh, my dear child." Maggie hugged Delia close again. "Your father was a very good man. This world will be a chillier place without Winston Williams. Such a loss!"

Delia cried even harder now—a mixture of overwhelming grief and sweet relief. It was good to know that her father had a good reputation, but heartbreaking to know she would never meet him. Maggie rocked her back and forth like a small child. Finally she held Delia back by her shoulders, looking her in the eyes.

"You get yourself out to your father's ranch, Delia. Do not get on that train and go home yet." She glanced over at Mr. Vincent then back at Delia. "You are *not* to leave Colorado until you've attended to your father's business. You hear?"

Delia blinked as she wiped her nose. "Yes. I—I'll do that."

As Maggie stood, Delia noticed her expensive looking gown of purple satin and brown lace. She also had on what appeared to be costly jewelry. She was obviously quite wealthy. "You're in the West now, Delia." Maggie smoothed the front of her dress down over her rather wide girth. "You must be strong. For your father's sake—as much as for yours."

"Thank you, Maggie," Delia said meekly. "I'll do my best."

After Maggie O'Neil left, Delia slowly stood. "My bags are packed," she told Mr. Vincent. "I'd like to leave at once, if you don't mind."

"Are you sure about this?" he asked with concern. "I thought for certain you'd want to go back east."

"Not yet," she firmly told him.

"As your father's foreman and best friend, I do not advise that you go to the ranch. It's possible that it could be dangerous."

"Dangerous?" She narrowed her eyes. "What are you saying?"

"Well, you do understand that your father was shot?"

"Yes, you said as much."

"What if it wasn't an accident?"

Delia wished that Maggie was still here, just to back her up. Then she remembered Maggie's words. *You're in the West now…you must be strong.*

"Mr. Vincent." Delia stood up straighter. "I am most determined to visit my father's ranch. If you are unwilling to take me, I will arrange for someone else—"

"I'll take you," he said begrudgingly. "But I just want to warn that it would be safer for you to go back home."

"I thought I was home." She looked evenly at him. Why was he so eager to be rid of her? "I believe Maggie was right. I know my father would want me to see his ranch while I'm here. And I would like to say goodbye."

Mr. Vincent just shrugged. "It's up to you."

Without waiting for him to launch further protests, Delia went over to the desk clerk, asking for someone to fetch her bags from her room and her trunks from storage. And then, using most of what money was left, she paid the hotel bill. As she buttoned her purse closed, she remembered her father's promise to give her return fare to Pennsylvania. She hoped that he'd thought to set it aside somewhere.

Mr. Vincent, it seemed, had ridden to town on his horse. As if he really had intended to send her back east without visiting her father's ranch. Consequently, she had to wait for him to hire a wagon from a nearby livery. As she waited, her determination grew. It was possible that Mr. Vincent truly did have her best interest in mind. And if he was her father's best friend and trusted employee, he certainly should. Yet something about this man didn't quite ring true.

As she rode up in front next to Mr. Vincent, she attempted to garner information regarding her father's death. Either he knew little of the facts or was reluctant to disclose them. She wasn't sure which it was, but her suspicions were growing.

"So you were very close with my father?" she said, hoping to extract more information.

"Well…he was my employer and friend."

Hadn't he claimed to be her father's best friend? Why was he softening his story now?

"Your father was looking forward to your visit," he said in a wooden-sounding voice.

"I was looking forward to it too," she said sadly.

"Too bad you couldn't have come out sooner." He clicked the reins, making the horses go a bit faster as they exited town. "But then I suppose you were too busy."

"If I had known about my father, which I didn't, I would've come much sooner," she explained with some aggravation. "I only learned about my father's existence last week. Apparently my parents had made an agreement that my father's identity would be kept from me until I finished my college education."

He gave her a sideways frown. "I heard you're an educated woman," he said with what sounded like disgust. "Can't imagine why anyone wanted to waste good money on that. Kind of like putting a gold ring in a pig's snout." He laughed as if this was a good joke.

"My *father* wanted to *waste* money on my education," she clarified hotly. "Apparently he believed that education was beneficial to *everyone*. And it's something I shall always be grateful for."

"Out here in the West, an educated woman is about as useful as a five-legged mule."

To this she said nothing.

"I'm sorry, miss." He sighed loudly. "I don't know why I'm being so cantankerous with you. I reckon I'm still reeling from the loss."

Her heart softened slightly. "Yes, I'm sorry for your loss too, Mr. Vincent."

"Call me Marcus," he said in a friendlier tone.

"Only if you call me Delia," she responded.

Now he smiled, and to her surprise she realized that he was actually quite good looking. Not nearly as handsome as Wyatt, but he was rather attractive in a rustic cowboy sort of way. "I'm sure it must be difficult to lose your employer and good friend."

"Winston Williams was like a father to me. Don't know how I'll get along without him."

At least you had him, she thought with a tinge of bitterness.

To her relief, neither of them spoke much for the duration of the trip. Instead, she just soaked up the surrounding countryside. Even before they were out of town, she could see that it was quite pretty. The farther they went, the more she could see that it wasn't simply pretty. It was spectacularly beautiful. Majestic snow-capped mountains provided a backdrop to the rolling green hills where a rainbow of colorful wildflowers bloomed, and the evergreen trees towered like giant sentries along the edges of a sparkling stream. It was amazing. No wonder her father had loved this land so much. She tipped her head back to look upward, and the sky was so vibrantly blue that it almost hurt her eyes. Inhaling a deep breath, she could taste the cleanness in the fresh air. She could understand why folks out here called this place a slice of heaven. And that provided a small consolation…if her father's life had to be cut short, at least he'd had all this.

Of course, he had been eager to bring her out here, to show her the incredible natural world he lived in. And yet she had arrived too late. And now she was crying all over again. Trying to conceal her tears from Marcus, she pretended to be gazing at the landscape, but all she saw was a blurry scene of green and blue.

15

As Marcus turned the wagon off one dirt road onto another one, Delia stared up at the tall ranch gate. Made of massive golden logs, the words *Double W Ranch* were painted across the top of the beam in bold black letters. "That's impressive," she said quietly.

"Uh-huh." Marcus glanced all around.

"How big is my father's ranch?"

He shrugged. "I dunno exactly, I reckon about six hundred acres."

"Goodness, that sounds enormous."

"Not compared to other ranches in these parts. Some of 'em number in the thousands." He jerked his thumb over a shoulder. "The Leaning R has around ten thousand acres."

"Oh?"

"Jerome Roswell, the owner of the Leaning R, runs several thousand head of cattle too. Biggest herd in these parts."

Delia looked over to the pasture on the right, where several dozen cows were peacefully grazing in lush green grass. "How many cows on this ranch?"

"Less than a hundred now. Winston used to run more. Before he decided to try other kinds of agriculture." Marcus frowned. "I tried to talk him out of that scheme. A cattle ranch is one thing—a farm is something else."

"I get the impression you don't approve of farming." Delia was taking it all in now—and the beauty was almost breathtaking. Besides the handsome mountains in the background and the towering pines, the rest of the property looked pristine and well cared for. Even the split rail fencing looked sturdy and well built. This ranch had been carefully tended over the years. Nothing like the rustic property she'd expected to find.

"This is cattle country," Marcus said stubbornly. "Shouldn't be fenced in."

"But what if the cows ran away?"

He chuckled. "Most cattle in these parts are raised on open range."

"Oh." She knew he was laughing at her. "But without fences, wouldn't the cows get into the crops?"

"Yup. That's why we put up the fences. If you want both cows and crops, it's the only way. I'm just saying I never thought it was the best plan."

"Well, I like the idea of a farm that raises both crops and animals. After all, people need a variety of foods. What's wrong with a farm that provides both?"

"Not as much money in it. And wastes too much water."

She pointed to a stream on the left. It was running into what looked like a large natural pond. "Looks like there's plenty of water here."

He shrugged.

"Sheep!" she exclaimed as she spotted a cluster of white woolly critters grazing contentedly. "And little lambs too! How bucolic."

"You *like* sheep?" Marcus's tone was chilly.

"Oh, I do. I think they're lovely to look at. And they provide us with wool. I like wool. And, although I don't like to think about it at the moment, but a lamb chop with a bit of mint sauce is rather nice too."

"You sound like your dad."

"Thank you."

"It wasn't a compliment, Miss Delia."

"I would think that if you disapproved of how my father ran his ranch, you would've sought other employment." She studied his profile, trying to discern his real nature. So far, he had done nothing to endear himself to her. She couldn't even understand why her father had hired him. Perhaps he was good at his job.

"Your dad was my friend."

"Yes, but now that he's gone?"

"I could get on at the Leaning R…if I wanted."

Before Delia could point out that Marcus might have to now, a black and brown dog came racing up to the wagon, barking with canine authority. "Who's that?" Delia asked.

"Your dad's dog. Hank."

"Hello, Hank," she called out. The dog trotted alongside the team, his tail wagging happily. As the wagon turned around a slow curve, Delia spotted a house up ahead. This was no one-room cabin! Although it wasn't as ornate as the home she'd left behind in Pittsburgh, this charming white farmhouse looked much bigger. Green grass and blooming flower beds surrounded the two-story house. Several rockers were on a wide porch that wrapped all the way around the house. With its dark green trim and red roof and brick chimneys, the place had a homey, welcoming look to it. In front of the house was a walkway lined with rose bushes just starting to bloom—and very beautiful.

"This is my father's house?" she said in unbelief and under her breath.

"This is it."

"I expected a small cabin." Beyond the house, Delia saw a large red barn and several other outbuildings, as well as a large corral and a number of handsome horses. Everything about this property was absolutely perfect—like a dream come true. Except that her father was dead.

As he pulled the wagon around the drive that circled in front of the house, she felt a large lump growing in her throat. She could feel her father's presence here—almost as if she could reach out and touch him—and yet he was dead.

"Miranda won't be expecting you."

"Miranda?" She wondered if that was a housekeeper.

Marcus frowned. "Winston didn't tell you about Miranda?"

"Did my father remarry? Is Miranda his second wife?"

"He did remarry. But his wife passed on a few years ago. Miss Miranda is his daughter."

"My father has another daughter?"

"Yup." He set the brake and hopped down.

As Marcus came around to her side, Delia was speechless. Her father had another daughter? Why hadn't he mentioned this in his letter? Why hadn't Uncle Enoch told her?

"Here you go," Marcus reached for her hand, helping her down. "Welcome to the Double W."

"Thank you." As Delia stepped onto the ground, the dog ran up to her with his tail still wagging. "Hello, Hank." She stooped over to let the dog sniff her glove. "Thank you for coming out to meet us." As she stood, she noticed a pale face peeking through the sheer curtains on the front window. It didn't look like a child's face. This was a young woman. "How old is Miranda?"

"Nearly seventeen. But I'll warn you, Miss Miranda thinks she's all grown up." He grinned. "I reckon she mostly is."

Imagine—a sister she'd never even heard about! Of course, she would be a half-sibling, but then so were the twins. "I can't wait to meet her," Delia said as Marcus started to unload her baggage.

"Well, then go on inside. I'm sure she's dying to meet you too."

Feeling slightly uneasy and a bit intrusive, Delia went up the steps to the porch. Hank remained by her side, almost as if he was escorting her to the house. Like everything else, the porch had a welcoming look. Besides the rockers, there were some small tables and a few potted plants. Very inviting. Instead of walking right in, Delia knocked on the door and after a few seconds a young woman with brown hair answered. Her brow was creased and her light blue eyes troubled. Of course, she too would be grieving the loss of her father.

"Miranda?" Delia asked hopefully.

"You must be Delia," the girl said in a flat tone.

"Yes. I'm so sorry for your loss, Miranda."

"Come in." Miranda opened the door wider, but when Hank started to go in, she stuck out her foot. "Not you," she said sharply. "No animals in the house."

Delia concealed her disappointment and smiled at Miranda. "I didn't even know I had a sister," she said as she followed her into a gracious foyer. A rectangular oriental rug was centered on a golden wooden floor and just beyond it was a sweeping staircase. "Marcus only just told me about you."

"I only heard about you a few months ago." Miranda pointed to what appeared to be a parlor. "Can I get you some tea or something?"

Suddenly Delia realized she was hungry. "Yes, tea would be most welcome. I left the hotel without breakfast. Thank you."

"Have a seat and I'll go tell Ginger. And I'll let Marcus know where to put your things."

After looking around the room for a bit, Delia sat down on a red upholstered chair. The parlor felt surprisingly cluttered and somewhat overdone—especially compared to the simple lines of the house's exterior. Everything in this room seemed to have tassels or fringe or ornate filigree. And the collection of porcelain statuettes looked like they were good at catching dust. This room had probably been decorated by a woman. Most likely, Miranda's mother.

Miranda returned, taking a seat across from Delia. "You're very pretty," she said with her brow still creased by a frown.

"You're very pretty too," Delia echoed. And, although it wasn't untrue, Delia probably wouldn't have stated as much if Miranda hadn't mentioned appearances in the first place. Miranda was certainly not unattractive, but she was pale and her features seemed tight and drawn. Her hair might be described as mousy, but perhaps just needed a good washing—and on closer inspection there appeared to be a hint of red in it, but pinned severely on top of her head, it wasn't the most becoming style. And her black gown, which she was probably wearing out of respect for their father, made her appear even paler. Plus the dress with its wide skirt was rather out of fashion.

"Marcus said he was going to send you back to Boston."

"Boston?"

"Or wherever you're from."

"Pittsburgh."

Miranda shrugged. "Yes, back East."

"I wanted to see my father's—I mean *our* father's property. He had wanted me to come out here. I felt I owed him this much."

"Well, you have seen it." Miranda narrowed her eyes. "At least you've seen the best of it. My mother always wanted the entrance to the house to make a good impression. She was from Charlotte, North Carolina and she often said that her family home had looked similar to this—before the war."

"It's very beautiful. I never expected it to be this nice."

"I'm afraid it will go downhill quickly with Dad not around. We've already lost most of the help."

"Oh." Delia didn't know what to say, but the lump in her throat was growing hard again. It was so difficult to take this in—her father was dead.

"I can see that you resemble Dad." Miranda seemed to be studying her.

"It's strange that I don't even know what he looks like. I've never seen a photograph...or anything."

Miranda got up and went over to an ornately carved wooden table and, opening the drawer, removed a folding frame made from tortoise shell. "Here." She handed it to Delia. "Meet Dad. That's my mother on the other side. She died in childbirth when I was twelve."

"I'm sorry for your loss," Delia said as she looked down at the photos. She felt a strange twist inside of her as she stared into the solemn face of a handsome man with wavy dark hair and intense eyes, which she could only assume were green like hers, based on what Uncle Enoch had said.

"Obviously they were both younger when those photographs were taken," Miranda said absently. "A few years after they married. I believe Dad was around forty and Mother was twenty-eight."

"They were a handsome couple," Delia said honestly. Something about her father did feel familiar to her. Perhaps it was because she could see a bit of herself in his eyes and high forehead. Or perhaps she had some long-gone memory from way back—something from her infant brain. The somber young woman on the opposite side had some resemblance to Miranda, although Delia felt perhaps she was prettier. Or maybe she was simply in love. Delia had heard that a woman in love grew more beautiful.

"Thank you." She handed the photos back to Miranda, who carefully slipped it back into the drawer.

"I get too sad when I see this," Miranda explained. "Better to keep it out of sight."

"Where, uh, is our father now?"

"He's been laid to rest in his library. That was his favorite place inside the house, so it seemed fitting."

"A library?"

"Do you think he shouldn't be in there?" Miranda asked with a troubled expression. "The undertaker suggested here in the parlor." She glanced around uncomfortably. "But I didn't think it a good idea."

"No, no, the library sounds just right." Delia couldn't imagine her father in this frilly room—alive or dead.

"Here you are." A plump, middle-aged woman with faded brown hair carried a tray into the room, setting it on the table. "Tea, and butter and jam sandwiches. It ain't much, but with Daisy and Susanna gone, it's the best I can do."

"Thank you, Ginger."

Ginger, instead of leaving, hovered by the door.

"This is Delia," Miranda said impatiently. "My father's *other* daughter."

"Pleased to meet you, Miss Delia," Ginger said warmly. "Welcome to the Double W. I'm so sorry about your father. It must've been a shock for you."

Delia thanked her, and then Ginger made her exit.

"She can be so impertinent," Miranda said as she poured a cup of tea, handing it to Delia. "And her cooking skills are unimpressive."

"She's not the regular cook?" Delia set a sandwich half on a small plate.

"No. That would be Daisy. And Susanna was her helper. But they both took off yesterday. Ginger is the head housekeeper, in charge of everything—and a busybody too."

"Did the others leave for good?"

"I think so. They were frightened…after Dad died. Everyone was upset. Ginger threatened to leave too, but I coaxed her to stay on. At least for a few days."

"Why was everyone so frightened?"

Miranda shrugged. "Perhaps they thought the shooter would go after someone else on the ranch." She took a bite of a sandwich.

"Is that a real possibility?" Delia asked. "Do you think our father's death was really intentional? Is there someone around here who is dangerous?"

"I really couldn't say." Miranda looked intently into Delia's eyes.

"But any man with a gun can be dangerous. At least that's what Dad used to say. Wouldn't you agree?"

Delia simply nodded.

"It's probably just as well that they all left." Miranda picked at the fringe of a velvet covered cushion.

"Why is that?" Delia asked.

"Because we probably can't afford to pay them anyway."

"Oh?" Delia remembered the state of her parents' finances back in Pittsburgh. They had been forced to part with household staff too. Was the whole country letting its servants go? "Why is that, if you don't mind me asking?"

"Because Dad invested every cent back into this land. He just never quit. He was always reading books and farming manuals, he wanted to improve everything…hoping this farm would start supporting itself eventually."

"From what I've seen, this property is lovely."

"Lovely doesn't pay the bills," Miranda said coolly. Now her eyes seemed to move over Delia, taking her in from head to toe. "You don't look much like a city girl to me."

"You mean because of my drab clothing?"

"Yes. I expected you to be much more fashionable."

Delia explained about her college wardrobe.

Miranda shrugged. "I suppose that makes sense. Although it's a terribly dreary dress." She looked down at her own frayed gown with a sad little smile. "I guess that's a bit like the pot calling the kettle black. This sad rag belonged to my mother, she wore it after her first husband was killed in the mine. As you can see, it's out of style too, but it's all I have for being in mourning. Do you have something appropriate?"

"Nothing in black." She looked down at her dark gray dress. "But this is close."

Miranda shrugged. "I suppose it'll do…for now."

After they finished their midmorning tea, Delia asked to view her father's body. It wasn't so much that she was eager to see him in such a state, but simply because she wanted to get the painful "meeting" over with. Everything felt so strange to her—almost as if she were stuck in a bad dream. If only it were so!

As Miranda led her to the back of the house, she acted like a proper hostess, pointing out the various rooms as if Delia were a welcomed guest. She started with the spacious front room where a tall fireplace had a mounted elk head hanging above it. Next was a large formal dining room with wallpaper with blue and yellow birds and trailing vines. This was connected by swinging doors to a butler's pantry that led into a spacious kitchen. Much bigger than the one back in Pittsburgh. In the rear of the house, on the right side, was a solarium, and finally they came to a tall closed door on the opposite side which, according to Miranda, led to the library.

"I won't go in with you," she said. "Feel free to stay as long as you like."

Taking in a deep breath, Delia pushed open the door, entering the dimly lit room that smelled faintly of cedar and candle wax. The heavy velvet drapes over the single window were pulled closed and the only light came from a flickering pair of candles in silver candlesticks. They must've been lit for some time because they were down to a couple of inches and the wax catchers were near to overflowing.

On a table in the center of the room was a dark wooden casket. Taking another steadying breath, Delia approached it, looking down at the lifeless face of a man who had been her father—the father she had never known…would never know. His hair, unlike the photo where he'd probably at least ten years younger, was tinged with gray. And there were traces of lines along the sides of his closed eyes. His brows and lashes, like hers, were dark. And there was a dark shadow of beard stubble on his squared chin, as if he hadn't shaved before his demise.

As she reached out her hand, laying it upon his chest, silent tears began to streak down her cheeks. "I'm sorry I got here too late," she whispered. "I would've come sooner…if I had known. I wish I had known." She took in a raggedy breath. "Thank you for everything you did for me, Father. All those years…I didn't even know it—you were helping my family. Thank you for everything. Thank you for being faithful to me when I didn't even know you existed. And thank you for allowing me to go to college for those two years." She closed her eyes as the sadness welled up inside of her. Why did it have to end this way? Why had she never been allowed the chance to look into his living eyes, to hear his voice, hold his hand? It seemed so unfair…so wrong…so heartbreaking.

She bowed her head, attempting to pray, but the words felt choked inside of her. *Why did God allow this to happen?* Why did he get her out here—so far from her home and so close to meeting her father—only to have it end like this? *Why? Why? Why?*

16

When Delia finally left the library, stopping by the kitchen to ask Ginger if the candles in the library should be replaced, she felt totally and utterly drained. Not to mention hopeless.

"Poor lassie." Ginger put a hand on her shoulder. "Comin' all this way to find your dear daddy gone. I'm so sorry, Miss Delia. And I'll see to them candles straight away."

"Thank you."

"Will you be the mistress of the house now?" Ginger asked as she opened a drawer, extracting several tall white candles.

"Oh, no." She shook her head. "I'm only a guest here."

Ginger's pale brows arched in question.

"I assume Miss Miranda is in charge."

Before Ginger could respond, the back door to the kitchen opened and short man with gray hair and a scruffy beard walked in and, not seeing her, began speaking to Ginger. "Now, I know the cook and half the servants have flown the coop," he said in a gruff tone. "But I need to know when to expect dinner. The men are hungry and after that pitiful excuse of a breakfast, well, I reckon we—"

"Excuse me, Caleb," Ginger interrupted him, pointing over to where Delia was still standing in the shadows of the doorway. "Have you met Mr. Williams's older daughter yet?"

When he turned to face Delia, his eyes lit up. "Well, I'll be. You must be Miss Delia." He stuck out his hand. "It's a pleasure to meet you, young lady. I've been looking forward to it. I'm sorry about the circumstance though."

She shook his hand. "You must be Uncle Enoch's good friend Caleb."

"I sure am. Caleb Johnson at your service."

"Uncle Enoch asked me to send you his regards."

"Thank you much." He nodded soberly. "Enoch ain't gonna like hearing the news about Winston, that's for sure." He frowned. "And I'm real sorry for your loss too, Miss Delia. Sorrier than I can say."

"Thank you. I'm still getting over the disappointment of not meeting him…in person." She swallowed hard, trying to hold back more tears. "I wish I'd come sooner."

"I s'pect you came as soon as you could. Weren't it just a week ago that Enoch went back East to fetch you? Seems to me you made right good time."

"Just not in time to meet my father," she said sadly. She looked at Ginger. "Excuse me for interrupting you. I'm sure you've got a lot to do, especially if you've lost some of your help."

"We are most assuredly shorthanded." She glared at Caleb. "And a mite of patience wouldn't be wasted. I haven't been in the habit of cooking for some years now."

"That is evident," Caleb growled back at her.

"Well, I hope you won't feel the need to wait on me," Delia said quickly to Ginger. "I can take care of myself. And if I can be of any help to you while I'm here, I'm more than willing." She grimaced. "Although I'm embarrassed to say that I don't really know how to cook, or much about housekeeping either—but I can take directions and I'm more than willing to learn."

"Don't you trouble yourself about me." Ginger waved her hand.

"With just you and Miranda in the house, it's not so much work. And once I get the hang of cooking for the men, I'll be all right." She frowned at Caleb. "I was just fixin' to start the midday meal, unless you'd rather do it yourself."

He grinned. "I'm good at cooking on the trail, but not so handy in a kitchen."

"So how many hands we got now?"

"I'm right sorry to say that, including me and Marcus, we're down to just four. Jeb, Simon, and Reese took off right after breakfast. And, just to be clear, it ain't due to your cookin' neither." He gave her an apologetic smile.

"Oh, my." Ginger pursed her lips. "That makes my job easier, Caleb, but not yours. That's for sure."

"I'm curious as to why so many people have left," Delia said carefully. "Miranda insinuated it was because they're afraid. In fact, Marcus suggested that it might not be safe here. Is that really true? Should I be concerned?"

Ginger bit her lip, and Caleb's mouth twisted to one side. "I can't say for sure, Miss Delia," Caleb began. "I reckon some of them might be scared, and some of them are just moving on to greener pastures. Hard to say."

"You mean because their employer is deceased? Are they worried their jobs are not secure now?"

"That's part of it, for certain."

"Does Miranda know how to manage these things? I assume she's in charge of things like payroll and hiring and such? Perhaps the workers are worried about being paid."

Caleb frowned. "I'm not sure Miss Miranda has a head for business."

"If Marcus gets his way, she won't need to," Ginger said quietly.

"What do you mean?" Delia asked.

Ginger put her hand over her mouth. "I'm afraid I said too much already. Forgive me, Miss Delia. Me and my big mouth."

"Well, excuse me for intruding." Delia started to back out of the kitchen, feeling as if she'd overstepped some bounds. "I suppose it's none of my business."

"Maybe you should make it your business," Caleb declared. "After all, this was your daddy's ranch, Miss Delia. Only seems natural you should want to know how it's been run. I know that your pa would be grateful."

She stepped back into the kitchen, nodding eagerly. "I would *love* to know how the ranch is run, Caleb. Already I'm so impressed with everything I've seen. Nothing would please me more than to see all that my father has done here."

"You know how to ride a horse?"

"Of course."

"How about if I give you a little tour this afternoon, right after dinner?"

"Thank you!" she exclaimed. "I'll be ready."

"And dinner will be ready at one," Ginger told Caleb. "Chicken and dumplings."

Delia waited as Caleb exited the kitchen before she addressed Ginger. "Do you know where I'm staying? Miss Miranda didn't mention anything."

"You're in the blue guest room," Ginger told her. "Go up the stairs then turn to the right. Last door at the end of the hallway. You let me know if you need anything."

As Delia passed through the dining room, she could hear voices up near the front door. It sounded like Miranda and Marcus, and they both sounded agitated.

"I told you not to bring her here," Miranda hissed at him.

"And I told you I had no choice," he retorted.

"What are we going to do with her?"

"I guess that's up to you. She's your sister."

"She is *not!* She's a complete stranger to me. You brought her here, Marcus, you deal with her."

"Stop acting like a child."

"How dare you!"

"It's time you grew up, Miranda. You always go 'round telling everyone that you're all grown up. Time you start acting like it." This was followed by the slamming of the front door and then angry footsteps and what sounded like she slamming of the parlor door.

Delia slowly counted to ten before continuing through the house. She didn't want her sister to know that she'd been eavesdropping—but really what else could she have done? To her relief, Miranda was nowhere to be seen as Delia hurried up the stairs. Then, following Ginger's directions, she went directly to the room at the end of the hallway—entering what had to be the blue room.

The walls were a soft robin's egg blue, and the heavy metal bed frame was a creamy white. The coverlet was blue and white and soft to the touch. The wardrobe, dresser, desk, chair, and side tables were all sturdy pieces of dark oak. Several attractive kerosene lamps were set about the room, as well as a big white pitcher and bowl for washing, with lace trimmed linens hanging on the towel bar. This seemed to confirm her earlier suspicions that there was no indoor plumbing.

Stepping past her trunks and bags, now heaped on an oriental rug in the center of the floor, she made her way to the window where a white lace curtain fluttered in the breeze. She pushed it aside to see this room was in the back of the house and down below was what appeared to be a fruit orchard with row upon row of lush green trees. Noticing some movement in the grass, she spied several snowy white geese meandering toward a large pond. Such a beautiful scene—it nearly took her breath away. Her father had created a truly wonderful haven. "A little slice of heaven," like Uncle Enoch had said.

As she unpacked her things, she pondered over her mystifying younger sister. For some reason, Miranda did not want Delia here. The obvious cause could be that Miranda was worried about sharing an inheritance with a half-sister. Although, Delia could not imagine that her father would've left anything besides return-trip train fare to her—not when he'd had another daughter living here with him all this time. A small wave of jealousy rippled through her. Oh, she knew it was ridiculous. It wasn't as if anyone had intentionally planned these things. Well, unless it was her own mother. In many ways, Delia still held her mother responsible for it all.

As Delia smoothed out her gowns, she wondered why she'd never considered the possibility of her father having other children. Especially considering that he, after finding gold, had become a man of means. And, judging by what she'd seen so far on his ranch, he was an intelligent businessman too. Not to mention he was quite handsome. Naturally he had married. Who could blame him? He must've been quite a catch!

And now, in the privacy of her own room—and such a lovely room—she allowed herself to have what she hoped would be her final cry over the loss of the father she had never known. Although as she let the tears of pain, disappointment, frustration, and hopelessness flow, she wasn't sure that it would be her last time. The image of her father lying lifelessly in his casket wouldn't leave her—as if she were still standing in the library. Why had God allowed it?

After another good cry, Delia dried her eyes and took out her stationery and pen. As promised, she would write Wyatt a letter, but since it was already past twelve, she would need to hurry. She kept the note brief, mostly telling of the disappointing news about her father…and how lost she was feeling.

She sealed the short letter just a few minutes before one o'clock. And then, still flushed from crying, she splashed some tepid water onto her face, straightened her hair, and went down for the midday meal. As Ginger had promised, it was chicken and dumplings and, although Marcus was present in the dining room, Caleb and his other two hands were not. Delia considered inquiring about this but decided to keep her questions to herself. After all, it wasn't as if servants ate with the family in her home back in Pittsburgh, but for some reason these people—at least Caleb and Ginger—seemed different. Almost as if they were family. But perhaps she was just grasping.

Marcus was seated at one end of the long table and Miranda at the other, with Delia on the side in between. Marcus and Miranda exchanged few words, mostly concerning the funeral service planned for tomorrow morning. And although they were careful not to include Delia in their conversation, she tried not to feel left out. After all, she was the interloper here. At least in their eyes.

"So what are your plans, while you are here?" Marcus suddenly asked her.

"Oh. Well, Caleb offered to take me on a tour of the property."

"Oh?" Marcus frowned. "Do you think that's a good idea?" he asked Miranda. "You told me there were restrictions for women in mourning."

"Speaking of that, Delia and I must go to town this afternoon," Miranda announced.

"What for?" Delia asked.

"To purchase our widows' weeds."

"But we're not widows." Delia nodded to Miranda. "Besides, you already have a black dress. I have this dark gray one. Don't you think they are sufficient for mourning clothes?"

"This horrible dress is so old that I fear it will fall to shreds by the time of the funeral service. Do you think it fitting that Winston Williams's daughter should appear in public wearing rags?"

"I agree." Marcus dropped his fork with a loud twang. "I'll get Cash to hitch up the wagon for you right now."

"I want the carriage," Miranda insisted.

"The wagon needs to be returned to town anyway."

"Then how will we get back?" Miranda demanded.

Marcus scratched his head. "Fine. I'll have Cash drive the wagon to town and you ladies can take the carriage and all come back together."

"But what about my plans?" Delia asked.

"What plans?" Miranda frowned.

Delia reminded her of Caleb's offer to show her around.

"You'll do that tomorrow," Marcus said sharply. *"After* the funeral."

"But I—"

"Surely, you don't want to dishonor our father," Miranda said. "You wouldn't go to his funeral, in front of all his friends, dressed like *that,* now would you?"

"No, I suppose not," Delia conceded. "I'll go to town with you, but first I must tell Caleb that I won't be coming." Excusing herself and promising to meet them out front in fifteen minutes, Delia went out to look for Caleb. She found him and two other men, as well as Ginger, just finishing up their supper in a mess hall housed in a separate building back behind the house.

Delia apologized for the intrusion then waited as Caleb introduced her to his two ranch hands. She politely greeted each of them—a young ruddy boy named Cash and a slightly older red-headed man named Silas—then turned her attention back to Caleb. "I'm sorry I won't be able to take the tour you offered," she explained. "Miranda feels it's vital that I go with her to town to get some mourning clothes."

"Mourning clothes?" He frowned.

She waved her hand down at her gray dress. "She insists we must wear black. I feel, since I am her guest, I must comply."

His frown deepened. "Miss Miranda is not the boss of you, Miss Delia."

Delia sighed. "It seems to me that she is the lady of the house."

"Things ain't always what they seem."

"Will you still be willing to give me a tour tomorrow? After the funeral service?"

"Of course, we can do it anytime you'd like." He followed her out, into the back yard. "But I gotta warn you, Miss Delia. It could be dangerous for you to go to town just now."

"What do you mean?"

He rubbed his grisly chin. "Anyone going with you?"

"Marcus said Chase will drive the borrowed wagon back to the livery. And Miss Miranda and I are to take the carriage." She glanced at her watch. "In fact, we should be leaving soon."

"I will drive you in the carriage," he insisted. "And we'll bring Silas along too. He's a good shot with the rifle."

"Rifle?"

"Best not to ask too many questions just yet, Miss Delia. Much of my suspicions are pure speculation. But I would rather be safe than sorry."

Before long, their entourage was headed to Colorado City. As much as Delia longed to be back at the ranch, she did enjoy the scenery along the way. And she hoped this might be a chance to draw out Miranda.

"What are your plans?" Delia asked. "I mean after the funeral. Do you intend to stay on and run the ranch?"

Miranda looked perplexed. "To be honest, I'm not sure."

"I can understand," Delia said soothingly. "I know it's difficult to rebuild one's life. But the ranch is such a beautiful place. I can certainly imagine you would want to live there for the rest of your days."

"You can imagine that because you've only just got here. Try living your whole life in these parts and tell me how you feel about it." Miranda folded her arms in front of her.

"Would you feel differently if you had someone by your side? Someone you cared for?"

Miranda softened slightly. "Maybe...."

"Is it my imagination or does Marcus Vincent fancy you?"

Miranda's blue eyes lit up. "Do you think he does?"

Delia nodded. "I most certainly do. I saw the way he looked at you."

"But he's always so sharp with me. He treats me more like a little sister than someone he has romantic feelings for."

"Perhaps that's just his way." Even as she said this, Delia felt a bit like a traitor. But she wanted to get to the bottom of this. Besides, if Miranda had feelings for Marcus, it would stand to reason that the two of them, together, could continue to run the ranch. And even though Delia didn't feel much respect for Marcus, she did care about Miranda…and the ranch.

Now Miranda let her guard down and began to talk about Marcus and how he had given her hope from time to time, even confessing that they had exchanged more than one kiss. "Don't you think he's the most handsome man ever?" Miranda asked as they were coming into town.

"He has the most striking blue eyes I have ever seen," Delia said honestly, without adding that those eyes felt as cold as steel to her.

Before long, the carriage pulled up to Miranda's favorite dress shop where, thanks to a savvy shopkeeper and seamstress, they were soon fitted for appropriate black gowns that would be altered and delivered to the Double W Ranch first thing tomorrow morning. And since the Post Office was nearby, Delia was even able to mail her letter. How long it would take to make its way up to Alaska was anyone's guess, but at least she had kept her promise.

The carriage returned home with Caleb at the reins and Silas sitting shotgun. Young Cash was perched on the back. Delia thought that Caleb had probably been overly cautious in bringing the extra men—especially when they were so shorthanded at home—but just as they were coming around a bend, she heard a couple of shots ring out from the direction of the mountains.

"Get down!" Caleb yelled as the horses were urged to a gallop and shots were returned from the carriage. While Delia and Miranda crouched down in the carriage, the horses continued along a straight stretch at a fast clip. Horrified at being in such peril, Delia reached for Miranda's hand, grasping it in fear. "Why are they shooting at us?" she demanded. "What's going on?"

17

AFTER THE CARRIAGE WENT AROUND A BEND AND INTO ANOTHER straight stretch, the shooting stopped. Several minutes passed with the team still galloping at full speed before Caleb called out. "Is everyone all right?"

"We are fine," Delia shouted from where they were still hunkered down on the carriage floor.

"Me too," Cash hollered from the back of the carriage.

"Looks like we're out of harm's way," Caleb yelled as he slowed the horses down some.

"What was that?" Delia asked Miranda as they returned to the padded seat. "Was someone trying to kill us?"

"I don't know." Miranda's eyes were dark—either with anger or fear, or maybe both.

"Then, tell me, is this a common occurrence around here? Do people often shoot at other people?" Delia tried to keep her voice steady as she smoothed her skirt.

"Some people might."

"Was that how our father got killed?" Delia could feel her hands still shaking within her soft kid gloves.

"Maybe."

"Does someone want *you* dead?" Delia stared at the Miranda, trying to determine her sister's inner thoughts and motives.

"It's possible," Miranda said crisply. She folded her arms in front of her as she turned to look out the side window.

Delia wanted to understand her half-sister—even hoped to become close to her—but this young woman seemed to be building a wall between them. Why did she resent Delia so much? Was there any way for Delia to win her trust, her friendship?

"I want to apologize," Delia said quietly.

"Apologize?" Miranda turned around. "What for?"

"I'm afraid I sort of forced myself upon you. Marcus encouraged me to return to Pennsylvania, but I insisted on coming out here. I really don't want to be an inconvenience and I honestly had no idea that I had a sister." She tried to smile but felt the falseness in it. "But I would like to get to know you better…before I go back East."

"So you do plan to go back East? To your home?"

"Of course." Delia sighed. "What else can I do?"

"I don't know…I suppose I assumed you might try to stay on here."

Delia shook her head. "Not without my father—I mean our father—still living. He was the reason I came out here."

Miranda's expression softened. "I'm sorry you got here too late."

They had turned into the Double W now and Delia's hands had finally stopped shaking. "Do you really think the men shooting at us were the same ones who killed our father?" Delia asked Miranda for the second time.

"It seems likely."

"Do you know why?"

"It's over water."

"Water?" Delia suddenly recalled Uncle Enoch mentioning that her father was having problems with his neighbors over water.

"Our property has water," Miranda said simply. "The creek and the natural pond. For the last ten years or so, Dad has steadily decreased his cattle herd and turned more land to crops. Some ranchers resent this."

"Resent it enough to kill someone?"

Miranda rolled her eyes. "You are new to the West, Delia."

"I'm well aware of this. But I also know that it's not as wild and lawless as it used to be. Even seeing Colorado City gave me the impression that the Wild West is a thing of the past."

"Don't be misled by impressions. There are many men out here who still live by their own law—they play sheriff, judge, and jury—and no one questions them. A neighboring ranch—the Leaning R—is owned by a powerful man named Jerome Roswell. He started cattle ranching three decades ago and sometimes acts like he's the king of Colorado. Or God. Roswell has been pressuring Dad to sell for years. Even more so last year because we'd been having a drought. This year we got good rain, but Roswell has been relentless."

"Did Roswell kill our father?"

Miranda sighed with exasperation. "No, of course not. At least not personally. You can be sure that when Dad was killed, Roswell was somewhere with a rock-solid alibi. Probably in the White Horse Saloon in Colorado City, maybe playing poker with the mayor and judge and chief of police. They're all good friends."

"Oh?" Delia didn't like the sound of this. "But perhaps one of Roswell's men killed our father, and maybe that same man—or men—were shooting at us today?"

"You're catching on." Miranda's smile felt condescending.

"So what can we do about it?"

"Do?" Miranda reached for the door handle as the carriage came to a stop in front of the house and, without answering, hopped out.

As Delia got out, she was greeted by her father's dog. "Hello, Hank." She bent over to scratch him behind his ears. "You taking care of things while we were gone?" He wagged his tail as he followed her up to the house. "Sorry, boy, guess you know the rule about animals in the house." As tempted as she was to sneak him inside, she knew Miranda wouldn't approve.

After making a tiny bit of progress in building sisterly relations, she didn't want to undermine her own effort. If only for her father's sake, she was determined to befriend the prickly Miranda. She thought it would make him happy to see that his two daughters were on good terms…that is, if he could see them. Delia looked toward the end of the house where the library was, where she knew her father was still laid out, and felt a fresh wave of sadness wash over her.

"Miss Delia?" Ginger approached wearing her usual faded apron. She wrung her hands. "You kindly offered to help me and, as much as I hate to ask, I'm afraid I must."

"Certainly." Delia nodded eagerly. "What can I do?"

"Well, Miss Miranda wants to serve supper after the funeral tomorrow morning and since Mr. Williams was a well-loved man, and his obituary ran in the newspaper, I'm afraid a bunch of folks will set upon us tomorrow and I'm not sure we'll be ready."

"You'll just tell me what to do and I'll try to do it," Delia assured her. "Let me go put my things away and I'll be right down." She hurried up the stairs, dropping off her purse, hat, and gloves then stopping by the bathroom that she'd discovered shortly before their trip to Colorado City. Earlier she'd assumed the door led to a bedroom, but seeing the door ajar, she'd discovered it was a rather nice bathroom. Much larger and even more modern than the one her parents had gotten installed in their home in Pittsburgh. Delia felt gratitude for her father's sensibilities—she had never dreamed there would be indoor plumbing in the Wild West. So many things she'd been wrong about.

"Here I am," Delia announced as she went into the kitchen. "How can I help?" She unbuttoned her cuffs and began to roll up her sleeves.

"Bless you, darlin'. I sent a message to my good friend Rosie in Colorado City," Ginger said as she vigorously stirred something in a large bowl. "I asked her to come over here with her two grown girls to help out—promised that they'd be well recompensed too. But Rosie said she couldn't bring her girls. Says everyone in town is gossiping about Mr. Williams's death. She thinks it's too dangerous out here, but she did offer to come lend a hand tomorrow."

"Is she right? Will it be dangerous?" Delia tried not to remember how frightened she'd been on the way home this afternoon.

"Dangerous?" Ginger shrugged. "I can't fathom why. Who would make trouble while Mr. Williams is being buried?" Ginger checked a pot on the big wood burning range. "After that, well, God only knows."

Delia considered telling Ginger about the gunshots exchanged on the road earlier but didn't want to upset her when she already had so much to handle for tomorrow. Besides, she reasoned, Caleb would probably inform Ginger. They seemed to be on friendly terms.

"Here." Ginger handed her a gingham apron. "I'll start you off with eggs. I need nine since I'm tripling the recipe. And I'll bet you know how to crack an egg." She chuckled.

But as Delia cracked the first egg, feeling it crumble in her hand as all the cold gooey contents dripped down the side of the bowl, she wasn't so sure. Trying to hide her lack of skill, she cleaned it up and picked the shells from the bowl. Next time she was more cautious. Eventually, she got the hang of it. With nine eggs sans eggshells, she proudly showed Ginger.

"Now you beat 'em."

"Beat them?"

"With our dandy new tool." Ginger winked as she opened a deep drawer. "Daisy bought it in town last year. She would never let me use it. But now I've used it a lot and I gotta admit, it's fun." She held up a metal contraption with a handle to crank it. "See, this turns the beaters." She turned the handle, making the beaters spin. "Isn't that fun?"

Delia put the beaters into the eggs and cranked the handle until the eggs were yellow and fluffy. "That's enough," Ginger told her. "Don't want to beat them to death. They're for the sponge cake. But you're so good at beating, I'll let you whip the meringue for the chocolate pies, and if you do a good job with that, I might let you make the angel's food cake."

"Really?" Delia asked hopefully.

"But first we need to get dinner started. You want to help with that?"

"Of course." Delia smiled. It was actually a relief to be here with Ginger in the kitchen. It kept her mind off of other more troubling things. Although, by the time she finished peeling the tenth potato, she wasn't so sure. "Do we really need all of these?" she asked as she frowned at the bucket of potatoes still waiting.

"Not for tonight, but we need them for tomorrow. I plan to make a heap of potato salad tonight. For tomorrow."

"Oh, I see."

"And we'll make coleslaw too."

"What else is on the menu?" Delia asked as she peeled another potato.

"Well, Caleb butchered a hog that will be cooked in a pit outside. That takes some of the workload off me. And then we'll have beet salad with the canned beets we put up last fall. And bean and corn salad and, of course, lots of desserts. And I'm hoping some of the folks attending the funeral will bring dishes too. That's usually what happens. But Miss Miranda wanted to be sure we offered a good spread...just in case."

"And Miss Miranda doesn't help in the kitchen?"

Ginger didn't say anything. The look she gave Delia said it all.

"No matter," Delia said quickly. "And I want you to know, I feel fortunate to help—I feel as if I'm honoring my father by doing this."

"You are a good girl, Miss Delia. And when we're not so busy, I'd like to talk to you about—"

"Miss Delia," Caleb said with what sounded like relief as he entered the kitchen. "I've been looking all over for you."

"I'm sorry," she said. "I've been in here with Ginger. Did you need me for something?"

"I just wanted to make sure you weren't upset. I thought you might've gone to hide in the cellar. I'm so sorry about what happened on our way home from Colorado City. If I'd known those outlaws were out there, I never would've allowed you two girls to go. As it turned out, I'm glad I went with you and took Cash and Silas along."

"What happened?" Ginger asked eagerly.

"Someone took pot shots at us," he told her. "Probably one of Roswell's men. They came from Eagle Bluff, but we couldn't spot the shooters. Cash and Silas returned fire and then we got away." He pushed his fingers through his scruffy beard. "I'm not sure if they were trying to kill us or just scare us. I reckon it's the latter." He frowned. "But you never know. I told the boys to be on the lookout, and I sent one of them to tell the sheriff. Not that I expect the sheriff to do much."

"Oh, my." Ginger wiped her hands on the front of her apron then peered at Delia. "And you weren't frightened by this?"

"Sure, I was frightened." Delia shrugged. "But what can you do?"

Caleb laughed. "Don't she sound just like Winston?"

"I do declare! She sure is her daddy's daughter."

"I know I promised to give you a tour of your daddy's spread," Caleb told her. "But with so much to be done, I don't see how I can get to it."

"Don't worry about that," she said. "I can explore on my own."

"I don't want you wandering too far from the house," he said with concern. "Might not be safe."

"All right." She nodded.

"And when things aren't so busy, I'll show you around," he assured her. "It's not easy running this place with so few hands. Not at all." Shaking his head grimly, he mumbled to himself as he went back out.

"Poor Caleb," Ginger said grimly. "If I think I'm busy in this house, he's got a whole lot more to take care of out there. And like me, he ain't no spring chicken neither. I just hope this job don't kill him."

As Ginger and Delia continued to work in the kitchen, Delia realized just how badly Ginger needed her help. It didn't seem possible that just the two of them could manage, not just the household, but all the preparations for the luncheon following the funeral. At one point Delia considered rousting out Miranda, insisting that she help out…then decided against it.

Delia noticed the dark clouds gathering out over the mountains again. "Looks like another thunderstorm."

"We been getting a lot of those lately. Can't complain though." Ginger pounded the raised bread dough down. "Not when they bring the rain with them. You probably noticed how green everything was."

"Yes, especially on the Double W. It looks just beautiful."

Ginger scowled. "You'd think with the good Lord providing rain for everyone—the just and the unjust—that even them greedy folk over at the Leaning R would be satisfied."

Delia just shook her head. It was more than she could begin to comprehend. Thankfully, she had so much to keep her busy that she didn't need to think about it. When it was time to set the table for supper, Delia made a suggestion to Ginger. "Instead of setting up a formal meal for Miranda, Marcus, and me, and then another dinner table for you and the others out back, why don't we all just eat together?"

"Eat together?" Ginger looked shocked.

"Yes," Delia continued. "We could use the everyday dishes and just keep everything simple. Less work for us to clean up afterwards."

"I'll admit it sounds real smart, Miss Delia." Ginger just shook her head. "But I would not want to see the fireworks show that would follow."

Of course, Ginger was referring to Miranda, but Delia kept her thoughts to herself as she went to the formal dining room to set the table. Delia had always known that servants worked hard, but until now, she hadn't been aware of just how difficult it was. She wondered if Miranda had any idea of how unrealistic her expectations were for one woman to accomplish all this.

"You best go clean yourself up for supper," Ginger said as she removed the roast beef from the oven. Part of the roast would be served for tonight with the remainder, along with two other roasts, served to tomorrow's guests.

"You're right." Delia removed her apron. "But first I want to say what a fine job you're doing, Ginger. I know that your real job was overseeing the household and that Daisy was the actual cook, but you're very organized and efficient. This household is lucky to have you."

Ginger smiled, pushing a strand of gray hair from her damp forehead. "You remind me so much of your daddy, Miss Delia. Always ready with a kind word, he was a true gentleman and a fine boss. And I just know he would've been so proud of you."

Delia felt slightly teary as she thanked Ginger then hurried upstairs. There was nothing that anyone could've said that would mean more to her than that—and she was grateful. Not only that, but it felt like just being here, in his house, around his employees…it was almost as if she was getting to know him.

As she passed by the spacious bathroom, Delia observed it was occupied, she assumed with Miranda since they were the only ones using the second floor. As much as Delia would've enjoyed using that room to freshen up, she was thankful for the pitcher and bowl in her room. But as she was drying her hands and face, she noticed that the top drawer in the dresser was askew and partially open. Upon closer inspection, it appeared as if someone had rifled through her belongings. The chemises and stockings that she'd carefully laid out in the drawer earlier had been moved around—as if someone had been searching for something.

With a racing heart, Delia reached into the back of the drawer, feeling around for the jewelry box that she'd wrapped in her shawl. To her relief, the shallow wooden box was still there and when she opened it, every piece of jewelry, aside from the topaz earrings she'd left with Julianne, was there. Even so, it was troubling to think that someone had trespassed into her room. Instead of putting the box back in the drawer, she put it in her hatbox, covered by a scarf, with her hats on top. For now that would have to do.

18

WYATT HAD NEVER BEEN IN SAN FRANCISCO BEFORE, BUT INSTEAD OF taking in all the sights as planned—and there was plenty to see in this beautiful city by the bay—he hired a wagon, loaded it with the cargo he'd transported cross-country by train, and had the driver take him directly to the piers. His goal was to see if he could get passage to Juneau by way of a different ship—a ship that was leaving sooner.

As they went through the city, Wyatt caught glimpses of the unique town, knowing that he was passing up the opportunity of a lifetime. Built upon a series of hills that dropped off into a glistening blue bay, San Francisco would be a fun place to explore. He'd already read about the town that had sprouted up as a result of the California gold rush of 1849. Since then it had grown and flourished and was often called the Paris of the West.

The architecture was stunning, and he'd heard that pleasures like theater and dining were as fine as anything back East or even in Europe. There was a Chinatown to be explored. And so much more. But he no longer cared about any of that. Perhaps he wasn't as much of a drifter as he'd been trying to make himself believe. Or perhaps he was in love.

At the docks, he asked the driver to wait as he went down to inquire about ships. Unwilling to approach just anyone, Wyatt waited until he spotted a pair of sailors that were neatly dressed, with the appearance of reputability. Of course, he realized that he could be wrong. For all he knew, these men were in the business of Shanghaiing strangers. He'd heard of such stories before.

"The *Cornelia* sails today," one of the sailors told him. "She heads north. Canada and Alaska. Then she crosses over to Russia and the Orient. You might be able to get passage on her."

"Unless she's already left port," the other sailor said. "I heard the *Cornelia* was departing this afternoon."

"Where's the *Cornelia* docked?" Wyatt asked eagerly.

"Down there a ways." The first sailor pointed west, describing the steamship.

Wyatt dashed back to the wagon, telling the driver which way to go as he climbed onto into the seat. "Hurry," he said. "No time to waste."

As the wagon rumbled down the dock, Wyatt said a silent prayer—if God really wanted him to get back to Delia, like Wyatt suddenly wanted to do, he asked for God's help. It wasn't long until he spotted a ship that seemed to fit the sailor's description, and as the wagon drew nearer, Wyatt saw the name on the bow. It was the SS *Cornelia*! "This is it!" he exclaimed to the driver. "Pull right up to the gangway. Wait while I go onboard."

It wasn't long before he located the first mate. "I have a small load of cargo to transport to Juneau," he said quickly. "Do you stop there on your way north? If so, do you have space for cargo—and a berth I can book?"

"Depends." The first mate frowned.

"On what?"

"On where your freight is located." He opened his watch with a frown. "We leave port in less than an hour."

Wyatt pointed down to the dock. "My freight is right there."

The first mate nodded. "Then you're in luck."

An hour later, the steamship was pulling out of San Francisco harbor. All Wyatt's crates, boxes, and barrels were below, and Wyatt was out on deck watching the blue Pacific unfurling before him. It wasn't until the view of San Francisco had shrunk to the size of a penny that Wyatt started to question himself. What about his original plan to spend a week in San Francisco, purchasing perishable goods to sell at great profit in Juneau? Now all he had was boots and socks and tools. No doubt there would be some demand for those items. Or so he hoped.

Still, he felt slightly stunned to think he had abandoned his original plan—and for a woman? A woman he had only known for three days. Had he lost his mind? And what would Jake say when he heard the news? What about his promise to spend two years up there working their claim? Had Wyatt been hypnotized by those emerald green eyes? Was Delia a siren like the ones who charmed Odysseus?

No, Wyatt, told himself. Delia was a fine woman, the kind of woman a man came across once in a lifetime. A woman who was worth more than gold. Like the pearl of great worth in the Bible—she was worth giving up everything for. Even if that was what Wyatt must do, he was determined. God willing, he would try!

19

DINNER WAS A SOMBER AFFAIR. NEITHER MIRANDA NOR MARCUS was inclined to conversation. Delia wanted to believe that their reticence was a result of their grief, but seeing their exchange of furtive glances convinced her otherwise.

"Ginger is working hard to prepare food for tomorrow's gathering after the funeral," Delia said as they were finishing up. "It's too big a job for just one woman."

"And…?" Miranda locked eyes with her.

"And…I've been lending a hand and I thought perhaps you—"

"I cannot believe you would expect me to play scullery maid," Miranda said hotly. "Especially when I am still deep in grief over the loss of Dad."

"I'm grieving for my father too," Delia said.

"You?" Miranda laid down her fork with a clang. "How can you grieve for someone you never knew?"

"Probably because I never got a chance to know him," Delia said simply.

"Well, you are welcome to work in the kitchen if you like," Miranda scooted her chair out. "But do not expect me to join you."

Before she could even stand, Marcus was out of his chair and by her side, helping her to her feet as if she were an invalid. Without as much as a howdy-do or an excuse-me, the two of them exited the room.

Delia actually wanted to throw something. And it wasn't that she was unaccustomed to rudeness. Her family in Pittsburgh, although refined in public and social situations, could be surprisingly thoughtless in the privacy of their own home, but Miranda might possibly be their equal in this regard. As Delia cleared the table, she wondered how her father—who everyone spoke so highly of—had raised such a selfish daughter. But then she reminded herself that Miranda was still young. Perhaps she would grow out of it. Besides that, Miranda's mother had died when Miranda was twelve. Maybe she hadn't been properly trained in matters of etiquette after that.

Delia carried the dishes into the kitchen and, seeing that Ginger wasn't back from her own dinner yet, proceeded to start cleaning them up. Although she knew little about housekeeping in general, she did know how to clean up after a meal since this was a chore that had been shared in her dormitory on the weekends when the some of the staff enjoyed time off. By the time Ginger came into the kitchen, the dinner dishes were clean and dry and Delia was putting them away.

"Oh, my—you are an angel, Miss Delia." Ginger reached for her apron. "But it grieves me to see you working in the kitchen like this. I know it's not what your daddy had planned for your visit." Ginger's eyes got moist, and she used the corner of her apron to wipe them. "Your dear daddy was so looking forward to meeting you. Did you see how nice the blue room looked? That was his doing. He wanted it all freshened up for you. Hired painters and got new linens. Do you like it?"

"I love it."

"Oh, good. He thought you'd enjoy looking out over the orchard. My, you should've seen it just a month ago—the blossoms on the trees were so beautiful."

As the two worked together, Ginger gave Delia directions and then rambled on and on, sharing interesting bits and pieces about the farm's evolution since she'd come to work here more than a dozen years ago. She talked about the vegetable garden and how it had grown and expanded over the years. "And then Mr. Williams decided to plant fruit trees. But he found out they needed help to pollinate. So he got beehives. And that's why we got so much honey." She continued telling Delia about how he'd stocked the front pond with trout and built a greenhouse and other interesting innovations. "Mr. Williams was always reading about farming and ways to make it better."

Delia smiled and then stifled a yawn.

"Oh, dear!" Ginger looked aghast. "I must insist that you go to bed, Miss Delia." She pointed a wooden spoon at the clock. "I had no idea it was so late, and I'm sure you must be plumb wore out."

Delia laid down the knife she'd been chopping cabbage with and sighed. "I guess I am rather tired."

"And me letting you handle a knife." Ginger picked up the sharp tool, shaking her head. "You just leave everything where it is. Looks like you were nearly finished with the coleslaw anyway. And you get yourself to bed, young lady."

"Will you turn in soon too?" Delia asked as she hung up her apron.

"Just as soon as I can. Don't you fret over me."

"Goodnight, Ginger."

"Goodnight, angel."

As Delia made her way through the darkened house, she felt strangely at home, almost as if everything here was familiar...a part of her life. But she also felt as if she were walking through a dream. By the time she pulled on her nightgown and stumbled into bed, she knew she'd have no trouble sleeping tonight.

Although tired, Delia rose early the next day. She quickly dressed then went down to the kitchen to continue helping Ginger. When she got there, she found Ginger slumped in a kitchen chair, her upper body across the worktable with a knife in her hand.

"Ginger!" Delia gasped in horror.

Ginger's head popped up. "What?" She blinked and looked around her.

"Oh, you're all right." Delia rushed to her side. "You scared me!" She didn't say that she'd thought Ginger was dead—could hardly bear to think such a thing.

"I'm sorry, darling. I must've dozed off."

"Have you even been to bed?" Delia asked.

Ginger sighed, stiffly standing. "Too much to be done."

"What is left to do?" Delia looked around. "Besides cleaning up."

"Not so much now. You can frost the chocolate cake when it's cooled off." She pointed to a bowl of white icing and two pans of chocolate cake, explaining how to layer them. "And I've got a batch of sweet rolls ready to go in the oven. They're for breakfast. Be sure to check them after twelve minutes."

"Yes. And you go rest for a while," Delia insisted. "I'll take care of things."

"But I—"

"Go take a nap." Delia said more strongly. "The funeral isn't until eleven. You should be able to get at least three hours of sleep."

"But Rosie is coming and—"

"Then Rosie and I will work together."

"And breakfast?"

"Rosie can help me with that."

"But—"

"No more buts." Delia gently pushed her away from the table. "If we really need you, I'll send Rosie to wake you up."

"All right." Ginger nodded sleepily. "If you promise."

Delia reassured her then went straight to work washing the pots and pans and utensils stacked by the sink. As she put things away, she was impressed with how much food Ginger had been able to prepare. The icebox, which was surprisingly large, was filled with various salads and a large platter of sliced roast beef. And the pie safe was full of desserts.

"Where's breakfast?" Caleb demanded as he came into the kitchen. When he saw Delia he scowled. "What're you doing in here? Where's Ginger?"

She paused from frosting the cake. "Her friend Rosie should be here soon. She and I can make breakfast. Hopefully before long." She glanced at the kitchen clock to see it was already half past seven.

"I just saw a wagon on the ranch drive," he said. "Probably Rosie."

"Morning," a female voice chirped from behind them. Delia turned to see a round-faced woman stepping through the backdoor. She and Caleb exchanged greetings. Then, as he was leaving, Rosie pointed at Delia. "You the new cook?" She removed her bonnet. "I'm Rosie."

Delia quickly introduced herself and explained the situation for the second time, but Rosie looked skeptical. "You don't belong in no kitchen, Miss Delia," she scolded. "Ain't right."

"It's just fine." Delia smiled stiffly. "And if you don't mind, I could use your help fixing breakfast right now. To be honest, I don't really know how to cook. Ginger has just been telling me what to do and I do it. But we need enough to feed…" She counted on her fingers. "Eight people—including you."

"Never mind about me, I already ate." Rosie reached for an apron. "Are you saying there are only seven people left on the Double W now?"

"That's correct." Delia pointed to the sweet rolls that she'd just removed from the oven. "Ginger made those for breakfast, but we'll need more to go with them."

Rosie made a tsk-tsk sound as she walked around the kitchen examining the various baked goods and foods, finally opening the icebox. "Well, well, Ginger *has* been busy." She rooted around in there for a bit, finally removing a hunk of bacon which she started to slice into. "Bacon and eggs and taters—nothing fancy, but then beggars can't be choosers, can they?" She chuckled. "You know how to make coffee, Miss Delia?"

"No." Delia grimaced. "But I know how to crack eggs."

Rosie laughed. "Then start crackin'. A dozen or so in a bowl, then give 'em a little stir, put in a pinch of salt and pepper, and I'll show you how to scramble."

"Are you a professional cook?" Delia asked as she cracked eggs.

"I was. Me and Ginger cooked for a mining camp on Cripple Creek." She chuckled. "Those were some wild times back then."

With the eggs ready in the bowl, Delia showed it to Rosie. "Should I start cooking them now?"

"Mercy, no. Eggs cook fast. They're the last thing."

"How about if I go set up the dining room?" Delia suggested.

Rosie waved her hand. "You do that."

Delia counted out seven of what Ginger had said were the every-day plates and cutlery and took them into the dining room. Her plan was to set up breakfast like a buffet—the way it was done at her old college dormitory. That way people could eat when they liked and no one would expect to be served. And being shorthanded, it would simplify everything. Even if some people, like Delia's own mother, would think it improper, this was, after all, the Wild West.

To Delia's relief, the workers, though somewhat surprised, had not complained. Dressed for the funeral in their Sunday-go-to-meeting clothes, they had on their good manners as well.

However, when Miranda finally came down to the dining room,

she scowled at the buffet Delia had set up. "What is going on here?" She glared at the hands still seated at the table.

"It's a breakfast buffet," Delia said as she set a biscuit on her own plate. "We serve ourselves. Very popular in Philadelphia."

Miranda tipped her head to one side as if considering this. "Really?"

"Oh, yes." Delia nodded as she put a pat of butter and dollop of jam on her plate. "And the luncheon after the funeral will be served buffet style as well. It's really the only option with your shortage of servants."

"Speaking of servants, why are we eating with them?" Miranda glowered at Caleb, Silas, and Cash, who were just finishing up.

"As I mentioned, we're shorthanded and there's much to be done today. It was just simpler." Delia sat down next to Caleb who was still at the table and, bowing her head, said a silent blessing.

"I suppose it's tolerable. For just *one* day," Miranda said primly. Then, as Marcus came in, she proceeded to tell him that buffet breakfasts were all the fashion in Philadelphia. Feeling mildly amused, Delia started to eat.

Caleb and the hands were just excusing themselves when Miranda sat down across from her. Noticing that Miranda was wearing a new black gown, Delia spoke up. "It looks like the dressmaker finished the alterations. You look very stylish."

"Yours is in your room," Miranda said crisply. "I suggest you get changed as soon as possible. And, if you have any respect for me or our dearly departed father, I beg you to stop helping in the kitchen. It is humiliating."

Delia wanted to point out that it might be more humiliating to invite the funeral attendees to a lunch with nothing to feed them, but she simply nodded. "I think everything is under control in there now."

"The men from the mortuary will arrive at ten," Miranda declared. "The service will be held in the family cemetery at eleven. I expect it will take about an hour. After that, we'll return to the house for our luncheon. I hope the guests will not linger too long. I'd like to have everyone cleared out of here by three." She glanced at Marcus as if she expected his help in this.

Delia wanted to point out that it might not be as simple as all that, but since Miranda was the lady of the house, she knew it wasn't her place. Once again, she simply nodded.

"I have checked the train schedule," Miranda continued in what sounded like a rehearsed speech. "Someone will take you to town at four o'clock. That should get you there not much after five. In time to get a ticket for the 5:50 train to Denver. Marcus suggests you spend the night in Denver then set out for Philadelphia, or wherever you're from, the following day." She took a bite of her biscuit.

Delia was speechless. Was Miranda actually throwing her out? Just like that? Delia hadn't even seen the whole house yet, let alone the rest of the ranch. But, she reminded herself, she was the guest here—how could she insist upon prolonging her visit if she wasn't wanted?

20

DELIA TRIED NOT TO TAKE OFFENSE WHEN SHE OBSERVED MIRANDA and Marcus being seated in the only two chairs in the family cemetery, directly across from the casket, which was now closed and covered with a large spray of red and white flowers. Everyone else, including Delia, stood behind these two, listening as Pastor Hall delivered a eulogy that any man would be proud of. Almost as moving as the eulogy was witnessing her father's dog sitting respectfully beside the casket. Almost as if Hank knew what was going on here today.

With what little Delia had learned about her father already, she wasn't surprised to discover that Winston Williams was known throughout the area as a kind and generous gentleman. A man she wished she had been able to know personally. The lump growing in her throat got bigger as they all sang her father's favorite hymn, "Rock of Ages."

Pastor Hall invited friends and neighbors to speak if they liked, and Delia was impressed with the number that did—and what they had to say about Winston Williams. Indeed, she could be proud to call this man her father—even if she'd never really known him in this life. Finally, as Pastor Hall read her father's favorite scripture, the Twenty-third Psalm, Delia's eyes overflowed with tears. That was her favorite too.

Pastor Hall closed the service with a short prayer. The service—which Miranda had hoped would be held to an hour—took nearly two. For this, Delia was thankful. Perhaps nothing would run according to Miranda's planned schedule and Delia would be "forced" to remain on the Double W for one more day.

As the funeral attendees began leaving the small fenced-in cemetery, Delia remained behind. Standing in the shadows of some pines, she waited until the guests were mostly gone before going up to the casket. Hank was still sitting next to the casket, almost as if he was waiting—as if he expected his master to whistle to him and tell him it was time to round up the cows. Delia sighed sadly as she gazed down at the small bouquet of wildflowers she'd collected alongside the creek earlier this morning. Already they were wilting. Such a paltry offering for such an impressive man. But at least it was from the heart. She felt the tears coming as she laid them on the casket.

"Even though I didn't know you, Father, and I can't remember you from my early childhood days, I can honestly say that I love you. I know it deep inside my soul. And I look forward to seeing you again." She placed a gloved hand on the casket, trying to contain her emotions. "Someday...."

Seeing the men from the mortuary now approaching with their shovels, she ducked her head down and kneeled next to Hank. "I know you're sad too, boy." She felt her tears falling as she petted him. "But I'll be your friend. And we should go now." Standing, she called out to Hank, inviting him to come with her. He started to go, but then he stopped. After returning to his post next to the casket, he sat down and waited. Unable to hold back her sobs at this sight, she hurried away.

Taking some deep breaths to recover from this breakdown, she retrieved her handkerchief and blotted her tears. Grateful for this solitude, she slowly walked down the hill toward the house. From this vantage point, she could see the people already gathering near the house. Some stood in small clumps, probably visiting and consoling one another. Others were forming what seemed a line of sorts—perhaps for the food.

As she got closer, she noticed Miranda and Marcus beneath the shade of a handsome stand of aspen trees, seated in a pair of wicker chairs. They made a handsome couple, appearing to be holding court, greeting the friends and neighbors who waited in a reception line.

Although she felt somewhat left out, she understood. These were people that Miranda and Marcus both knew, but they were strangers to Delia. It wouldn't be her place to greet them. Still, it hurt being on the outside. Especially since it seemed to emphasize all that she had missed out on—and that the one person whose love and acceptance could've made such a difference in her life was gone.

Despite Miranda's command that Delia refrain from the kitchen, it seemed the one place where she'd felt comfortable and welcome and so, with Miranda distracted, Delia sneaked back inside. But the kitchen was now bustling with not just Ginger and Rosie, but a number of other helpful women as well.

"Out of here," Ginger told Delia in a gentle but firm way. "We have plenty of hands now. You go mingle with your father's friends."

Delia just nodded, but instead of following Ginger's orders, she went up to her room and allowed herself what she promised would be her last good long cry.

After about an hour, Delia washed and dried her face and, determined not to keep playing the helpless victim, went down to meet some of her father's friends. Her plan was twofold. First of all, she would find out more about her father, gathering snippets of memories that she could carry along with her when she was forced to leave. But she might also, by engaging in conversation, encourage the guests to linger and chat and thus delay her departure, at least by one day.

By now people were eating. Although some were still filling plates from the buffet table, most were seated at the tables and chairs that had been arranged around the yard. Delia went to the end of line, waiting her turn to fill a plate and then looking around, hoping to find an empty seat. She was about to give up when she noticed a woman wearing a large black hat waving to her. "Over here," she called boisterously.

As Delia got closer, she realized this was Maggie O'Neil from the hotel. Was it only yesterday? So much had transpired since then.

"Miss Delia Williams," the woman said warmly, nudging the young man beside her to his feet. "You're nearly done, Jackson. Give the lady a seat."

"Sure, Mom." The young man jumped to his feet, pulling out the chair for Delia as Maggie O'Neil did a quick introduction, explaining that Jackson was her son.

"Thank you," Delia told him.

Maggie pointed across the table to where a tiny white-haired woman was picking at her food. "And that's my ma, Pearly Smith." She winked at Delia. "She's deaf as a post, but she enjoys getting out amongst people."

Delia smiled at the old woman. "Nice to meet you, ma'am."

"And this fine-looking man," Maggie said as she grinned at the grizzled old man sitting on her left, "is my husband, Rocky O'Neil."

Delia smiled. "Pleased to meet you, Mr. O'Neil."

"Call me Rocky or I won't answer," he said in a friendly tone. "And I'm real sorry for your loss, young lady. Winston Williams was a good man."

"Thank you." Delia nodded as she picked up her fork. "Did you hear how your wife rescued me at the Elk Horn Hotel yesterday morning?"

"That'd be my Maggie." He chuckled. "Always sticking her nose in other peoples' business."

"I beg your pardon, old man. Why wouldn't I help Winston's daughter? The girl was in need of counsel. I simply gave her my two cents' worth."

"For which I'm most grateful," Delia assured her.

"That Marcus Vincent wanted to put Delia back on the train," Maggie quietly informed her husband. "Even before coming out here to see her daddy's ranch." She turned back to Delia. "What do you think of the place?"

"I love it. It's amazing. I still haven't seen everything yet." She lowered her voice. "And I might not get to if Miranda has her way. My sister wants me on the 5:50 train to Denver this afternoon."

Maggie's brows arched. "But you've barely arrived. Why would you leave so soon?"

Delia felt a tinge of guilt for her reckless disclosure. "I suppose it might be out of concern for my safety," she said quietly. And now she told them about being shot at yesterday.

"My word!" Maggie shook her head. "Sounds like the Double W needs to hire itself some protection." She turned to Rocky. "Maybe you could help round up some additional security for Winston's girls."

"I'll ask around the mine," he told her. "Some of the fellers might be willing to come out here for a spell."

Delia knew she'd overstepped her bounds now. "Well, I suppose you should speak to Miss Miranda about that. She's the lady of the house now."

"And you're in agreement with that?" Maggie peered curiously at Delia.

Delia didn't know what to say. Did it matter whether or not she agreed?

"Where is Horace Griswold anyway?" Rocky looked around the yard.

"He was at the graveside service," Maggie said. "But I don't see him now."

"Who's Horace Griswold?" Delia asked.

"Your father's lawyer," Rocky told her. "I 'spect he's got a will that'll need to be read. You better stick around long enough to hear it."

"Didn't Miranda tell you about that?" Maggie's eyes narrowed slightly.

Delia shook her head. "I just assumed that Miranda would inherit the ranch. After all, she's the daughter who grew up here. I'm the outsider. It seems only natural that Miranda should continue to run the place."

"Speak of the devil," Maggie said with what seemed a forced smile. "Hello, Miranda. It's good to see you, although I'm sorry for your loss."

"Maggie and Rocky O'Neil," Miranda said in a friendly tone. "I missed you folks earlier, but I just wanted to thank you for coming. I know Dad would be grateful. You two were very dear to him."

"It was a good service," Maggie told Miranda. "For a good man."

Rocky stood up. "Looks like I'm done here, if you ladies'll excuse me." He pointed to his chair. "Maybe Miss Miranda would like to join you."

"No, thank you," Miranda said. "I only wanted to say hello."

"I was just telling Delia that she better stick around for the reading of the will," Maggie said abruptly.

"Oh?" Miranda slowly eased herself down in the vacant chair with a perturbed expression on her face. Beside her, Pearly Smith was dozing off with a fork still in her hand.

"Horace will have to come out here to read the will, won't he?" Maggie pressed.

"I, uh, I haven't had time to even consider that." Miranda sniffed loudly, reaching for her handkerchief. "I've just been so upset over losing Dad." She dabbed her eyes. "I never gave much thought to a will. I rather doubt that Dad even had one. He always said that if anything happened to him, the ranch would go to Mother and me." She made another sniff. "But then I lost Mother when I was twelve…and now Dad too. I suppose I'm an orphan. All I have left now is this ranch."

"And your sister," Maggie said wryly.

"*Half*-sister," Miranda corrected.

"Well, I feel certain your father had a will. And I'm just as certain that Horace plans to get everyone together to read it." Maggie nodded toward Delia. "And you, my dear, cannot go rushing back East before it gets read. Your father would not like that. Not one bit."

Delia nodded. "I hadn't really thought of it like that. I'm sure you're right, Maggie. I'll definitely stay until the will is read." She looked hopefully at Miranda. "Maybe in a few days?"

Miranda abruptly stood. "I'll check with Mr. Griswold on that."

"So I suppose that means no one will need to take me to the train station today," Delia told Miranda before she could leave.

She shrugged. "I suppose not."

After Miranda was gone, Maggie chuckled. "There," she proclaimed. "That should help keep you around for a while." Maggie was waving to someone else now. Delia glanced over to see that it was her son Jackson.

"Jackson is a mite shy," Maggie said quickly, "but he's a good boy. And an excellent marksman."

"Marksman?" Delia was confused.

"With a rifle." Maggie asked Jackson to sit down again. "I was just telling Maggie that you're a good shot."

Jackson shrugged.

As Maggie explained to him how the carriage had been shot at yesterday, Delia felt a gentle nudge on the side of her leg. Looking down she saw that it was Hank. He'd seated himself right next to her feet. Touched by his presence, she reached over to gently scratch his ear, and it wasn't long before he laid his head in her lap. She could barely hold back her tears.

"And the Double W is running short of hands right now," Maggie continued, still directing her conversation to her son. "So I 'spect you could take a few days off to help out round here, couldn't you? Your dad would probably agree to that."

Jackson seemed to consider this. "I reckon he would." He smiled. "If you talked to him."

"Then it's settled," Maggie declared. "Jackson will stick around to help keep an eye on things here. At least until the will is read."

"Do you think there will be more trouble?" Delia asked as she stroked Hank's smooth head.

"Hard to say. But with Jackson around, I think you'll be a whole lot safer."

"Do you think it's possible...." Delia lowered her voice. "That the Leaning R is behind this? That they shot my father over water? I just find that so barbaric, so hard to believe."

"It's happened before," Jackson said somberly. "It'll likely happen again."

"The West ain't as wild as it used to be, but there's still some folks that take the law into their own hands when it suits 'em." Maggie took her last bite of chocolate cream pie, smacking her lips. "Oh, my! That was good."

Although Delia was no longer concerned about being shipped off on an eastbound train anytime soon, she could tell that her presence at the Double W was unwelcome. At least with the lady of the house. Miranda seemed intent on freezing Delia out. Besides blatantly ignoring her after the guests from the funeral departed, Miranda decided to avoid her at mealtimes as well. Delia couldn't help but overhear the conversation since she was already in the kitchen, washing up things after the big luncheon.

"Since Delia insists upon eating with the help in the dining room," Miranda instructed Ginger, "I want my meal delivered to my room. And just so you know, I have changed rooms."

"Changed rooms, Miss?" Ginger looked confused.

"I have moved my things into my parents' old room. It's more spacious and has a better view. Now, regarding my meals. I want them delivered at these specific times." She handed Ginger a card. "And I want them delivered by you—not her. And I expect you to use the good china on a silver tray. And I want the empty tray picked up in exactly one hour. Do you understand?"

"Of course, miss." Ginger tucked the card in her apron pocket. "But if you are wanting such grand treatment, you might have to look into finding more house staff. As you know, I cannot manage all the housekeeping and the cooking by myself."

"You have her to help you, don't you?" Miranda narrowed her eyes at Delia.

"Yes, but it isn't her job to—"

"Are you talking back to me?"

"I'm telling you how things is, miss." Ginger looked defiantly at her mistress.

"Fine. I will do my best to find new servants as soon as possible. In the meantime, is it too much to ask that I take my meals in my room?" She sighed wearily, holding her hand to her chest as if in pain. "I am in bereavement, Ginger. I've tried to keep a brave front for the sake of everyone, but I feel I need some time to myself."

"All right, Miss Miranda. I will do what I can," Ginger said subserviently.

After Miranda left the kitchen, Ginger let out a long exasperated sigh. "I 'spect she'll want me to start bowing and calling her 'your highness,' next."

Despite her irritation, Delia could only laugh.

"But what I said is true, we need to hire more staff."

"Did the others really leave out of fear?" Delia asked as she dried a large bowl.

"The truth is I'm not entirely sure. Not about everyone." Ginger lowered her voice. "I got a feeling that some of the men got paid off by Mr. Roswell to leave. He offered them better wages at the Leaning R. And then I think some others left because they're worried the ranch will be sold by Miss Miranda. But some of the women, well, I suppose they were scared. Rumors were flying that there was going to be more shooting and killing and maybe the whole place would get burned to the ground in the night." She shuddered. "That's enough to scare anyone."

"But not you?"

Ginger grinned. "I'm a tough old bird. Takes more'n rumors to scare me." She looked around. "'Sides, I like this place. Being in charge of housekeeping is the best job I've had. Well, it used to be. Now that I gotta wait on Queen Miranda, I'm not so sure no more."

"Is there any chance we could talk some of the old staff into returning?" Delia asked. "Perhaps offer some sort of incentive."

"If they believed this place was safe and not about to be sold... maybe they'd come back. Some of 'em, anyway."

"Then that's what we need to do," Delia declared. Although she had no idea how this would be accomplished—it sounded impossible. At the same time, she knew her father wouldn't give up. After all, he'd built this place up from nothing but bare land. She hated to see it all falling apart all because he was no longer here.

21

WITH MIRANDA CLOISTERED IN HER ROOM THE MORNING AFTER THE funeral, Delia felt more freedom to explore the house. And, after helping Ginger with the breakfast dishes, that is just what she did. The large front room had a very masculine feel to it. Not only because of the majestic elk head mounted above the stone fireplace, but the furnishings were heavy and dark, the upholstery was leather, and the room smelled faintly of tobacco. Even the original oils, in their ornate gilt frames, were primarily landscapes of nature. Some had wildlife like buffalo and elk. And one tall painting with a grizzly bear on his hind legs was actually a little frightening.

Even so the room had a friendly feel to it and, in Delia's opinion, was much more comfortable than the overly decorated parlor. Delia could imagine her father entertaining his friends and neighbors in the spacious room. She could almost hear their voices, discussing farming techniques, reminiscing about the old mining days, swapping livestock stories, arguing over politics, or even speculating on the weather. Although she didn't know much about her father, based on things she'd heard at his funeral yesterday, she knew that he'd enjoyed a good full life. That was reassuring.

Next she went to see the solarium. Although a bit warm due to the morning sun that was washing across the terracotta tiled floor, it was a pretty room with its various green plants. But on closer inspection she realized that some of the leaves were turning brown around the edges and wilting from thirst. She used her finger to test the soil, discovering it was bone dry. So, going to the kitchen, she explained the situation and Ginger gave her a watering tin.

"I haven't given that room a thought since the master's death. It was Max the gardener's job to tend it. But the poor man has a lot more than that to care for now."

"I'd like to open the windows and doors in there too," Delia told her. "If no one minds."

"Yes, by all means, open it up. That should've been done several days ago. Mrs. Williams always loved the solarium, and she was the one who originally oversaw it. But since her death, it's gone downhill. The mistress had the green thumb. Every plant seemed to thrive under her care. She could even grow orchids. Oh, my, they were beautiful. And the room would smell heavenly. Course, the orchids are long gone now. But Max tried to keep the palms and ferns alive."

"I'm happy to care for the solarium, at least while I'm here."

"Bless your heart, Delia. You are your father's daughter."

Not exactly sure what she was doing, but fairly certain she couldn't hurt anything too badly, Delia carefully watered all the plants, even pinching off dead leaves—something she'd seen their own gardener doing, back when they had one. It took several trips to refill the watering tin, but by the time she finished the plants seemed grateful. And with all the windows opened, it was less stuffy.

Before she left, she paused to survey the room, trying to imagine what her stepmother—Miranda's mother—might've been like. She realized it was probably unfair to assume that Miranda and her mother were very similar. Because from what Delia knew of her father, she couldn't imagine him marrying a woman who wasn't his match. She liked the image of her stepmother in here tending to her plants. Delia reached out to rock a rocker. Like all the furniture in here, it was wicker, and the floral cushion, though faded from the sun, had probably once been bright and cheerful. Like the world that Mr. and Mrs. Williams inhabited. This room had probably been a delightful spot to enjoy a cup of hot tea on a cool winter's day.

With her work in the solarium done, Delia returned the watering tin then ventured to the other side of the house. More than all the other rooms, the library intrigued her the most. But she hadn't been in there since the day she'd arrived and viewed her father's body laid out there. As she stood in front of the closed wooden door, she tried not to think about that. Miranda had said the library was their father's favorite room. And in all likelihood it would be Delia's favorite room as well.

She slowly pushed open the door, unsure if she was truly ready for this, but to her relief the drapes were fully drawn and without the casket and the candles, it was actually a surprisingly pleasant room. With morning sunlight flowing in, she was able to see the bookshelves and, taking time to peruse the titles on the spines, she could see that her father was quite well-read. Of course, this was bittersweet. It was one more reason to be sad about never sharing a conversation with him, but at the same time glad to know that he, like her, enjoyed good literature. She felt certain they would've become fast friends.

She could imagine them in here together, discussing a book they'd both read. Perhaps it would be a lively discussion, each expressing their opinion, free to disagree. She went over to the massive desk beneath the window, and seeing various pieces of paperwork spread out across the top, she quite naturally felt curious.

What were the things that concerned him most shortly before his death? Was he, like Miranda had suggested, worried about the financial state of the farm? Was the property truly in dire straits? Despite her curiosity, she knew it was wrong to poke around. Instead, she picked up a paperweight, which was actually a stone that had been sliced in half. The outside was rough and dark, but the inside was a beautiful polished stone that shone brilliantly.

"What are you doing?"

Nearly dropping the paperweight, Delia turned to see Miranda glaring at her with her fists on her hips. "I'm sorry," Delia said.

"I asked you a question," Miranda demanded. "What are you doing in here?"

"Just looking around." Delia nervously set the paperweight back down.

"Don't you mean *snooping* around?"

"I was only—"

"Stay out of Dad's desk," Miranda said hotly. She pushed past Delia to get to the desk, looking all over it as if she thought Delia had poured ink on everything. "Did you *take* anything?"

"No, of course not." Delia held up her empty hands.

Now Miranda swept up the paperwork in a messy bundle, holding it to her chest as if she was protecting something precious.

"Please, excuse me," Delia said in embarrassment.

"And, please, stay out of this room," Miranda said in a slightly less hostile tone. "I would've locked the door except I don't know where the key is."

"I won't come back in here," Delia promised as she backed out. "I'm sorry to have intruded." Then, feeling like a small child that had just been reprimanded, she retreated to her room. And there she stayed, writing a letter to her mother explaining about her father's death, and then she wrote a second letter to Wyatt, pouring out her confused frustration and grief.

She wrote page after page to Wyatt. Writing so vehemently that the ink pen splattered a couple of times. Instead of starting over with a clean sheet of paper, she simply continued. By the time she finished, she was tempted to throw the whole mess away, but was worried someone might find it and read it.

Instead she slipped it into an envelope, securing it with her wax and seal. Still unsure as to whether she should send it, she did feel better for getting the words out. And if she did send it…perhaps Wyatt wouldn't receive it for months, if at all. He might even find it good entertainment for some cold Alaskan night. Then she would send him another letter, assuring him not to worry, probably informing him that she was on her way back East by then.

As she carried the letters downstairs, she wondered why she had felt so resistant to going East yesterday. Wouldn't it be better to be on her way home than remaining here where she was so obviously unwanted? But there was that business of the will—Maggie had been so insistent that she remain. Knowing how well her father had looked after her during her childhood and even paid her tuition, she supposed it wasn't unlikely that he might've left her something more. Although she remembered what Miranda had told her the first day she'd come—that every cent had been invested into the farm and there wasn't even enough left to pay the hired help. That wasn't good.

But she hadn't come to Colorado in the hopes of securing an inheritance. She had simply wanted to meet her father—even if he was living in a one-room cabin. As Delia dropped her letters into the wooden box by the front door that was marked MAIL, she knew that she would be grateful for a few books from her father's library and a train ticket back to Pennsylvania. Nothing more. Although, if she could talk Miranda into it, she would be happy to take home a photo of her father. That would be more than she'd had less than two weeks ago—back when she didn't even know about Winston Williams and the Double W Ranch.

Feeling slightly lost and a little sad, Delia wandered into the kitchen, asking whether Ginger needed help preparing the midday meal.

"Thank you for asking, darlin', but we got all these fine leftovers. I think they will see us through today and maybe most of tomorrow. But if you want to make yourself useful, I got a suggestion."

"Yes," Delia said eagerly. "What can I do?"

"Seeing you might have a green thumb like Mrs. Williams, I suggest you visit the greenhouse. So much was coming on good out there, but with Max the gardener gone—I just hate to think what'll become of it. I asked Caleb about it this morning, but he's got his hands full with the livestock and only two hands to help him. And that Marcus, well, I'm sure he won't lift a finger to help in there."

"I'd love to check on the greenhouse," Delia told her. She looked down at her black satin gown, knowing that it would probably get ruined if she were to be working with soil and water. She'd already stained it with water while working in the solarium. "Would anyone mind if I changed into a different gown, one more suitable for garden work?"

"I don't see why not." Ginger pointed to the black band pinned around her sleeve. "Since you'd be working like us, you could just do what we're doing. I've got plenty of black fabric if you want it."

"Perfect!" Relieved to get out of the house—and away from her stepsister—and hoping to make herself useful, Delia hurried up to change her dress. And before long, she was happily strolling through the surprisingly large greenhouse. The first thing she did was to open the doors and windows to let fresh air flow through.

Before long, she found herself being shadowed by Hank. And, although she knew she probably sounded silly, she conversed with him. Asking his advice over some of the gardening tasks, she imagined he was giving her direction. Seeing him lapping water out of a full bucket, she realized that was probably a good place to begin with the plants as well. And dipping the watering can into the rain barrel again and again, she eventually satisfied the thirsty plants.

She had just discovered a dusty gardener's log, when she heard the supper bell ringing. Reluctant to leave this magical place behind, she realized that she was actually hungry. As she approached the house, tailed by Hank, she noticed Caleb talking to a man dressed in a dark jacket. When she got closer, she could see it was Maggie's son, Jackson O'Neil.

"We got ourselves our own policeman," Caleb told Delia as they went inside. "And just in time for lunch."

"Howdy, Miss Delia," Jackson tipped his hat with a shy smile.

"Are you really going to protect us?" Delia asked as they went inside.

"I put my guns on the front porch." He reached down to pet Hank.

"Anyone shoot at you on your way out here?" Caleb asked as they passed through the kitchen, headed to the dining room where Delia had told Ginger to continue serving the meals.

"Nah." Jackson shook his head. "But then I doubt those Leaning R boys would figure out I was coming here."

Before long they were all seated at the dining table where, as usual, Marcus sat at the head of the table. As Delia placed her napkin in her lap she wondered...was that her father's chair? And if so, what right did Marcus have to sit there? Caleb said a short blessing and soon they were eating and visiting. She could tell the workers were enjoying this stint in the regular dining room—and it really did make Ginger's work easier. Plus each of these men was doing the jobs of several. Didn't they deserve some special treatment? And, although it wasn't her place to call the shots, she figured as long as Miranda was hiding out, she might as well.

She could tell by Marcus's grim expression that he was not in favor of the new dining arrangement. Perhaps like Miranda, he should opt to eat in his room too. Although she didn't think anyone should be forced to deliver meals to the bunkhouse.

The men visited with Jackson, listening as he explained his plan to primarily guard the house. "Ma said I need to make sure the women stay safe," he said quietly.

"That's right," Caleb agreed. "Appreciate it."

After lunch, Delia returned to the greenhouse, perusing through the gardener's log to try and determine which plants might be ready to be moved outside—because that was her plan. According to what

had been done last year, it was high time the tomatoes were planted in the garden. She just hoped she was up to the task. She read
through Max's notes to find out where he'd planted them and how
far apart. All in all, it sounded rather simple. But the truth was she'd
never planted a single thing in her entire life.

"What if I mess them up?" She asked Hank. Of course, his only
response was a wagging tail, going thwack-thwack against a metal
bucket. "So I should just give it a try?" She picked up what, according to the wooden stick, was a "big rainbow beefsteak tomato."
Maybe she should just start with one and see how it went—and, if
the plant's tender stems survived her inexperienced hands, she would
cautiously continue.

But by the time she finished digging the hole, removing the fragile plant from the pot, putting it in the hole then packing it down,
she realized it wasn't that hard. And it was strangely satisfying to see
the small green plant comfortably situated in the garden bed. She
hoped it would grow large and produce lots of lovely big rainbow
beefsteak tomatoes. She smiled as she went back to get more pots of
tomatoes. The more she worked, the more she could understand why
her father had enjoyed growing things.

By the time she finished with the last tomato plant, it was nearly
time for dinner. Her back ached from bending over and her gown
and her hands were a filthy mess, but as she gathered up the terracotta pots back to take back to the greenhouse, she felt inexplicably
happy. Looking at the rows of small green tomato plants, she felt like
she had really accomplished something. At the same time, she felt
sad to know she would probably never see the plants with tomatoes
growing on them, she would probably never taste the fruit of her
labors. But perhaps that didn't matter.

22

SEVERAL DAYS PASSED IN A SURPRISINGLY COMFORTABLE ROUTINE. So comfortable that Delia began to feel really at home. She continued helping Ginger as needed, but her favorite chores were the outdoors tasks in the company of Hank, who had become her constant companion. At least when they were outside, since Miranda wouldn't allow him in the house. But Delia soon discovered she loved working in the greenhouse and garden, helping things to grow.

Then, after visiting the chicken coop and meeting the hens, she insisted on taking over the care of them as well. Feeding and watering her new fine feathered friends was fairly easy and collecting the eggs was surprisingly fun and, although cleaning out their nesting boxes in the hen house was a bit messy, she soon discovered an old pair of leather work gloves that helped. Other than a bad-tempered brown hen she'd named Bitty, Delia rather enjoyed the chickens.

By her second week on the Double W, she had even enticed Cash to teach her how to milk a cow and, although it was work, it was rewarding. She could understand how her father had wanted to change his cattle ranch into a working farm. The idea of producing a wholesome variety of food was rewarding. She couldn't understand why anyone would oppose the idea of a farm.

"You got the hang of it, Miss Delia," Cash told her on her second day of morning milking. "You keep this up and I'll let you take over all them cows."

"Why not?" she offered as she squirted a stream of warm white milk into the pail. "Especially since we're so shorthanded around here. I really don't mind."

"I reckon Caleb would appreciate having me available to help with the herd more these days."

"That's understandable." She pressed her head into the side of the cow the way Cash had shown her, watching as the pail slowly filled, feeling the warmth of one of the barn cats rubbing against her leg. By now she knew these were working cats. Their job was to keep the mice away. And she was relieved to discover that Hank got along with the barn cats. Just like one big happy family—out here anyway, it was something else inside the house with her moody sister.

"Especially this time of year. Almost time to start driving the herd out to the upper west range."

"Why's that?"

"It's where they graze for summer. Allows the lower meadows time to grow back and get green before winter."

"That makes sense. Is it fun driving the cattle? I've read about cowboys, driving a herd for hundreds of miles."

"Well, we don't go anywheres near that far. Takes a few days to get to the upper west range. But it's right pretty up there. I only did that cattle drive twice, but it was a good time."

"It sounds adventurous."

"It's the best part of working on the Double W," he said wistfully. "Riding out there on the open range, driving the cows, sleeping under the stars. Your pa said I could stay out there all summer with 'em this year. But now that he's gone, well, I don't know."

"I wish I could do something like that."

"You wanna stay with the herd all summer?"

She laughed. "Well, maybe I would. But, no, I meant I wish I could do the cattle drive with you fellows. I think it sounds exciting."

"You know how to ride a horse, Miss Delia?"

"Sure," she told him. "Caleb promised to take me for a ride to see the whole property…but I know he's been busy. I hate to trouble him."

"Maybe you can help us drive the cattle," Cash said. "Although I never heard of a lady cowboy before—well, there's that Calamity Jane, but I don't reckon you'd call her a cowboy even though she can ride and shoot real good. I saw a Wild West show last year."

"And there's Annie Oakley," Delia offered. "And I happen to think that women can do a lot more than most men give them credit for."

"I don't know about that, but since you're Mr. William's daughter and you know how to ride…seems like it would be all right for you to drive cattle with us—just this one time."

"Do you really think so?" Delia sat up straight on the milking stool. "It would be so wonderful to go back East and tell my friends that I was a cowboy on my dad's ranch." She laughed at the thought of it.

"I'll ask Caleb for you," Cash promised.

As Delia carried the heavy milk pail to the ice house, she realized that she hadn't seen Miranda for several days and then only in passing. It wasn't that Delia minded so much since Miranda was usually in a foul mood, which could be attributed to grief, but Delia still felt disappointed they were not getting better acquainted. Delia felt her father would've been disappointed. Perhaps it wasn't too late.

Although Miranda continued to take her meals in her room, she did occasionally spend time in the parlor in the evening. Usually with Marcus—and with the door closed. Although Delia questioned whether this closed-door practice was proper, she knew that it wasn't her place to correct her sister. She also knew that Miranda, being a headstrong young woman, probably wouldn't listen to Delia anyway.

So far, Delia hadn't seen or met the lawyer. She hadn't heard a single word about the reading of the will. She had asked Miranda about this several times when she could get her to pause long enough for a quick chat. But Miranda's answers were vague and varying. One time she suggested that Horace Griswold was out of town and that the will would just have to wait. The next time she reminded Delia that there was no estate—aside from the land, which had been promised to Miranda.

Delia wanted to believe her sister—wished she could believe her—but something about this did not ring true. So when she spied Miranda coming out of the parlor this morning, Delia stopped her. "Good morning," Delia said pleasantly.

"Good morning," Miranda answered quickly, heading for the stairs.

"I wanted to ask you about Horace Griswold," Delia said as she followed her up. "Is he back in town yet?"

Miranda turned to Delia with a blank stare. "I do not know why you insist on questioning me about this," she said in a slightly wounded tone. "I already told you that there is no estate to inherit because there is no will."

"No will?" Delia frowned. Miranda had never said this before.

"Did you not hear me?" Miranda stopped on the landing with a creased brow. "There is no will," she said simply.

"How do you know this?" Delia questioned.

"Because I looked all over Dad's office for it," Miranda explained. "Not finding one, I sent a note to Horace." She held up her hands. "He has nothing."

"But Maggie seemed certain that he—"

"How on earth would Maggie know?"

"I'm not sure, but—"

"Dad had planned to make a will," Miranda told Delia. "He

spoke of it to me. But he was so busy. I guess he just never got around to it."

"That seems odd." Delia ran her hand along the smooth stair railing. "From what I know of our father, he was an intelligent businessman. My impression is that he was very careful with details. Almost meticulous. I would think he would've had his affairs in order...before his death."

"Dad didn't expect to get shot down at the age of fifty-two," Miranda said hotly.

"What about the paperwork you removed from his office?" Delia locked eyes with Miranda.

"Are you accusing me of taking Dad's will?" Miranda narrowed her eyes.

"I'm just saying it's odd...him not having a will. Especially since he had a lawyer. You said as much yourself. And he must've known the value of his land. He would've wanted to—"

"I already told you." Miranda's voice was laced with irritation. "He had planned to leave the ranch to me, his only child. He said so time and again. Ask Marcus. He heard it enough. But, of course, you must question me." Miranda sniffed. "It's not enough that I lost Dad. You want me to lose the only home I've ever known too?"

"No, not at all. And I can certainly understand why our father would leave you the ranch, Miranda. You were the child who grew up here, but you are not his *only* child," Delia reminded her.

"So you think you can just show up here and, because you're older, you can take it away from me?" Miranda's voice grew shrill.

"Of course not."

"Then why are you still here?"

"Because I thought there was going to be a reading of the will," Delia answered calmly.

"There is no will!"

Delia slowly nodded, unsure of what to do next. She felt that familiar lump in her throat again but was determined to remain strong. "Then I think perhaps I should go home. Go back East," she said sadly.

"Yes," Miranda agreed. "There is no reason for you to stay here."

Delia could think of a hundred reasons to stay here. But none that her sister would understand.

"Marcus can take you to the train," Miranda said eagerly. "Even today, if you like."

Delia didn't know what to say. Everything in her wanted to remain on the Double W, to continue helping and working...feeling at home. But how could she justify this when Miranda so clearly wanted her gone?

"I'll even help you pack," Miranda offered.

"But I—"

"And we can have Jackson go with you into town. He can ride shotgun. Just to make sure you get there safely."

"But—"

"Come on, Delia." Miranda grabbed her hand, tugging her toward the stairs. "You go start packing and I'll let Marcus know of your plan. It's been good that you've spent this time with us, but there really is no point in you remaining here longer. I don't want to seem inhospitable, but the Double W is having difficulty making ends meet and one more mouth to feed, well, it is one more mouth to feed." Miranda smiled, but it seemed disingenuous. "But I am pleased to have met you. And I must apologize for being so out of sorts. It is not easy to lose both your mother and your father and then feel that someone has come to take away your home. Surely, you understand."

Delia wanted to understand. But Miranda was a hard one to read. "May I ask for something before I go?" Delia asked in a weak voice. "Something to take with me...to remind me of my father?"

"Certainly," Miranda said cheerfully. "Name it."

"I'd like to take some of my father's books with me."

"Oh, sure. Take as many as you like. I'll ask Ginger to find a box for you to pack them in."

"Thank you." Delia felt surprised by Miranda's generosity, deciding to push for one more thing. "And I would like a photograph of my father. Although if you only have the one, I will understand if you—"

"It's all yours," Miranda said. "I'll get it and bring it up to your room when I come back to help you pack."

Delia considered asking for the dog as well. She would love to take Hank with her. Except that she had nothing to offer the dear dog. As far as she knew, she didn't even have a home to return to— how could she take a poor dog along with her?

So it was that, after just two weeks on the Double W, Delia was on her way back to Colorado City to catch the 2:40 train to Denver. She had a box of carefully chosen books, the photograph of her father, an envelope containing her return fare, and a heavy, heavy heart. Miranda and Marcus had been in such a rush that she hadn't even been able to tell Caleb, Silas, and Cash goodbye. And Ginger had broken down in tears at the news, so upset she couldn't even talk. Not that she would've gotten the chance since Marcus and Miranda had been rushing Delia out to the carriage, worried that they wouldn't make it to the station in time. When Delia saw Hank running up toward them, she felt her heart was breaking. "You're a good dog," she whispered as she petted him. "A really good dog."

"Again, I apologize," Miranda said in a surprisingly kind voice. "I have not been myself since Dad was shot." She dabbed her eyes with her delicate handkerchief. "I'm sure, even though you were not close to him as I was, you must understand my sorrow."

"I understand. And I thank you for your hospitality. I've left my parents' address on a card in the bedroom…perhaps we'll keep in touch. We are, after all, sisters." Delia forced a shaky smile as she reached for the carriage door.

Miranda reached out to give Delia a quick, stiff hug then stepped back and waved her handkerchief, bidding her farewell. Delia couldn't bear to look out of the carriage, to see the meadows or the house…or the beloved brown and black dog running alongside the horses. As promised, Jackson rode shotgun next to Marcus. Delia was grateful for the solitude in the carriage by herself, allowing her tears to flow freely so that by the time they got to the train station, she felt oddly calm—drained, it seemed, of all emotion.

Marcus waited in front while Jackson, with the help of a railroad worker, unloaded her things, but before Delia went to the ticket counter to purchase her fare, Jackson took her aside. "I don't want to be out of line, Miss Delia," he began, "but something about all this doesn't set right with me."

"How do you mean?" she asked without really caring.

"Well, I've been at the Double W ever since the funeral, keeping watch on the house like my ma told me to and, as far as I could see, Horace Griswold never came out to the house. I can only assume that means he never held a reading of the will."

Delia sighed. "There is no will."

Jackson frowned. "No will?"

She just shook her head.

"You know that for a fact?"

"Miranda told me."

"But she—" Jackson stopped himself, nodding to where Marcus was approaching them.

"Ready to go?" Marcus asked Jackson.

"I forgot to tell you that I plan to stay in town," Jackson told him. "I promised Ma that I'd have supper with her at the hotel tonight."

"Suit yourself." Marcus tipped his hat to Delia.

"And if you still need me, I'll be back to the Double W tomorrow."

Marcus rubbed his chin. "Well, seeing that we haven't had any signs of trouble this past week, I reckon we can get along without you, Jackson." He smiled. "But we do appreciate your help." He tipped his hat to Delia now. "Have a good trip home, miss. It was a pleasure to meet you."

"Thank you," she said somberly.

After Marcus left, Delia turned to go to the ticket counter, but Jackson stopped her again. "If my ma were here, she would tell you that something about this smells fishy, Miss Delia."

Delia nodded slightly. "I know. I smell it too. But I'm not really sure what it is. And I don't see that there's anything I can do about it. Miranda wants me gone."

"One thing you can do is to not get on the train until you've talked to Horace Griswold," Jackson declared. "And I happen to know where Griswold's law office is located."

Delia tipped her head to one side, considering this. "I guess it couldn't hurt to meet Mr. Griswold."

Jackson grinned. "I'll ask the stationmaster to put your baggage in storage for now, Miss Delia. Until you know exactly what you want to do."

"Thank you." As she heard the shrill train whistle, watching the Denver train pulling into the station, Delia felt a strong sense of relief to know that she would not be on the 2:40 after all. Perhaps she would be on the 5:50. But in the meantime she just might get some solid answers.

23

Jackson suggested they walk to the law office. "It's only a few blocks from here," he told her as they set out. "And you couldn't ask for better weather."

"I really appreciate you helping me like this," Delia told him as they walked. "It's very generous." She was actually starting to feel a bit uncomfortable though, curious as to why Jackson was being so accommodating. Had she sent him the wrong signal?

"Ma asked me to help you," he confessed as they waited to cross the busy street.

"Why?"

"Because your pa and your uncle were good friends with my parents—back in the early mining days. Your Uncle Enoch and my pa filed the first claim on Cripple Creek. They had to watch each other's backs. Then your pa came along and proved a good friend too. My parents feel beholding." He grinned. "Plus Ma likes you."

"I like her too."

"There's the law office." Jackson pointed to a two-story building next to a barber shop. "Hopefully Griswold is in."

As it turned out, not only was he in, he was very happy to meet

Delia and not too busy to speak with her. "I have been looking forward to making your acquaintance, young lady." He warmly grasped her hand. "I'm so very sorry for your loss." He glanced at Jackson. "Are you planning to join us today?"

Jackson chuckled. "Not particularly. I thought I'd run over to the Elk Horn. Ma's staying there for all of June and she sent me a note saying she wants to talk to me."

"Probably about the trouble up at the mine," Mr. Griswold said grimly.

"Trouble?" Jackson's brow creased.

"Go ask your ma. She'll fill you in."

"Thank you for bringing me here," Delia said. "I hope everything is all right at your dad's mine."

Jackson tipped his head. "I'll find out."

"Please, take a seat." Mr. Griswold said as he closed the door to his office.

"Thank you." She sat down and sighed. "I hope you don't think me too forward for showing up like this." She quickly explained about Miranda rushing her off to the train. "Jackson insisted I should come speak to you before leaving."

"Jackson was right." He narrowed his eyes slightly. "Are you and Jackson…well, he's a fine young man. Are you and he, uh—"

"No, no, not at all," she said quickly, understanding the implication. "Jackson's family, as I understand, was on friendly terms with my father. Jackson's mother, Maggie, encouraged him to help us. He's been out at the ranch this past week. Keeping a lookout for… dangerous men. Probably from the Leaning R Ranch. Perhaps the same men who shot my father." She frowned. "Is anyone investigating my father's death? Do you happen to know?"

"You bet they are." He stroked his bristly gray mustache. "I've got my own suspicions about it too. That was one reason I couldn't stay for the luncheon after your father's funeral. I had to check into something."

"Do you believe it was someone from the Leaning R Ranch?"

He pursed his lips. "I have my doubts about that. Oh, I know they've been squabbling over water for years. And I know Roswell tried to buy your father out. But I just can't see Roswell going that far—as to shoot a man in the back. Your father was a good man. Even a skunk like Roswell knew that."

"So could it have been an accident? Some have insinuated as much."

He frowned. "I've seen the evidence and I find that difficult to believe."

"And it wouldn't explain why most of my dad's ranch hands have been frightened away," she added. "Or why someone was shooting at us last week."

"From what I can figure, and after talking to the lawmen on the case, your father was clearly murdered, Miss Delia."

She sadly shook her head. As much as she appreciated hearing what was probably the truth, it did not make her feel better.

"But that's probably not why you're here." Mr. Griswold leaned forward. "Is it?"

She sighed. "Miranda has informed me that our father made no will, but I must confess—and I don't like saying this—something about her demeanor makes me question her integrity."

"Miss Miranda said there wasn't a will?" Mr. Griswold scowled.

"That's what she told me this morning. She said she'd searched through our father's things, and that she had contacted you, and that there is no will. She also says that our father said, many times, that he would leave the ranch to her. First to her and her mother, but when her mother passed on, he would leave it entirely to Miranda. And I can understand this. After all, she was been born and raised on that property and—"

"Hold on, little lady." Mr. Griswold stuck a hand in the air. "I can see that it's high time someone straightened you out."

Delia nodded. "Feel free."

"First of all, there *is* a will. I have the original in my safe and your father has a copy in his safe back at the ranch."

"Oh?"

"And let's be clear on this—do you truly believe that Miranda is your father's daughter?"

Delia considered this. "To be honest, I was rather confused about it at first. Miranda is nearly seventeen, and that would mean that my father married her mother almost as soon as he arrived in Colorado. While I suppose that's possible, it did not seem highly plausible. According to Uncle Enoch, my father was mining in his early years out here. Seems to me it would've been difficult having a wife and a baby while working a claim in the mine, although I suspect some men manage."

Mr. Griswold chuckled. "You remind me of your father, Miss Delia. The way your brain works."

"Thank you."

"Your presumptions were correct. Your father didn't marry Abigail until he had made his fortune in the mine and purchased the land for the Double W. He was just building the house when Abigail was widowed. Her husband was killed by a cave-in at the mine. Miranda was about five years old at the time. Your father married Abigail a couple of years later. And although your father was a very good dad to Miranda, she is not his by birth. And, from what I know, Miranda was not overly fond of ranch life either. She made no secret of the fact that she wanted Winston to sell everything to Roswell and move to the city."

"Oh my." Delia was shocked—trying to absorb all of this information—and yet knowing it had the ring of truth to it. Miranda was not her half-sister, and yet she had allowed Delia to believe that she was.

"I'm sure you are stunned by this. I can see it in your face."

"I—I don't know what to think."

"I told Miranda on the day of the funeral that I could come back that evening to read the will, but she said you were both too grief-stricken to hear just then. A few days later, I sent word to her again, but she wrote back that it was still too soon. She asked me to give you a couple of weeks." He grimaced. "And then she tells you there is no will and tries to send you back East before you even knew what was in it."

"What is in the will?" Delia asked curiously.

"I'd prefer to read it in front of both of you. As well as some of your father's trusted workers that he's made provisions for. I hoped to get everyone together at the house. Like I know your father would've wanted."

"Of course." Delia frowned. "Although I can't imagine how Miranda will react when she finds out I'm still in town. Or that I met with you. I doubt I'll be very welcome at the Double W now."

Mr. Griswold scowled. "You might not even be safe."

"But I thought you said Roswell wasn't—"

"I'm not talking about Jerome Roswell, Miss Delia."

Delia turned to the sound of someone knocking on the door. "Oh, I almost forgot." Mr. Griswold stood. "I'm due in court at 3:30." He waved to the man on the other side of the door. "That's my partner Mr. Stanfield. I'll have to excuse myself, Miss Delia."

"I'm sorry to have taken so much of your time." She stood too.

"I don't want you to go back to the Double W," he said as he reached for his hat. "Stay in town for now. And come back here tomorrow to meet with me." He glanced at an opened date book. "Around two o'clock tomorrow I can give you about an hour. We need to put together a plan, little lady." He reached for her hand again. "A real pleasure to meet you. Your father would be proud."

She thanked him and then watched as he and Mr. Stanfield hurried on their way. Unsure of what to do next, Delia decided to head back to the Elk Horn Hotel. She hoped she could afford a night or two there until she got things figured out better. Mr. Griswold's warning about returning to the Double W had gotten her attention.

And hopefully she'd cross paths with Maggie O'Neil again. She knew she could trust that woman.

At the hotel, she checked in and gave her baggage claim tickets to the front desk clerk. "I plan to be here for a day or two," she said. "Maybe longer."

He assured her that was no problem. And she hoped he was right. But she also knew that the rooms in this hotel were not inexpensive and the money in her envelope would disappear quickly if she stayed here too long. Perhaps she should look for some form of employment.

"Miss Delia!"

Delia stopped in her tracks, spotting Maggie O'Neil quickly approaching from the other side of the lobby. "Good afternoon," Delia said. "I'm so happy to see you."

"Have you heard the news?" Maggie's eyes were filled with concern.

"What news?"

"There's trouble at the mine," she explained. "As hard as my Rocky tries to make sure that the shafts are safe, you just never know. And, of course, mining is a dangerous business. Well, some of the workers are going on strike this week. They're threatening the workers that won't go along with them. Such a mess." She paused to reach for a small fan, waving it over her flushed face.

"I'm sorry to hear that."

"Anyway, I just sent Jackson up there to give his pa a hand with the rabble-rousers. I was about to call Horace Griswold to relay that message to you. Jackson felt bad for leaving you there like that. My apologies."

"No apology needed," Delia assured her. "I'm so appreciative of Jackson for directing me to Mr. Griswold, rather than letting me get on that train."

"Do you have time for tea or an early supper?" Maggie asked eagerly. "I missed my luncheon entirely. And you can tell me how it all went at the law office. Jackson was quite concerned for you."

As the two women ate a light early supper, Delia shared some, but not everything, that Mr. Griswold had told her. She sensed that Maggie was entirely trustworthy, but still believed that discretion was important. Especially for the sake of her father.

"Oh, I knew that Miranda wasn't your real sister," Maggie said lightly. "I thought you knew that too. I'm surprised."

She shook her head. "No…I assumed she was my half-sister."

"Well, I don't like to speak ill of anyone, but Miranda made no secret of the fact that she does not like ranch life—not one bit. Although she seems to appreciate what the proceeds from a working ranch can buy. Miranda does like expensive things. But she's been threatening to leave the Double W for some time now. Winston even offered to send her to some sort of finishing school, if you can imagine that. Well, of course, she said no. So he asked her to wait until she was eighteen or married before she left. I think he hoped that she'd get some good sense by then. But, if you ask me, the girl is a flibbertigibbet. Cares more about clothes and jewelry and money than she does about people. Why, she even tried to get her hooks into my Jackson last year." She chuckled. "But he's got too much sense to fall for a pretty face." Maggie pointed at Delia. "Although I suspect he might fall for yours."

Delia felt a stab of guilt. "Jackson is a good, kind, generous man," she said carefully. "One that I would value as a dear friend… but I…."

Maggie looked disappointed as she held up her teacup. "But he's not your cup of tea, eh?"

Delia smiled apologetically. "The truth is I think my heart belongs to another."

"Another?" Maggie's brows arched.

"I've hardly let myself think of him," Delia confessed. "And I might be a fool for allowing myself to fall for a man I barely know." And, like an uncorked bottle, she poured out the story of her and

Wyatt, telling how they'd first met at the Pittsburgh hotel, how she'd assumed he was a detective. How they'd later met on the train and even how he rescued her in Kearney. "Wyatt calls himself a drifter," she said sadly, "but he's so much more than that." She explained how well read he was and the many varying jobs he'd had and places he'd been. "I find him most interesting."

"And how does he feel about you?"

Delia sighed. "I thought he might fancy me…a little. But he's in Juneau, Alaska now, selling boots and shovels and working a claim with his buddy Jake."

Maggie laughed. "He's a miner just like my Rocky. Well, Delia, if it's meant to be, I pray the Good Lord brings him back to you. And if it's not meant to be, well, perhaps in time you'll give my Jackson a second look."

Delia smiled faintly. "Perhaps."

"I expected to stay here at the Elk Horn for all of June and perhaps most of the summer, while our house is being built here in town." Maggie wiped her mouth with her napkin. "But since there's trouble at the mine, I s'pect I'll head back up there tomorrow. Oh, Rocky, might not like having me up there in the middle of the danger, but it won't be the first time. And our house up there is sturdy enough. Besides, I'd rather be with my loved ones in the midst of their troubles than down here by myself just worrying about them."

"I can understand that."

"But I'll keep you in my prayers, Delia. I'm afraid you're going to have your own troubles too."

Delia just nodded. "I'm fairly certain of it."

"But Horace Griswold is a good man. He'll see you through this business with your stepsister. You can count on him."

After Delia got to her room, she removed her hastily packed clothes from her case, sending all of her college dresses, as well as some other things, down for cleaning. Ginger had offered to help with this back at the ranch, but seeing how busy that poor woman was, Delia had refrained. It would be a relief to have them cleaned now. And, as plain and drab as those gowns were, she felt they had been highly serviceable for chores like tending chickens, milking cows, and gardening. She wouldn't mind having some everyday dresses in lighter weight fabrics as well. If her budget would allow it, she might see about purchasing a couple of sturdy cotton dresses.

Although it felt restful to be in the hotel, Delia was surprised at how much she missed her father's ranch. Looking out her window to the orchard below, strolling through the meadow gathering wild-flowers, chatting with Ginger in the kitchen…even doing the chores! She missed it all.

To occupy herself, she decided to write a letter to Wyatt. She had already written him six letters, almost every other day. For the most part, after her first two letters which had probably sounded quite frantic, she had tried not to complain too much. She wrote very little about her curious relationship with Miranda and barely mentioned the perceived "danger" they were in. Instead, she had written about the ranch and the animals and farming. She knew that, because Wyatt had been a farmer in Oregon, he would probably appreciate hearing those things.

Today, she wrote more frankly, explaining about her stepsister's deceit and the meeting with her father's attorney. She explained about temporarily staying in the hotel and how there was trouble at nearby mine that was owned by the O'Neils. And finally, she told Wyatt just how much she missed him. And, instead of saying "truly yours" like the past letters, she signed this one with "love, Delia."

As she sealed the envelope, she doubted that he'd even received her first letter yet. He'd said it took three weeks to get mail to Juneau. But she'd hoped to have a message from him by now, sent during his week in San Francisco. Coming by train, couldn't it have made it here? Unless he hadn't cared to write. What if he'd forgotten all about her?

24

THERE WAS NO DENYING THAT THE LAND OF THE MIDNIGHT SUN WAS completely enchanting—not simply because the daylight seemed almost endless in June, but also because of the pristine natural beauty of the land. Rugged snowcapped mountains dropped into the stunning blue waters of the bay. The sky was bluer than blue. And the wildlife was amazing. Already they'd seen several bears and numerous moose. And the fishing was beyond fantastic. This place was a nature lover's paradise. At least during summer. Wyatt wasn't too sure what he'd think of the region in the dead of winter.

Despite all the natural beauty that Alaska could offer, Wyatt still found himself longing for something else. He wanted to be with Delia. More than ever after getting a letter from her this morning. Even as he and Jake stood on a rise overlooking the bay, observing a pod of killer whales, Wyatt found himself wishing he could share this moment with Delia. He felt certain she'd appreciate it.

"Let me guess," Jake said with an ironic edge to his voice. "You are thinking about that woman again—the *delectable Delia.*"

"What if I am?" Wyatt said defensively.

"Here you are in one of the most magnificent regions I've ever witnessed, and you are so moonfaced over a female you can't even appreciate it."

"I appreciate it," Wyatt argued. "I was just imagining showing it to Delia."

Jake laughed. "Well, the sooner that ship gets up here to take you back to San Francisco, the better it will be for both of us."

Wyatt softened. "So you're not irked at me for leaving you in the lurch like this?"

"You promised me your half of the claim after you go," Jake reminded him. "And if I strike color while you're boarding the SS *Clarissa*, you're the one who might be feeling a mite bit irked."

"Well, I've still got five days to work it," Wyatt pointed out. "Maybe we'll get lucky before then." He chuckled, knowing the odds were stacked against this.

"Then we better get back at it," Jake said as they turned to walk back to their claim. "At least you got lucky selling all your goods. I can't believe you moved all your merchandise in just one week, Wyatt. Almost makes me wanna give up mining and go into merchandizing."

"What'd I tell you?" Wyatt said.

"That miners need boots and socks and shovels," Jake mimicked his friend.

"Well, it was a sure thing." Wyatt bent down to get his pickaxe and shovel. "If I had to make my living in the mines, I'd probably starve to death." He grimaced as they went into the dark cave they'd been working on.

"At least you could say you'd done something interesting," Jake said as he lit a lantern. "You've had adventures."

As Wyatt swung his pickaxe, he realized that he wasn't as keen on doing "something interesting" as he used to be. Oh, he still wanted some excitement and adventure…it's just that he wanted to have Delia by his side as he experienced it. Based on Delia's letter, there was plenty to be had in Colorado. And unless he was mistaken, Delia needed him badly. That letter was a clear cry for help.

As he reached for his shovel, he remembered his thrill to discover a letter had come from her—arriving in less than two weeks too. But he'd been shocked upon reading her emotional words. Delia's father had been killed and, unless he'd misunderstood, the neighboring rancher was responsible for his death. Over water rights. This was not good. As soon as he finished reading the letter, Wyatt inquired about ship passage going south. His plan was to get to Colorado as swiftly as possible.

As he shoveled some of the rock debris out of the way, he imagined a future with Delia. If she'd decided she didn't want to remain in a place where a good man was shot in the back over water, they could always head out to his ranch in Oregon. He'd use his earnings from selling supplies to get to work building a house straightaway. Or maybe she'd want to come back up here to the Alaska Territory, where he might be able to make some more money. Although it seemed a little rough for a cultivated woman like Delia.

As long as they were together, he didn't much care where they landed. All he wanted was to be able to take care of her. Sure, it would be nice if he could do it in a fashion she was accustomed to. He knew that she'd grown up in comfort. If worse came to worst— and if Delia wanted—he would probably even be willing to go back to work in his uncle's boot factory. Oh, it wouldn't be his first choice, but it was a sacrifice he could make for a fine woman like Delia. Wouldn't his aunt adore her?

As he tossed a shovelful of debris out of the way, Wyatt felt saddened to think of Delia's father being slain like that—just one day before Delia's arrival. He knew that had to hurt—a lot. Poor Delia had never gotten the chance to meet and know her flesh and blood father. But at least she was getting acquainted with her sister…and seeing the ranch her dad had built. That had to count for something.

His biggest fear was that Delia could be in danger. If some crazy rancher was going around shooting innocent folks over water, well, that did not sit well with him. Not at all. For that reason he was bound and determined to board the SS *Clarissa* next week. In the meantime, he would work as hard as he could with Jake on their claim. Not because he had any illusions or expectations to see even a speck of gold. He didn't. It would simply help pass the time, and when it was all said and done, he could say he'd tried. Not for very long, that was for sure, but he'd given it his all. He gave his pick a hard swing, breaking off a good-sized chunk of rock, pausing to study it a moment then going after it again.

From what he could tell, Jake had been mistaken to stake his claim over here. Most of the miners were on the other side of this hill and several of them had already struck gold. Still, he told himself, this was as much about being with his best friend as anything else. It was about keeping his promise. Already they'd had a good week of working hard all day. But it hadn't been all work. They'd taken time to see some sights, enjoying an occasional good meal of salmon or elk in the fast growing nearby town.

They'd had some great discussions, lying on their bedrolls, watching as the sun finally set around ten o'clock, although the sky remained light for the next hour. And then being surprised when the sky grew light again just a few hours later. If the next five days were as enjoyable as the others had been, that was riches enough. Not only that, but Wyatt had a nice little bundle of cash to take back with him. It might not be enough to do all the improvements he'd wanted for his ranch, but it would be a start.

As Wyatt picked out another chunk of stone, examining the opening that his last swing of the pick had exposed, something there in the rock gave him pause. "Hey, Jake." Wyatt tried to keep his voice level as he ran his finger over a narrow irregularity in the stone wall.

"What?" Jake stopped swinging his pick.

"Get yourself over here."

Feeling the excitement that always came whenever they thought maybe they'd found a nugget or a vein—even though they were usually wrong—Wyatt picked up his lantern in the hopes of seeing it better.

"What is it?"

"Look at this." Wyatt pointed at the yellow streak snaking through the middle of a section of rock.

Jake held up his own lantern now, illuminating the streak which now glistened like gold. "Interesting."

Wyatt picked up the piece of stone that he'd just chipped away, seeing that this streak ran though it as well. "Let's take some of this outside and see it it's the real thing."

Together they picked and pried, pulling out several good-sized chunks before they hurried outside to examine the pieces more closely in the bright sunshine.

"This is it!" Jake shrieked, jumping up and down like a schoolboy. "You found it, Wyatt! *Eureka,* you found it!"

"Shhh!" Wyatt warned, holding onto Jake's shoulder to steady him. "You want the whole world to know? You know about claim jumpers." Wyatt looked over to the nearby ridge, hoping no miners were lurking there.

"It's the real thing!" Jake declared. "We did it, Wyatt!" He grabbed Wyatt by the hand, dancing around in the rubble.

"You gotta keep quiet," Wyatt urged him. He knew the closest claim was at least half a mile away, but anyone could be around here. He'd heard of these interlopers—greedy men who waited until a hardworking miner made his lucky strike, then they'd swoop in like vultures and take over. Any celebrating could draw attention—the wrong kind of attention.

"I know. I know." Jake grinned down at the chunk in his palm. "But it's hard to contain myself." He held it up to the light. "Look at this, Wyatt. This is *good* stuff."

"We gotta get as much out of this lode out as possible. And as quickly as we can," Wyatt said. "Before anyone tries to make trouble.

You know what can happen. There are only two of us to defend this claim. And there are a lot of hungry miners out there—some with the scruples of a sidewinder."

Jake grew more sober. "Yeah, you're right. Let's get to work. Not time to waste now."

"And we don't tell anyone." Wyatt looked all around him as they returned to the cave. "Just like always."

"So you still wanna jump that boat to Frisco next week?" Jake asked in a teasing tone as they went inside. "Wanna give this all up for a girl?"

"I'm thinking about it." Wyatt led the way to where he'd discovered the gold vein. From what he could see it was fairly long—at least four or five feet. And it was possible that it would lead to other veins, or maybe not. You never knew. But there was no denying it was a good find. A real good find. "Why don't you go to work on the pieces down there?" Wyatt pointed to the rocks down on the cave floor. "I'll keep picking at this." Wyatt swung his smaller pick now, dislodging a chunk of rock from beneath the vein to expose the gold better.

"If you leave, like you say you're gonna, I plan to hold you to your promise." Jake said as he picked through the pile of rocks. "You leave me here on my own, Wyatt, and this claim is mine, remember?"

"I remember." Wyatt frowned as he slipped a piece of gold into his pocket.

"Look at this piece." Jake held up a chunk nearly as big as his thumb. "Can you believe it? We've done struck gold!"

"Keep your voice down," Wyatt warned. Then he grinned, punching Jake playfully in the arm. "There'll be time to celebrate later."

As the pair worked, prying out varying sizes of gold chunks, Wyatt wondered if he was going to stick to his plan after all. Was he still determined to leave Alaska, to get to Delia as quickly as possible? Or did it make more sense to stay here and work this claim until it quit producing? That way he could go to Delia as a rich man.

Pausing to wipe sweat from his brow, Wyatt remembered what he'd said about not caring about riches anymore. Despite his experience with Maryanne—or perhaps because of it—his values had changed. Or so he'd thought. He studied a piece of gold before slipping it into his other pocket. Did he still believe that? Or was he, like so many other miners, getting caught up in gold fever?

The two of them worked for hours before they finally decided to take turns, allowing one of them to catch some sleep while the other one worked and kept watch for claim jumpers. They continued like this for the next couple of days, working around the clock together and in shifts, taking turns fixing food and sleeping, but continually digging out the vein until both of them were so exhausted they could barely talk or reason.

"We need food," Wyatt told Jake on the third day.

"I know, but I don't want to leave this." Jake wiped a dirty hand across his grimy brow.

"I'll go fetch some provisions," Wyatt offered.

"Don't talk to anyone," Jake urgently warned.

"If I don't talk to anyone, I'll look even more suspicious." Wyatt sighed wearily.

"Yeah, well, I guess you know what to do."

"And you keep your rifle handy," Wyatt warned. "Just in case."

As Wyatt walked to town with their pack mule, he felt divided. As if someone had driven a pickaxe straight down his middle. On one hand, he was sick of spending all this time in the dark, tired of mining and dirt and picks and shovels—all he wanted was to get out of this place and back to Delia. On the other hand—how much gold did their claim hold? What if he was a fool to walk away?

"Looks like you're all in. Been working hard?" A slightly disreputable man named Jeb met Wyatt in front of the mercantile with a suspicious look. "You seeing any color yet?"

"Mostly seeing a lot of dirt and dust and rocks," Wyatt said with nonchalance. "But I'm giving it my best shot. Especially since I plan to head outta here in a few days. Wanna make my best attempt before I give up for good." He laughed. "Can't say I'll miss it much either. Mining's hard work."

Wyatt kept up his unsuccessful act with others as he picked out some unimpressive provisions at the mercantile. Like everything else up here, food was ridiculously expensive. If he'd stayed in San Francisco longer, like he'd meant to originally, he would've brought up plenty for him and Jake—with plenty to sell for profit. But he hadn't wanted to waste the time down there. Now he was paying for it.

As Wyatt loaded a hunk of bacon, numerous tins, parcels of rice and beans and coffee into a flour sack, he noticed how filthy his hands were. And he remembered that he hadn't shaved or bathed in days. He must look a sight. Tying the sack shut, he wondered what the refined Delia would think of him now. Somehow he knew she'd see past the grime. Still, would she want him to leave this all behind—just to return to her? Or would she prefer he stay put and make his fortune first? He just did not know.

As he led the mule back to their claim, he considered Jake. He felt guilty about leaving his friend and partner behind. They both knew it was dangerous to strike gold when you had just one partner, but even more so when you were alone. Maybe it was wrong for Wyatt to abandon his best friend. He honestly didn't know. And as he unloaded the supplies in the tent, he was so tired that he wasn't even sure he could figure it out. So he silently prayed—asking God to direct him somehow.

For the next two days, the partners continued working the vein, slaving around the clock and barely speaking to each other. It was a strange sort of existence, working in the darkness of the mine, coming out into the almost continual sunlight. Wyatt wondered if this was the kind of experience that could drive a man to madness.

Finally, on what was supposed to be Wyatt's last night in Alaska, the vein seemed to be dwindling down to nothing. Was it possible they'd gotten everything their claim had to offer? Or was there another vein buried just a little deeper in the rock behind it? In their old mining days they would quite naturally have assumed the latter. Still, Wyatt wasn't sure he cared anymore.

"The *Clarissa* arrives tomorrow," Wyatt told Jake as the two of them sat down to eat their bacon and beans together. Although it was midnight, the sky was still light and Wyatt felt like he'd lost all sense of time. Day was night and night was day.

"You getting on it?" Jake asked. "Sailing away for good?"

"I don't rightly know." Wyatt shook his head with uncertainty… or perhaps just plain weariness.

Jake ran his hand through dirt encrusted hair and frowned. "You said you were leaving."

Wyatt felt confused. "You *want* me to leave?"

"You said you were going," Jake said again. "I just figured you were."

"Yeah, but do you really *want* me to go?" Wyatt demanded. "To leave you here on your own? With claim jumpers who might kill you for your gold?"

Jake shrugged. "I'm not worried."

"So you honestly want me to go?" Wyatt asked for the third time. Here he'd been worried about abandoning Jake and now it seemed his best friend couldn't wait to be rid of him.

"You said you were going, Wyatt, so why don't you just go?" Jake said loudly. "I thought you were a man of your word."

Wyatt was dumbfounded. Did Jake think he could kick him off his own claim now? Just because they'd struck gold? What kind of friend was he anyway? Wyatt knew this kind of disagreement could turn ugly—even amongst the best of friends. He studied Jake for a long moment. Maybe he didn't know this guy as well as he thought.

"Fine," Wyatt said abruptly. "I'm leaving tomorrow. I'll take my half of the gold and you get my half of the claim."

"Fine." Jake said in a grouchy tone.

They finished eating then worked awhile longer. Breaking apart rocks without speaking until Jake decided to take a shift of sleeping. And then it was Wyatt's turn. By mid-morning the next day, Wyatt felt more tired than he'd ever been in his life. As he washed himself off in a nearby stream, he also felt sad. This wasn't how he'd wanted to end things. Finally, with his knapsack packed, and heavy with gold, he went to find Jake.

"I hope you hit the mother lode," Wyatt said to his old friend. "I really do."

Jake frowned. "You do?"

"If that's what makes you happy." Wyatt adjusted a strap of his heavy pack. "I'm leaving the tent and my tools and stuff with you. I even left some books behind. In case you get the hankering to improve your mind."

"Thanks." Jake's smile was sheepish. "Sorry about growling at you last night."

"No problem." Wyatt reached to shake his friend's hand. "And more than just getting rich, Jake, I hope you'll find a life that's satisfying." He grinned. "And I hope you find a good woman too. I'll be praying that you do."

Jake laughed. "Well, if things work out like you hope with Delia, you might inspire me to follow your example. Who knows?"

"Take care." Wyatt clasped Jake's shoulder. "And stay in touch. I wrote down the address in Colorado—where Delia is—I put it in on top of the books in the tent. I hope you'll write and let me know how it goes."

"So if the claim keeps paying and I become a millionaire, you'll come back here looking for me?"

Wyatt just laughed. "There's more to life than riches, Jake. I think you know I believe that—and I think on a good day, you believe it too."

Jake looked uncertain. "Maybe…I'll let you know."

Wyatt just shook his head. "Good luck, Jake. You'll be in my prayers." As he turned to walk down to the hill toward town, Wyatt said a quick silent prayer for his friend—asking for God's protection and direction. Then he prayed the same prayer for Delia—and for himself.

Before long, he was down by the bay where—not wanting to take any chances of missing the boat—he planned to stay put. And he planned to keep his knapsack right with him. Looking like a decrepit miner, frayed and dirty and down on his luck, Wyatt doubted that anyone would pay him much mind, or guess what the contents of his knapsack was worth, but he wasn't taking any chances either.

He sat down on the dock, leaning his back against the knapsack that he'd set against the pier, as he watched for the boat. He knew it would dock and unload and head on its way within the course of an hour. These ships waited for no one, and he didn't intend to miss it. The idea of wasting one more week in Juneau—one more week between him and Delia—was more than he could bear. As he waited for the ship, he had no doubts that he'd made the right decision about leaving Alaska. As promising as their claim might be, it wasn't enough to hold him here a single day longer. *Delia needed him.* And he needed her…more than he needed riches.

25

SEVERAL HOURS BEFORE SHE PLANNED TO LEAVE FOR HER APPOINT-
ment the following afternoon, Delia heard the shocking news. Horace
Griswold had been shot. According to the morning paper, Mr. Griswold had been murdered by someone who'd broken into his office
last night. Apparently Mr. Griswold had been working late when the
break-in occurred. The law office had been ransacked and an undis-
closed amount of cash had been stolen, but so far there seemed to be
no leads in the case, and no explanations for why the perpetrator had
wanted the well-liked elderly attorney dead. The newspaper made it
sound as if he'd simply been in the wrong place at the wrong time.

Horrified over the death of such a kind man, Delia didn't know
what to do or who to turn to. She checked with the desk clerk to see
if Maggie O'Neil was still registered, hoping to get some advice from
her, but to her dismay, Delia was informed that Maggie had checked
out early that morning. Probably before the newspaper came out.

Delia knew that Mr. Griswold had an associate, but she couldn't
recall his name and, under the circumstances of losing his business
partner, Delia wasn't even sure it was proper for her to make an inquiry of him. Just the same, she decided to walk by the law office.

Perhaps in the hopes she might run into him. But seeing the law office's broken windows in the process of being boarded up and the black wreath on the door, she knew she would have to wait.

"Poor Horace Griswold," an elderly gentleman was saying to a woman. "Such a kind man—and being shot down in cold blood like that." He grimly shook his head. "I heard Mr. Stanfield telling the police that they never kept more than fifty dollars in there. To think Horace was killed for such a pittance. A shame and a waste."

Delia shuddered as she continued walking past. She knew it was probably just a coincidence that Mr. Griswold had been murdered within hours of speaking to her. And yet the crime felt strangely connected to her. But why? As she hurried back to the hotel, she thought about her father's death—and how Mr. Griswold had been certain it was not an accident but murder. And now he'd been murdered too. Was that just a coincidence? Somehow, she didn't think so.

In her hotel room, Delia decided to write a short letter to the law firm. When she'd overheard the bystander's mention of the name of Stanfield, she knew that was Mr. Griswold's partner. She addressed her letter to him, writing of her dilemma regarding her father's ranch, the "missing" will, and her disagreeable stepsister, explaining about how she'd planned to meet with Griswold later today—finally stating her need of counsel.

After the letter was sent, she knew she would just have to wait for a response. And, although the money in her envelope would not cover much more than a week in this somewhat expensive hotel, she decided that the best thing to do was to simply stay put.

Horace Griswold's death was the talk of the town and, staying in the hotel, it was impossible not to hear the various versions of what had happened and why. By the evening of her second day there, she still hadn't heard from Mr. Stanfield. However, she did learn that a funeral service was scheduled for Mr. Griswold, for tomorrow, and she planned to go.

Dressed in her black mourning gown, Delia slowly walked to

church the next day. Although she hadn't known Mr. Griswold well, she had respected him and felt that she was honoring her father by attending this funeral. After the service, where Mr. Griswold was remembered and honored by many, a tall middle-aged man with a full gray beard approached her. "Excuse me for my presumption," he said politely, "but you were pointed out as the daughter of Winston Williams. Is that correct?"

"Yes." She nodded. "I am Delia Williams."

"I'm pleased to make your acquaintance, Miss Williams. I want to express my sincere sympathy for your loss. Your father was a good man." He grasped her hand.

"And you are?" She peered into his pale blue eyes, trying to see behind them.

"Forgive me, Miss Williams. I'm Jerome Roswell. I own a neighboring ranch."

She pulled her hand away from him with a slight gasp, feeling almost as if she'd been bitten by a snake.

"I realize that—"

"Miss Williams." Marcus Vincent stepped to her side in a way that almost felt protective. "I was surprised to see you here today."

"I—uh—I didn't catch the train."

Marcus smiled at her. "I must say I'm most pleased to see you." He glanced at Jerome Roswell. "Is this man giving you trouble?"

Delia didn't know what to say.

"I was simply introducing—"

"You don't need to tell me what you're up to, Roswell." Marcus narrowed his eyes. "But don't you think a funeral service is a poor place to conduct business? It's no secret that you're determined to purchase the Double W, but out of respect for the dead, you—"

"Excuse me," Mr. Roswell growled, barely tipping his head toward Delia. "Sorry to have troubled you, miss." Before she could respond, he quickly moved away.

"I'm sorry you had to be subjected to that." Marcus shook his

Delia and the Drifter

head. "But it's not surprising that Roswell would attempt such a thing. That man's a scoundrel—through and through."

"It was so shocking," she confessed, "to look into the eyes of... of—"

"A killer?" Marcus said quietly. "I understand. Everyone knows that Roswell thinks he's above the law. Just because he's got the biggest ranch in these parts, he runs roughshod over everyone. And now it looks like he's set his sights on you, Miss Delia. I'm sorry."

Delia was speechless. She'd never felt like Marcus Vincent cared much about her before and suddenly he was being so kind. "I'm surprised to see you here too, Mr. Vincent," she said. "Were you friends with Mr. Griswold?"

He nodded grimly. "Yes. Your father and I were both good friends with Horace. I still can't believe he's gone—that they're both gone. Two of the finest men around." He glanced over to where Mr. Roswell was talking to some men. "And I have strong suspicions as to who is behind it."

"Mr. Roswell?"

"You already know that everyone believes that he was behind your father's death."

"Yes. But Mr. Griswold too? What motive did Roswell have?"

"Horace was one of your father's best friends. Winston confided in Horace regularly. I suspect that Horace had information that would lead the law straight back to Roswell."

"Mr. Griswold did mention that he was doing some research on the case." She tried to remember what he'd said to her. As she recalled he didn't seem to think the Leaning R was involved.

"Even more reason for Roswell to be worried." Marcus's brow creased with concern. "And I'm worried about you, Miss Delia. I felt much better thinking you were safely on a train. Do you realize what danger you're in right now?"

"What are you insinuating, Mr. Vincent?" She glanced nervously over to where Mr. Roswell was having an intense conversation with several men.

"Roswell is determined to get the water from the Double W," Marcus said quietly. "He doesn't want anyone to get in his way, including you."

"What about Miranda?" Delia studied his expression carefully.

"I suspect she's in danger too. Even though she's only Winston's stepdaughter, Roswell might see her as an obstacle."

"So you know that Miranda isn't his daughter?" For some reason she hadn't expected this.

He nodded. "Of course. And I would like to keep protecting both of you—for the sake of your father—but I can't very well do that on the ranch and in town. For that reason, I strongly encourage you to return to the ranch with me."

"I would be glad to do that, but I'm afraid my sister will not welcome me."

He grimaced. "Miss Miranda hasn't been herself since your father was killed. If you return with me, I promise that I'll attempt to talk some sense into her."

Despite her longing to go home to the Double W, and not wanting to spend all her money at the Elk Horn Hotel, she felt reluctant... uneasy.

"Caleb would be so happy to have you back, Miss Delia. He told me that Cash invited you to help us drive the cattle next week. He wasn't sure it was such a good idea, but we're so short of hands that I think I can talk him into it." He grinned. "Cash seems to think you're a good horsewoman."

She shrugged. "I know how to stay in the saddle."

"A side-saddle?"

"I can ride side or astride."

Marcus looked impressed. "Then I encourage you to come home with me, Miss Delia. Ginger has been pining for you too. Even the dog has been sad."

Remembering Hank's head in her lap on the day of the funeral was what pushed her to accept the invitation. "It'll take me about an hour to pack and check out of the hotel," she said.

"I'll have the carriage ready and waiting outside."

To her relief, her clean laundry had been returned to her room and she packed up everything and, with the help of the bellboy, got it all back down to the lobby where Marcus was waiting. "I must hand it to you, Miss Delia, you do not dillydally." He reached for her smaller bags, leading her out the front door. "When you say you can be ready in an hour, you are ready in an hour. An admirable trait in a woman." He opened the door of the carriage for her, helped her inside, then saw to the loading of her luggage.

As Marcus drove the carriage toward home, Delia wondered if perhaps she had misjudged this man initially. For some reason she had not trusted him from their very first meeting, that first day when he'd wanted to send her back to Pennsylvania. Of course, she later learned this was for her own safety, and having been shot at, she understood the reasoning. In fact, he had even warned her it could happen again. "Be sure and get down if you hear me yell," he'd told her. "Although I'm probably in more danger than you since I don't have anyone riding shotgun."

Promising to pray for their safety, Delia tried not to think about what she would do if he was wounded...or worse. Now, as the carriage thundered toward the ranch, Delia reminded herself of the fact that her father, a good, wise businessman, had hired Marcus Vincent. And, unless memory failed her, it had been about ten years ago. Didn't that imply that her father trusted him—and if her father trusted Marcus, why shouldn't she? Perhaps her only real concern had been Marcus's interaction with Miranda. But even that seemed somewhat unfounded now. What business of hers was it anyway? Perhaps it was time she gave this man a second chance. After all, he was risking his life to get her safely back home.

Delia couldn't have been happier as they passed beneath the

Double W gate. And yet she was when she heard the excited barking of Hank as he ran out to meet them. Waving out the window, she called out a hello, watching as he ran alongside the horses, almost as if he thought he was driving them home.

She felt a damper on her happiness when Miranda stepped out onto the porch with a puzzled frown. As Marcus jumped down from the driver's seat, Miranda's gaze was fixed on Delia. She was clearly not glad to see her.

"I brought Delia home to keep her safe," Marcus called out as helped Delia down from the buggy. Delia bristled at this familiarity—Marcus usually referred to her as *Miss* Delia. But this was a practice he'd already adapted with Miranda, so perhaps he thought it was acceptable with Delia too.

"Miss Delia," she said firmly under her breath.

He just grinned.

"I thought you were on your way back East." Miranda scowled darkly as Delia strolled up to the house with Hank running alongside her. "What happened?"

"I ran into *Miss* Delia at Horace's funeral," Marcus explained. "I made her come back with me. Too dangerous out there right now."

"At least no one shot at us." Delia knelt down to properly greet Hank.

"But why are you here?" Miranda asked pointedly.

"I spoke to Mr. Griswold about the will." Delia stood, looking directly at Miranda. "Before he died."

"There is no will," Miranda insisted.

"You're wrong. Horace said he had one in his safe."

Miranda's blue eyes grew wide. "Did you see it for yourself?"

"No, he wanted to read it to everyone all at once. You and the employees and me. All together."

"So he didn't show it to you?" Miranda pressed.

"No, but—"

"Then how do you know there is a will?"

"Miranda!" Marcus exclaimed in a scolding tone. "If Miss Delia says that Horace said there's a will, then surely there is a will."

"But you—"

"And I'd think you'd be ashamed of yourself for not treating your sister in a more civilized manner." Marcus was standing in front of Miranda now, glaring at her with an expression that Delia could only describe as disgust. "Or maybe she's not your *real* sister. Maybe you two aren't related at all. Maybe you are simply *stepsisters*. Perhaps because Miss Delia is really Winston's daughter, and you are not, well, maybe you wanted to be rid of her."

"Who told you that?" Miranda demanded. "That she's not my real sister?"

"Your *step*father."

Miranda narrowed her eyes. "I don't believe you."

Marcus shrugged. "Believe what you like."

"But you said—"

"I'm sure I said a lot of things that I no longer mean," he said coolly. "I'm starting to see you in a whole different light, Miranda, and quite frankly, I'm not liking what I see."

"But I—"

"And if I were you, I would start treating your older sister with a lot more respect."

Miranda looked enraged, but instead of lashing out, she spun around and stormed back into the house.

"My word!" Delia looked at Marcus in wonder.

"Sorry to make such a scene, but I just felt Miss Miranda needed to be put in her place. And I'm sure that Winston would've approved."

"I must admit to feeling confused," Delia said. "But at the same time I'm relieved. It is always good to bring the truth to light."

"You go on inside," he told her. "I'll see if I can find Cash to help unload the carriage."

"Thank you." She smiled.

"And I would recommend you steer clear of Miss Miranda for a spell. She's obviously out of sorts now. Best to let her cool off and come to her senses."

Delia nodded. "I'm sure you're right."

As she went inside, instead of going up to her room, she headed straight for the kitchen where Ginger broke into tears of happiness. "I feel like the sun just came out again," Ginger exclaimed. "Having you back here, Miss Delia, it's like a breath of fresh air."

Delia hugged her. "I'm so glad to be back too. I feel like I just came home."

"Caleb will be so happy."

"Why don't I run out to see him?" Delia suggested. "Marcus promised that I can go on the cattle drive with them next week. Do you think Caleb will really let me?"

"Land o' mercy, child—I don't know why you'd want to do that. Driving cattle is hard work. Men's work."

Delia smiled. "I just really want to do it. It sounds exciting."

"I said it before and I'll say it again." Ginger chuckled as she shook her head. "You are your father's daughter, Miss Delia. You surely are."

As Delia headed out back, she was quickly joined by Hank. "So where's Caleb?" she asked him as she strode out toward the barn and corral. "We've got to convince him to take us cattle driving." Hank just wagged his tail, but Delia could tell he understood.

26

DESPITE MIRANDA'S HOSTILE DEMEANOR AND ICY STARES, DELIA FELT more at home at the Double W than ever. And the first thing she did, after greeting everyone and checking on the garden and the chickens, was to write another letter to Mr. Stanfield. She informed him of her new whereabouts and invited him to visit the ranch for the reading of the will.

She also wrote a letter to Wyatt, but she kept it brief since she was beginning to question his interest in her. She assumed he hadn't written from San Francisco now, since it was going on three weeks. And she wondered if she'd overblown their short-lived relationship in her "violet" influenced imagination. It seemed quite likely that her beloved drifter had chosen the lure of the open road and next great adventure. Certainly, the wilds of Alaska were more compelling than pursuing a relationship with and "educated" woman.

She remembered his seeming dismay when she'd confessed about her education. Almost as if he'd been intimidated. Hadn't her mother warned of this? Maybe it had scared him off. Or perhaps he had simply been enjoying a brief interlude…a diversion for entertainment on the long train trip.

Delia was aware that love could be a one-way street. She'd seen the foolishness of Violet, falling again and again, only to be disappointed. Delia had warned herself—plenty of times in college—*don't be a violet.* And yet wasn't that exactly what she'd done? Fallen foolishly in love?

However, she told herself as she laid out her riding habit, she would not become a *shrinking* violet. If she'd fallen in love so easily, she would just as easily fall out. She was a strong woman. Right now, she felt ready to mount a horse and drive cattle with a bunch of rough and rugged men. Ready to eat dust, be encrusted with dirt, and so saddle sore that she'd be crying for mercy—at least that's what Caleb had told her. And she was ready to bathe in the creek, cook on an open fire, and sleep beneath the stars. Unladylike, yes, but it would be an adventure! And a good distraction from fretting over Wyatt's disinterest in her.

Before embarking on this adventure, Caleb had insisted she must spend some significant time in the saddle. He wanted her to prove herself to him. Both as a horsewoman and cowhand. So the next day, after she'd completed her regular farm chores and weeded the garden, she went out to the corral to work with the horses. To start with, she wanted to decide which horse best suited her. To do this, she needed to get to know the horses—up close. By the end of the day, she decided on a bay mare named Lady. But when Cash saddled her up with her deceased stepmother's old side-saddle, Delia put her foot down, insisting she planned to use a regular saddle.

His confused frown looked doubtful.

"Look," she told him. "I know women traditionally use those silly contraptions, but I would rather break tradition than break my neck."

He grinned. "You got something there." But he pointed to her riding habit, and what still resembled a full skirt. "What about that?"

She quickly explained that with Ginger's help, she'd already altered her riding habit into a split-skirt. "So don't concern yourself about me."

Caleb chuckled as he went in search of a saddle that would fit both her and Lady.

"Well, you may be Lady," Delia said as she curried the mare's gleaming brown coat, "but I do not plan to ride like a lady. And I expect you to hold your own too. We'll show those buckaroos that being female does not mean being weak."

After several days back on the ranch, doing chores and working with Lady, Delia received a note from Mr. Stanfield. Without any explanation or apology, the note simply stated that her father had left no will with their law firm.

Of course, this made no sense. Especially after what Horace Griswold had told her. But there were even more reasons that Delia questioned the letter's validity. For one thing, the wording of the communique didn't utilize the vocabulary one would expect from an attorney of law. Besides that, the note was handwritten on plain white stationery with no letterhead. And it wasn't that she expected something more formal, but she had been impressed by the Caligraph typing machine at the law office, exactly like ones that she and other students had shared at the university. Even if Mr. Stanfield had chosen to pen the note himself, she just was not convinced this was the handwriting of a lawyer. And, unless she was mistaken, the stationery had the faint scent of lilacs—very similar to the perfume favored by Miranda.

Was it possible that Miranda had discovered Delia's letter to the lawyer in the letter box—before one of the men made an errand trip to town with it—and that her unscrupulous stepsister had opened and read it then penned her own forged response? To get to the bottom of this, Delia recruited Ginger to help. Without giving away her suspicions, she got Ginger to get Miranda into the kitchen under the guise of helping with a choice of the evening's dessert. While

Miranda was in the kitchen, Delia went into her room—actually the master bedroom that Miranda had usurped shortly after her stepfather was killed—with the intent to snoop around.

Feeling guilty as well as flushed with excitement, Delia made a beeline for the desk by the window. It didn't take long to confirm her suspicions. Not only did she find matching stationery, the curly handwriting, which she discovered on another note, was identical. And then—the icing on the proverbial cake—Delia's original letter crumpled up and tossed into the wastebasket beneath the desk.

Gathering her evidence, Delia hurried from the room and prepared to confront her stepsister. She didn't have a particular plan in place, she simply wanted to get to the truth. Finding Miranda in the parlor, Delia insisted that Miranda meet with her in their father's library—and before Miranda could question this, Delia stormed off.

"Why would you do this?" she asked Miranda when she finally showed up. Delia held out her evidence, waiting for Miranda's response. "And there's no use denying it, since I know you did."

"Because you just never give up." Miranda glared at Delia. "You come in here one day after my dad dies and—"

"He was *my* dad too."

"Yes, but I'm the one who was here *all those years.*"

"And that was a hardship?"

"I never *wanted* this," Miranda waved her arms around. "I would've traded all these cows and horses and chickens and pigs for a civilized life in a city somewhere. Like where you grew up—*Philadelphia.*"

"I grew up in Pittsburgh."

"Well, yes, wherever—any city is better than this stinking farm!"

Delia wanted to tell her that this farm smelled a whole lot better than the murky skies of the steel town she'd left back East, but that was beside the point. "Being unhappy here does not make it acceptable for you to lie and forge letters and—"

"I wanted out of here!"

"Then you should go."

Miranda narrowed her eyes. "Not without what's coming to me!"

Delia had to bite her tongue on this one.

"What's going on in here?" Marcus burst into the library with a concerned expression. "I could hear you yelling clear in the dining room."

"This is your fault!" Miranda yelled at him. "You were supposed to be with me—and now you've betrayed me—just because you think Delia will inherit everything. You are a great big lying—"

"You're talking nonsense." Marcus folded his arms in front of him. "As usual." He turned to Delia. "Care to explain this little squabble?"

Delia held up her crumpled letter to Mr. Stanfield, explaining Miranda's counterfeit response. "She knows there's a will, but she doesn't want me to see it."

"Probably because your father left everything to you," Marcus said calmly.

"Do you really think—"

"Shut up! Both of you!" Miranda screamed. "You both make me sick!" And before anyone could say another word, she stormed out of the room.

"I'm sorry she's being so difficult," Marcus said. "I don't like to say it, but she's always been spoiled."

Delia didn't like to say it either—but she feared he was right. "So I will write another letter to Mr. Griswold's associate Mr. Stanfield," she said. "And hopefully you can assure me that it will get there."

"I will happily deliver it myself."

"Oh, that's not—"

"I was heading into town anyway. I planned to leave shortly. I need to round up some supplies for the cattle drive and check on some things. I can easily drop off your letter too. By this evening, if you'd like."

"If you're sure it's no trouble."

"It's the least I can do," he assured her. "The truth is I feel somewhat responsible for Miranda's bad behavior recently. I've probably indulged her too much. I suppose I felt sorry for her. First her mother dies...then her stepfather. She seemed lost to me. I tried to reach out to her. But I think she misunderstood my attentions."

Delia just nodded.

"Miranda has a lot of growing up to do yet," he continued. "I know you're not that much older than her—but you seem so much more mature, Miss Delia." He smiled. "I can't help but admire that."

"Thank you."

He pointed to her father's desk. "My guess is that you will inherit the ranch, although I could be wrong. I want to offer my help with any of the business responsibilities. I was your father's right-hand man, so I'm sure I can answer your questions or, if you like, just handle the bookkeeping until you decide what you want to do. Especially since it's nearly payday now."

She studied him closely. "There is something you could do, Mr. Vincent—"

"Please, call me Marcus. Your father always did. We never went in for formalities around here." He smiled. "Just one of the things I respected about Winston. He treated everyone equally."

"That's good to know." She nodded. "Now, what you could do for me—for the ranch I should say. Can you please ask around town, see if there are employable people, ones who aren't afraid to come out here? Colorado City is a big place. Surely, there are those in need of work. We are so shorthanded, and after looking over the gardens and orchards and dairy, not to mention the livestock, I cannot imagine how this isn't a self-supporting business."

"That's always been your father's goal." Marcus picked up small bronze sculpture of an Indian maiden that was sitting on the corner of her father's desk, examining it closely.

"I just don't understand where my father kept his books."

"Books?" Marcus waved to the full bookshelves.

"I mean ledgers, for bookkeeping. Surely he kept track of expenditures and profits and such."

Marcus set the statue down with a blank expression. "You'd think so."

Delia waved her hand. "Sorry to trouble you with that." Suddenly she regretted speaking to him of the ranching business—as if she'd let her guard down.

He moved closer to her. "It is no trouble, Miss Delia."

She stepped back. "So I assume that you will look for workers to come out here to lighten the load?"

"If any can be enticed, I will certainly try."

"Thank you. Now I will write another letter to Mr. Stanfield." She sat down at her father's big mahogany desk, reaching for pen and stationery. "If you'll excuse me, please."

For the second time, she wrote her inquiry regarding the will and when she handed it over to Marcus, he assured her that it would be delivered to the law firm as soon as possible. After Marcus left, Delia looked around the library. She searched every nook and cranny, removing books, looking behind paintings, pulling back curtains and rolling back carpets…hoping to find a cleverly hidden safe somewhere. But as far as she could see, there was nothing like that in this room.

Supper was even quieter than usual, with Marcus in town and Miranda sulking in her room. Delia had already told Ginger it was no longer necessary to cater to Miranda by delivering her meals. "No more mollycoddling her. If she's hungry, let her come down here to eat." Just the same, Delia appreciated the peace and quiet. It gave her time to think. The more she thought, the more she knew it was imperative to get her hands on her father's will. And she couldn't believe it wasn't somewhere in this house.

After helping Ginger with the supper dishes, Delia returned to searching through the quiet house. By now she suspected her father had creatively concealed his safe. And why not when his ranch was fairly isolated, not to mention the unscrupulous neighboring Leaning R Ranch? No wonder he'd been so careful.

Delia didn't think that Mr. Griswold would have mentioned a safe if one didn't exist. It had to be here somewhere. As well as all the paperwork that would go with a ranch of this size. There would be ledgers and journals and records of payroll. There had to be. Except that there just wasn't.

Finally, after searching through every room on the first floor, looking behind every painting and cabinet and even rolling back the carpets on the floor, she gave up. As far as she could see, there was no such safe in this house. Unless it was upstairs and that seemed unlikely. As she went to bed, she wondered if perhaps Miranda had gotten it right. Maybe there truly was no will.

27

THE NEXT AFTERNOON, AFTER FINISHING HER CHORES, DELIA PUT ON the riding habit with the neatly split skirt. By now she felt perfectly comfortable on Lady and at ease in the western saddle, and so she asked Caleb to take some time out of his busy day to give her a full tour of the Double W.

He agreed, and before long, she and Caleb, with Hank happily running alongside, were galloping their horses across a pasture and over a stream and up a mountain trail. Caleb proved a good guide, showing her the best views, and pointing out where the property lines lay, explaining the value of sections of trees for lumber, where the water came down from the mountain, where her father had hoped to plant new crops, and finally pointing toward the upper western range where he explained they drove the cattle herd to graze openly. "We keep 'em up there for most of the summer," he said.

"Yes, I heard about that."

"We'll be heading off in a few days, Miss Delia."

"Marcus suggested I might accompany you on this cattle drive," she said a bit timidly. "I know you can use an extra hand."

"Oh, Miss Delia, you don't wanna go driving them dusty old cows with us. That's man's work."

"I think it would be a grand adventure. Something I will remember when I'm an old lady."

"It's nasty, hard work." He spat over his shoulder. "You're stuck in the saddle all day—so long that your hind end feels like you're sitting on hot coals. And you're eating so much dust that your teeth turn brown as mud. You barely stop to rest or get water or wash up. At day's end, you cook your own food over a smoky fire and you're so hungry that you eat your beans even though they're still crunchy. Then you're so tired you can barely keep your eyes open, but it's time to take turns watching the herd at night. When you finally do get to go to sleep, it's on the lumpy ground, and you hope and pray you don't wake up with a rattlesnake in your bedroll or a hungry ol' bear drooling down on your chest. Surely, you don't want to do all that, now do you, Miss Delia?"

"Tell me the truth—have you ever awakened with a rattlesnake in your bedroll?" She tried to hide her horror at this image.

"Well, no, but—"

"How about a bear?"

"Well, we seen sign of 'em plenty of times. And cougar too. Don't kid yourself, Miss Delia, them beasts are out there." He shrugged. "But truth be told, they're probably more scared of us than we are of them."

"Then I am convinced, Caleb. I would like to go on this cattle drive. I would like to say that I did something like this—at least once."

"I'll wager you'll never want to do it again." He chuckled.

"So, please, let me go with you, Caleb. Just this one time. If my father were here, I would be begging him to go just like I'm begging you. And for some reason I think he would want me to go. I truly do."

Caleb seemed to consider this. "Well, put like that, I don't know how I can turn you down, Miss Delia. I reckon you're right about your daddy too. He probably would've been glad to have you on a cattle drive with him. He was funny like that."

"Funny like what?"

"Oh, Winston always believed that women should have more opportunities than they got. He thought they were pert near equal to men." Caleb chuckled.

"Really?" This intrigued Delia. "That's very interesting."

"Don't you go telling no one this, little lady, but your daddy even believed that women should get the vote." He looked thoroughly scandalized. "I reckon it was something his mama taught him as a boy, but it must've stuck somehow. I've even overheard him saying as much to Miranda not so very long ago. I warned him about putting such wild ideas into a young gal's head. But your daddy just laughed at me."

"My daddy sounds as if he were a very fine man," Delia proclaimed. "And I will take this as his permission for me to accompany you on the cattle drive. I'm going!"

"Well, don't you go whining and complaining about the conditions once we're on the trail. There will be no turning back, I assure you. It takes two long days to get there and two long days to get back. We always get back to the ranch on the third of July. And the next day we celebrate with a big old barbecue for the Fourth." He frowned. "Although, considering all that's gone on, we might not have the barbecue after all."

"Well, I'm looking forward to the cattle drive," she declared. "Every bit of it."

By the time they got back to the house, it was nearly suppertime. Delia had just enough time to change out of her riding clothes and get back downstairs to help Ginger. Of course, Ginger, like Caleb, was doubtful about a woman going on a cattle drive, but after a few go rounds, she gave in. "I reckon if any young lady can handle such a thing, it would be you, Miss Delia." She grinned at her. "But what a beautiful girl like you sees in something like that is plum crazy."

After supper, where Miranda was once again absent, Delia went upstairs and heard a curious noise. She paused on the landing, thinking it was an animal in pain—although she'd just given Hank some table scraps out the back door so she knew it wasn't him. Straining to listen, she decided the sounds were definitely human, and since they were coming from the master suite bedroom where Miranda was holed up, she knew it must be her. As much as Delia disliked eavesdropping, she felt concerned. And so she pressed her ear to the door to hear what indeed sounded like sobbing.

Tapping lightly on the door, Delia called out to her. "Miranda, it's just me. Can we talk?"

"Go away!"

"Please, Miranda," she said urgently. "I need to speak to you. Let me in!"

After a short wait, she heard the doorknob click and the door cracked open. "What do you want?" Miranda growled in a gruff voice.

"To talk to you." Delia gently pushed the door open, entering the room. The first time she'd been in this space, she had been so set on finding the stolen letter that she'd barely noticed the details. Now, she glanced around to see a large, well-appointed room with lovely furnishings, but in a complete shambles. Miranda's housekeeping skills were sadly lacking.

"I know you've been crying," Delia said gently. "I was hoping that you would talk to me about it."

"Why should you care?" Miranda glared at her with red puffy eyes.

"Because, like it or not, we are sisters…sisters of a sort. Even if we are not related by blood, my father did marry your mother and, I think, he was like a true father to you, Miranda. Am I right?"

Miranda barely nodded, sniffing and tugging at the edge of the sleeve of her long white nightgown, a garment which appeared to be in need of a good laundering.

"And I am certain that my father loved you…as his daughter." Delia tried not to feel envious about something that was neither of their faults. "I'm sure that on a good day—if you were not pouting or acting like a spoiled brat—you probably brought him real pleasure."

Miranda's lips curved up ever so slightly. "We did have fun at times."

"See." Delia pushed a damp strand of reddish hair away from Miranda's eyes. "And the truth is I am probably a bit jealous of you."

"*You're* jealous of *me?*" Miranda looked incredulous.

"I'm sure I would've gladly traded lives with you. I know you think I had all the privileges and advantages of the city, but the truth is I was never really happy there. My family life was…well, shall I say disappointing."

"Really?"

Delia nodded soberly. "But that's not what I want to talk to you about."

Miranda motioned to a pair of rose colored chairs by a bay window. "Do you want to sit?"

"Thank you." Delia took a chair. "What I want to say is that I really wish we could have a truce, Miranda. Deep down I don't have any hard feelings toward you, but you keep treating me like I'm the enemy. And I honestly don't believe I am."

Miranda looked uncertain.

"Ever since we met, I've been wanting to get to know you better. I'd like to hear more about your mother and how she and my father met. How old you were, what you remember…that sort of thing. I'd like to hear about the creation of this ranch and all that went into it. I feel like you're a very important key to my father's story, and I'd love to hear anything you'd care to share with me. I'd love it if we could become friends. I believe our father would have loved that too. In fact, I'm certain of it."

"You honestly mean that?" Miranda's blue eyes grew large and hopeful. "After all I've done to you, you'd still want to be friends with me?"

"Of course I would." Delia smiled. In some ways Miranda reminded her of Julianne at home. The girl could be such a brat sometimes and then totally endearing at other times. Maybe that was the nature of a little sister. "So tell me, how old were you when your mother married my father?"

"My real dad died when I was five," Miranda began. "The mine collapsed on him. A lot of miners died. It was really sad."

"I can imagine." Delia thought about Wyatt working that mine up in Juneau, hoping he was safe from cave-ins and other dangers.

"It was a couple years later, when I was seven, that Ma married your father. He had just finished building this house. And the truth is I thought I'd died and gone to heaven when we first came out here to live. I'd never seen a place so fine—even indoor plumbing! I wanted to live here forever."

"But now you don't?"

Miranda frowned. "I'm not sure what I want anymore. Sometimes I want to go far, far away and sometimes I want to stay put. I get so confused."

"I think that's normal at your age. I've been confused too."

"You don't seem like a person who ever gets confused."

"Trust me, I do." Delia sighed. "And you've been through a lot at your age. How old were you when your mother died? I think you told me, but I forgot."

"Twelve." Miranda shuddered as she pulled her legs up inside her nightgown, tucking her chin over the top of her knees. "It was the worst day of my life. Mother was screaming and screaming—I still have nightmares sometimes. I've never heard anything so horrible."

"Oh, my!"

"The doctor thought he could save the baby...it turned out to be a boy. But they both ended up dying. I can't even go into the room—it's the one on the other end of the hallway—I swear I can still smell the blood in there. Ginger tells me I'm crazy, but I really can smell it, Delia."

Delia grimaced. "I can imagine that."

"I never ever want to have a baby."

"Oh, but it might not be like that for—"

"No, I mean it. I don't want any babies. I even told Marcus that, and he said he didn't care." She frowned. "He acted like he wanted to marry me, but now I know he just wanted the ranch."

"I'm so sorry, Miranda."

"I don't care. I hate him now anyway." All previous warmth was replaced by an icy stare. "You can have him if you want."

"No thank you." Delia firmly shook her head. "I haven't the slightest interest in Marcus. Not in the least."

Miranda narrowed her eyes. "I don't believe you."

"I'll tell you a secret then. I met a man in Pittsburgh. We traveled west on the train together." She sighed. "He stole my heart."

Miranda's brow creased. "Where is he now?"

"Alaska. Mining for gold."

"Will he ever come back for you?"

"I don't know." Delia felt an ache deep inside of her. "I hope so, but the truth is he's a bit of a drifter."

For several minutes they both just sat there in silence. Miranda was the first to speak. "What will I do?"

"What do you mean?"

"I mean where will I go if I don't live here anymore?" Miranda's blue eyes were filling with tears again.

"Why wouldn't you just continue living here? It's such a lovely place to live, and there's plenty of room."

"Because I know the ranch is going to belong to you."

"How can you *know* that?"

"It was just a feeling to start with, but Marcus said the same thing. That's why he didn't want to bring you out here at first—well, and because he didn't think it was safe. But from the moment I met you, I knew it was for real. The ranch was going to belong to you."

"We don't know that for sure. And even if this property has been left to me, I would never throw you out. In fact, I would share the ranch with you. I'm sure that's what our father would want."

"You would really do that?" She used her nightgown sleeve to wipe her tears.

"Yes. You have as much right to this ranch as I do. You've lived here most of your life. And we could share it, Miranda. There's so much still to be done here. Perhaps you could learn to run the house and I could oversee the land. I'm sure we could make it work—and we could make it pay too."

"Do you really think I could run a house? All by myself?"

"Ginger and I would help you get started, but you could learn."

"What if I got married?"

Delia laughed. "Well, then we'd figure something else out. Goodness, there's plenty of land out there—I just saw it today. You and your new husband could build a house or something. Perhaps he'd want to work on the ranch as well."

Miranda looked hopeful as she considered these possibilities. Suddenly she popped out of her chair and threw her arms around Delia's neck.

"I'm sorry I was so horrible to you," she said. "It's just that I was scared. Really, truly frightened. I felt certain you would want to get rid of me—and I didn't know what I'd do or where I'd go."

"I'd never do that." Delia hugged her back. "I want us to be sisters and friends, Miranda. I want us to honor the memory of our father. From here on out, even if I should inherit everything like you keep saying—and remember that is uncertain—but if I should, you need to know that I want to share this ranch with you. It's big enough for both of us."

Miranda let out what sounded like a relieved sigh.

"I just wish we could find that will." Delia stood up, walking around the room. "I've looked all over for the safe. Do you think it could be in here?"

"I've looked throughout this room already," Miranda confessed. "But look around more if you like."

"What about the paperwork you removed from the library?" Delia asked. "Remember on the day after the funeral? Is it possible the will was in there?"

Miranda shook her head. "I already looked through them. They were just some invoices and business papers. And I put them back in the top drawer of his desk."

Delia poked around the room a bit, but it seemed clear no safe was hidden in here. "Do you think it's somewhere outside of the house?" Delia asked as she straightened the painting she'd just peeked behind.

"I wondered about that too. I even looked around the barn and stable, but that just doesn't seem like Dad. I think it has to be in the house."

"If there is a safe." Delia frowned doubtfully.

"I'm sure there is," Miranda said. "I heard Dad talking to Mother about it once—before he went to Denver for a few days."

"And you don't remember where?"

She shook her head. "I wasn't paying attention. Sorry."

"Well, Marcus has taken my letter to the lawyer—the *second* one." Delia smirked at Miranda.

"Sorry about that too. I just felt so desperate."

"I hope that Mr. Stanfield will bring the original out here for us. I'd really like to get this business wrapped up." Delia shrugged. "For all we know the entire ranch could go to you, Miranda."

Miranda tilted her head to one side. "Do you honestly think so?"

"Who knows?" Delia waited a moment, wishing that Miranda would make the same offer to split ownership of the ranch like she'd just done, but Miranda said nothing. Perhaps it hadn't even occurred to her. Or perhaps it never would.

"Well, you should go down and get some dinner," Delia told her as she reached for the door. Before leaving, she pointed inside the disheveled room, where clothes were scattered and dirty food dishes were strewn about. "I don't want to sound bossy, but you should clean up in here. It's not right to turn your parents' room into a pigsty."

Miranda rolled her eyes then nodded. As Delia went to her own room, she was more than a little perplexed. Although she felt she'd made progress with Miranda, she wasn't sure the congeniality went both ways. Perhaps Miranda still resented her—or maybe she still hoped to inherit the entire ranch. And if that was how their father had wanted it, Delia would stand by it. If only they could get their hands on that will!

28

As the sun was going down, Delia sat on the front porch with Hank by her side. Enjoying a cup of tea and the lonely sounds of a hawk circling overhead, she watched as shades of coral, pink, and lavender painted the sky and the mountains. It was almost too beautiful for words. And, not for the first time, she could feel her father's presence…as if this was a pleasure he had enjoyed too. She could imagine him sitting out here at the end of a good day, drinking it in.

Her serenity was cut short as she noticed a wagon and several horses coming down the ranch road at a fairly fast pace. Thinking it might be men from the Leaning R ready to create more trouble, she set down her teacup and was about to dash into the house, when Hank trotted down the steps and down the road to greet them.

Judging by his excited bark, these were not foes. And, as the wagon got closer, she was relieved to see it was their own ranch wagon being driven by Marcus. Although she didn't recognize the three men on horseback riding with him.

Before long they were all stopped out in front of the house and Marcus was introducing the three men to her. "This is Roy and Owen and JT." He explained that they used to work for a big ranch east of Denver. "They just arrived in Colorado City yesterday."

"We met up at the Silver Dollar," Roy told her. He was the biggest of the three and had a look of toughness about him, like he'd lived hard and would eventually pay the price for it. "Your man Marcus here bought us drinks and we became fast friends." Roy laughed loudly.

"We told Marcus we was thinking about doing some mining," Owen added. This guy was rather nondescript, the kind of face a person could easily forget.

"But Marcus said they got labor troubles up at the mine." Roy pushed his dusty dark hat back, giving Delia a slow head to toe look that made her uncomfortable.

"Marcus talked us into coming out to the Double W instead," JT finished with a shy smile. He was the slightest of the men, but something about his demeanor seemed trustworthy. Or maybe it was simply that his shirt looked clean and pressed. Probably new.

Although Delia wasn't sure what to make of these three men, she was relieved that Marcus had found hands willing to come to the ranch. However, she felt disturbed to see that all three of them had firearms on their person. JT's wasn't so alarming, just a holster with a single gun. But Roy and Owen both had a pair of revolvers in their holsters.

"So are you cowboys or gunslingers?" She forced an uneasy smile as she reached for her tea, hoping to appear more nonchalant than she felt.

"Don't mind Miss Delia," Marcus told the men. "She's a city gal. I doubt she's seen much in the way of firearms back East." He turned back to Delia. "I wanted to find men who were handy with guns."

She nodded. "Yes, that makes sense in light of the Leaning R."

Marcus grinned at the men. "You won't be frightened off now will you?"

"We can take care of ourselves." Roy removed a revolver, spinning it around in his fingers like he really was a gunslinger.

"But don't worry, Miss Delia, we're cowboys too," JT reassured her.

Just then, Marcus spotted Cash strolling through the side yard. He whistled through his teeth, waving the young hand over to them. After a quick introduction, he told Cash to show the men around. "Get 'em situated in the bunkhouse and tell Ginger to stir up some grub too. I promised them a good dinner."

"Will do." Cash nodded.

"And tell Silas to see to the wagon and team," Marcus commanded.

After the others left, Marcus joined Delia on the porch. "Didn't expect to take so long in town." He helped himself to the rocking chair beside her. "But it's not easy finding hands that aren't afraid to stand up to the likes of Jerome Roswell and his men."

"Did you get any trouble from them on your trip?"

He cleared his throat, leaning back in the chair. "As a matter of fact, someone did take some pot shots at me on my way into town. They were either bad shots or just trying to scare me."

"Oh, dear." Delia frowned. "I'd hoped it was over."

"Least nobody troubled us on the way back. Maybe they didn't like the looks of those boys' firearms." He chuckled.

"Maybe not." Delia didn't much like them either. "And you delivered my letter to the law office?"

"I sure did." Marcus shook his head dismally. "Couldn't get it there until this morning, but I handed it directly to Mr. Stanfield. And then I decided that since I was already there, I might as well wait for his response."

"Oh, good. Did he send a letter for me with you?"

"Nope. He just said to tell you that there's no will in their law office."

"No will?" Delia's heart sank. "How can that be?"

"Seems that when the break-in occurred, that night when Horace got shot, a bunch of stuff—not just money—was taken. Including your father's will."

"What does that mean? What do I do if there's no will?"

"I asked Stanfield about that. He said that the ranch most likely will be passed down to Winston William's next direct descendent." His pale brows arched slightly. "As far as I can tell, that would be you, Miss Delia. Right?"

"I suppose so. But Mr. Griswold spoke specifically of a will," she persisted. "One that made provision for his workers too. Surely, that would include you. And I'm certain it made provision for Miranda as well. There has to be a will."

Marcus just shrugged. "That may be, but without an actual will, you'll probably never know. At least you know the ranch is yours. That's something, don't you think?"

"I don't think I'll be truly satisfied until I see my father's will. I've looked everywhere for a safe." She picked at a frayed piece of black lace on her mourning gown. Already the garment needed mending. "And I just don't understand why my father's other record books— ledgers, payrolls, and such—weren't in his desk or in the cabinet in the library." She peered curiously at Marcus. "You didn't remove them, did you?"

He opened his eyes wide, revealing a startling shade of blue. "Of course, not, Miss Delia. Perhaps you should ask Miranda. She's the one who's had access to everything in the house. And she's clearly been out of sorts with you. Wouldn't surprise me a bit if she took everything out of Winston's library and hid it somewhere—just to spite you."

Delia stood. "I will ask her again. Thank you."

"And now that we got some extra hands, there's no reason we can't set out for the cattle drive the day after tomorrow. Caleb had suggested delaying it a day—and coming back sooner since we've been so short-handed. It'll be nice not to be in such a fired-up hurry."

"That does sound good." She nodded. "And Caleb has given me permission to go along."

"Good." Marcus grinned. "I must admit this will be a first for me. A lady on a cattle drive. I hope you don't regret it, Miss Delia."

"Caleb already told me of the dirt and deprivations," she said as she headed for the door. "No whining or complaining is allowed."

Marcus chuckled. "Maybe you can cook for us."

"Don't count on it."

"No matter, JT already offered to manage the meals. He's experienced."

"That's a relief. Goodnight, Mr. Vincent."

"If we're going to be driving cows together, I might have to insist you call me Marcus."

"Fine. *Marcus.*" She held her head high, determined to maintain a cordial distance from him as she went into the house. Despite his recent helpfulness, she still wasn't sure about him. And his friendliness did not put her at ease. She had no intention of encouraging more familiarity by inviting him to omit the 'Miss' from her name. Delia remembered something her mother used to quote: "Familiarity breeds contempt." In this case, it could be true.

As Delia went upstairs to her room, she wondered once again if her father's safe might be somewhere on the second floor. Although she was fairly certain it wasn't in the master bedroom, she hadn't checked the other rooms yet. Not wanting to appear intrusive or be caught snooping, she decided to speak to Miranda first.

When Miranda opened the door, Delia was pleasantly surprised to see that she'd straightened the master bedroom some. "Sorry to bother you, Miranda, but I just found out that our father's will was stolen from the law office when Mr. Griswold was killed."

Miranda frowned. "Now what?"

Delia explained her plan to search the second floor. "I know there are more bedrooms up here. Do you mind if I look around?"

"Feel free, but I know it's not in my old room. And I already looked in your room and the other guest room." Miranda's expression grew troubled. "There's only one room I didn't look in…"

"Is that the room where your mother…passed away?"

Miranda just nodded. She stepped into the hallway, pointing to the door at the far end. "You can look if you want, but I'm not going in there."

Delia put a hand on her shoulder. "I understand. And I doubt it will be there anyway."

Delia had never been afraid of ghosts or spirits, but she did feel a strange sense of coolness as she opened the door to the bedroom. Odd considering the heat of the day. Of course, that could be a result of being on the east side of the house. It hadn't had the afternoon sunlight to warm it. Even so, she felt a shiver going through her that had nothing to do with temperature as she went inside.

Attempting to shake it off, she looked around the room. It was smaller than her room and fairly stark, but tidy. The walls were painted a pale watery green. A narrow bed with a metal bed-frame was against the wall with a pastel patchwork quilt on it. A faded yellow gingham curtain had been hung over the window. There was a braided rug on the floor and a few other furnishings. But nothing to suggest it housed a safe.

Still, Delia felt curious about this room…and the sad history contained within its walls. She suspected that little had changed in here since the day Abigail and her baby had died. There was even a wooden cradle opposite the bed. Perhaps this was going to be the baby's nursery. The general feeling in here was deep melancholy…a place of heartbreak and disappointment. No wonder Miranda avoided it.

Delia felt like a trespasser as she poked around, first looking behind a couple of pictures on the wall. One print was of a mother and child and the other of a landscape with a waterfall. Delia scooted the small dresser away from the wall then looked behind and under the bed, beneath the braided rug, and even behind the cradle. Finally she went to the largest piece of furniture. It was a large wardrobe with a mirror on the front. It was heavy and difficult to move, almost as if its feet were fastened to the soft pine floor. She was about to give up when the piece finally budged. Reaching her hand behind it, and hoping not disturb spiders, she ran her fingers over the wall where, to her surprise, she felt an irregularity. Something cold and hard and metal!

Feeling hopeful, she pushed the wardrobe out far enough to ascertain there was indeed a wall safe! Naturally, it was locked, but at least she'd located it. She wondered why her father had felt the need to hide it in a place like this. Was it because of the Leaning R? Or was there someone in the household he didn't trust? Miranda perhaps? Had he had chosen a room that he knew she would never enter? But why?

She pushed the wardrobe back into place and then, deciding she would keep this to herself, exited the room. To her relief Miranda was nowhere in sight and her door was closed. Delia slipped to her room, trying to decide how to best handle this.

By morning, she had made up her mind. She would get someone to drive her to town and enlist the help of Mr. Stanfield. Because of the extra hands Marcus had brought home last night, she didn't feel guilty for asking Caleb to allow Cash to drive her. And the sixteen-year-old was happy to be chosen. She told him she wanted to leave before breakfast, but that Ginger would give them something to eat on their way. That way they could get to town as soon as the law office opened.

To her relief, Mr. Stanfield was just arriving when they got there and he had no appointments until the afternoon. He called the locksmith, and it was soon agreed that they would all return to the Double W together. "If all goes well, and the copy of the will is in the safe as you hope, we should have the reading of the will read finished before one," he assured her. "I know I will be glad to have this business behind me."

As soon as they got to the house, Delia hurried upstairs to explain to Miranda about the safe. "I would've told you last night," she said, "but it looked as if you had gone to bed. And then I left early this morning before you were up."

It took the locksmith about thirty minutes to get into the safe. Sure enough, the will and few other legal documents were inside it. But there was no cash, no gold, nothing of monetary value.

Shortly before noon everyone, except for the three new ranch hands who Delia presumed were outside working, was assembled in the library for the reading of the will. Mr. Stanfield slowly read what sounded like a typical beginning of a last will and testament. According to the date, it had been created less than two years ago. It didn't take long to discover that the ranch in its entirety had been left to Delia. However, there was a provision in there for Miranda as well. It seemed that Delia, if she accepted responsibility for the ranch, was to act as Miranda's guardian until Miranda was eighteen. At that age, Miranda's prepaid college tuition, at the same university that Delia had attended, would be available to her.

There was also provision for Caleb and Ginger to remain on the ranch for the remainder of their days, even if they were too old to work. And some other provisions and incentives, linked to the success of the ranch, had been put in place for other employees as well. It was obvious that Winston Williams believed in the ranch and wanted to motivate his workers to see his vision too.

"'I regret that my cash holdings have diminished during the past few years,'" Mr. Stanfield continued reading the last portion of the will. "'Everything has been invested back into the ranch and the farm in the hopes that it is about to become completely self-supportive and eventually profitable. In the event that I meet my demise, it is my hope that my daughter Delia Williams aka Blackstone will continue in the work that I have begun. And in the likely event that the Double W Ranch does begin to make a profit, it is my hope that my daughter will act as a fair and generous trustee to her stepsister Miranda Williams, at least until the time that Miranda comes of age, finishes college, or marries.'"

Mr. Stanfield finished reading the last details of the will, mostly information about the law firm and Colorado law, but all Delia could think about was that she'd been put in charge of Miranda. Was she really up to the task? What if Miranda resented having her stepsister as a trustee? It sounded like the makings of a mess.

"Any questions?" Mr. Stanfield was saying.

"Are you saying there is no money?" Miranda demanded. "Nothing?"

"Other than what's in the Double W bank account, for the daily running of the ranch, and part of the ranch holding, that's correct. There is no money."

"I thought you knew that," Delia told Miranda. "It's what you told me."

"It's what Dad used to say, but I never thought he was serious."

"Everything has been invested in the land," Mr. Stanfield said.

"And you will be provided for during your time at the university," Delia pointed out. "And after that I'll—"

"What if I don't want to go to the university?" Miranda exclaimed. "How can I be forced to do something I don't want? What sort of women go to college anyway?"

"According to this document, it seems that your stepsister Delia attended the same university." Mr. Stanfield glanced uncomfortably at Delia.

"That's right," Delia said calmly. "It's a highly respected school, and I think it would be a wonderful opportunity for you, Miranda."

"Maybe it was wonderful for someone like you. Perhaps you don't care if you turn into an old maid, Delia. Everyone knows that overly educated women turn into spinsters. No man wants to marry—"

"I hardly think that Delia is destined to be a spinster," Marcus said sharply. "You would do well to follow your stepsister's fine example, Miranda."

"So that's it." Miranda stood with clenched fists and tears glistening in her eyes. "I'm to be forced out of my home, to go to some horrible old school, without a choice—"

"No one will force you to do anything," Delia firmly assured her. "You will be welcome to stay here as long as you—"

"I do not *want* to stay here!" Miranda yelled as she rushed from the room.

"I apologize for Miranda's outburst," Delia told Mr. Stanfield. "Thank you for reading the will. I assume you will take it back to your office to keep on file?"

He assured her that it would be placed in the bank safe. "We're currently utilizing their security until our office is restored." And then, despite Delia's invitation for Mr. Stanfield to join them for dinner, he thanked her, explaining his need to return to town. She didn't blame him considering Miranda's behavior.

As the rest of them sat down to dinner, the general mood was light. Caleb and Ginger seemed to greatly appreciate being remembered in the will. But Delia felt increasingly uneasy. Finally, unable to stand it any longer, she asked Ginger to help her prepare a tray to take up to Miranda. And, carrying it up herself, Delia tapped gently on her door, letting herself in. Miranda was face-down on the bed.

"I know you're upset," Delia said quietly as she carried the tray to the table by the window. "And I do understand. But you need to know that what I told you before is still true. Although the ranch is legally mine, I believe it belongs to *both* of us, Miranda. I want you to stay on here for as long as you like. You and I will share it."

Miranda sat up, looking at Delia with moist eyes. "Do you really truly mean that?"

"Of course, I do. You have my word. This ranch is your home as much as it is mine. No one will ever force you off of it. Whether you go to college or not is your choice. But I will continue to encourage you to consider it. I'm very thankful that I had more school-ing. I know our father had great respect for learning. I'm sure he believed he could give you no greater gift than a formal education." She smiled hopefully.

"That might be true for you. But I do not intend to go to col-lege."

Delia placed her hand on Miranda's shoulder. "That is your choice." She nodded to the tray. "Now, please, eat. You're starting to worry me with your temperamental dietary habits."

Miranda's blue eyes lit up slightly. "So you really do care about me?"

"You know that I do." Delia considered pointing out that she was Miranda's guardian now—at least until the willful girl turned eighteen—but decided not to push things. "After all, you're my sis-ter."

"Thank you." Miranda sniffed loudly. "I suppose I need a sister."

But as Delia left, she knew that Miranda was not an "easy" sister, if there were such a thing. Perhaps she'd calm down and see rea-son eventually. Maybe she'd even reconsider going to the university. From what Delia could see, Miranda had a good sharp mind. But, like Marcus and Ginger had pointed out, she was rather spoiled. Delia could only hope that she'd grow out of it in time.

29

By the morning of the cattle drive, Miranda seemed to have turned a corner. She'd shown up at every meal yesterday. And she'd been politely conversing with Delia and the others. She'd even offered to help Ginger and Delia with the supper dishes last night. It actually gave Delia a great deal of hope. As she put on her father's cowboy hat, the one she'd found hanging on a hook in his library, she felt it was going to be a good day, a good cattle drive.

"Is that Dad's hat?" Miranda asked as she trailed Delia out of the house.

"It is." Delia handed Miranda her saddlebag as she tied the stampede strings beneath her chin. "It's much better than my own hats. And this light tan color will be good for keeping the sun from getting too hot."

"I must say that I think you are very foolish for doing this silly cattle drive." Miranda handed her back the saddlebag as they walked toward the corral. "A lady does not go on a trek like this with a bunch of men."

"We are short-handed," Delia reminded her, pausing to call out to Hank, who was busy herding a goose.

"But Marcus got those three men from town to help. Why do they need you too?"

"He got those men so that we wouldn't have to leave the ranch shorthanded. Or unprotected. Caleb told me it takes at least five hands to get the cattle safely to high country—and that only leaves three hands to keep the farm chores going while we're gone." Delia hoisted her loaded saddlebag behind the saddle on Lady, leaning down to secure it and then tightening the saddle cinch beneath the horse.

"You honestly think you can be of help driving cows?" Miranda asked as Delia checked the bridle. "That they would even notice if you were not there?"

"Caleb explained to me how everyone has a position, how important it is to keep the cattle boxed-in so to speak." Delia glanced over to where Cash and Silas were talking to Caleb by the stable. None of them looked too happy. "I wonder what's troubling them."

"I can tell you," Miranda said dryly. "They're furious because they don't get to go."

"What do you mean? Of course, they're going."

"No, they're not. Marcus said they have to stay behind to work the farm."

"But why—"

"I'll tell you why." Marcus came up from behind her, making her jump. "Caleb, Cash, and Silas are familiar with working the farm. These new guys haven't had time to figure it all out. Besides that the new hands are experienced *cowboys*. Plus they're armed. They can help keep us safer out on the open range."

"But Cash was so looking forward to driving cattle with us." Delia frowned to imagine the sixteen-year-old's disappointment.

"He's a kid. He can come next year."

"But doesn't Caleb always go on the drive?" Delia demanded. "Why would—"

"Caleb's getting old. Look, I already gotta take a city gal along.

You want to stick me with an old man and a young'un too? We're driving cows, Miss Delia, not going out for a picnic."

"Well, I—"

"And we're burning daylight." Marcus yelled to the hands that were just getting into their saddles, "Let's get moving—now!" He glanced back at Delia. "If you've changed your mind, just say so now. I figured you might chicken out."

Delia straightened her spine, staring him directly in the eyes. "I am *not* afraid."

"Then let's move it." He swung up into his saddle and, without another word, urged his horse to a gallop, heading toward the pasture where the herd was gathered and ready to go.

Delia glanced over to where the other hands were mounting their own horses. They also had a couple of packhorses, loaded with supplies. The group set out to follow Marcus. Delia glanced nervously over her shoulder, realizing that it wasn't too late to back out. She could easily call out to Cash, invite him to take her place, which he would gladly do. Then she could remain behind to help with the farm chores as usual. Really, what difference would it make?

Except that the men might perceive her as scared—the weak woman—unfit to run the Double W. If she wanted to win their respect and prove that she was ready to take her father's place and run this ranch like it was meant to be, she needed to do this, and she needed to do it right. With confidence and enthusiasm and skill and grace. Besides, she reminded herself, it would be an adventure.

As she got into the saddle, she remembered Wyatt's talk of adventure. A drifter, who hungered for excitement—he wouldn't be the least bit intimidated by something like this. She smiled to think of what he'd say when he got her letter describing her adventures of driving cattle with a bunch of rough cowboys. She'd even brought writing materials along, just in case she ever had a free moment to write to him. Perhaps Wyatt would begin to see her in a different light too. Or maybe she was just delusional, imagining this relationship with a man she barely knew. Perhaps her short stint with Wyatt had been just that—*a short stint.*

"Well, you be careful out there," Miranda called out her warning. "Don't go getting yourself hurt or eaten by a wild animal. There's cougars, wolves, bears, rattlesnakes—all sorts of dangers out there!"

"I'll be fine. You be careful too," Delia called back. "Don't forget we're still on the lookout for the Leaning R. Stay close to home. Be watchful."

Delia waved as she nudged Lady with her knees, calling out for Hank to keep pace with her. She felt glad for the dog's loyal companionship as he trotted alongside. Yesterday, Caleb had assured her that the dog was up for the task, telling her how Hank had always ridden with her father. But she felt even more grateful for the dog as she followed the new hands over to where the cattle were waiting on what was quickly becoming an overly grazed section of pasture. It wasn't that she didn't trust these men exactly. More that she didn't know them.

As she went up to the front of the herd, waiting while Owen and JT started to roll back the barbed wire fencing where they would let the steers out, she wondered if she was acting responsibly. What if she was wrong to go on this drive? Was she just trying to prove something? Was her decision more about pride than prudence? What if her rightful place really was back on the ranch? Helping with Miranda and the daily chores?

"Ready to go?" Marcus called out to Delia.

"Ready when you are," she called back, although she felt anything but.

"You'll ride up front. You'll take the right side. I'll take the left. You won't be eating so much dust that way." He grinned. "At least to start with."

She nodded, reining her horse to the right and trying to remember the tips that Caleb had given her yesterday. "Come on, Hank," she called. "Let's go round up some cows." Excited at the task ahead,

Hank gave out some happy yips and within minutes they were off. With the other drivers alongside and in back, it wasn't long until the whole herd, like one surprisingly graceful—albeit noisy—body of water was moving. It was truly a sight to be seen, and Delia hoped that she'd be able to describe it appropriately for Wyatt. Although she suspected, based on what stories he'd shared, he'd already seen a cattle drive for himself. Maybe even lots of times.

As the herd continued moving, she still felt a little uneasy. Was she foolish to participate in the cattle drive? She wondered how her father would've advised her. As they started up the hill, the cattle mooing and lowing as if they were unsure or perhaps simply eager, she said a quick silent prayer, asking God to lead her.

Focusing on her horse and the cattle, keeping an eye out for Hank, who clearly knew what he was doing, she started to see this cattle drive in a whole new light. It was actually rather fun. And somewhat amazing to think that just the five of them, and a dog, were able to control this herd of steers.

Riding at the front of the herd, with the sun beating down on her father's hat, the solid feel of dependable horse beneath her, and a good dog by her side, it all somehow felt just right. If she truly intended to be a rancher—like her father had hoped—doing this cattle drive wouldn't be too much for her. As she approached the rise, keeping her position like Marcus had instructed, she thought about her father—realizing that, in his own way, he had been preparing her for this for years, and she'd never even realized it.

As the day progressed, Delia discovered that driving a herd was a rather slow and tedious process. The goal, Caleb had told her, wasn't to run the cattle, especially since some were recently weaned calves, but simply to move them. "Steady and sure," he had told her. And with everyone doing their part, and with a good horse that knew what to do, it gave a person time to think. More and more, Delia's thoughts were with her father—understanding why he loved this kind of life and marveling at the way he had prepared her for it. It was as if he'd known.

For starters, her father had made certain that his own mother, a dear woman Delia had known as Great Aunt Adelaide, was an integral part of her life. The old woman had steadily imparted wisdom and common sense and confidence into Delia—from a very early age. She had also seen to it that Delia had riding lessons—something that Delia's mother had never fully supported. At least not until she learned that women from wealthy families often rode horses—although they rode sidesaddle. And then Delia's father had ensured that she get an education too. It suddenly felt clear—he had done all this to help equip her for the life that she now felt she was destined to lead. Running this ranch. Somehow he had known.

The only thing wrong with this picture—well, besides the fact that her father was missing—was she couldn't quite see where Wyatt would fit into all this. He had made it clear to her from the beginning that he was a drifter, always looking for the next exciting opportunity, in search of adventure. And even if he got the drifting part of him satisfied, which might never happen, he still had his own ranch in far off Oregon. It seemed highly likely he would have emotional ties to the place his parents had settled when he was just a boy. Surely, if he decided to grow roots, he would want to grow them out there. It was foolhardy to imagine he would change…for her. Would she be willing to give this all up for him? She didn't feel ready to answer that question. Besides, no one was asking her!

At the end of the first day, which was long and hot and exhausting, Delia did not feel as if she'd disappointed anyone. And despite being coated with dust and more tired than she'd ever been in her life, she wasn't willing to give up. In fact, she felt rather pleased with herself for keeping up with the men. And as she crouched down in front of the mountain stream to wash up before dinner, she thought this was a lifestyle she might learn to enjoy. Well, aside from being saddle sore. That would take some getting used to.

She laughed as Hank plunged into the stream, lapping up the water as it swirled around him. "That's the right idea," she told him. "If it were just you and me, I'd strip down and join you."

"You look like you're holding up all right," Marcus told Delia as they were taking turns filling their plates with the grub JT had prepared.

"I'm doing just fine, thank you." She went over to sit on a nearby log, gingerly sitting down to eat.

"We decided that since you're a lady, we won't expect you to keep watch on the herd tonight. We'll split it up between the four of us."

"But I'm willing to—"

"It's the way we're doing it," he said sharply. "You don't carry a firearm and even if we loaned you one of ours, I'll bet you don't know how to shoot."

"I could learn."

"Not out here, you can't. And if a wild animal tries to get a calf in the middle of the night, you'd probably end up shooting yourself in the foot. That wouldn't help much."

She just nodded. "I suppose you're right. Maybe by next year's cattle drive, I will have some shooting skills."

The men had a good laugh over this and, trying not to show her irritation, she finished her food then offered to wash up the dishes for everyone. Since no one protested, she gathered up all the enamelware dishes and pans and made her way back to the creek. As she scrubbed the greasy dishes, she decided that perhaps this would be her contribution. Instead of doing a night watch on the herd, she would make herself the cleanup crew. Surely they would appreciate that.

Delia had expected to be uncomfortable on her first night sleeping out in the open air. But Caleb had given her a pocketknife yesterday, explaining how to cut pine boughs to create a mattress of sorts. On this she laid a thick quilt she'd found in a closet and, being that she was quite tired, she discovered it wasn't really too bad as she pulled the woolen blanket up over her clothes. With Hank snuggled up right beside her, she felt relatively safe—and with the sound of the fire crackling nearby and the voices of the men swapping unbelievably tall tales, she stared up into the bright stars overhead and started to relax. It wasn't long before she felt herself drifting to sleep.

The second day was a repeat of the first. Delia and Hank stayed in position near the front of the herd on the right side, keeping the cattle moving along the path that Marcus, on the opposite side, seemed to be directing. But, really, she decided later in the day, it was almost as if the cows knew where they were going. As if they were looking forward to reaching the higher, cooler pastures where they would graze for the next couple of months. Even Hank seemed to know the way.

Besides being hot and dusty and dirty—and feeling as if the saddle had turned itself into a piece of hardened granite—it was not that difficult. Still she was relieved when the day came to an end and even more relieved when Marcus announced that the next day they would reach their destination by midday and that everyone would get a nice long rest.

By the third day, the idea that they wouldn't be riding all day long was very welcome to Delia. Unless she was imagining it, even Hank was getting tired. So much so that she grew worried he might get trampled by a cow, so she picked him up and carried him on horseback with her for the last hour of driving. "I'm tired too," she told him as she used her horse to push a wayward cow back into the herd.

It was early afternoon when they arrived up on top of the high meadow. The cattle seemed to know just what to do, casually spreading out into the wide, grassy area. It was surprisingly satisfying to see the herd on the open range. So peaceful after the long dusty drive. She could imagine her father standing up here, watching this sight with a sense of fulfillment.

"What keeps the cattle from wandering off after we leave?" she asked Marcus as they started making camp. "And what about cougars and bears?"

"We always leave a man to guard the herd," he told her. "Owen will take the first shift. Then JT will come spell him in a couple weeks. And so on."

"It's not a bad life," JT said as he set the coffee pot on the fire. "Lonely, but we're used to it."

"Always glad to see women folk when we get back," Owen said in a way that made her uncomfortable. Already she was well aware of their enjoyment of off-color jokes which were usually initiated by Roy. A part of her wanted to challenge them on this, and at the same time, she didn't want to stir anything up. But next year, she told herself, she would pick her cowboys to make this ride. That is, if she was going up with them. Based on the way her backside felt, she wasn't too sure.

While JT was getting dinner started, Marcus and the others announced they were going to bathe in the creek. "You're welcome to join us," Roy said to Delia with a smirk.

"Thank you, but I will wait until I get home to bathe." Delia attempted to give him a very chilly look, longing to lecture him on respect, but knowing it probably wouldn't help.

"I never thought a lady could make a ride like this," JT said after the others left. "I gotta hand it to you, Miss Delia, you are a tough little lady."

"Thank you," she told him. "I can see that it's not an easy trip and I'll admit that I'm wearier than I can ever remember being. But I'm glad I made it. It's beautiful up here, and it's an experience I'll always remember. Although I am looking forward to getting home."

"Marcus said since we got this afternoon to rest up some, he wants to press home in two days instead of three. You think you can take that—two long days in the saddle?"

"That sounds good to me. I figured we would make better time going down without the cattle to drive. I'd be happy to get home a day sooner."

After the men returned from their bathing looking fresher and cleaner, Delia felt a little jealous. Still, she knew she wasn't comfortable bathing in the creek. Not with these fellows anywhere nearby. Instead, she would settle for washing up like she'd done every night. She considered taking Hank along with her, but he looked so relaxed lying in the shade that she went by herself. She was just finishing when she heard something behind her. Worried that it might be a bear or cougar, she stood up quickly, preparing to scream.

"Oh, it's just you," she said with relief as Marcus approached her. "I thought you were a wild animal."

"Just making sure you're all right," he said as he came closer. "We've seen sign of both cougar and bear up here. You can't be too careful."

"Thank you for telling me." She dried her hands and face on her linen towel, which was now the color of trail dirt. Her creek-side cleanup made her feel a bit better, but she was certain her face was still smudged and her neck felt gritty. Beneath the felt hat, her hair was so coated with dust that it was no longer chestnut, but more like the color of mud. Not that she particularly cared about her appearance.

After all, wasn't this supposed to be "a cattle drive and not a picnic"? She considered reminding Marcus of his own words when she noticed that he was all cleaned up. His wheat colored hair was still damp from his recent bath in the creek, and he'd even put on a fresh shirt and taken the time to shave. She hadn't expected that cowboys on a cattle drive would go to such effort—and it rather irked her.

"I must say you've done a good job," Marcus said with a broad smile. "Didn't know you had it in you, Miss Delia. But then you are quite a woman."

She smiled stiffly. "Thank you." Stepping past him, she was eager to get back camp and away from him. But he stopped her by placing a hand on her forearm.

"I wanted to speak to you, Miss Delia. Alone, if you don't mind."

She stopped and looked directly at him. "What is it?"

"Well, as I was saying, you are a fine woman. I could see that from the moment I met you that you were someone—"

"You mean that day at the Elk Horn Hotel? Right after my father was shot? When you tried to put me back on the train headed east? Without even seeing the Double W?" she challenged. "That day when you told me your opinion of an educated woman? That I was about as useful as a five-legged mule or a gold ring in a pig's snout, I believe was how you so delicately put it."

"Aw, Miss Delia, I'm sorry. I was just being ornery. I was still upset over what happened to your dad. Everything was sort of mixed up just then."

She studied him closely and, although a part of her wished he was telling the truth, wanted him to be on the up and up—just for the sake of the ranch—she seriously doubted it. Still, she didn't want lay all her cards on the table, not with two long days of trail riding ahead of them. "I can understand that," she said more gently. "We were all upset just then. You and Miranda and myself. I'm sure we said and did things we didn't really mean." She forced a smile. "No hard feelings."

"Glad to hear it." He grinned back at her, flashing those alarmingly blue eyes as if he thought he could woo her with his looks. Perhaps this tactic had worked on other women. Miranda had certainly bought into it.

Feeling more than a little uncomfortable, Delia started heading back toward camp again. "I've really enjoyed the cattle drive," she said evenly as she walked. "I can see why my father employed you, Mr. Vincent—"

"Please." He touched her arm again. "Call me Marcus."

"Yes…Marcus." She walked a bit faster. "You're very good at

driving cattle. I'm sure my father appreciated your skills." She turned to give him what she hoped looked like a polite but impersonal smile—the way a boss might do. "I appreciate your skills too. I'm sure that good cattlemen aren't that easy to find." Well, she wasn't that sure of this, but it sounded good, and it was getting her closer to camp.

"Delia." Marcus suddenly reached for her hand, stopping her just outside of the camp. "Please, I want to talk to you."

She looked him straight in the eyes with the distinct feeling that this man was probably just as dangerous as a bear or a cougar—perhaps even more so! Somehow she knew, deep inside of her being, that she needed to deal with him carefully...cordially...but firmly.

"Please, Marcus," she said evenly. "You are making me *most* uncomfortable. You know that I'm a lady. I was educated in the city and trained in the manners and etiquette of civilized society. People who respect decorum and restraint. I am not accustomed to being rough-handled like this." She glared down at his hand grasping hers.

To her relief, he removed his hand with a startled expression. "I beg your pardon, Miss Delia. Being out here like this, I nearly forgot you were a lady."

"If the conversation you wish to have with me is *not* relevant to work, I suggest you wait until we're back at the ranch to have it."

"Because it wouldn't be proper out here?" He sounded genuinely apologetic.

"Precisely." She looked him squarely in the eyes. "You do understand my meaning, don't you?"

He nodded eagerly. "Yes. I didn't consider propriety. I'm sorry, Miss Delia. I will wait until a better time and place. Please, forgive me."

"Thank you," she said crisply and then, without giving him another look, she hurried back to camp. She had no doubt as to Marcus's intentions. He believed he could win her over. He planned to propose marriage. And as soon as she walked down the aisle and vowed to honor and obey, Marcus would take over the Double W Ranch—and her life. But if this man thought he could charm his way into her heart, he had another think coming.

30

To Wyatt's relief both the steamship trip to California and the subsequent train ride to Colorado proceeded without incident. It had been a bit unnerving to travel with so much money on his person and not something he would recommend in the West, where outlaws and con men were still too common, but it seemed necessary under the circumstances. The circumstances being that he was in a hurry to get to Delia.

He'd been glad to exchange his gold for cash in San Francisco. The assayer, recommended to him by Jake, had been very fair. With a much lighter knapsack, and his cash secured in a money belt, he'd continued on his way. Not bothering to change from his rough mining clothes, he enjoyed playing the part of the poor drifter. And, after all, wasn't that who he truly was? As a result, no one suspected he had a small fortune on him.

It wasn't until he arrived in Colorado City on the midday train that he began to breathe a little easier. As he walked down the street of the bustling town, he realized that, although it felt like a year, it'd only been one month since he'd last seen Delia. They'd parted ways in Denver and she'd come here on her own. It was almost as if he could feel her presence in this place, could imagine her walking down this very street. Or maybe he was just that eager to see her.

With no time to waste, he purchased a new set of clothes. Nothing fancy, but because he'd sold most of his belongings in Juneau, it was time to replenish his wardrobe with clothing that looked appropriate to ranch life. Next he visited the bathhouse and then he got a haircut and a shave. Feeling almost like a new man, he headed down to the livery stable where he purchased himself a good horse and slightly used saddle.

Before leaving town, he stopped by the blacksmith to check on a loose horseshoe then, following the smithy's directions, Wyatt headed down the road toward the Double W Ranch. It was late in the day and looked like a summer thunderstorm was about to kick up, but according to the blacksmith, he should reach the ranch before sundown and if he was lucky, before the downpour as well.

He thought he was familiar with Colorado country, but he'd never been in this part before and it was surprisingly beautiful. Even with the dark clouds roiling around the rugged mountaintops, it was still spectacular. But not wanting to reunite with Delia looking like a drowned rat, he nudged his horse into a gallop.

He'd only received the one letter from Delia while in Alaska, but he suspected that was the result of the slow-moving mail. He hoped that she'd received the letter he'd written back to her, announcing his plan to return to Colorado as quickly as possible, but he wouldn't be surprised if he'd beaten it there. He'd written a second letter shortly before leaving Juneau—simply because he wanted to feel connected to her. And then another short note from San Francisco, in the hopes it would get here before him.

For some reason time seemed of the essence. As if he had to get there fast—if he was too late, she might be gone. That was his worst fear—that he would miss her completely. And then he'd be unable to locate her again. He'd even dreamt that he was a lifelong drifter last night, searching the whole world over for the woman he loved and never finding her.

Instead of dwelling on the frustrating dream, he remembered the contents of her letter. He'd read it so many times that the paper had grown thin and the ink had faded. After the shocking death of her father and the discovery of a sister, Delia had sounded upset and uncertain about a lot of things. In fact, she had seemed rather lost and alone—and in need. As dismayed as he was over her difficult situation, he had liked feeling that she needed him. For weeks he'd imagined himself showing up and becoming her hero.

But as the clouds grew darker, his thoughts seemed to follow suit. What if Delia wasn't even there? What if he'd sacrificed everything and come all this way, to find out she'd already departed? And if she'd left, where would she go? He knew that she felt unwelcome with her family in Pittsburgh. But it was possible she'd gone back East. Although he hoped and prayed she hadn't.

After he'd gone what seemed about the right distance, he began to look for signs of the Double W Ranch. He didn't know what to expect exactly. For all he knew it would be an undeveloped parcel of land with no road and a lean-to shanty on it. Or perhaps it would be similar to his ranch—somewhat developed with a small rustic cabin in need of work. And, if so, he was ready to work. He was, he felt, ready for anything. As long as it involved Delia.

This region had some similarities to where his parents had settled in Oregon, and yet it was different too. The mountains here seemed to go on forever in a rough and rugged way. And the sky seemed bigger too—if that was possible. As he came to a grassy meadow that was surprisingly green, especially compared with some of the dryer spreads he'd just passed, he realized that this place must have more access to water. He felt surprised to see that this section was fenced and the meadow had a small flock of sheep on it. Based on what he'd seen on his way out here, he'd assumed this was cattle country. Cows and sheep didn't usually mix.

Suddenly he noticed a ranch gate made of pine timbers. The words DOUBLE W RANCH were painted across the top beam, and he knew he was there. Turning onto the road and riding past the peacefully grazing sheep, Wyatt felt perplexed. Hadn't Delia described her dad as a cattle rancher? And yet he had sheep. To add to his confusion, there were what appeared to be dairy cattle grazing on the other side of the road. Both cows and sheep on the same ranch?

Eager to see Delia, he considered spurring his horse into a full run but decided against it. Better to take it easy. Especially since those dark clouds seemed to be holding back. Besides, he reminded himself, he needed a moment to think and get his bearings. His original plan, ever since he decided to return to her, had been to proclaim his undying love and immediately propose marriage. He'd imagined himself down on one knee as he asked for her hand. But now he wasn't so sure. Especially since they'd spent such a short amount of time together. What if he overwhelmed her?

Wyatt knew that Delia was a sensible woman. Sensible bordering on cautious. He remembered how frightened she'd been of him at first. But then she'd assumed he was a detective. He chuckled to remember it. But besides that, Delia was a college-educated woman, and she just didn't strike him as the impulsive type. He certainly didn't want to scare her off by being too pushy and eager.

Best to go easy and give her time to get to know him all over again. And, besides, what if she wasn't even there? For all Wyatt knew she could've sold her father's ranch to the highest bidder, perhaps the neighbor who'd been hankering for the water rights all along, and headed back East. But somehow he didn't think so. And the more he saw of this place, the more confident he felt. The property was stunning—and incredibly well maintained too. Surely Delia would've wanted to remain here. Even if the house turned out to be a little rustic, he had the funds to improve it. They would do it together.

As he rounded the corner of the road leading into the ranch, he saw something white up ahead. Blinking to see better, he was surprised to see it was a house. A great big white house with a steep red roof and several dormers in it. As he continued toward the building, he noticed the creek meandering through the green meadow next to him, and the pond that it flowed into. No wonder the neighbors were jealous!

Behind the house, the barn and outbuildings were substantial. The fences looked solid and the whole place had an air of respectability to it. Delia's father hadn't been lazy. He'd also invested a lot of money into this place. It was slightly overwhelming. Especially considering that Wyatt had expected to find her struggling to get by—needing him. Based on what he was seeing, Delia was set up just fine.

As Wyatt got closer to the house, he saw her—standing outside in front of the house in her pale green gown, she had her back to him. Suddenly he didn't know if he could continue concealing his eagerness. He no longer wanted to go easy like he'd intended. He was glad she had her back to him, seemingly unaware that she was being watched. He could hardly take his eyes of that pale green dress, the one that made her emerald eyes glow richly. She had on a wide brimmed hat and appeared to be picking roses from a hedge that grew alongside the path that led up to the house. If he was an artist, he would want to paint a picture of this scene. Delia in her green dress and sun hat, a basket over her arm overflowing with red roses. It was heavenly.

Thinking it would be fun to sneak up on her, he stopped his horse out on the road and, slipping out of the saddle he slowly made his way toward her. It felt like stalking a buck in the woods. Except that he had to control himself from breaking out into delighted laughter at how completely oblivious she was. Finally, from about twenty feet away, he sprinted forward, grabbing her from behind, he scooped her into his arms like a child. "Delia!" he said happily, but just as quickly he realized it was a mistake. The redheaded woman let out a startled scream and her roses went flying.

He set her back down in the ground in horror. "I'm so sorry, miss," he stammered. "So very sorry. I thought you were someone else. Please, forgive me."

Recovering herself, she straightened her gown—which looked identical to Delia's gown—and studied him with what seemed curiosity—not fear. "Who are you?" she asked with wide blue eyes.

"I'm Wyatt Davis. I'm a—a friend of Miss Delia Williams. I understood that she lives here. I mistook you as her."

"Yes. Delia is my older sister. I am *Miranda* Williams." She removed her garden glove and stuck out a hand. "I'm most pleased to meet you, Mr. Davis."

"You can't imagine how embarrassed I am." Wyatt briefly grasped her hand then kneeled down to gather the tumbled blooms. "I was convinced you were Delia. Unless I'm mistaken, Delia has a dress very much like that."

"That's because this *is* her dress," Miranda said coyly. "But you won't tell her I borrowed it now, will you?"

"If you don't tell that I plowed you over thinking you were Delia." He chuckled nervously as he laid the roses back in her basket, pointing to the garden-sheers still in her other hand. "I'm lucky you didn't slay me with those."

She giggled. "I considered it. Until I saw your face. That's when I decided that a man as handsome as you couldn't possibly be a murderer. Besides you used my sister's name, so I figured you must know her."

He smiled nervously, noticing that her hair was nearly the same shade of red as Maryanne's back in Oregon. Perhaps there was something about women with hair that color—similar to a polished copper kettle—something that a savvy man should know to steer clear of. He stepped back cautiously. "So...where is Delia?"

"Delia is gone...." Miranda spoke in a furtive tone, turning as if she were about to go up onto the big porch that wrapped around the house.

"Gone?" Although uninvited, Wyatt followed her. "Where is she?"

"I hate to admit it, but she is off doing something that no self-respecting lady should be caught doing."

"Excuse me?" Wyatt was shocked.

"I'm sorry." Miranda turned to face him with a warm smile. "Would you like to come inside? I can explain the whole thing to you."

In the same instant they both looked toward the mountains as a flash of lightning lit up the dark clouds, followed by an ear-splitting crack of lightning.

"You better get up here," Miranda called. "Maybe you're hungry. We've already had dinner, but I'm sure Ginger could fix you a plate."

"If it's no trouble." Wyatt followed her up the steps, removing his hat and trying to make sense of what she'd just told him. He couldn't imagine Delia doing anything disrespectful.

Another lightning bolt sliced through the sky, followed by a loud boom, and Miranda hurried to open the front door. "Come in," she called.

"Let me attend to my horse," Wyatt said suddenly. "The storm might startle him."

Miranda pointed him toward the corral, and he hurried over to the horse, calming him with his voice as he walked him over to where several other horses were waiting. By the time he'd removed the saddle, setting it under cover in the nearby stable and marveling at what an impressive ranch this place was turning out to be, it was just starting to rain. Grabbing up his knapsack, he sprinted to the house and, seeing the front door still open, went inside.

Miranda was waiting for him with her basket of roses still over her arm. Although she made an attractive picture there, she was a dim shadow compared to Delia. Not that he wanted to compare the two sisters.

"I assume that if you came to see my sister, you will be staying with us for a spell?"

"Well, I don't know." Wyatt was dumbfounded as he closed the front door.

"Don't concern yourself." She smiled in a coquettish way. "Ginger is here too. She cooks and cleans. And some of the ranch hands are around too. It's not as if we're alone."

"I'd be perfectly happy in the bunk house—"

"Nonsense. Delia would want you to be our guest, Mr. Davis." She pointed toward the stairs. "There is an available guest room—the third door to your right. Feel free to make yourself comfortable while I go see about getting you some supper."

Unsure of what to do, but not wanting to leave without seeing Delia and not eager to return to town in the rainstorm, he accepted her offer by heading up to the guestroom. And, after a quick clean up, he hurried back downstairs. His goal was to find out exactly what was happening with Delia—and why Miranda had made such a strange comment about her sister.

Miranda met him in a comfortable looking room where an elk head trophy was mounted above a big stone fireplace. "Welcome to the Double W," she said graciously. "You supper is right this way, sir."

Wyatt followed her into a large dining room where a formal looking place setting—and a tempting looking meal—were already waiting at the head of the table. "You didn't need to go to so much trouble," he said uneasily.

"I wanted to," she told him as she set a blue and white china vase in the center of the table. "If you don't mind, I'll just arrange these roses while you eat. I'd like to hear more about you and why you are here."

"And I'd like to hear more about where Delia is," he said as he placed the linen napkin in his lap, taking a moment to bow his head before he picked up a fork. "This looks good. Thank you."

"Ginger's cooking skills are improving." Miranda smiled as she clipped a rose stem, dropping it into the vase. "So are you the man Delia met on the train?"

"Did she mention me?"

"She spoke of a man who was headed for Alaska."

He nodded as he chewed a piece of roast. "That would be me."

"Why are you not in Alaska?"

"Because I am here." He forced an uneasy smile. "Now, please, tell me, where is Delia? You said something troubling earlier. About Delia doing something disrespectful. Although, quite frankly, I find that hard to believe."

"I said she was doing something no self-respecting lady would do." Miranda snipped another rose stem.

"What would that be?" He frowned at her.

"Delia has gone on a cattle drive." She wrinkled her nose with disgust.

Wyatt chuckled in surprised relief. "Is that all?"

"Is that *all*?" Miranda looked horrified. "She is gone for six days with four men—three who are strangers to her—and you say, 'is that all?'"

Wyatt wasn't so sure now. "Why would she go with strangers? Whose cattle are being driven? Where did they go?"

"Ah-hah, so you see my point." She held a rose in the air. "You are just as concerned as I am."

"Well, I—"

"It is our herd being driven, of course. And Marcus, our foreman, is with her. Of course, he would be with her—after all, Marcus is in love with my sister. But the other three men, well, they are ruffians that Marcus found in town the other night. At the saloon, I heard him saying. And if you ask me, they are a very rough looking bunch. They all were wearing gun holsters with guns."

Wyatt wasn't sure how to respond. Much of what she said was concerning. But how much of it was true? This Miranda didn't seem completely trustworthy. And now she was claiming that Delia was out with a bunch of men, for six days, one of them was in love with her, the others were strangers armed with guns. Although, to be fair, most cowboys carried guns.

"I'm afraid I'm a little confused," he said slowly. "Are you honestly concerned for Delia's safety?"

"Perhaps I'm more concerned for her reputation," Miranda said with a smirk.

Wyatt laid down his fork, pushing back his chair. "Tell me which way they went and I'll go out to find her right now."

"No, no, no," Miranda said quickly. "Forgive me, Mr. Davis. Delia would say I'm being dramatic. It's just that I think it is unwomanly to dress like a man and ride a horse the way she does, and go off like that with a bunch of strange men." She peered curiously at him. "Wouldn't you agree?"

He shrugged, trying to envision this—it just didn't sound like the Delia he'd known on the train. "Depends."

"Depends on what?"

"On the woman." He hesitantly picked up his fork again. "I would trust Delia in any situation. Well, as long as I could trust the people around her." He frowned to remember the time she'd been accosted in Kearney.

"But you're *not* certain, are you?" Miranda pressed him. "You're worried too."

"Maybe I *should* go looking for her." He laid down his fork.

"No, no." Miranda laughed. "Forgive me. I think I just miss her. I'm sure she is perfectly fine."

He wasn't so sure, and he didn't care for this game she was playing. "When are they supposed to come back?"

"Tomorrow." She focused her attention on arranging the roses. "They said three days up and three days back."

Now he pushed his chair back, standing up. "I think I'll head out to meet them. If you directed me to where they started, I'm sure it would be easy to pick up their trail."

"It's a deluge out there." She pointed to the window now streaked with rain. "Plus it'll be night soon. Even if you could follow the trail in the dark and the storm, it would probably take all night just to find their camp—if you could even find it. And then it would be morning and time to ride again. Why not just wait until tomorrow?"

He nodded. That actually made sense. "So this man, Marcus—is he a trustworthy sort?"

Miranda looked as if she was considering her answer. "He was my father's foreman. His righthand man."

"Yes?" Wyatt wasn't convinced.

"So he must be trustworthy, don't you think?"

"You say that this foreman, Marcus, that he's in love with Delia?" Wyatt watched her closely now, trying to discern if she was being honest or not. Something about this girl did not feel genuine to him.

"Well, he hasn't proposed marriage to Delia yet, but I'm guessing it's just a matter of time. He always comes to her aid and defends her against anyone who questions her. No one would be surprised if they decided to marry."

The tender beef he was swallowing suddenly felt like a small hard rock in his throat. "And do you know how Delia feels about Marcus?"

She shrugged as she plunked the last rose into the vase. "We don't talk much about things like that. But she does seem to trust him. She ran off with him, didn't she? Even after I warned her not to." Miranda's smile was apologetic. "Now let me go fetch you some dessert. Ginger made pies today."

"No thank you." Wyatt's appetite was gone.

"I'm sorry," Miranda came over next to him. "I know I've said all the wrong things. Delia would probably chastise me for speaking so recklessly. Truly, I am sorry. Please, forget all that I've said. I'm probably just out of sorts because they've all left me behind. And I suppose you heard that my Dad passed away a few weeks ago. It's been a difficult month."

"I'm sorry."

She smiled warmly. "Please, have a piece of cherry pie, Mr. Davis. Ginger will be hurt if you refuse."

"All right," he said with reluctance.

By the time he finished his dessert and a cup of coffee, it was dark outside. And, although he was uneasy about Delia being out there in the dark and the storm, with four men, he realized it was foolishness to set out to find her. Miranda was right, by the time he reached them, if he didn't lose their trail in the darkness, it would be time to set out for the day. Better to wait for morning. Especially considering they would be home tomorrow.

"Thank you for the delicious meal," Wyatt told Miranda as she refilled his coffee cup, setting her own cup adjacent from him and sitting down.

"Now, tell me about Alaska," she said eagerly. "What were you doing up there?"

"Mining for gold," he said woodenly.

Her eyes grew wide. "Did you strike it rich?"

He acted as if this was a ridiculous conclusion, pausing to sip his coffee, and knowing he would keep this information to himself.

"My Dad struck it rich."

Wyatt nodded. "So it seems."

"Well, he was broke when he died," she said in a dismal way. "Put every cent into this ranch."

"From what I can see he did things right. This ranch is very impressive."

"I suppose…if you like farming." She peered closely at him. "Do you?"

He shrugged. "I might."

"I'd offer to show you the place," she said, "but it's too dark outside. I can show it to you tomorrow though, if you like. There's lots to see and—"

"I'd like that," he said quickly. Mostly he would like escaping this flibbertigibbet. Didn't she know that she talked too much? He downed the last of his coffee.

"I can give you the tour of the house," she said eagerly. "As the woman of the house, I should've offered that to you earlier. Forgive my lack of manners."

"Forgiven. So *you* are the woman of the house?" Wyatt studied her as she considered her answer. Was she saying that the ranch had gone to her—not to her older sister?

"Of course, it's still rather new to me. I mean I was always the woman of the house after mother died. But Dad was there to help. Now he's gone...and...well, it's not been easy."

"So you are the woman of the house?" he repeated himself for clarity sake.

"I most certainly am," she declared rather hotly. "You can even ask Delia if you don't believe me."

"I've no reason not to believe you." It actually made sense that Miranda would've inherited this place. After all, she had been here all these years with her father. And although he felt a bit bad for Delia's sake, he was happily relieved for his own. Was this selfishness on his part? He wasn't even sure. But he didn't mind knowing that Delia had nothing. Already he'd been worried that he would be unable to compete with the incredible place her father had created. But if she was penniless, perhaps she would be even more willing to cast her lot with him.

After she finished her coffee, Miranda announced it was time to give Wyatt a tour. And he didn't really mind seeing the rooms or hearing how her dad had helped to design and build it. Seeing the lay of the rooms and some surprising innovations, he could tell that Delia's father was intelligent and thoughtful. And Miranda seemed to enjoy giving him a thorough and complete tour of everything.

"It's all very impressive," Wyatt told her as they were finishing up. "So well thought out and highly livable."

"I remember how happy I was to discover we would have indoor plumbing," she told him as she lingered at the foot of the staircase. "What was your favorite part of the house?"

"Definitely the library."

She wrinkled her nose. "I should've guessed that. Men always seem to like it. It was Dad's favorite place too. Although, oddly enough, it's Delia's favorite place too."

Wyatt didn't feel surprised by this. "Would you mind if I borrowed a book to read while I'm here?"

"Not at all. Help yourself."

"Thank you." He smiled. "Maybe I'll go pick one now. Thank you for the tour and I'll bid you goodnight."

However, she was not that easily gotten rid of. Miranda insisted on following him back to the library, chattering at him as he perused the book spines. So much so that it was hard to concentrate. But he finally selected a book about designing houses.

"Do you want to build a house someday?" she asked curiously as she trailed him back through the large front room to the stairs.

"Perhaps. I have a piece of land in Oregon that could use a new house."

"How interesting. What sort of—"

"If you'll excuse me," he cut her off as he stepped onto the stairs. "It's been a long day, I'd like to do some reading, and I have letters to write."

"Letters?" she said teasingly. "Are you one of those men with a girl at every port?"

"No. Just to my aunt and uncle and my mining partner in Alaska. I promised to write them after I got settled."

"So are you settled?" Miranda asked in what was clearly a flirtatious tone.

"I am. For the night anyway. Who knows where I'll be tomorrow."

"Delia said you were a drifter," Miranda said lightly. "Where will you be drifting to next, Mr. Davis?"

"Depends."

"You're a man of mystery, aren't you?"

Wyatt just laughed. "And you're a girl full of questions, aren't you? Goodnight, Miss Miranda. Thank you for your hospitality." As Wyatt went up to his room, he knew he'd have to watch out for that one. Even though he had absolutely no interest in the pesky young girl, he knew she was the kind who could be dangerous. Not only that, she was Delia's sister. And he planned to keep a safe distance from her.

31

After a restless night, Wyatt rose before the sun. His goal was to get out of this house without any more interaction with Miss Miranda. He wanted to find the cattle trail that he hoped would lead him to Delia. Even if they were nearly home, he relished the thought of meeting her out there on the open trail. He was impatient to be with her, to look into those emerald green eyes, and to discover where he stood with the woman he loved. He couldn't wait!

He'd just reached the corral, where he'd left his horse last night, when he ran into an old man and the muzzle of a rather large shotgun.

"Who're you and what're you doing on the Double W?" the old coot demanded with narrowed eyes.

"I'm Wyatt Davis. A friend of Miss Delia Williams. I was Miss Miranda's guest last night and I want to follow the trail that was used to drive the cattle a few days ago. I hope to find Miss Delia and accompany her safely back here."

"Oh." The man lowered the shotgun. "Sorry about that, but we've had trouble round here. Can't be too careful with strangers."

"Understandable." Wyatt frowned. "Speaking of strangers, what sort of men were they—the ones who drove cattle with Miss Delia? If you don't mind me asking."

The old man frowned. "I can't rightly say. Three of the hands were brand new. The fourth one, well, I can't really say."

Wyatt pursed his lips. "Well, then I'm going up there to find her. I'll just follow the cattle trail and—"

"Wait, son." The man put his hand on Wyatt's shoulder. "You might be able to follow the trail up there, but that's not the same way they'll be coming back down. When we're not driving cattle, we usually take a different route. Quicker that way. And we don't always take the same route. Depends on the weather. Flash floods and whatnot. And with these afternoon thunderstorms, hard to say."

"Oh."

"I'd offer to show you myself, but there's too much needing doing round here. Shorthanded like we are." The old man stuck out his hand. "Excuse my bad manners, son. I'm Caleb Morris. I was good friends with Delia's dad. Used to be foreman...until I got too old."

"Pleased to meet you. You don't seem too old to me."

"Winston feared I was working too hard." He rubbed a grizzled chin.

As the two them tended to the horses in the corral, Wyatt quickly explained how he'd met Delia and where he'd been.

"So you're a miner?" Caleb lit up as he threw a flake of hay into the corral. "Delia's dad and his uncle and me—we were all miners too. Those were good ol' days."

"I've been a miner as well as a number of other things," Wyatt confessed. "I was starting to think I was just a drifter...but meeting Delia—I mean *Miss* Delia—made me question that."

Caleb chuckled. "Miss Delia is quite a special little lady. Her daddy would be right proud of her. If he'd lived long enough to meet her." His grin faded.

"There you are!" Miranda came striding toward them. Today she had on a black dress, probably out of respect for her deceased father.

"I thought you were going to let me give you a tour of the property this morning," she declared.

"Well, I was about to ask Caleb for a tour." Wyatt exchanged glances with the old man. "I figure he can answer all my farming questions. Right, Caleb?"

Caleb had a knowing grin. "That's right. We got just enough time to see a good bit of it before breakfast." He nodded to Wyatt. "You can give me a hand with the chores."

"Glad to."

Caleb pointed to Miranda with a crooked smile. "And you're welcome to join us if you'd like, Miss Miranda. But I know you've never cottoned to the chicken coop. And you've never been too fond of feeding pigs or milking cows."

"Oh, but you're wrong," Miranda said. "I just never had the opportunity to spend much time with the animals before. I'm happy to join you for the tour."

So it was that Wyatt was led around by Caleb with Miranda eagerly following and asking lots of questions. Her nonstop chatter exposed two things. First of all, this girl was smarter than she appeared, and secondly, she knew next to nothing about her family's farming business. But it was amusing to hear Caleb giving her the go round.

Caleb had just challenged her to take on the milking when a clanging bell made her jump up from the milking stool. "Breakfast time," she chirped.

"For the workers anyway," Caleb said to her. "But maybe that includes you today, Miss. I don't reckon I ever seen you up this early before. Not even when your daddy was alive."

As they walked back to the house, Caleb explained how they'd been shorthanded since Winston's death. "Miss Delia's been helping out. She got real good at a lot of the chores. Works as hard as a man and never complains about it neither."

"If you'll excuse me," Miranda said to Wyatt when they reached the back porch, "I want to give Ginger a hand in the kitchen. She's shorthanded too."

"Well, don't that beat all," Caleb exclaimed. "That girl's turning over a new leaf. Must be her big sister's influence. It would make their daddy proud."

After washing up, Wyatt joined the others in the dining room for breakfast. As Miranda set food on the table, she explained to Wyatt that they didn't always eat together like this in the dining room. "It's just because we're shorthanded."

He nodded. "Caleb mentioned how you lost workers after your father's death."

A young man named Cash chimed in now, explaining how many workers had been scared off. "I was a mite worried," he confessed. "But Silas and Caleb talked me into staying on."

"Can't blame anyone for being worried." An older hand named Silas explained about a time the women had been shot at in the carriage. As Miranda filled coffee cups, she told of how frightening it had been.

"Happened right after Mr. Williams was killed," Silas said as reached for the hotcakes. "I returned fire. Couldn't spot the shooter, but it came from Marshall's Ridge. That borders the Leaning R."

"So that rancher's willing to kill?" Wyatt asked. "Over water rights?"

"He's been after our water here for years. But I never thought Jerome Roswell was a murderer." Miranda returned to the kitchen.

"Yeah, but some of them Leanin' R boys might be killers," Cash declared.

"What about the law?" Wyatt asked. "Why isn't someone investigating Mr. William's death?"

"Winston's lawyer was looking into it," Caleb explained.

"But he got murdered too," Cash said.

Silas shook his head. "Makes us think the Leaning R's behind it."

They continued discussing this as they ate, speculating over various theories as to who had done what, but not agreeing over much of it.

"All right, enough gossiping like a bunch of old biddies." Caleb stood. "Time to get to work." He pointed to Wyatt. "You wanna help out? This is our busiest time of year. Plenty to be done."

"I'm glad to lend a hand." Wyatt finished his coffee. Sure, he'd rather head out to meet Delia, but based on what Caleb had said, he knew his chances of finding her were slim. "Just tell me what needs doing."

"Ever dipped sheep before?" Silas asked as they headed outside.

"Can't say that I have."

Caleb chuckled as they walked through the yard. "It's a stinky, nasty mess."

Unsure of what he'd gotten himself into, Wyatt just shrugged. Maybe doing some messy work would be a good way to keep Miranda at bay. That girl was getting way too friendly.

"Silas is in charge this year," Caleb dug his elbow into Silas's ribs.

"You might wanna put on some old clothes," Silas told Wyatt. "By the end of the day you'll know why."

So Wyatt agreed to meet him in the sheep pasture in a few minutes. Glad that he'd kept his old mining clothes, which were still dirty, he changed and then, relieved not to cross paths with Miranda, he found Silas standing in front of narrow manmade pond that had fencing alongside of it. "This is where we dip 'em." He explained how they would herd the sheep single file through the water that had been treated with something that would kill parasites.

"Interesting." Wyatt studied the set up.

"Mr. Williams learned about this in his farm journal. He said it was how Scots clean the wool. And I gotta say that come shearing time—which we're running late on this year—it makes for better wool."

Before long the two of them were leading the unsuspecting sheep down the ramp and into the disgustingly smelly water. At first they went willingly, but almost as if the other sheep had gotten wind of the procedure, it became increasingly difficult. Soon Silas and Wyatt felt like they were running some sort of a sheep rodeo.

Instead of stopping for the midday meal, Silas sent Wyatt in to ask Ginger to send their lunch out to them. As Wyatt walked to the house, he knew he was a sight to be seen. Hopefully Delia wasn't about to arrive home. He didn't really want to meet her like this. Wiping his hands on the back of his blue jeans, he asked Ginger if the cattle drivers had gotten home yet.

"Oh, they aren't expected home until tomorrow," she told him.

"Tomorrow?" He wanted to question why Miranda had told him today, but thought better of it. He hadn't completely trusted her—now he knew why.

"That's right. Tomorrow on the third of July. That's how they always done it. Then we usually have a big celebration on the Fourth" She frowned. "Won't be so grand this year. Not with Mr. Williams gone...and being shorthanded."

Wyatt tried to disguise his disappointment as he returned to the sheep pasture, reminding himself that it was just one more day. Besides, he hadn't wanted to meet her looking and smelling like this anyway. "Lunch is on its way," he told Silas as he rounded up the next sheep.

It wasn't long before Miranda came out carrying a picnic basket and wearing a big smile. However, as she got closer and saw the condition of the men, her smile quickly evaporated. "I'll just set this here," she called out as she put the basket on a rock.

Silas called out a thanks, but Wyatt ignored her, keeping his eyes on the un-dipped ewe that was about to make a break for the pasture and trying not imagine how Miss Miranda would look if she accidentally got dipped in the nasty smelling brown water.

Neither of them said much as they ate their lunch. "How long do you think it'll be until we're done?" Wyatt asked Silas. Although he could guess since they were barely half done with the herd. And it seemed the process was going slower now.

"I sure hope we finish up by sundown," Silas said in a weary voice. "I don't wanna do it again tomorrow."

"I don't want to do it again *ever*," Wyatt confessed. And so he worked harder than ever and, to both of their surprised relief, they got the last sheep through the dip not too long after the supper bell rang.

"Thanks for your help." Silas shook hands with Wyatt. "Couldn't have done it without you."

"It was a good learning experience," Wyatt admitted and although that was true, Wyatt was certain he never wanted to put this lesson to use again.

It took a full hour for Wyatt to clean himself up enough to go down for dinner. He figured the others would be finished by now, but perhaps Ginger would fix him a plate of leftovers. And then he could retire to his room to relax and read—and look forward to tomorrow when Delia would get here. And at least he'd worn himself out by working with Silas today. He would sleep well tonight!

"There you are at last." Miranda smiled expectantly as he came down the stairs. "I've been waiting for you."

"Waiting?" Wyatt didn't like the sound of that.

"For dinner." She smiled sweetly.

"Isn't everyone done eating by now?"

"Not everyone. Right this way, Mr. Davis." As she led him toward the dining room, he noticed that she was no longer wearing the black gown she'd had on this morning. In fact, unless he was mistaken, she'd borrowed another one of Delia's gowns. The striking lavender gown was a little long on Miranda and, although he was no expert, it didn't seem to fit quite right. Delia had worn that gown like a queen on the night they'd dined in Chicago.

"There you go." Miranda waved to the chair at the head of the table, waiting by the chair adjacent from her as if she expected him to play the gentleman and pull it out for her. Reluctantly, he complied.

"Are you wearing Delia's dress?" he asked as he sat down in his chair.

"Have you seen *all* of my sister's gowns?" Miranda demanded as she waved her napkin into her lap.

He studied the emerald earrings she had on, certain he'd seen those before too. They had caught his attention because they matched Delia's eyes. "Do you sisters share everything?"

"Not everything." She smiled coyly as she reached for a little brass bell, giving it a tingle. Next she reached for a crystal decanter which appeared to be filled with port, but before she could fill a glass for him, he covered it with his hand.

"No thank you," he said firmly.

"Oh?" She frowned as she put the stopper back. "Dad enjoyed a glass of port after a hard day's work...sometimes."

"I might enjoy one too," Wyatt said. "But not tonight."

"What's wrong?" She pushed her lower lip out in a pout.

"You told me Delia would be home today," he said.

"Oh?" Her brow creased. "Well, I got my days mixed up. It seems they'll be home tomorrow."

"So I heard."

Before long Ginger came in, serving them their soup course. After she left, Miranda filled her own glass with port, taking a generous sip then giggling.

"Are you even old enough to drink that?" he demanded.

"Don't be such a stick in the mud, Wyatt."

He bristled at her using his first name. Prior to this she'd been calling him Mr. Davis. Hurrying to eat his soup, he was determined to finish this meal as quickly as possible. And, at the risk of being rude, he was considering taking his main course off to his room with him. He would've exited without it, except that he was ravenous.

"I'm very sorry I got the days mixed up regarding Delia's return," she said penitently. "I hope you will forgive me."

"You seem to apologize a lot." He put his spoon in his empty soup bowl.

"I suppose it's because I'm always making mistakes." She looked upset now. He hoped she wasn't about to cry. "I realize I'm not anything like Delia. Goodness knows she is perfect in every way."

He didn't miss her sarcasm, but even so he didn't respond, didn't want to take her bait. And thankfully Ginger was now bringing in the next course. "Good soup," he told her as he handed her his bowl. "Thank you."

"Well, you worked hard today, Mr. Davis. Seems the least I can do." She grinned at him. "Did you know that Miss Miranda helped me in the kitchen? That was sure nice." Carrying the used soup bowls out she returned to the kitchen.

"Do you often help in the kitchen?" Wyatt asked partly to make conversation and partly out of curiosity. Miranda didn't seem like the kitchen help type.

"Ginger is teaching me to cook," she said primly. "She says every woman should know how to cook—no matter her status in life. Even a wealthy woman with lots of servants should understand the basics of food preparation."

Wyatt wasn't really listening to her as she rambled on and on, but before long, Ginger returned with plates filled with delicious looking food. And without saying a word to Miranda, he dug into the massive steak. As soon as he finished, he was getting out of here. And, as soon as Delia got home from that trail drive, he was going to proclaim his love and beg her to go away with her. Leave the "lady of the house" to manage her ranch without them.

31

DELIA HAD NEVER BEEN SO EXHAUSTED IN HER LIFE. EVERY BONE IN her body seemed to be aching. And she was coated from head to toe in trail dust. Even her eyes and her teeth felt gritty. She couldn't begin to imagine what she must look like, but it did amuse her to imagine what her mother would say if she could see her right now. Or what she would say if she knew that Delia had just spent five nights in the wilderness with a bunch of rough cowboys. She would be scandalized.

However, when it was all said and done, Delia felt pleased with her accomplishment. Besides doing her part to drive the herd—without complaining—she had kept Marcus in his place. She had also managed to discern what she felt was the true character of the three new hands. And by tomorrow, Roy would be paid off and sent packing. Owen might decide he wanted to leave too—after he found out about Roy. But JT was a keeper. That boy seemed good and true and worth having around. She hoped that he'd become friends with Cash and Silas and want to stay on.

As they rode up to the house, she felt a wonderful wave of relief wash over her. She was so glad to be home! And it did feel like a homecoming when she saw the welcoming golden lights coming from the windows of the big farmhouse. The idea of taking a hot bath and sleeping in a comfortable bed made her feel slightly light-headed. Not to mention a good meal. JT had done a fine job cooking over the campfire, but she was tired of the three Bs. Bacon and beans and biscuits.

"You're back," Cash said as he emerged from the kitchen with a slop pail for the pigs. "A day early."

"We made good time," Delia told him.

"I'll see to your horse, Miss Delia." Cash set down the bucket and reached for her horse's bridle. "You're not even too late for supper. Miss Miranda is still in the dining room."

"Thank you." She slid from the saddle and headed inside. It seemed late for dinner, but at least the food wouldn't be put away yet.

"Miss Delia!" Ginger exclaimed as Delia entered the kitchen through the backdoor. "You're a day early."

"I am." Delia peered over to the stove. "Anything left?"

"There will be." Ginger's eyes grew wide as she looked more closely at Delia. "Goodness, Miss Delia, I'm glad I haven't used up my hot water yet. I'll put some more on and take this kettle upstairs for your bath."

"Thank you." She looked down at her filthy clothes. "I'd like to eat first. The men will be hungry too. We're all dirty so we should eat in the mess hall."

"Yes, I'll get it set up right away. Especially since Miss Miranda and her young man are having a fancy dinner there." Ginger nodded toward the dining room door then giggled.

"Her young man?"

She nodded as she put a cast iron pan on the stove. "Showed up two days ago, and Miss Miranda has barely let him outta her sight. A very nice young man too. He seems to bring out the best in our girl."

"Where did she meet him?"

"Can't say." She shoved some kindling into the stove, stoking the fire. "But Miss Miranda is acting like a different girl."

"A different girl."

As Ginger got more steaks ready to cook, she described how Miranda was helping in the kitchen. "She's turned over a new leaf. Even gathered the eggs this morning and you know how she hates going in the hen house. And she told me she might try milking tomorrow. Don't it beat all?"

"It surely does." Delia helped herself to a biscuit. Light and fluffy, it was nothing like a camp biscuit.

"Mr. Davis sure does bring out the best in our girl."

"Mr. Davis?" Delia stopped chewing. "What's his first name?"

"I can't recall." Ginger frowned as she put a dollop of grease into the pan. "Starts with a W though, just like your daddy."

"Wyatt Davis?" Delia set the half-eaten biscuit on the counter.

"Yes, I do believe that's right. Do you know the gentleman?"

Without answering, Delia left the kitchen, going through the butler's pantry, she barely opened the door into the dining room, peeking through the crack. The room glowed with the flickering of candles in silver candelabras. The clean white tablecloth was set with the best china. A lovely bouquet of red roses graced the center of the table with a decanter of red wine nearby. The setting was perfect—for romance!

But it was the back of the man seated at the head of the table that captured Delia's full, stunned attention. *It was Wyatt!* And although she knew Miranda was in there with him because she could hear her talking, she couldn't see her. Pushing the door a bit more open, she peered around the edge to see that Miranda was sitting to the left of Wyatt—and she was wearing Delia's dress!

"Am I dreaming?" Delia demanded as she stepped fully into the dining room.

Miranda's fork dropped from her hand with a loud clang, and

her mouth gaped open in shock. Wyatt leaped from his chair, turning around to see Delia.

"Hello, Wyatt," she said in a cool, controlled voice.

His eyes grew huge as he stared at her, reminding her of how horrible she must look. "Delia, is that really you?"

"Yes. We came home a day early." She frowned at Miranda. "Clearly you weren't expecting me."

"I can't believe it's you." Wyatt started to chuckle.

"You look absolutely ridiculous." Miranda began to laugh too. "You should see yourself, Delia. It's really funny and—"

"I'm so glad I can amuse you both." She felt like a pot that was about to boil over.

Still smiling, Wyatt started toward her, but she held up her hands to stop him. "I'm covered in trail dust. I suggest you keep your distance." She looked from Miranda to Wyatt, trying to absorb what she was seeing. "It looks like you two are enjoying a lovely meal. Please, excuse me for interrupting you. Tell Ginger, I'll take my supper in my room. *Goodnight!*" She moved past them, hurrying out the other door as Wyatt called out for her to stop.

"Wait, Delia. Don't go! Let me talk to you."

She was already through the main room then dashing up the stairs, headed straight for her room. Closing the door behind her, she leaned against it, trying to catch her breath. Oh, she knew she was being childish. And judgmental. But she was just too weary—and too shocked—to think clearly.

Standing next to the door, she started peeling off her soiled trail clothes, letting them drop to the floor one by one. She still couldn't believe that Wyatt was really here, and she knew she should be happy about it. But seeing him down there with Miranda like that—well, it was just very disturbing. It felt as if the writing was on the wall.

Stripped down to her chemise and bloomers, she gingerly reached for her dressing gown and, quietly opened the door to listen and feeling that she was alone upstairs, she made a beeline for the bathroom.

Prepared to take a cold bath, she felt a happy wave of relief to see that Ginger had already brought a kettle of hot water up. As Delia started filling the tub, she tried to sort through her thoughts.

It wasn't even surprising to think that Miranda would've been attracted to Wyatt. But that she should go after him in such a blatant way like that—well, it was not very sisterly. And to wear Delia's gown? That was just wrong. But those things aside, where did Wyatt stand in all this? He had appeared quite comfortable sitting at the head of the table with Miranda catering to him like he was lord of the manor.

Satisfied that she had enough water for her first bath—she intended to have two—she turned off the tap and reached for the kettle. But before she poured the hot water in, she caught a glimpse of her face in the mirror above the sink. Blinking in horror at her dirt caked face and dust coated hair. She barely looked human. It was no wonder Wyatt had laughed at her. Who could blame him?

She poured enough hot water into the tub to warm it then, reaching for a bar of soap, slipped in and started to scrub. After a few minutes the water was so brown that she knew it could no longer get her clean. So she emptied the tub and began the process all over again. She was ready to go in for a third time—even if it was with cold water—when she heard a gentle tapping at the door.

"Miss Delia," Ginger called. "I got more hot water for you."

Holding a towel over her, Delia hurried to exchange kettles with her. "Thank you!"

"And I put your dinner in your room."

"Bless you!" Delia wanted to inquire about Miranda and Wyatt but simply closed the door. There was no point in putting Ginger in the middle of it.

Finally, Delia eased herself into the last tub full of nice warm water. She'd infused this with the rosehips oil she'd discovered in the cupboard. With her clean hair wrapped in a towel, she relaxed in the fragrant water and tried not to think about anything. Of course, this was impossible. All she could think about was Wyatt. He was here!

She had so many questions. Why had he come? When had he arrived? How long could he stay? And most importantly—what was going on between him and Miranda? Her mind went round and round over these troubling thoughts until she realized the water had grown tepid and despite the warm summer night, she was shivering.

She took her time toweling off then, with her dressing gown which now needed laundering wrapped around her, she slipped back to her room where, to her delight, dinner was waiting. She blocked out all thoughts of Wyatt and Miranda as she hungrily ate and then, seeing that it was well past ten o'clock, she fell gratefully into bed. Whatever needed sorting out would have to wait until morning. But before she drifted off to sleep she prayed a quick prayer—asking for God to lead her in his will, no matter what it was.

Wyatt knew he'd handled everything all wrong. In the first place, he should've taken supper in his room like he'd planned. He'd known that Miranda was trouble. Secondly he never should've laughed at Delia. Big mistake. Even though she'd looked hilariously adorable all covered in dirt. In fact, even like that—Delia in her dusty disheveled riding clothes and Miranda dressed like royalty—Delia was hands-down the winner. At least in his heart. Delia's little sister didn't hold a candle to her.

Despite him exiting the table right after Delia, he hadn't been willing chase her down and storm her room. He knew she wouldn't like that. And so he'd retired to his room, listening to the hallway just in case she happened by—in the hopes he could step out and apologize. But he never heard a peep. She was probably going to avoid him. Who could blame her? She had to be plumb worn out after that cattle drive. And then he'd been caught with Miranda, looking like a fool. As badly as he wanted to talk to her, to explain himself, he also wanted to give her time…to allow her to clean up and cool off and get a good night's rest.

Even though he was fairly worn out from his long day, he felt restless. Pacing the floor of the guest room, he tried to imagine what tomorrow would hold. Would he find out that, like Miranda had suggested, Delia had allowed the foreman named Marcus to steal her heart—or would she still have feelings for him?

He could barely stand to think that he had made this trip for naught. The first time he'd been wrong about a woman—Maryanne in Oregon—hadn't been all that hard to recover from. He'd been over her by the time he'd been halfway back East over the Oregon Trail. Getting over Delia…well, that would probably take about seventeen trips around the world…and a lifetime.

Delia woke early the next morning. Feeling surprisingly refreshed, she dressed in her "widow's weeds" as Miranda had called their dresses, and slipped downstairs. The house was quiet. And, although Ginger had laid out some things for breakfast, she was nowhere to be seen. Delia slipped outside, going through the backyard, and up the hill behind the house, she had one goal in mind. She'd been planning to do this since the first day of the cattle drive.

Standing by her father's grave, she let out a long sigh. "I felt like you were with me…helping me on the cattle drive," she began quietly. "As if you were leading and guiding me and protecting me." She smiled sadly. "Or maybe it was simply that you'd already done so much to prepare me throughout my childhood. It felt as if you had been getting me ready for this—to run your ranch someday. And I just want to say that I believe I'm up to the task now. I think I can do this, Father. And I want to thank you for trusting me with it. I promise to do my best—and to honor your memory as I continue to build upon what you began." She took in a deep breath, looking up at the mountains and the crisp blue sky. Today, she felt, was going to be a good day.

As she walked back down to the house, she silently prayed. First she thanked God for getting her safely through the cattle drive. Then she asked God to help her to figure out why Wyatt was here—and to determine what she should do about it. As she got closer to the house, she made a decision. If Wyatt had somehow developed an interest in Miranda, which she found very difficult to believe, she would give them her blessing and send them on their way. And even if her heart was broken—and it would be—she would lose herself in work.

And there was plenty of that to go around, she reminded herself as she stopped by the chicken coop to gather eggs. With a full basket, she was just letting herself out when she saw him walking toward her. Her heart did a little flip, and it took her full concentration not to drop the basket of eggs as she continued walking toward him. Why did he have to be so doggone handsome?

"I've been looking all over for you." He reached for the egg basket, carrying it for her as they walked toward the house.

"I was up at the family cemetery," she explained.

"Oh." He nodded grimly. "I'm so sorry for your loss. I wrote to you about it, but I'm not sure you got my letter."

"No. I didn't."

"Is there a private place where we can talk?" Wyatt glanced over to where some of the hands were starting to trickle out of the bunkhouse. "There are things that need saying and sooner is better."

"Yes." She pointed to the washing up table by the backdoor. "Leave the eggs there. Someone will take them inside." As she waited for him, she braced herself for whichever way this was going to go. She had just declared to God that she wanted his will. And even if God's will did not include Wyatt in her life, she still wanted God's will. As hard as it would be to let this man go—the man who made her feel so warm and happy every time she looked into his eyes—she was prepared to do it.

32

When Wyatt returned she led him to a trail she'd found shortly after arriving here. As they walked, she looked around, curious as to where Hank was keeping himself this morning. Perhaps he was worn out from the cattle drive. The trail led to a nice vantage point where a rustic wooden bench had been placed and, she'd discovered, it was a good place to think and be alone.

"I suspect my dad created this little retreat," she said as they both sat down on the bench. "It's almost as if I can feel his presence up here."

"It's beautiful." Wyatt gazed down over the valley where the farm was situated. "Everything around here is beautiful." He turned to look her. "But it all dims compared to you, Delia."

She couldn't help but smile. "I bet you weren't thinking that last night."

"You'd be surprised then." He confessed to her that, even covered with mud, she had looked more beautiful to him than any woman he'd ever seen.

"Including Miranda?"

He just laughed. "Poor Miranda. She is living in her sister's shadow and she knows it. Parading around in your gowns and jewelry."

"She wore my jewelry too?"

He described the emerald earrings. "I recognized them…I remembered how they matched your eyes."

"You're very observant."

"When it comes to you, I am."

She felt her heart softening even more. "Why are you here, Wyatt?"

For a long moment, he didn't answer. "So you never received any of my letters?"

She shook her head.

"Well, when I got your first letter, up in Alaska, I knew I had to come back."

"Come back?"

"To you, Delia. You'd already captured my heart, but I went up to Alaska anyway. I knew I needed to finish up my business there. And I thought you needed time to get acquainted with your dad. I thought maybe I'd just put in six months. Or maybe just the summer. But when I read your letter, I knew I had to come help you. I came back on the next boat." He shrugged. "And here I am. I hope you don't mind."

She felt her lips curling into a smile. "I don't mind at all. But I'll admit I was a little taken aback last night."

Now he explained how Miranda seemed to have set her sights on him from the get-go. "To be fair, I probably started it." He confessed about how he'd mistaken her for Delia and swooped her up. "She was wearing your pale green gown and—"

"She wore that dress too?" Delia shook her head in wonder.

"I even spent yesterday dipping sheep to keep her at a distance," he said. "Well, and I wanted to help."

"You dipped sheep?" She was incredulous. "The men had just

been complaining about that before we left for the cattle drive. They made it sound like it was the worst chore in the world."

He nodded grimly. "It was pretty bad."

"Well, thank you for doing that."

"My pleasure." He reached for her hand. "I pretended I was doing it for you, Delia. Even though I know that Miranda has inherited your dad's ranch."

"What?" She tilted her head to one side. "Is that what you heard?"

"Miranda said she was lady of the house." He frowned. "I assumed that means she inherited and, considering everything, well, it made sense."

"Except that Miranda is my father's stepdaughter. Because of that, he left the ranch to me."

Wyatt looked shocked...and dismayed.

"Does that trouble you?"

"The ranch is all yours?" he asked quietly. "Not Miranda's?"

"Yes. But I'm to look after Miranda. And I told her she could stay on as long as she likes and I even said I would put her in charge of the house, which might be why she called herself the 'lady of the house.'" Delia laughed. "Although that hardly makes it permissible to go parading around in my clothes." She looked down to where Wyatt was still holding her hand. "So, knowing that I own the ranch, Wyatt, does that change your feelings toward me?"

"No, of course, not." He looked into her eyes. "But I have to admit that I liked the idea of showing up here and whisking you away. I mean if you were alone in the world and had nothing." He sighed. "Like in some of the books we've both read, I wanted to be the hero who rescued you."

Delia felt torn now. As much as she loved Wyatt, she wasn't sure she could give up the ranch for him. Was that what he was asking her to do?

"Delia, I love you," he said solemnly. "I believe I've loved you almost since the moment we met—when you were wearing your school-girl dress and afraid that I was the hotel detective."

"That seems so long ago…yet it was only a month."

"A lot can happen in a month."

"I'll say." She felt herself getting lost in his eyes.

"I wasn't going to say these things at first," he continued. "But after the debacle last night with Miranda, I feel that I must. I love you, Delia. And I want to take care of you for the rest of your life. But I'm worried that you don't need me so much now. Seeing that you've got your own ranch and all." He looked out over the land below them.

"I love you too, Wyatt." She spoke so quietly she wasn't sure he could even hear her.

"You do?" He turned back to her with eager eyes.

"Yes. I think it was sitting on the back of the train that I first knew it. And I was determined not to be a violet."

"A violet?" His brow creased.

She explained about her friend Violet in college. "I didn't want to succumb that easily to love."

"If you ask me, you didn't succumb easily at all." He took her other hand in his. "You held me off quite admirably."

"I'm not holding you off now," she said.

And then he leaned in and kissed her and she kissed him back and for several minutes they melted into each others' arms and, for the first time in her life, Delia felt as if she were truly at home. Not a home with a roof and a floor, but a home where her heart would be safe and cared for.

"I do love you, Wyatt," she murmured when they finally pulled apart. "And if you wanted me to give up the ranch to go with you—to Oregon or Alaska or wherever you wanted to go—I know I could do it." She looked out over the land she'd grown to love. "I'm not saying it would be easy, but I could go with you." She turned back to him, smiling into his eyes. "I could even be a drifter."

He laughed. "After seeing you covered in dirt last night, I believe it." He was about to kiss her again when they heard someone yelling down below.

"Sounds like trouble," Wyatt said as they both stood.

"We need to go back."

Holding hands, they hurried down the trail to discover Marcus in front of the horse corral with a grim expression. The gate was wide open, and all the horses appeared to be missing.

"Someone left the corral open and the horses are out," he told Delia. "We need to go round them up."

"I'll help," Wyatt offered.

"Good, you go help Caleb and Silas." He handed Wyatt several lengths of rope. "They spotted a bunch of them headed for the cow pasture, but since that fence is down, there's no telling how far they might go. I think your horse was with them too. You'll have to run to catch up with 'em."

Wyatt grabbed the ropes and took off running toward the cow pasture.

"I think your horse went that way." Marcus pointed Delia toward Marshall Ridge, the section of rough terrain that divided the Double W from the Leaning R. He handed her a section of rope. "You might have more luck catching Lady. I'm going to head over to the river. I'm guessing some of the horses went there."

"Have you seen Hank?" she asked as she looped a rope over her arm.

"I think he might've taken off with the horses. Maybe he's with Lady."

"That makes sense." She headed off in the direction Marcus had pointed to. As she called out for Hank, she wished for her riding habit, although it was still filthy. But trudging through the high grass in the black satin gown wasn't easy. Plus the sun was getting warm and she hadn't even bothered to put on a hat.

"Lady," she called out, hoping she might be able to entice her horse back to her. "Hank?" she yelled, hoping that he might let out a yip to reveal his whereabouts. As she continued pressing through the rough field and into the area where there was more rocks than grassland, she remembered Caleb's warning about being careful for rattlesnakes in landscape like this. So far she had never seen one, but according to Caleb, the deadly snakes liked rocky places like this. The thought of one jumping out at her made her nervous.

She hurried along, eager to get into the tree line where she thought she might be safer. She'd just reached the shadows of the evergreens when she heard a rustling noise behind her. Thinking it might be a snake, although there was no rattle, she turned around slowly, not wanting to startle it. She hoped it wasn't some other wild animal—a cougar or bear.

"Oh, it's just you," she said in relief as she realized Marcus was striding toward her.

"Sorry to frighten you," he said as he continued up the hill.

"I thought you went to the river." She paused to push a strand of hair from her damp forehead.

"I decided to come help you instead." He smiled in a way that made her feel uncomfortable. "Nice to see you got yourself cleaned up after the cattle drive. You were really a sight yesterday." He chuckled in a way that made the hair on the back of her neck bristle.

As he moved closer, a silent alarm went off inside of her—something about this was wrong—all wrong! "I'm fine on my own," she assured him, stepping back. "You really should go look for the other horses."

"I just want to talk to you, Delia." He kept moving toward her with an intense expression.

"This isn't the time to talk." She continued to back away—until she backed right into the solid trunk of a tree.

"There now. Just stay put and hear what I have to say."

"Marcus, I—"

"I want you to marry me, Delia. I wanted to tell you that—"

"I'm sorry, Marcus. I never meant to mislead you. But that will never happen. I cannot marry you."

"I was afraid you would say that." He continued standing just inches from her, but the expression on his face was so cold that, despite the heat, she felt a chill rush through her.

"Now, if you'll excuse me." She attempted to push past him.

"Not so quick, little lady." He reached into his holster and pulled out a shiny revolver.

"What are you doing?"

He grabbed her by the arm, spinning her away from him. "You just start walking." He shoved her toward the ridge. "Up there."

"What—" She felt the hard stab of the gun muzzle in her back.

"Just shut up," he growled. "And walk fast. Unless you want me to shoot you right here."

With trembling legs, she proceeded to walk in the direction he was pushing her. "Marcus," she said as calmly as she could. "Why are you doing this?"

"Just walk," he said in a flat tone.

"You would kill me simply because I won't marry you?" She tried to keep the tremble out of her voice. "I—I doubt that you even love me."

"Who said anything about love?" He gave a harsh laugh.

"Then why are you doing this?"

"To get you out of the way."

She considered this as she struggled through the rough terrain. Amazingly, it was starting to make sense. With Marcus's pistol pressed into the small of her back, she was putting the pieces together in her mind. It was like Miranda had insinuated—Marcus simply wanted the ranch. And he didn't care what it took to get it.

"If you kill me, the ranch will go to Miranda," Delia said slowly, the full realization sinking in. "And you think that you can get Miranda to marry you. And then the ranch will belong to you."

"That was how it was going to be before you came along and

messed everything up," he admitted. "And that would've been easier. Because if you ask me, you're too smart for your own good. See what comes from being too educated?"

She didn't say anything for a couple of minutes. "You killed my father too, didn't you? With him out of the way, you could marry Miranda and have the ranch."

"See what I said about being too smart."

"And you killed Horace Griswold too," she said finally. "But I'm not sure why. Just to get your hands on the will?"

"I didn't plan to kill Horace. I just needed to see the will, to see which one of you girls was going to inherit. So I could make my plan. Horace just happened to be working late. He got in the way."

Delia knew her fate was sealed now. Marcus had sent all the men in different directions searching for horses that he must've let out himself. No one would think to look over here. "Lady didn't even go this way, did she?"

"Nah. She's probably down by the river with the rest of 'em by now." He shoved her toward what looked like a deer trail going along a steep ridge. "Take that path there."

"What will you do when the others ask how I got killed?"

"Blame the Leaning R. Just like always. And being you'll be found so close to their ranch and in the same place where there's been trouble before—it'll be believable." He chuckled. "But that's assuming you'll be found. Might be that the coyotes and wolves will have taken care of your remains before anyone thinks to come looking up here."

Delia's mind was still spinning, trying to think of a way out of this. "What if you're wrong about Miranda?" she said suddenly. "What if she refuses to marry you?"

"Why would she refuse?"

"Because she's in love with Wyatt."

"You mean that guy you took off with this morning?"

Now Delia quickly explained how she'd found Wyatt and Miranda last night. "Miranda is clearly in love with Wyatt. With me out of the way, nothing will stand between her and him."

Marcus actually stopped walking now, grabbing more tightly to her arm. "You're lying, Delia. You think you can outsmart me."

She turned to face him. "I swear to you, Marcus. As God is my witness. I felt certain that Miranda was in love with Wyatt when I found them together last night. Ginger even told me as much."

Marcus scowled darkly.

"There has to be another way out of this," she said gently. "A way to—"

"I know." He brightened. "I'll just have to kill Wyatt too."

A rush of panic ran through her—why had she mentioned Wyatt to him? Somehow she had to stop him. "You can't kill everyone."

"Turn around and keep walking," he growled.

Delia knew she was out of answers. Marcus was determined to get what he wanted, no matter who stood in his way. Desperation and fear twisted inside of her—she was helpless and she knew it. All she could do was to pray. And as she fumbled up the trail, with Marcus swearing at her and shoving her forward, that's what she did.

She wasn't just praying for her own safety, but for Wyatt's as well. She even prayed for Miranda because Delia knew that if she disagreed with Marcus, she would be in severe danger as well. Not for the first time, she wondered why her dad had ever hired this evil man.

She stumbled slightly as they came to the top of the ridge but, catching herself, she stood up straight and, looking down, was shocked to see a fairly steep drop off down below. Probably where he planned to dispose of her body. She gulped and looked away.

"This is far enough."

She turned around to look at him, wondering if there was some way to talk him out of this—she was smart, surely she could think of something. "What if I agreed to marry you?" she tried in desperation. "You and I could run the ranch together."

He just laughed. "You think I'm stupid?"

"No, or course not...." Just then Delia noticed a movement to her right—a dark shadow near a tree. Not wanting Marcus to look that way, she stared down at the ground, trying to gather her thoughts, hoping to stall him. "You can't keep this up without getting caught, Marcus. But you could get away from here," she said desperately. "I could give you money and you could—"

"There's no money and you know it."

"I could get my hands on money," she said quickly. "I could sell the place to Roswell. I could give you half and—"

"Why should I take half when I can get all of it?"

She glanced to her right again. There was definitely something over there. Could it be help? Or just a wild animal? Even the distraction of a hungry bear or cougar would be welcome right now. "So you plan to sell the ranch?" she asked him.

"You think I wanna be a rancher?" He laughed harshly. "I know exactly how much hard work that is. Been doing it for two years now."

"*Two* years?" she questioned. "You said you'd been here for ten years."

"And you believed me. You're not as smart as you think you are, Delia."

"Because I believe people?" She knew she needed to continue stalling him as she glanced to the right again. This time she saw nothing, but she was still determined. "I'm curious about something," she said quickly. "Why did my father hire you?"

"What difference does it make?" He glowered at her. "Let's just end this now."

"You can't even grant me one last dying wish?" She looked at him with sorrowful eyes.

"What?" he growled.

"Well, seeing how you don't even like ranching—why would

my father hire you? It makes no sense and I'd just like to know the truth—before you kill me."

"Fine." He put his face close to hers. "If I tell you the truth, maybe you'll reward me with a little something before I finish you off."

Feeling sickened by this, she forced a smile and nodded, hoping he believed her.

Still holding tightly to her arm, he pulled her closer to him, talking quietly in an intimate tone that was completely incongruous with his words. "I met little Miranda in town one day. Her flashy red hair caught my eye and when she started flirting with me, I asked around about her. When I heard she had a rich daddy, I figured I'd hit the jackpot. But she was only fifteen then, so I knew I'd have to bide my time. I came out to apply for a job at the ranch, and Miranda begged her daddy to hire me on. Naturally, he did. And I worked real hard these past couple of years. Harder than I ever worked in my whole life."

"And you were good at it too, weren't you?"

His eyes were like steel as smiled smugly. "I'm good at whatever I turn my hand to."

"Even murder?"

His smile vanished.

"Too bad you didn't decide to turn your hand to something good." As Delia said this, she realized the shadow to her right was Miranda. Standing out in the open now, Miranda had a rifle in her hands and a deadly expression on her face as she aimed the rifle directly at them. Was Miranda in cahoots with Marcus?

"Drop the gun!" Miranda yelled loudly.

"What the—" Marcus turned to see.

"I said *drop the gun*, Marcus!" She peered down the barrel of the rifle like she was ready to pull the trigger.

"Aw, you don't even know how to shoot that thing," he yelled back.

"I do too. My daddy taught me."

"You'll never hit me from there." He wrapped his left arm around Delia, pulling her close and positioning her like a shield, he turned his revolver onto Miranda. "Drop your gun or you're both dead."

In the same instant a shot rang out and Delia felt Marcus jolt and his grasp on her suddenly loosened. His gun fell to the dirt as he went limp. As Delia leaped away from him, Marcus tumbled sideways, careening over the narrow ridge and plummeting down into the deep crevasse below.

Falling to her knees, Delia crumbled to the ground—breaking into frightened tears.

"Are you all right?" Miranda knelt next to her, laying down the rifle. "Did you get shot too?"

"No, I'm all right. Just shaken." Delia clung to Miranda as they both stood up. "Thank you for saving my life!" she exclaimed. "I can't believe you shot him, Miranda! That was amazing."

"I *didn't* shoot him!" Miranda exclaimed. "I can't hit the broad side of a barn and I don't even think the rifle was loaded."

"What happened then?"

"Delia!" Seemingly out of nowhere, Wyatt came rushing toward them, a rifle in his hand. "Did he hurt you? Are you all right?"

"I'm fine," Delia answered in a shaky voice. "But what—where did you come from? What happened?"

"You're the one who shot Marcus!" Miranda pointed at his gun.

"Yeah." Wyatt leaned over to peer down the crevasse, slowly shaking his head.

"Excellent shot." Miranda nodded her approval. "My Daddy would've been impressed."

"Is he—is he dead?" Delia asked in a choked voice.

"I'm afraid so," Wyatt said gently. "That was a long way to fall."

"Oh—dear!" Delia started to cry.

"There was no avoiding it," Wyatt explained.

"Wyatt saved your life," Miranda declared. "You should be thanking him, Delia."

"Yes," Delia sobbed. "Of course, I'm grateful, Wyatt. But it's just so sad and shocking—a man we knew is dead."

"Marcus was going to kill you!" Miranda said hotly. "He was a lowdown snake that—"

"Let's not speak ill of the dead." Wyatt gathered Delia into his arms, looking down into her face with a concerned expression "You're white as a sheet," he said gently. "You're sure you're all right? You weren't grazed by the bullet or—"

"No, no, I'm fine. Just shaken." She leaned into his chest, letting the tears fall.

They stood there holding onto each other for a long moment, until Miranda finally spoke up. "Well, I suppose you two want to be alone." She folded her arms across her front with an exasperated sigh. "I'll go tell Caleb what happened—send somebody to get the sheriff."

"No, Miranda, please don't leave. Not yet." Delia drew in a raggedy breath, trying to bring her thoughts back to the present—not on the lifeless man at the bottom of the crevasse. "We have something we need to tell you first." Delia glanced up at Wyatt and he just nodded.

"We are going to be married."

"I figured as much." Miranda picked up her rifle and started heading down the hill.

"Wait, Miranda," Delia called out. "We need to talk."

"About what?" Miranda frowned at her.

"I need to hear your story—what made you come up here?" Delia said as they joined her. "Let's all walk down together."

With Wyatt on one side and Miranda on the other, Delia listened as they both took turns sharing what it was that sent them up her looking for her.

"I got up earlier than usual," Miranda began in earnest. "Truth be told, I was hoping to run into *him.*" She reached across Delia, jerking her thumb at Wyatt as she rolled her eyes. "So I was out back when I noticed Marcus was letting all the horses out. At first I figured he was moving them to a pasture. But then it looked like he was shooing them down to the river, which made no sense. It felt like he was up to something. So I kept watching. That's when I noticed him frowning up the hill." She pointed over to the vantage point where Delia had taken Wyatt. "He looked like he was really fixated on something. I realized it was you two and from what I could see—and Marcus must've seen it too—you two were *kissing!*"

"I forgot that it's not exactly private up there," Delia admitted to Wyatt.

"Anyway, I was keeping my eye on Marcus," Miranda continued. "I noticed him taking Hank into the bunkhouse, where he must've locked him in. Then Marcus came out wearing his holster and six-shooter. That's when I got really worried. I figured he was going after Wyatt."

"A reasonable suspicion." Delia shuddered to remember Marcus's plan to kill Wyatt after her.

"But then Marcus started yelling to everyone, saying that the horses ran off. Well, I knew that was a big fat lie—so I kept out of sight and watched while he sent everyone off in the wrong directions. Then I saw him heading toward the river, but then he doubled back. I could tell he was following you, Delia. And the way he was walking, well, it just made me feel sick inside. So I grabbed Dad's rifle and took up here after you."

"And I'm so glad you did!" Delia slipped her arm around Miranda, giving her a sideways hug before she turned to Wyatt. "But I'm curious. How did you know to come up here?"

"Miranda and I must've been on the same page about Marcus," he began. "I'd nearly reached Cash and Silas, without a horse in sight, when I got to worrying about you, Delia. I didn't like how Marcus had been so eager to get rid of me. Then I remembered he was wearing a gun. Just didn't set right with me. So I headed back."

He gave her a hand as they went down a steep bit of trail, helping Miranda too.

"Of course, you were nowhere to be seen by then. But Ginger was standing out in the yard with a fretful look. She asked if I knew why Miranda had run up the hill with her dad's rifle. Well, I didn't know what to think about that, but figured I'd find out. I spotted Miranda working her way up one side over there." He pointed to the west side of the hill. "So I decided to work my way up the other side. And that's when I found you about to be murdered by Marcus. I knew I had to wait for just the right shot, but having Miranda there to distract Marcus from the other direction helped a lot."

"Really?" Miranda smiled. "I helped?"

"Couldn't have pulled it off without you," he assured her.

By the time they reached the bottom of the hill, Delia had told her side of the story as well, describing how she'd gotten a complete confession from Marcus. "He killed Father and Mr. Griswold," she said sadly. "And after he killed me, he planned to kill Wyatt and marry Miranda."

"As if I would've married that good-for-nothing sidewinder." Miranda kicked a stone with her button-top shoe. "I wish I'd never met the snake!"

Delia wished Miranda had never met him too. But she wasn't about to rub her sister's nose in her mistakes. Hopefully she would learn from them.

"I'm going to check on the horses," Wyatt said as the three of them stood on the front porch. "And then I'll ride into town and fetch a lawman."

"Sounds like a good plan. But please have breakfast first." Delia smiled meekly, still trying to dispel the shaky feeling inside of her. "By the way, thanks again for saving my life today." She turned to Miranda. "You too."

Wyatt leaned over to plant a kiss on Delia, sending happy shivers down her spine. "I will see you later."

"Come on," Delia put an arm around Miranda's drooping shoulders. "Let's go inside and see if Ginger needs help with breakfast."

Miranda didn't say a word as they went up the steps and into the house, but as they stood in foyer, she burst into tears. "I am such a miserable mess, Delia. Everything that happened—Dad and Horace's death—it's all my fault."

"You can't take the blame for Marcus's murderous ways," Delia told her.

"But I invited him into our lives," she sobbed. "It was because of me that Dad took him on. And Marcus ruined everything."

"At least he's gone now." Delia let out a long sigh, trying to erase the images of him from her mind.

"But that's not all." Miranda let out a choked sob. "You've been so good to me, Delia, and then I tried to steal your man. I dressed up in your clothes and wore your jewelry and managed to make a complete fool of myself. I'm so sorry. I really am. Will you ever forgive me?"

Delia just hugged her little sister. "Of course, I will. We're sisters, aren't we?"

"Yes. We are." Miranda wiped her tears with her sleeve. "I've made a decision."

"Yes?"

"I do want to go to college. I think Dad was right about me needing more schooling. Do you think that college will let a foolish girl like me in?"

"Of course, they will!"

"When can I go? I'd like to start right away."

"Classes don't start until early September."

"That's two whole months away."

"Just enough time for you to help me plan my wedding." Delia looked up to see Wyatt entering the front door, announcing that the horses had all been rounded up. "Unless that's too soon for you?"

"What's too soon?" he asked.

"Delia wants to marry you before I go to college in September," Miranda announced with a bit of impudence. "Is that too soon?"

"*Today* isn't too soon for me." Wyatt slipped his arm around Delia's waist, pulling her closer to him. "But I'll let you pick the date, darling." He was leaning in for another kiss.

"I am really going to let you two be alone *now.*" Miranda turned to run up the stairs.

And then, with no one looking on, Wyatt leaned down and kissed her again—long and hard and good. So good that she felt dizzy by the time their lips parted. "What about an Independence Day wedding?" she suggested in a slightly teasing tone.

"Works for me." He nodded with approval. "But that's tomorrow...you sure you don't mind?"

"There might be fireworks," she told him dreamily.

He chuckled. "And if not, we'll make our own."

She laughed, and they kissed again.

ALSO BY MELODY CARLSON

Made in the USA
Monee, IL
23 June 2022

98442137R00187